WHERE HORIZONS END

A SEAN WYATT THRILLER

ERNEST DEMPSEY

138 PUBLISHING

JOIN THE ADVENTURE

Visit ernestdempsey.net to get a free copy of the not-sold-in-stores short stories *Red Gold, The Lost Canvas,* and *The Moldova Job,* plus the full length novel *The Cairo Vendetta,* all from the critically acclaimed Sean Wyatt archaeological thriller series.

You'll also get access to exclusive content, private giveaways, and a chance to win signed copies.

While you're at it, swing by the official Ernest Dempsey fan page on Facebook at https://facebook.com/ErnestDempsey to join the community of travelers, adventurers, historians, and dreamers. There are exclusive contests, giveaways, and more!

Lastly, if you enjoy pictures of exotic locations, food, and travel adventures, check out my feed @ernestdempsey on the Instagram app.

What are you waiting for? Join the adventure today!

For my friend Jason Chatraw, the kind of guy who will wear the colors of a rival team to support a friend... no matter how much he may hate the color orange.
#GBO
#VFL

PRIMARY CHARACTERS IN SERIES

Sean Wyatt: International Archaeological Agency field agent. Adriana Villa's husband.

Tommy Schultz: Founder of the International Archaeological Agency specializing in discovery, recovery, and securing ancient artifacts for preservation and study. Husband to June Holiday.

Adriana Villa: Master thief specializing in the recovery of lost or stolen masterpieces from World War II. Wife of Sean Wyatt.

Diego Villa: Adriana Villa's father and private intelligence consultant.

Tara Watson: IAA field agent and co-lead investigator of the Paranormal Archaeology Division at IAA. Wife of Alex Simms.

Alex Simms: IAA field agent and co-lead investigator of the Paranormal Archaeology Division at IAA. Husband of Tara Watson.

Dak Harper: Relic runner/treasure hunter for professional video gamer Boston McClaren. Former Delta Force.

Emily Starks: Director of The Axis Agency.

June Holiday: Axis field agent and wife to Tommy Schultz.

Joe and Helen McElroy: Axis field agents.

OTHER CHARACTERS

Gwen McCarthy: President of the United States

Malcom Barnwell- Founder and CEO of a major weapons manufacturer for the United States Military and friend of Tommy and Sean.

"Guard closely the issues of your heart, for everything you do flows from it."
Proverbs 4:23

PROLOGUE
XINJIANG, CHINA | 887 A.D.

Q in Zongquan squinted against the bright, uninterrupted sunlight as he stared across the barren earth toward the temple ruins. A gigantic mountain, bigger than any Qin had seen in many seasons, towered into the sky behind it, nearly two days' ride from where he stood.

"We should not be here," his advisor, Pa Yin, warned. "This is a cursed place, General."

Qin scoffed at the comment, spitting into the dry dirt next to his horse. The animal didn't seem to notice, keeping its proud head high and facing forward.

"I don't believe in curses, Pa," Qin countered. "Superstition has no place in the mind of a leader."

Pa merely nodded his agreement, afraid to argue the point with his commander, the man who had his sights squarely on the emperor's throne.

"This place was destroyed by Arabs," Qin went on. "Not some supernatural force, or a monster from legends. An army of religious zealots wiped it out, along with all the monks who lived here."

He'd heard the story about this place more than once. Shikshin had been a thriving Buddhist monastery for nearly a thousand years, as far as he knew. There were some who claimed it had only been established much more recently, but Qin knew the truth. This place had been a religious center for those traveling along the ancient Silk Road, and had provided sanctuary for those who needed it.

But the history of the Shikshin temple wasn't why Qin and his entourage were here.

He'd started a rebellion against the Tang Dynasty, and while he wasn't the first, he knew he was the strongest. Unlike the others before him, though, Qin was willing to do anything to claim the throne.

His legend swelled around the country, striking fear into the hearts of the people. The rumors passed from one prefecture to the next with the speed of a falcon, carried on the terrified lips of bards, soldiers, women, even children.

Qin's troops had lashed out in a horrifying shock-and-awe campaign in which he directly ordered his men to murder, rape, pillage, and burn villages to the ground if they would not bend the knee to him—and sometimes, he would do all that even if they did bow.

He had never wanted a reputation for kindness. Mercy was for the weak, and Qin had no intention of showing weakness to those he meant to rule.

"Are we even sure this is the place, great General?" Pa asked. He immediately regretted the question. Standing a few inches taller than Qin, Pa's imposing stature caused many to respect him purely for his height. He commanded Qin's forces with unquestioned loyalty and ruthlessness, all of which made his concern about entering the temple ruins all the more baffling to the general.

Qin slapped his lieutenant on the back and grinned. "What's the matter with you? I've never known you to be afraid of anything—the man who faced two dozen of the emperor's soldiers with only his sword, and dealt death to every one of them."

"Soldiers I can handle," Pa offered. "The mortals of this world cause me no fear. It's those of the other worlds that I fear, my General. Against them, my sword is useless."

Qin studied him for a minute, as if uncertain whether his second-in-command was being serious.

He quickly realized Pa's sincerity was genuine. "Very well," Qin said. "I'll go in alone. You and the men stay here, and wait for me."

The general stomped away, never looking back for one of the men to call his bluff. Pa glanced around at the other ten warriors. Their eyes remained locked on their commander, or perhaps they were focused on the ruins and the terror it promised from the mythical curse.

With a sigh, Pa turned to one of his officers and said, "Shen Cong, you, Zhu, and the others stay here and keep watch. If we're not back before dusk, get help."

The man replied with a curt nod.

Pa turned and hurried after his general, hoping not to face the leader's wrath at his initial indecision.

"I knew you would come," Qin said without looking over his shoulder.

Pa slowed down next to the general, bobbing his head. "You are not just my general," he said. "You know that."

He spoke the truth, and Qin knew it. The two had been close friends since they were eleven years old, and that friendship had allowed Qin to have a second pair of eyes and hands wherever his conquests led. He knew that Pa could think like him, react like him, and handle any situation, military or otherwise, with the same line of thinking that Qin would use. It was an incredible advantage to have against a foe, and that fact never slipped by Qin.

"You have always been a good friend," Qin said. "Sorry I have to speak to you like a dog in front of the others."

"Never apologize, old friend. I know why you do it. We must keep the men in line, no matter the cost. Any slip on our part, any cause for doubt with your leadership, and all will be lost."

Qin agreed with a nod as they passed the ruins of huts; ancient homes devastated by the invaders who trampled this land so many years ago. Straight ahead, the remains of a dilapidated temple stood before them.

Faded round pillars stood at the front of the crumbling building. Matching steps led up to the main entrance, or what was left of it. Parts of the walls had fallen in, while others remained intact. The roof was long since gone, the parts left by invaders having been taken by time and weather.

The dry air blew across the little plateau where the ancient ruins stood, kicking up dust devils that twirled like filthy ghosts across the ground before evaporating into the air.

"Do you think it's still here?" Pa asked, glancing over at his friend with an undeniable hope in his eyes.

"I don't know," Qin confessed.

The honesty only slightly shocked Pa, but the answer did more so. If the general wasn't certain they would find their prize here, why had they come so far? Perhaps the man was merely hedging his bets, unwilling to commit fully to his best guess.

"All of my studies have brought us here," Qin continued. "I have read the ancient texts a hundred times over. This is the place where they hid the heart."

Even hearing the word come from his friend's lips sent a quiver through Pa. They'd first heard of the Heart of Shambala when they were mere children. At first, the idea of roaming the world in search of the rare jewel brought ideas of wealth and fame to the boys' minds. They imagined returning to their village as heroes, and with enough money to do anything they wanted for the rest of their days.

The thought never occurred to them that finding the heart would give them something far more important than gold or fame. That is, until Qin's fourteenth birthday, when he heard an old man in the village tell the story about the seven lost realms.

Qin and Pa sat around the firepit, eating roasted chicken, listening as the bard regaled them with tales of ancient lands that flowed with gold and silver, and where the people aged slower than in the rest of the world.

When Qin asked the wrinkle-faced old man where these realms were, the storyteller only chuckled, gazing at Qin with eyes that betrayed his true knowledge. "No one knows, boy. All but one of them were destroyed long ago."

Despite the man's words, Qin knew he wasn't telling the whole truth. As a result, Qin set about learning as much as he could from the legends of the old kingdoms, and the strange people who lived supernaturally long lives.

He and Pa pretended they were great soldiers, exploring the land for treasures and mystical places—most often comprising the hidden realms.

Then one day, Qin found out the old man was dying and went to pay his respects—as well ask one last question.

Stopping at the foot of the temple steps, Qin recalled the way the old man's skin hung from his face and neck. All semblance of color had long since gone, and the pale, papery look to the flesh affirmed the knocking of death on the storyteller's door.

When the young boy stepped in the room, the bard smiled at him, then beckoned him to come closer. Hesitantly, Qin approached the bedside and looked down at the man with pity in his eyes.

"Do not worry about me, young one," the man said. "There is a great future ahead for you." He turned to the other people in the room and asked them to leave. After a moment of consideration, they did as requested, leaving the young boy alone with the dying man.

When he was certain no one was listening, the old man called Qin even closer and rolled over a little in his bed, despite the obvious discomfort. He took a long breath through the nose, and then spoke.

"You have an amazing future, young Qin," the man began.

Qin shook his head, insistent the guy was wrong. "I doubt it. I don't come from a wealthy, prominent family, and we have no connections to the royal bloodlines."

"And yet, a great battle will you lead against tyranny."

Qin scowled at the comment, not fully understanding where the old man was going with this. "I doubt it," Qin countered. "I don't come from a prominent family, and anything I achieve in this life will be by my own efforts, through my own sweat. Even with that, there is only so much someone like me can accomplish."

The old man nodded, but Qin knew his agreement was only half-hearted. There was something else in the man's eyes, a secret he'd been longing to share.

"You must find the Heart of Shambala, young Qin. It is the only one of its kind, and will lead you to the last of the seven lost realms."

Qin stood there unbelieving of the words the man spoke. "Teacher," he said, "I wouldn't know where to start. And I'm only a boy. Many people have searched for the heart, and for the lost kingdoms. Most never return."

The old man narrowed his glazed eyes, and a childish grin crossed his lips. "You will find it. And it will help you in your journey to lead a new dynasty." Before Qin could protest, the man continued. "There is a temple that was destroyed long ago by invaders. It was a place of peace." Suddenly, the old man's body shook and leaped as a terrible cough overtook him.

The episode lasted nearly a minute before he finally calmed down enough to finish speaking.

"Would you like me to get the physician?" Qin asked.

"No. It is my time, Qin. You must go. Find the ancient Buddhist temple. Within its walls lies the secret to the lost kingdom."

"What kind of secret?"

The man swallowed hard against another fit of coughing that racked his chest. "A passage. It contains the heart. But beware, young one. That place also holds a terrible curse. You must be cautious."

Qin recalled his initial reaction, one of both curiosity and fear. The man had died moments later, and Qin never had the chance to ask him anything else. But he'd heard enough, and the man had left him with one last vital piece of information. A map pointing to this location.

After the man's death, Qin's life went on. He became an officer in his village, and then a great military leader, and governor. He never had time to go in search of the treasure the old man discussed. But Qin followed the man's prophecy, eventually laying claim to the throne of China and declaring himself emperor.

Several military defeats, however, led him to retreat, and to regroup. Rather than drive himself crazy wondering how he'd lost it all, Qin refocused his attention on finding the Heart of Shambala. He'd been distracted for too long and in the midst of his conquest had forgotten the key that would make him not only the most powerful man in China but in all the world.

He stood at the base of the steps and stared at the entrance to the temple. "This is it, my old friend. What we heard about so long ago. Somewhere in there," Qin said, pointing through the entryway, "is the heart."

A gurgle escaped Pa's lips.

Qin turned to his friend in surprise at the strange sound. Shock filled Qin's eyes as they fell on an arrow protruding from Pa's lips. Pa turned to Qin, staring back in terror as he fell to his knees, grasping at the projectile jutting out of his throat.

Qin whirled around to face the threat, his mind immediately believing they had been followed here by one of his enemies.

Instead, he found his own men, standing in a line across the pathway to block Qin's escape.

"What is the meaning of this?" Qin demanded.

Shen Cong stepped forward, a baton in his right hand. One of the other men held a bow in his hands, another arrow notched and pointed directly at Qin's chest.

"This is the end of your ridiculous rebellion," Shen answered, stepping close to Qin. "We have suffered enough, bled enough, died enough in your quest for power. It's over, Qin. We just want to go home to our families."

Qin huffed at the statement. "You rats. You would rather live under the oppression of a tyrant?"

"That is what you've become, General," Shen answered. Before Qin could respond, Shen whipped the baton around hard, striking Qin in the shin.

The heavy blunt weapon hit the leg hard, cracking the bone within. Qin collapsed in agonizing pain, but he only allowed a grunt to escape his parched throat.

"You are making a mistake," Qin spat. "We could have lived like gods in this world. All of us. Now, you will perish just like everyone else."

Shen whipped the baton at the other leg. He felt it crack hard against the bone and flesh. This time Qin couldn't resist the urge to yell as the tibia broke.

Staring down at the general with disgust, Shen shook his head and motioned to two of the other soldiers with his free hand. The men shuffled over to the fallen leader, and hovered above him awaiting their orders.

"You will be taken to the true emperor," Shen stated. "We will be received as heroes of the empire, and will be richly rewarded."

Qin mustered his strength. Clenching his jaws, he shook his head slowly back and forth. "You're making a grave mistake, Shen. And for what? Wealth? Fame? Those things fade, Shen." He spat the words between desperate, heaving breaths.

"At least they are real."

Qin ground his teeth in anger. He wanted to rip his sword from its sheath and cut his betrayers down one by one. The fantasy flashed through his mind's eye for several seconds and then was gone, replaced by the agonizing pain in his broken legs.

Forlorn, he glanced over at his childhood friend, Pa, who lay prostrate on the ground, eyes staring blankly back at him.

Resignation filled Qin, and he tore his eyes from Pa to face his mutinous officer. His stare would have consumed Shen with fire if he could have willed such magic, but all Qin could muster were a few last words before the soldiers dragged him away to what he knew would be a quick trial and a torturous execution.

"Shambala is real, Shen. And may the curse that protects it fall on your head."

1

COSTA RICAN JUNGLE

Sean knew there was no way he could get the bloodstains out of his khakis, not with the thunderstorm dumping rain on the jungle above. Fortunately, it wasn't his blood. The snake had appeared out of nowhere, dropping from a tree branch less than five feet away. He hadn't bothered to stop and ask the serpent if it was venomous or not, opting instead to go with the *a dead snake is a good snake* mindset. Not a terrible idea in a place where even the frogs could kill a human with their powerful toxins.

The animals were the least of Sean's predatory concerns. He wasn't the only one down in the tunnels of an ancient Olmec temple.

Sean had worked for months on this project, spending countless hours looking through aerial scans of an area that covered a few hundred square miles. He'd read a few legends regarding the Olmecs in this part of Central America, but their mysterious disappearance from history left more questions than answers. Historians had done their best to document the Olmec civilization as much as they could, but there was always something missing, one last piece of the puzzle that could give closure to the rise and fall of their empire.

Working for the International Archaeological Agency in Atlanta gave Sean the opportunity, and tools, to discover places like this—

and other treasures that the world hadn't seen for hundreds, sometimes thousands, of years.

Usually, his primary job was securing and delivering artifacts from a site to a museum or lab. But every now and then, he stumbled onto a challenge he couldn't pass up, and from time to time that landed him in a steaming pile of trouble.

Which is how he ended up in Costa Rica with a priceless golden statue in the satchel hanging from his shoulder. The straps dug into muscle as Sean looked around the tunnel with the flashlight in his left hand, his Springfield .40-cal pistol in the right.

Sean peered with blue-gray eyes into the darkness. The tunnel straight ahead continued beyond the reach of the flashlight's beam. To his left, and right, the tunnels branched off in either direction.

His gut told him to keep going straight, and he thought it was the way he'd come in. But Sean had lost his sense of direction within twenty minutes of descending into the underground temple, and that was in no small part due to his pursuer.

He decided to go straight, and sprinted ahead down the corridor. The beam from his flashlight danced around wildly on the walls and floor, and Sean didn't give any thought to the signal it would give to the man chasing him.

At the end of the passage, Sean skidded to a stop, where the only options were to go left or right.

When he turned his head to the right, however, he realized his options had been cut to one.

"Get him!" a familiar voice shouted in a Spanish accent.

Two henchmen charged ahead of their master with Sean's chief pursuer close behind.

Sean whirled and darted in the other direction, opting to flee rather than fight. He could have fired his weapon, but in the stone corridor, he'd have been lucky to come out of there with a fraction of his hearing intact. He hadn't had time to slap on one of his box suppressors. Initially, Sean didn't really think he'd need it.

That was a mistake.

Straight ahead, Sean saw the dim glow of moonlight and caught a whiff of fresh jungle air mingling with the musty smell from the temple.

Sean hoped the men following him had the same concerns about discharging firearms in the corridor, but that hope was quickly squashed when a bullet ricocheted off the wall to his left, sending sparks across his vision.

He instinctively ducked his head and pumped his legs harder. The end of the passage beckoned just ahead, another fifty feet away. Fresh, misty air washed over him, and the sound of a waterfall filled the tunnel, drowning out the sounds of the men behind him.

The roar grew louder as Sean neared the end. The moisture made the stone floor slick, and dangerous, and he had to be careful not to slip so close to his goal.

Another bullet bounced off the wall to his right, and Sean ducked again just as he reached the end of the corridor. He slowed down cautiously before getting to the edge. His old enemy crept up on him, crawling up his spine like a spider, tingling his senses with a venomous fear.

The tunnel opening dropped three hundred feet down next to a waterfall. The falls spewed white foam, sending a cloud of mist all around the cliff face, enshrouding his escape. It was little wonder no one had ever located this passage, save for the skeletal remains of long-dead explorers Sean found inside.

Sean spun around, keeping his heels safely a foot away from the edge. He was grateful for the breeze blowing into the tunnel, as one of his irrational fears with heights was that a gust of wind might blow him over the edge and send him plummeting to his death. He extended his pistol, pointing it at the men as they rushed toward him.

"Stop right there," Sean ordered. He still didn't want to fire the weapon, for more than one reason. Killing was never Sean's first choice in any scenario, but these guys had brought it on themselves when they fired the first shots. "Not another step!"

The two men slowed to a grind, with their leader nearly running into them from behind.

The gunmen held their weapons at their hips, aimed at Sean.

"You have nowhere else to go, Sean," the leader taunted. He stepped between his men, bravely or stupidly, Sean wasn't sure which. The breeze funneling through the passage blew through the Spaniard's thick, black hair. His maroon rain jacket flapped at his sides and behind him. "Drop the statue, and perhaps I'll let you walk away. No reason for anyone to die today."

Sean felt the weight of the satchel tugging against his shoulder, a constant and uncomfortable reminder of why he was here.

"I'm sorry, Benny," Sean offered with heartfelt insincerity. "You have to be faster. I'm taking this to a lab for analysis. Maybe you can see it again someday at a museum or something."

The man's right eye twitched, but other than that he made no sign of indignation. Sean knew Benitzio Torres from several similar meetings in the past. Torres was a treasure hunter, and had made a significant fortune with two of his finds. Like so many, though, he wasn't satisfied with enough money to set him up for life. He always wanted more. As a result, Torres found himself constantly searching for the next lost treasure.

Sean knew what a fruitless venture that would prove to be, even if he weren't occasionally in Torres' way.

The men behind Torres kept their guns trained on Sean. They knew he couldn't take out both of them before one got off a shot. He might be quick, but no one was that quick.

Torres also knew this.

"You're outgunned, Sean," Torres informed him over the constant, machine-like churn of the waterfalls. "You could kill me, or one of my men, but you will drop before you can take out another."

"Yeah, but at least I wouldn't have to deal with you popping up on my tail whenever I'm in the middle of a project." Sean tightened his grip on the weapon and hoped Torres could see the action in the darkness. With both flashlights on him, Sean figured it was hard to miss.

"Come now, Sean," Torres said, boldly taking another step forward. "You won't kill me. If you wanted to do that, you would have done it long ago."

"I don't want to kill anyone," Sean replied coldly.

"Your track record begs to differ."

Sean had to admit: The guy had him on that one. He'd left a body count in his wake over the last ten years, and that was following a career that demanded he use lethal force. This gig was supposed to be a step back from that.

But working for the International Archaeological Agency had more than its share of adventurous missions, and more close calls than Sean could count. He tilted his head toward the radio on his shoulder and spoke clearly so his partner would be able to hear him over the sound of the waterfall.

"You know if you shoot me, Benny, I'm going to fall right out through this opening," Sean flicked his head back to indicate the precipice. Just the slight movement of his head caused Sean to feel as though he would tip over and fall to his death. That's how it always felt when he was near somewhere high like this. Gravity seemed to work twice as hard, and only on him. It was an irrational, paranoid fear but one he had never been able to release his entire life.

"Then, what do you propose we do, Sean?" Torres asked. "Stand here in a stalemate until Judgment Day?"

"Or you could just give up. Unlikely, I know."

"I could have my men shoot you. It's a fifty-fifty chance you fall through the opening."

Sean chuckled uncomfortably. "I would make sure I did," he said.

"I see no need in us going around and around about this, Sean. It's simple. You're trapped, with no way out except certain death. Give me the statue. Take the loss this time. Honestly, it's someone else's turn to win for a change."

"Oh, I see," Sean realized. "You're tired of losing."

The bland, unimpressed look on Torres' face didn't change.

"Time to let someone else have a trophy?" Sean continued. He shook his head. "Except you're doing it to sell to someone on the black market."

"That's not true, Sean," Torres said in a twist Sean didn't expect. "I'm not going to list it on the antiquities market."

Sean knew there was a catch, so he said nothing and waited instead.

"I already have the buyer in place."

There it is, Sean thought.

"You didn't think I would come all the way down here to the jungles of Costa Rica for a fabled, ancient golden statue without someone to sell it to, did you?"

"Crossed my mind. You haven't always been the best decision maker, Benny. Let's be honest."

A thin smile swept across Torres' face. "You are correct about that, Sean. I have made mistakes in the past, but I have learned from them." He stepped toward Sean without fear. "Give me the statue. You lose this time, Sean. Maybe you'll get the next one."

Sean sensed movement off his right shoulder and heard a low clapping sound. He grinned devilishly back at Torres. "Sorry, Benny. Can't let you have it. And I gotta run. My ride is here."

A confused scowl crossed the Spaniard's face, and his lips curled in an unspoken question.

Sean inched his heel backward toward the cliff, and then Torres understood.

"It's not worth it, Sean. Keeping me from having it makes no difference to you—according to your screwed-up way of thinking."

Sean laughed on the inside, but he decided to play up the man's assertion. He shook his head vehemently. "Don't come any closer, Benny. I swear, I will do it. I will jump. Please don't make me jump, Benny." Sean nudged the wall with his shoulder to keep his balance.

While he made a show of being terrified on the outside, deep down, he felt a familiar paralysis gripping every muscle in his body. All he wanted to do was drop down on the ground and crawl back through the corridor the way he came, but that wasn't an option. Besides, his ride was waiting. Sean just didn't want to take the first step to get on board.

"Stay back!" Sean warned with genuine fear in his voice. "Don't make me do it, Benny!"

Torres held up both hands, suddenly concerned that Sean might actually jump. Not that he cared about Sean Wyatt's life. He could jump if he wanted. Torres only wanted him to leave the statue there in the tunnel if he was going to kill himself.

"Take it easy, Sean. Just relax. Okay? We're not going to hurt you. Right, boys?" Torres glanced over his shoulders at his men. Both shook their heads vigorously.

"You're lying," Sean said, nearly conjuring tears in the process. "If that was true, you wouldn't be shooting at me."

Torres looked at his men again and nodded. "Lower your weapons."

The henchmen, confused and irritated, did as ordered and let their pistols drop to their hips.

Sean felt the tip of his heel reach the edge of the cliff. A shiver of terror coursed through him, but he fended it off with a quick breath in and locked eyes with Torres. "I'm sorry, Benny. But I can't let you have this. It belongs to history, not in some private collection."

He reached his hand around the corner of the tunnel opening, carefully digging his shoulder and chest into the rock to keep his balance. He felt his weight shift, and a horrific vision of falling into the misty doom below passed through Sean's mind. He leaned forward to correct himself, then stuffed the pistol into his belt and returned his hand to the outer wall.

"Sean," Torres said, a look of pity washing over him. "What are you doing? Do you really think you're going to climb to safety out there? That rock wall is completely wet. You won't get one grip before you slip and fall to your death. Just leave the statue. It's not worth dying over."

"I agree, Benny. It's not." Sean shoved his hand a little farther out through the hole and found what he was looking for. The cable smacked against his palm and he wrapped his fingers around it, winding the vinyl coating around his wrist before gripping it hard with his fingers. "Okay, Schultzie. I'm on."

"Roger that, Sean," Tommy said through the earpiece in Sean's right ear.

Sean smirked at Torres, then gave a salute with his hand that held the flashlight. "Gotta go, Benny. See you next time."

Torres stepped forward as Sean kicked his legs out.

For a second, the Spaniard felt a wave of shock at the sight of Sean jumping out of the passage. Then, his surprise turned to rage as he saw Sean swing upward, a black cable wrapped around his right wrist and hand.

"No!" Torres shouted. He sprinted toward the opening, but slowed as he neared the dangerous edge.

He planted his right hand on the corner and dared to crane his neck out of the tunnel enough to look up and see Sean running up the sheer cliff with the satchel over his shoulder.

"Wyatt! I will get you!"

Sean barely heard the threat as he ran up the rock wall, the cable pulling him fast toward the top, almost faster than he could move his feet.

"Almost there, Tommy," Sean said into the radio.

"What?" Tommy asked. The pace of the cable tugging Sean up the cliff abruptly slowed, and Sean found himself standing at a sharp angle with nothing but a cord wrapped around his arm to keep him from dropping like a stone.

"Don't stop!" Sean commanded. "Keep going!"

"Oh, okay." The cable jerked Sean's arm so hard it nearly dislocated his shoulder, but his momentum continued upward, even as Torres' men below started firing their pistols at the ascending target.

Sean heard some of the bullets crack the air as they sailed by, and he pumped his feet faster, zigging and zagging across the face of the rock to make for a more difficult target.

Finally, after a significant amount of pain in his forearm and an exhausting climb, Sean reached the top of the cliff. The speed of the cable pulled him up and over the edge, and he struck the ground hard.

The second Tommy saw his friend, he cut off the winch on the front of the SUV and hurried over to where Sean landed on the ground amid a cluster of shrubs and trees.

"You okay, buddy?" Tommy asked as Sean picked himself up and unwound the rope from his wrist.

He looked down at the red marks and the pattern imprinted on his skin. Then he met Tommy's gaze. "Yeah, I'm good. Glad you had that winch."

Tommy's eyes narrowed, and he nodded. "And you used to make fun of me bringing rope everywhere."

"Great, so the tow cable is your next thing?"

"You never know," Tommy said with a wry expression.

Sean dusted wet debris off his pants and rain jacket. The moon beamed in the sky to the east, while dark clouds directly overhead continued to leak rain onto the jungle.

Tommy trudged over to the cliff's edge and glanced over. He turned back to his friend with a curious look in his eyes. "I'm impressed, man. You're normally so terrified of heights."

"Does it look like I'm comfortable with them now?" Sean asked. His wet, pale face betrayed his true sentiments.

"No, you definitely look like you've seen a ghost, or something scarier than a ghost. What's scarier than a ghost?" Tommy thought for a second while Sean walked over to the SUV and threw open the passenger door.

"We need to go. Those guys will be coming for us."

"Relax," Tommy insisted. "They'll have to go all the way through the labyrinth again. Now, what is scarier than a ghost?" He touched his thumb to his chin as if in deep thought.

"Cool," Sean said and climbed into the driver's seat. "I'm leaving without you."

"Hey!" Tommy snapped and rushed to get to the SUV before Sean backed it away from three huge boulders.

He huffed as his back hit the seat in the passenger side of the truck, and Sean stepped on the gas. The four tires spun in unison, kicking mud, leaves, and sticks up behind the vehicle.

"So, you got it?" Tommy asked, his eyes wandering to the army-green satchel on the floor at his feet.

"I did," Sean said, keeping his eyes on the narrow ruts that passed for a road in these parts. "Have a look for yourself."

Tommy swallowed back his excitement and bent down. He gently unzipped the top zipper and pulled back the folds of the bag. Inside, a yellow gleam caught his eye, and for a second, he didn't believe what he was seeing.

"You got it," Tommy said. A thread of disappointment tickled his tone.

"What's the matter?" Sean asked. "I thought you would be happy."

"I am," Tommy insisted. "I am. I just would have liked to be down in the tunnel with you." He looked down at his wrist with the cast on it.

"Well, maybe next time you decide to go to a jump park, you'll be more careful. No offense, pal, but I'm thinking things like training for the Ninja Warrior series, or any sort of stuff like that is probably a young person's game."

Tommy relented with a sigh. "Yeah, I guess you're right. But how come you can still do all this stuff?"

"I'm not as weak as you," Sean said with a straight face, keeping his eyes locked firmly on the two ruts ahead.

Tommy's face reddened, and he twisted to the side to face his friend. "What did you just say?"

Sean held back as long as he could, then erupted in laughter. "I'm messing with you, man. Take it easy."

Tommy shook his head, unimpressed. "You called me weak."

"It's a joke, Schultzie. Relax."

"You're lucky I have this cast on," Tommy replied, turning his head to look out the window. "Otherwise, you'd be in trouble."

"Never pick a fight with a guy in a cast," Sean muttered.

"That's right."

The cab fell silent for a minute while Tommy's gaze fell downward to the satchel once again.

Inside, the statue of the Dragon God of the Olmecs stared back up at him, and the bulging, vacant eyes almost felt like they were alive, in a zombie-esque sort of way. Tommy quickly zipped the bag closed again and focused his attention on the bumpy path.

Then Tommy glanced back over his shoulder through the SUV's rear window.

Sean noted his concern. "By the time they find their way out of there," he said, "we'll be in the air."

"Oh, I know," Tommy said, turning around and facing forward once more. "I just wish I could have seen the inside of that place." He squeezed his fingers over and over, flexing the tendons and muscles in his forearm.

"You'll be back in the game before you know it," Sean said. He jerked the wheel to the left, then back to the right to avoid a huge boulder jutting out into the trail on the side.

Tommy agreed with a nod. "Will be nice to get back out there, into the thick of it."

Sean snorted. "This incident with Benny was the first close call we've had in a while. I wouldn't expect another one anytime soon."

"It's not the close calls I want," Tommy corrected. "Just being able to get into these places, see these things that no eyes have seen for so long..." His voice drifted off.

"I know, Schultzie." Sean rested his head against the cushion behind his skull. "I know."

2

CHINA, JIANGXI- TWO MONTHS LATER

J u Chen stood at the edge of the cliff, watching without emotion as the archaeologist dangling from the rope below tried to make sense of the message carved into the rock.

"What does it say?" Chen yelled down. She kept her arms crossed, more as a symbol of her fearsome persona than to protect her against the cold wind streaking across the Huaiyu Mountains.

"The inscription is very old!" the man on the rope answered. His voice sounded tight and weak, gripped by fear. "It's endured much weathering, and is nearly faded completely. But it looks like a map. It's truly incredible! I'm amazed someone put this in such an obscure location, but that's how these things go."

Werner Fischer was one of the top experts in Europe when it came to studies of the ancient Far East, and his work with the history of China had brought him awards, accolades, and even a small amount of fame—none of which, however, helped pay his modest debts.

Fischer lived a simple life but had been married four times. The last two wives had taken him for nearly everything he had, including most of the money he'd earned for making appearances or selling books. The books he'd published didn't bring in much revenue, but they gave him clout, and had played a big part in landing this particular gig with Chen and her boss, a man the German archaeologist had still yet to meet.

"*Nearly* means you can still read it," Chen answered, conjuring the spirit of her employer with the response. He was cold that way, and she knew he appreciated her intolerance of both weakness and pathetic excuses. They hadn't come this far only to walk away because they couldn't read the script etched into the rock.

The archaeologist grunted his irritation but said nothing, instead returning to the painstaking work of rubbing the inscription onto the paper in hopes of getting a good print of the ancient message.

He pressed the paper against the surface, rubbing against it with the coal in his other hand.

Chen could sense his apprehension. Had it been her on the end of the rope, she might have felt the same way, but the difference between the two was that Chen wouldn't have let someone else see her fear. In the world where Chen grew up, letting others see your fear was like letting a lion see you limping at the back of a pack of antelope.

Fischer's eyes widened as he completed the rubbing. He shook his head in disbelief, pinning the paper to the rock so the wind wouldn't blow it away. "Wait a minute."

"Are you finished?" Chen asked, seeing the archaeologist staring blankly at his handiwork. She didn't care for the confused, irritated look on his face.

"Yes," the man nodded absently. He extended the sheet up to her, and she took it from him, staring at the paper as she held it to the cloud-diffused sunlight.

He kept his hand extended for a few seconds, then realized she wasn't going to help him back up. Fischer scowled at her lack of manners, though he'd already come to expect such behavior from the woman. She was bossy, and rude, without an ounce of polite disposition.

Fischer scrambled back up the cliff face, thankful at least that the sherpa belaying him was still paying attention to the rope. Once over the top edge, Fischer unhooked the harness from the carabiner and stood up straight. He looked at the woman holding the rubbing; she was still analyzing it with narrowed eyes.

"Can you read it?" he asked, genuinely curious.

"Of course I can read it," she snarled, firing him a sidelong, half-offended glare.

The barb deflected off Fischer, and he went on the offensive. "Then you know what it says."

"Obviously."

"So, what are you going to do? It's obviously a fake or a prank of some kind. And we both know the place it's referring to doesn't exist."

Chen rounded on him instantly. So fast and sudden were her movements, they happened in a blur. Fischer found it impossible to react quickly enough before she was inches from his face.

Her hot breath escaped from blaring nostrils as she locked eyes with him, staring into his as if she might smack him like an insect and toss him in the trash.

"You should watch your tongue," Chen warned. "The truths that remain hidden from humanity are the most powerful of all. There's a reason some things have been kept a secret from human eyes. Things people weren't meant to understand or access."

"Pfft. I suppose you and your boss are the exceptions? The rules apply to everyone else?" He rolled his eyes, which was the wrong move.

Chen grabbed him by the jacket collar and shoved him toward the edge of the cliff. Fischer suddenly realized how naked he felt so high up without any sort of rope or harness attached to him. The sickening epiphany struck him that, if she wanted, Chen could merely shove him backward, and he would likely be unable to keep himself from falling to his death.

"The rules," she said, "are for those too weak to break them and make their own. For those of us who can break through, we can achieve an even greater existence."

"Pretty deep in it, huh," he said nervously. His voice shook in his throat, as if the words themselves were too afraid to climb out and be heard by the powerful woman.

Chen was smaller than Fischer by four inches, but of the two, she possessed skills that his strength and reach couldn't overcome.

"You would be wise to keep your disparaging thoughts to yourself," Chen snapped, pushing him farther toward the edge.

"What seems to be the problem, Ju?" The new voice entered the conversation from one of the tents standing amid the trees and rock formations a dozen yards away.

Chen turned her head to face the man who'd asked the question; her employer. He stood at the orange-and-gray tent's entrance, towering over it like a crane in a pond, and his eyes fixed on her like she was the only fish left in the water.

Her grip loosened on the archaeologist's collar. "My apologies, sir."

"I overheard the discussion," Benitzio said, stalking slowly toward the two on the tips of his toes. He moved with a grace that could have easily been mistaken for softness or even as dainty, but the man was anything but. "It seems you have taken offense to our colleague's opinions on the purpose of our quest."

"Not offense," Chen refuted. "He doesn't understand." She returned her gaze to the fear-stricken man, who was now only feet away from the edge and starting to think there was a real possibility she might shove him over.

"And this is your method of convincing people we're in the right?" Torres asked. He shook his head, and her fingers let go of Fischer's jacket.

Torres walked over to where to the two stood, and he patted Chen on the back. She took the gesture as condescending but allowed it beneath a smoldering exterior.

"Now, what is it we've found here?" Torres asked, his attention settling on the rubbing in Chen's other hand.

She held it out for him, and he accepted, poring over it within a second of taking it from her hand. Benitzio's head snapped toward the cliff, then back to the archaeologist. "This?"

Fischer nodded. Chen melted into the background, falling silent as her employer took over the conversation.

Fischer shook and pointed angrily at the rubbing. "The poet was half-mad when he wrote this. I don't think there's any reason we should give any credit to this being a legitimate claim."

Tao Yuanming, a Chinese poet from the fifth century, had written about a great many things in nature, as well as from his imagination. A legend suggested that his burial place was somewhere here, in the mountains of Jiangxi Province.

"Your thoughts have been noted," Torres said absently, his focus returning to the paper. The script written in Chinese characters stared back at him, revealing a message that hadn't been seen in centuries.

"This is a fool's errand," Fischer went on. "People have spent their life's fortunes on this quest. It doesn't exist. Only someone as mad as the poet was at the end of his life would pursue this. On top of all that, if it really existed, someone would have discovered it by now with satellite images or LIDAR. Heck, even random photos from a wandering spy plane would have produced the location."

Torres had heard all of those excuses before, but he remained undeterred, as did the man who funded this entire operation. What Fischer didn't realize was that Benitzio Torres wasn't the one in charge. Oh, sure, he gave the orders on the expedition, but he answered to someone far more powerful and wealthy, and that man wouldn't accept the cliché excuses that Fischer dredged up.

"Phu?" Torres said, catching the sherpa's attention. "Could you go collect some more firewood. We'll need it for this evening's campfire. I fear a cold snap is approaching."

The guide nodded with a snap of his head and disappeared into the forest a few seconds later.

"I think it's better," Torres went on, returning his focus to Fischer, "if the help isn't around to hear our discussion."

Fischer stiffened his stance, but Torres didn't back down. The Spaniard stared at eye level with the German, his gaze following his long, pointy nose like the sights of a rifle.

"I appreciate the sentiment, Benitzio, but I don't think you require my services any longer. I won't be part of some ridiculous treasure hunt for the forgotten utopia of legend."

"I understand," Torres agreed. "You're quite right, Herr Fischer. A man of your accomplishments and education can't be bothered with a ridiculous hunt for some mythical lost kingdom. After all, what would your peers say if they found out you were searching for Shangri-La? I imagine you'd be laughed out of the club."

The statement caught Fischer off guard, and he expressed his confusion with narrowed eyelids and a wrinkled forehead. "Well, I wouldn't say it's ridiculous," he countered. "It's just that if this mythical place really did exist, someone would have already found it."

"Yes, of course you're correct, Dr. Fischer," Torres agreed, putting his arm around the man's shoulder. "It's just that, well, this tells us the location of the Heart of Shambala. I'm sure you read that."

"I did." Fischer's face darkened.

"And I'm sure that's why you must think we're searching for the ancient utopia so many others tried to find."

"Well, if that isn't what you're looking for, then what could it be?"

Torres grinned slyly and turned the archaeologist around, albeit with extra effort. "Look out over these sacred mountains," Torres said, extending his left arm out as far as it would go. He pointed as he swept the entire scene, as if showing it all to Fischer for the first time. "It's beautiful here, isn't it?"

"Yes, but I don't see how that—"

Torres cut Fischer off. "The world once looked like this everywhere, until people ruined it." The German's offense at being interrupted went ignored by Torres, who could not have cared less at this point. "But there is a place where the technology of the Old World can fix the new, can take us from the brink of extinction to thriving once more—free of diseases, hunger, pain, sadness."

Fischer twisted his head to look over at Torres, who stared out at the landscape, pure admiration glistening in his eyes.

"What are you talking about?" Fischer argued. "You can't really believe all of that?"

Torres snapped from his daydream in an instant, as though he'd been in some far-off land, or in another dimension. "No, of course not, Werner. I don't have any illusions about what this place can be used for, or how it will change the world."

"Yes, well...Wait, what did you say?"

"Shangri-La holds the secrets to the most powerful technology on the planet, my good professor. How else would they be able to remain invisible to the planet? They must have something that keeps them hidden, a device or a resource that makes them unseen."

Fischer searched Torres' eyes for any sign of reason left, but he found none. All he saw was madness, unadulterated and ravenous.

"I'm sorry?" Fischer leered. "What are you talking about? That is not what we, what you, told me this was about. It almost sounds like you want to exploit this mythical valley." He raised a finger, pointing it at the bridge of Torres' nose. "You said we were investigating the disappearance of an ancient tribe from this region, and that you had evidence for this group. Not this."

"I see," Torres accepted. "I was hoping that you'd be excited about this project, about bringing to light something that had been suppressed from the public for so long. This was your chance to expose a great truth, to share with the world a light that had been extinguished so long ago. I suppose I was wrong about that."

"You were wrong to assume I wouldn't figure out you're trying to get me on board with a wild goose chase," Fischer snapped. "I'm leaving."

He started to walk away, but Torres stopped him with a firm hand against his shoulder. "Then before you leave, we should have a drink."

"A drink?" Fischer did nothing to suppress his suspicions.

"Of course," Torres said. "Do you think I hold it against you that you won't continue on this journey? I can find another archaeologist, Werner. I assure you. You were my first choice, obviously." Torres ambled over to a backpack sitting next to the stone firepit and plucked a bottle of whiskey from within. He set the bottle down on a nearby tree stump, then produced two tin cups from the backpack.

Torres made quick work of pouring the drinks and replaced the cork back in the bottle before handing Fischer one of the cups.

The German accepted with hesitation but decided not to be rude. Perhaps he feared Torres, and that would certainly have made sense given the man's blatant suspicion. His decorum, however won out over fear.

"To new roads and new adventures," Torres said, raising his cup. He tipped it back and drank it all in one gulp, watching nonchalantly as the archaeologist consumed his.

Fischer looked down at his empty cup when he'd swallowed and nodded his approval. "Now that is good whiskey," he said. "I've never been much for bourbon, but this is excellent."

"Might as well have another," Torres said. "Will make my pack lighter on the way out if there's less to carry."

Fischer grinned at the comment. "Now you're starting to sound like a German."

Torres disarmed him completely with his returning smile. He splashed the cups with bourbon again, this time filling Fischer's to the top but his own only halfway. His task done, Torres returned the cup to Fischer, who raised it and this time offered the toast.

"To history," he said. "Real, evidence-based history. Let it always light our way." He bobbed his head, gauging how well Torres received the barbs.

For his part, the Spaniard didn't even flinch.

"Prost."

"Salud," Torres replied. He sipped his whiskey, watching as the German dumped his into his mouth, then swallowed.

"Ah," Fischer exclaimed. "Well, I am glad you see things my way. I suppose we should head back to the vehicles before it gets dark. I don't know about you, but I have had about enough of sleeping in a tent on the ground and could do with a comfortable bed."

"Indeed," Torres agreed. "You must be dead tired."

He stood and set his cup down on the stump, angling toward Fischer, who stood between him and the cliff's edge.

Fischer wasn't paying attention, his gaze focused in the bottom of the empty cup. "What kind of bourbon did you say this was? It's very good."

When he looked up from the cup, he found Torres a few feet away and closing. The determined look in the Spaniard's face sent a wave of fear through Fischer, but in the split second he had to think, Fischer figured he was just being paranoid, an effect that would only heighten with the absorption of booze into his bloodstream.

That sentiment vanished in a flash as Torres slapped his hand on the German's shoulder and spun him around to look out over the mountains and valleys.

"It's certainly beautiful, isn't it, Professor?" Torres asked, a jovial kind of drunkenness teetered on the question.

"Yes," Fischer affirmed, nervous. "It certainly is. It beats working in a lab or an office all of the time."

"Or a classroom, I imagine."

"I enjoy teaching when I get the chance, but most of what I do is research. Occasionally, I miss the students."

"I'm sure they miss you, too," Torres said, gripping the man's shoulder tighter.

Fischer half turned his head to look at the Spaniard who'd hired him for this project. "Are you okay, Benitzio?"

"Me?" Torres asked, facing Fischer with a mentally absent, clownish grin. "I'm fine. I just can't understand why someone who was an accomplished archaeologist, so close to the discovery of some-thing incredible that would change the course of history, would do something so rash, so tragic."

Fischer's eyebrows lowered, pinching together to express his confusion. "What are you talking about?"

His answer came in an abrupt show of force from the arm wrapped around his back and the hand gripping his shoulder.

Before he could react, Fischer felt himself shoved forward toward the precipice only ten feet away. Chen watched from the shadows of the trees as her master drove the impudent archaeologist toward the precipice, the victim unable to stop it.

"What are you doing?" he shouted, but his answer came in another push, this time stronger, and in his middle back.

Fischer tried to resist, to regain his balance by flailing his arms around or planting his feet on the rock, but he couldn't fight Torres' strength, and the German could only yell in desperation as he felt air under his foot with the next step forward. Then, gravity hooked him, tugging on his weight toward the ground far below.

His screams heightened, then faded, as he fell—until the sound abruptly stopped. Then, the mountains wrapped Torres and Chen in reverent silence. The smell of evergreens filled Torres' nostrils as he leaned his head back and sucked in a deep breath. The effort to shove Fischer over the cliff hadn't taken long, but the few seconds still required effort.

Chen got the feeling the reason for her boss needing the breath might have been the altitude, but it could have also been a gesture of relief.

"What's next?" She risked the question, knowing Torres preferred to keep things rolling rather than stagnate.

He stepped closer to the rocky edge and leaned out, staring down at the broken body on the ground below. Fischer's arms and legs splayed out in awkward directions, with the neck bent in a grisly, unnatural position.

Torres retreated from the drop and faced his assistant. "We have what we need," he said plainly. "That should tell us how to find the heart."

Chen wasn't so sure, and she let him see that in her eyes. "The clue doesn't give us much to go on. It's a vague reference."

"Vague?"

Torres diverted his gaze to the scenery beyond the precipice. He stared for nearly a minute before speaking again, feeling certain that he was clever enough to figure out a dead poet's riddle. "Read it out loud to me," he said in a hushed tone.

She took the paper from his hand and looked at it again. "Seven stars cradle the Heart of Shambala, protecting the way for those who would seek the gates to the sacred valley."

He looked over at her when she finished and sidled next to her to view the document again. "Such a short message and yet so powerful."

"And neither of us knows what it means," Chen added.

"No. We don't." He relented, folding his hands behind his back and raised up on his tiptoes for a second, then lowered back down. "And we need to figure it out before someone else does."

"Who else is looking for this?"

"No one that I know of. But that can always change."

3

ATLANTA

Sean finished scrolling to the bottom of the tablet's screen and shook his head. He let out an audible "Ugh" and then picked up the white porcelain coffee mug sitting next to his right elbow.

Pearl Jam's song "Corduroy" played in his headphones, and he reached over to his phone to turn the volume down as he stared at the headline again.

With the music lowered, he pulled up the text messaging app and sent a quick text to Tommy Schultz, the head of the International Archaeological Agency and his best friend of nearly three decades.

He got a reply within thirty seconds.

"Yes, I saw. So strange," was all Tommy offered.

Sean stared in disbelief at the screen, the headline still seeming like something out of a bad dream. *Werner Fischer, dead from a hiking accident at 65.*

The second Sean saw the headline, he felt a tsunami of pain hit him. Sean had met Fischer around ten years ago, just before Tommy was kidnapped by the man who called himself "The Prophet."

The article said that investigators found alcohol in the late archaeologist's bloodstream, and that he likely lost his balance while enjoying the view.

"What was he doing in China?" Sean wondered out loud.

"What was who doing in China?" a woman's voice asked from the other end of the kitchen. Her Spanish accent still sent a flurry of goose bumps over Sean's skin. He turned and looked over at his wife, Adriana Villa, where she stood in a Doors T-shirt and a pair of tight shorts. She held a cup of coffee near her waist and raised it to her lips, waiting for Sean's answer.

"Sorry," Sean offered. "A guy Tommy and I knew just died. Archaeologist. Good dude. Brilliant researcher. He was only sixty-five."

"What happened? You said he was in China?"

"Yeah. Looks like he fell off a cliff. Hiking accident."

"In China?"

"Looks like it. Jiangxi Province. He was in the mountains there. Beautiful area."

"Yes," she affirmed. "It is pretty there."

"You've been?" Sean sounded surprised, when in reality he knew his wife had been nearly everywhere. It shouldn't have been the slightest shock to him that she'd been to those sacred mountains.

"That area, yes. Once. It's pretty vast."

Sean chuckled. "Vast?"

She cocked her head to the side after a sip of coffee and fired her best *you should stop talking* look. "A lot of people don't realize how much land there is in China. They see the overcrowded cities and think the entire country looks like that. Much of it is still natural or agrarian."

That much Sean knew, but he didn't feel the need to assert that.

"What was he doing in that part of China?" she asked, both out of genuine curiosity and to needle the bull.

Sean couldn't resist the bait. Or he was still too groggy from sleep fog to catch her jab. "That's what I just said...Oh, okay. You got me. Good one."

She offered a sultry grin as a reward.

"Anyway," he continued, "I didn't know that much about the man's personal life, like that he was an avid hiker, for example."

"Was he?"

Sean rolled his eyes and tossed his head to one side. "I have no idea. Look, my point is that I knew him professionally. And he was a really nice guy on the occasions we worked together, or when I bumped into him at a conference. Class act."

"Was he alone?" Adriana pried.

Sean's eyebrows shot up. "Actually, that's a good question. I would imagine he'd have been with someone. And I know he enjoyed his booze, but to be wandering through the mountains of China, drinking by himself...that doesn't seem like him."

Adriana rolled her shoulders and took a sip as if it was nothing to consider.

Sean knew better. "What?" he pressed. "You thinking foul play?"

She swallowed. "I didn't say that."

"Yeah, but you insinuated it. Who would want to kill an archaeologist?" He immediately realized his mistake when the word slipped out.

Adriana lowered her head, peering at him with the darkest chocolate eyes he'd ever seen. "Seriously? You're going to ask me that? How many times have people tried to kill you or Tommy? Or people you're associated with?"

"Okay. I get it. But still..." He turned his head to look at the screen once more. "Fischer wasn't like us." *Then again, neither were so many people that had died mysteriously, or were outright murdered in their line of work.*

The thought sent a flutter through his gut, twisting it with sadness. How many innocent people had been hurt, or killed, through the years for no other reason than greed or ambition? Sean reckoned that could be said of all human history since the dawn of time. People had always been willing to harm others to get what they wanted. He'd heard some mention that in the current era, folks were more selfish than they'd ever been. Sean disagreed. As a student of history, he knew well how humans had acted all along. The vehicles and weapons they used to carry out their devious plans had changed, but the motives, the intentions, the evil selfishness were all the same.

"You okay?" Adriana asked. There was no teasing in her voice, only sincere concern. Her posture stiffened to a more attentive stance.

Sean snapped out of it, realizing he'd been staring at the floor, thinking about so many things from his personal history, and beyond. "Yeah. Sorry. Just thinking about human psychology through the ages. It never seems to change. And good people like Werner are collateral damage."

She arched an eyebrow. "That's a bit heavy for seven forty-five in the morning." Then she nodded. "But you're right, of course." Tilting her head to the side, she asked, "Does that mean you think maybe it was foul play?"

Sean snorted. "I don't know. But is it messed up that our first instinct with stuff like this is to immediately question the official narrative?"

Adriana shrugged. "Maybe. I've heard people get more cynical with age, old man." She flashed a flirty smile.

Sean shook his head. In other circumstances, he would have stood up, walked over to her, and wrapped his arms around her. As it was, he only half chuckled. The weight on his heart pulled him back to his previous thoughts.

"I'll check around," he said. "I'm sure I have a resource over there who could find out something."

"I'm sure you do."

He caught her mischievous tone. "If I didn't know any better, I would say someone was jealous."

"Jealous?" She laughed. "Of what?"

"You tell me. You're the one who's jealous."

Adriana rolled her eyes and tossed her sleek brown hair back. "You're so dumb," she joked.

"And you married me," he quipped. His eyes squinted with his grin, completely disarming any resistance she still possessed.

She left the safe confines of the counter and sashayed over to the breakfast table overlooking the courtyard behind their home in

Buckhead, a suburb of Atlanta. "You certainly have a mouth on you," she said. "I bet you got in all sorts of trouble when you were a kid."

His left shoulder shrugged off the accusation. "Nah, I was an angel. Never got in any trouble."

"Sure you were." She took a sip of her coffee and shook her head. "Sorry if I don't buy that. I bet you were a huge brat."

"I got into some mischief in school. Horsing around, making silly noises or talking too much in class. That last one never went away, even in college. I remember my best friend's mom was one of my professors for English literature, and she got onto me about talking in class over dinner one night at their house. That was embarrassing, but I never did anything serious."

She eyed him suspiciously. "I'm still not convinced. I feel like you might have been something of a bully."

He shrank back from the statement. "I was not...Well, maybe I was a touch competitive in sports."

"There it is."

Sean shook his head. "Can we please get back on the subject? Do you want to go to China with me or not? We could get a nice hotel in Hong Kong, then head up to the mountains. Maybe there's a cabin there or something. Might be a chance to have a little romantic getaway on the other side of the world."

She shuffled closer to the point her knees brushed against his. "We've been on the other side of the world." She paused. "But a little romance with Sean Wyatt? I'll definitely take that." She bent down and looped her arm around his neck, then kissed him gently on the lips.

Her perfume filled his nostrils with the scent of roses and vanilla, and his eyes nearly rolled back at the intoxicating smell. The touch of her lips felt like tiny pillows against his, and he relished the moment.

Then, as quickly as it began, it ended as Adriana stood up straight again. "Book the trip, cowboy. I'll start packing."

"If I can get us a flight."

"Just take the IAA jet. Tommy's not using it this week, is he?"

"No, I don't think so."

She sensed the hesitation in his voice. "No. Don't even think about it."

"Think about what?" He looked up at her, genuinely puzzled.

"About asking Tommy if he wanted to come along for the ride. He doesn't like being a third wheel any more than you would."

"I was going to see if June wanted to go, too. They could use a little alone time together."

She cocked her head to the side, scowling in confusion. "How could they be alone if they were with us?"

"I don't know," he said with a shrug. "I thought we could split up once we got there."

Adriana put a hand on her hip and then bent down close to him again. Her nose nearly touched his, and he could feel her breath on his lips. "Let's just the two of us go. I can book the flights. No need to use the company plane."

"Are you sure?"

She nodded. "Yep. You should start packing."

Adriana turned and sauntered back through the kitchen and out the doorway, heading toward the staircase.

He shook his head as she left his sight. Then he flapped his lips. "Man, I am weak," he muttered.

"Don't worry!" she shouted from another room. "I won't tell anyone! Besides, you're only human!"

Sean huffed a laugh to himself, wondering how she'd heard his comment from so far away. Then he turned back to the laptop and stared at the screen, reading the headline over again. "I guess we're coming to find out what happened to you, Dr. Fischer. I just hope there's nothing to find."

"You still going to that demonstration your friend is putting on for the military?"

"Crap," Sean muttered to himself. "Yeah, I guess so. Tommy's going with me, so that should be good. Maybe it will give us a chance to debrief about this whole thing with Dr. Fischer."

"Okay, do you want me to look for tickets while you're out?" She reappeared in the doorway and leaned against the frame. She wore a look of concern with her morning outfit.

"No, hold off on that until I get back. Let's see what Tommy thinks about all this first. And there's the memorial to consider. We may have a funeral to attend before we do any international travel."

"Yes, I suppose I forgot about that. Well, let me know when you hear anything. I'll keep an eye out on flights."

"Thanks."

Sean stared at the last remnants of coffee at the bottom of his mug and sighed. This was supposed to be a relaxing Sunday morning at the house. He wished he could sit out by the pool all day and just take it easy, but that wasn't going to happen. He and Tommy had to drive out to the middle of nowhere for an exclusive military demonstration.

Malcolm Barnwell didn't extend invitations like that very often, in no small part due to the fact that the military tried to keep as many things as possible under wraps. Wouldn't want to let any enemies accidentally get wind of a new experimental weapon prototype.

Even though Sean and Tommy were trusted friends, there were some things Malcolm couldn't allow due to national security—even though Sean had done more than almost any single person to make sure that security was maintained.

Today, however, appeared to be an exception. Which, in Sean's mind, meant Malcolm needed something from them. The question as to what he could want nagged at Sean's brain.

The billionaire had any number of people at his disposal, and an endless stream of resources from experts in medicine, engineering, physics, weapons design, and beyond. He was basically Santa Claus for the military, and had a full complement of elves always working on the next and newest toy in the workshop.

Still, Sean couldn't recall the last time Malcolm had extended an invitation to watch a demonstration. Until he and Tommy arrived at the range later that day, Sean knew he probably wouldn't have his answer.

4

SOUTH GEORGIA

T he army convoy rolled along the bumpy, dirt road. A cloud of dust followed each vehicle's wake, combining to form a veritable dust storm of swirling light brown that churned into the clear blue sky. When the caravan of armored vehicles stopped, a warm breeze rolled down the surrounding green hills to the west and quickly dispelled the dusty cluster.

Malcolm Barnwell stood on a wooden deck built into the side of one of the hills a few thousand yards away from the road, and from the targets sitting on it.

He watched the lead vehicle through binoculars, then shifted his focus to the three vehicles behind it.

Barnwell nodded and then turned to his audience. High-ranking officers from four of the military branches stood in rapt attention as they waited for the test to begin.

"So, I don't think I have to tell you gentlemen what we're looking at. You're all familiar with this particular armored chassis platform, what it's made out of, all that. These are some of the toughest transports we have."

The officers said nothing, though the guy from the navy seemed a little grumpy. It might have had something to do with his being from

North Dakota. Up there, they didn't experience the kind of heat and humidity that South Georgia cooked up.

Beads of sweat rolled down both sides of the man's weathered face. The wrinkles on his forehead were like ski moguls for perspiration, and Malcolm wondered when the guy was going to give in and dab his skin with a kerchief.

Malcolm paced in front of the men, placing the binoculars on a table set up beneath the white tent he'd arranged for the exhibition. A little shade was the least he could provide against the sweltering heat. Well, that and a cooler full of bottled water.

"What you're about to witness is the dawn of a new era in smart warhead technology. With this new compound, weight is reduced by sixty percent. I don't have to tell you what that means for your planes," he glanced specifically at the air force and navy guys. "And an increase in firepower capability is only the beginning."

"What's this compound made of?" the Marine huffed. His question sparked a cluster of laughter from the others.

Malcolm chuckled, too, lowering his head as if he hadn't expected the question, which of course, he had. He ground his teeth against the irritation but didn't counter the man's joke. People were so predictable. He imagined the Marine, and probably the others, were the same kind of people who'd walk out onto their front porch, see their neighbor washing his car, and crack the clichéd joke, "While you're out there, can you wash mine, too?"

He'd seen it all, and Malcolm Barnwell had been selling high-tech weaponry for over thirty years. He thought it interesting how rapidly weapons evolved but people never seemed to.

Except Sean Wyatt.

Malcolm glanced over at his longtime friends Tommy and Sean standing behind the row of officers. Those two knuckleheads were special guests, which was a touch unorthodox for these kinds of things, but Malcolm knew the two enjoyed a good explosion. And since they'd been in the area—relatively speaking—he thought an invitation was in order.

Sean and Tommy watched with rapt fascination; their eyes locked on the parked vehicles. From this distance, they looked more like big toys sitting out in someone's yard.

"He sure is a showman," Tommy whispered, leaning close so only Sean could hear the comment.

Sean's lips curled on the left side, offering a wry smirk. "All part of the sales gig," Sean replied.

"Without further ado," Malcolm announced, his voice swelling with adrenaline-fueled drama, "I give you the Omega ZX-3."

He spun around and put his hands up as a stage actor might with the curtain pulled back. For a couple of seconds, the people in attendance merely stared out at the vehicles on the road.

Silence spilled over the hillside. The officer from the army wrinkled his forehead, then looked over at one of the men next to him, wondering what was supposed to be happening.

He was about to ask when suddenly, there was a pop from downrange. The audience leaned in closer, each of them staring expectantly toward the vehicles.

Then, four bright orange explosions consumed the vehicles in an instant. The blasts thundered over the valley and up the surrounding hillsides. Tree branches shivered and waved from the concussion.

Within seconds, the fires from the explosion consumed the vehicles, leaving nothing but torched husks.

The officers clapped their approval as the fire team rolled out onto the range to douse the remaining flames.

"I thought you said it was in a plane," the air force guy said.

"Yes," Malcolm confirmed, whirling around with all the flare of a ballet dancer. "We have Omegas for planes, surface-to-air, and surface-to-surface weapons. What you just saw was one of our rockets."

"I didn't see a rocket. I barely even heard anything, other than that little pop. Sounded like a potato cannon."

Malcolm grinned, knowing he'd already won. "Exactly."

The air force general paused for only a second, realizing what the ironmonger meant. "Outstanding."

Malcolm paced again, this time from right to left. "The Omega is called that because it's the last weapon of its kind that you'll need. Capable of auto-targeting multiple enemies, the Omega can do the work of four weapons for the price of...well, two."

The officers laughed in unison as Malcolm cast them a mischievous, sidelong glance.

"A boy's gotta eat."

"With the money we pay you, Malcolm," the army general said, "you need to be taking us out to eat."

"Funny you should say that, Frank," Malcolm quipped. "I took the liberty of having catering brought out." He motioned behind Sean and Tommy to a large table being setup by six caterers in white jackets and matching chef hats. "I trust filet mignon is okay with everyone."

The navy commander shook his head. He snorted before saying, "You sure know how to impress, Malcolm."

Malcolm turned to him, took a step closer, slapped him on the shoulder and said, "That's why you come to me and not the other guys, Jerry." He extended his right arm toward the catering table. "After you."

The officers formed a short, single-file line at the serving line while the caterers removed the metal lids from the dishes and began filling plates with potatoes, peppered green beans, and steak medallions smothered in onions, butter, and a dollop of Boursin cheese.

Sean and Tommy greeted their friend with broad grins as Malcolm approached them. "You two should get something to eat." He leaned closer. "I wouldn't let these military guys go first. There won't be anything left. Have you ever seen how they eat?"

Sean laughed and looked back at the short line. "I think you'll have enough today. Looks like you had them bring out everything they had."

"I'll refer to my previous statement."

The three shared another laugh. When the laughter faded, Malcolm looked back at the range, where the fire crew sprayed a combination of water and a fire retardant onto the smoldering husks that were previously military vehicles.

"I have to say, Malcolm," Tommy started, "those are some pretty impressive bombs."

"Yes, well, we take pride in what we do." Malcolm resisted the urge to correct his friend referring to the weapons as bombs. The ones they'd just witnessed weren't technically that, but he chose to ignore the error and continued. "Those warheads will help save untold numbers of American lives. We'll be able to take out multiple targets with a single ordnance. They'll be more cost effective than traditional weapons, too, which will give the federal budget a much-needed discount."

"Maybe we could push some of that money toward other areas of need," Sean added.

"Absolutely. Schools, health care, stuffing some of the money back in the Social Security mattress that has been raided over the last few decades." He turned and motioned to the table that was quickly clearing up. "You two get something to eat. Let me finish up with business, and I'll get back to you two."

"Sure thing, Malcolm. Do your job." Tommy gave him a rough shake with his hand on the man's collar, and then let him go to head toward the spread.

Malcolm winked, ambled over to one of two tables prepared for the meal, and sat down with the officers who were already seated. Glasses of cold sweet tea sat on the tables beside every set of white plates and silverware.

Sean and Tommy went through the now empty line, piled food on their plates, and returned to an empty table that had—apparently —been set up just for the two of them.

Sean listened unintentionally to the conversation between the officers and Malcolm as they discussed deployment, cost, and delivery times. He smiled to himself as he listened to Malcolm close the deal.

He reminded Sean of the *Saturday Night Live* bit with Alec Baldwin—always be closing. It was a pure salesman's mantra, and one that Malcolm had grasped early on in life. He understood better than most how to schmooze with the people controlling the money. And Malcolm knew the best ways to extract that money. These guys were decision makers. Getting the funding for the projects or the weapons they desired was a matter of red tape. People talk all day about restructuring the budget, cutting military spending, but in the end, these guys in uniform always got what they wanted. One way or the other.

"How soon can we have these weapons in the hands of soldiers?" the guy from the army asked.

"We're accepting deposits today. Then it's just a matter of delivery time. I'll trust you gentlemen to do the right thing and pay upon receiving the goods."

The group laughed.

Sean shook his head and forked a cluster of green beans into his mouth.

"He knows how to work the room, doesn't he?" Tommy asked, reading his friend's mind.

After Sean swallowed the veggies, he bobbed his head in agreement. "Yep. He's the master."

Tommy chewed on a piece of steak, watching Malcolm with mesmerized interest. When the meal was done, the military officers said their goodbyes, thanking Malcolm for the delicious food and the incredible display.

After the men were gone, Malcolm joined his friends at the table. He loosened the already loose black tie around his neck and picked up a yeast roll from a basket in the center of the table. He tore the bread in half and took a bite.

"You know," he said, still chewing on the roll, "I never get tired of this gig."

"I was going to ask," Sean said. He cut a piece of steak and looked at it for a second, admiring the perfectly seared outside and the pink inside. "I would imagine a meal like this is tough to get used to." He offered a wry grin with his sarcasm.

Malcolm chuckled. "Yeah, well, these meals aren't every day, you know. But I have a lifestyle I could only have dreamed of when I was younger."

"I'm sure," Tommy agreed. "You grew up in a tough situation. You're the living embodiment of the American dream."

Malcolm lowered his head, face blushing. "Well, I've been lucky."

"Yeah right," Sean countered. "You busted your hump to get where you are. People who win the lottery are lucky. You worked your way to the top. It's admirable. Don't disparage that."

"Well, I appreciate that," Malcolm said, humility framing his words. "Very kind of you, Sean."

"Hey, you earned it. We're proud of what you've accomplished."

"Yeah," Tommy concurred. "And it wasn't always easy. Back in the 'nineties, you really struggled."

"Almost folded up shop," Malcolm said. "If it hadn't been for a couple of small contracts that kept us open for business, we would have gone under. Then we got that one law enforcement deal that pushed us into the mainstream."

"You think you're ever going to go into small arms—rifles, pistols, that sort of thing?" Sean asked.

Malcolm shrugged. "Maybe, but that space has so many players in it now. These days, it's so easy for anyone to build those kinds of weapons. Or at least assemble them. I know a few of those guys who do that, like our friend at Dawn of Defense in North Georgia. But I'm in a good niche where I am. Barnwell Armaments is a billion-dollar company now, and with this little demo you two just witnessed, I won't have any worries for a very long time."

"That's good to hear," Tommy said. "Almost sounds like you're getting ready to retire."

"Retire?" Malcolm answered with a huff. "I'm in my prime."

The three shared a laugh before Malcolm continued. "I'm only fifty, you young whippersnapper," he said in his best grumpy-old-man voice. "I have plenty of years left to do good work."

"Speaking of," Sean switched gears, "what's next for Barnwell Armaments? You looking into any of this new tech? Magnetic propulsion, that sort of thing?"

A serpentine grin slid across Malcolm lips. "Sure, I can talk about some of those things. I just need you two to sign an NDA form first."

"Always the wise guy," Tommy said with a laugh.

The table fell silent again, and the air filled with the sounds of birds and cicadas. Sean's face turned serious. He'd been biding his time before asking the question, but he wanted to give Malcolm time to take care of business, and calm down for a minute after giving his big pitch.

"I have to ask," Sean began, cutting the thick humid air with the deep version of his voice. "This is the first time you've ever invited us to one of your demonstrations." He paused, letting the question finish itself in Malcolm's mind.

Sean wasn't disappointed.

"And you're wondering, why now, right? Why this time?"

"Something like that," Sean affirmed. He picked up a glass of tea and took a sip. The ice cubes jingled against the side of the glass when he set it back down.

Malcolm offered a wide grin, cocking his head to the side as he pointed a finger at Sean. "Can't slip anything past you, can I, Sean?"

"He does have a point," Tommy added.

Malcolm waited a few seconds to answer, popping the second half of the yeast roll into his mouth to chew on both the bread and his response.

"You boys know me too well," he said after swallowing the bread. "I suppose there's no beating around the bush."

"I thought you preferred a more direct approach anyway," Sean injected.

"Very true, my friend. You know me too well. And I assume," Malcolm said, pausing to take a sip of tea, "you figured I invited you here for a reason other than to watch a bunch of things blow up."

"You'd be correct."

Malcolm threw up his hands. "Astute, as always, my friend. I knew I wasn't going to get any intel from any of my military connections, much less the people I know in the CIA."

"This sounds juicy," Tommy mused. "What's going on, Malcolm?"

"Actually..." the billionaire said. His face darkened, and the casual demeanor in the man's eyes vanished in an instant. "I was hoping you could tell me."

5

SOUTH GEORGIA

Sean exchanged a questioning glance with Tommy then let his friend take the lead. The IAA was, after all, his baby. Tommy had formed the organization as a way to honor his parents when he believed they'd died in a plane crash. It was only later he discovered they'd been held prisoner for several years in North Korea after being captured during an expedition.

Tommy took the look from Sean as his cue and asked the first question. The eyebrow arched over his right eye, and he cocked his head at an angle as he peered at their friend Malcolm. "Hoping we could tell you what?"

The grin he received from the ironmonger piqued Tommy's interest even more, as if the billionaire's previous statement wasn't enough. "You two know that I'm involved in several other ventures. One of them being in your neck of the woods." He took a swig of tea, then said, "Archaeology."

"Yeah, we know. And you're behind on your donations."

Sean snorted at his friend's wit.

Malcolm laughed, too. "That's true. I am. And I need to be better about that. All kidding aside, though, I've recently funded several expeditions, some of them on the other side of the world. Like the one in question."

He allowed his words to hang in their minds for a few seconds before continuing. Malcolm knew how to play an audience of a thousand or a mere two. He could swing them from one side of the drama to the other like a clock pendulum.

"I recently funded an expedition into China, Jiangxi to be precise. Do you know it?"

"I've heard of it," Sean said. "One of the few places I haven't been."

"Same," Tommy echoed. "Heard of it but never actually visited." He stopped as the realization hit him. *No,* he thought, trying to convince himself that wasn't possible. *Or was it?* "A friend of ours was over there recently..." He fought off the emotions surrounding the strange death of Werner Fischer and ended his sentence abruptly.

"Oh?" Malcolm wondered, tilting his head to one side.

Tommy lowered his eyes, unwilling to say anything else until he could collect himself.

Sean took over when he saw his friend wasn't going to keep going. "Werner Fischer," he said. "Good guy. We just found out this morning that he died while on an expedition. And he was over in China, in Jiangxi, actually."

Malcolm eyes widened. "Yes," he said. "Werner's death was beyond unfortunate, and extremely tragic."

"How did you know about that?" Tommy asked, lifting his gaze once more to focus on Malcolm.

The billionaire shrugged. "Because I funded the research and the trip."

Sean and Tommy exchanged another look, but this time it was one of confusion.

"I didn't realize you knew him," Tommy managed.

Malcolm nodded, the look in his eyes growing distant as he shifted his gaze to the table underneath his elbows. "I didn't know him as well as you guys. I doubt I did, anyway. I'm not an archaeologist. Y'all have a community, a tribe. You see each other at keynote talks or conferences or whatever it is you guys do when you're not scraping dirt and rocks with brushes."

The two guests shared a laugh at the comment.

"But yes," Malcolm continued, "I knew Werner as an expert in his field. I hired him to take on this project, in part because you two weren't available. On top of that, you don't normally take on jobs from someone else. You do your own thing."

"Glad someone read the fine print on the website," Sean joked.

A round of laughter circled the table before Malcolm spoke again. "Yeah, well, I also know how you guys operate. You're not some treasure hunters for hire. I appreciate that."

"Of course you do," Tommy said. "You run a historical preservation foundation you probably pour millions into every year."

Malcolm whistled. "Yep, we do put a lot in."

"Right." Tommy inclined his head. "So, you said you funded Fischer's trip?"

Regret painted Malcolm's face a pale, crestfallen color. He lowered his eyes to the table and nodded. "Yeah. I had no idea, boys. Honestly. I didn't think it would be anything dangerous. There was no way we could have foreseen something like that happening."

Sean shook his head, sticking out his lower lip in solemn agreement. "Nope. Nothing you could have done. Werner was his own man. If there were risks involved, I'm sure he knew about them. Horrible way to go, though, falling like that."

A sickening feeling fluttered across Sean's skin, causing goose bumps to ripple across his arms. Sean's fear of heights had earned him quite the ribbing from Tommy throughout the years, but Sean felt like he'd made progress, too. That didn't mean he was ready to go BASE jumping with his buddies, but he'd faced his greatest fear many times and come out unscathed—mostly.

The thought of someone in a similar line of work falling to their death on a mountainside brought all those old fears back to the front of Sean's mind. He imagined the horror of slipping over the cliff's edge, tumbling for what must have felt like minutes, desperately hoping to land safely on something. Sean had fallen a few times from low heights, off a ladder or the back of a couch. The thing he always recalled was the feeling of sheer terror at not sensing anything stable behind him. The air beneath felt like falling into a void, like a bottomless pit, and that instability shook Sean. He never wanted to feel that way again, and so he took precautions, such as not getting anywhere close to a long drop.

Perhaps his measures were out of paranoia, irrational actions that made him look ridiculous. Sean didn't care. He'd always been afraid of heights and figured he always would be no matter how many times he climbed a rock face with a harness and rope, or how many times he fought someone on the top of a building. That deeply rooted fear was never going away, and Sean had to just make good with that fact.

"Yeah," Malcolm agreed, whipping Sean back into the present moment. He hadn't realized he'd gone silent for a somber minute. "Horrible," Malcolm continued. "Hard to believe it."

"I still can't believe he's gone," Tommy admitted. "Doesn't seem real."

"No, it doesn't. Werner was a good guy, and extremely intelligent. Terrible for him to go out the way he did. And so senseless."

Sean sighed and allowed a new thought to enter his mind. "You said you funded this expedition?"

Malcolm nodded. "Yep," he said with a slap of his knees. "Well, my foundation did. I contribute a little, but the foundation does most of the heavy lifting in regard to money."

"Humility is a weird suit for you to wear, Malcolm," Tommy said, raising his glass of tea with a mischievous smirk.

It produced a snort from the billionaire. "Well, it's the truth. I won't take credit where it isn't due."

"It's your foundation," Sean argued. "But we're getting off track. You said you were hoping we could tell you something. Does this have to do with what happened with Werner?"

Malcolm pointed a finger at his guest. "While that isn't why I invited you two here, I must admit I'm curious to hear your thoughts or theories about what could have happened to poor Werner."

Sean and Tommy stole a quick look at each other. Sean spoke first. "I thought he accidentally fell off the side of a mountain."

"That's the official word," Malcolm said, the sound of skepticism scraping his voice.

"You don't believe that?" Tommy asked.

"No, it's not that. I just want to get your take on it."

Malcolm held his glass close to his mouth, watching his guests in anticipation of hearing their thoughts on the mysterious death of Dr. Fischer.

"It sounds suspicious," Sean said, "but these things do happen. I had a friend in college die the exact same way. She and a guy she was seeing were up hiking around on some high cliffs in East Tennessee. From what I heard, they were jumping over a little gap between the rocks along their path and she slipped. There was nothing her boyfriend could do." The horrific memory rammed its way into Sean's head, and he winced at the thought. He hadn't even been there, but his overactive imagination filled in the blanks as if he'd seen the whole thing. "None of us thought that the boyfriend had done anything like push her over the edge. We didn't suspect foul play."

"So, you don't now?"

"That all depends," Sean continued. "What would the motive be?"

"I guess that's where you two come in," Malcolm segued. "Fischer was working on something incredible. But," he raised the index finger he seemed so fond of using, "most people would say what he was looking for was a fool's errand, a desperate grasp at a wild goose chase."

Tommy crossed his arms, completely hooked. "What are you talking about, Malcolm? What was he looking for that would cause you to think someone might have killed him to get it?"

"I don't think someone might have killed Werner Fischer for what he was looking for. It's what I believe happened."

The assertion swept over the conversation, accompanied by a hot wind from the valley.

"What makes you think that?" Sean pressed.

"Because of where he was—in the Chinese wilderness—for starters. He would have hired on help, too. I know we gave him the budget for that. I think it's possible that Werner may have hired a guide or some other sort of expert to help him. This assistant could have learned about what Werner was trying to find and decided to steal it for himself. If he found it, I mean. Last I heard from him, they were going to investigate a site in the mountains. It was there he fell. I received word from one of his research assistants here in the States the second she found out."

"What are the investigators saying?" Tommy wondered.

"Same thing you heard. Werner's death was an accident. They haven't changed that story, and I haven't received any communications to the contrary."

"Despite that report, you believe he was murdered? By who?" Sean asked. "And why? Did they find whatever they were looking for?"

"I don't think so," Malcolm answered. "There's no sign of anything there that they might have found interesting."

"And you still haven't told us what they were trying to find."

"I didn't mention it?"

The two guests shook their heads, their eyes locked squarely on Malcolm. "My mistake, gentlemen. I thought I said something. I'm actually a little surprised Werner didn't mention it to you, considering the nature of this particular expedition."

He was building it up, just like he did with the military officers who were there earlier. Malcolm set down his tea and folded his hands in his lap. "They were looking for Shangri-La, boys."

"I'm sorry, did you just say he was looking for Shangri-La?" Tommy wore a much more dumbfounded look on his face than Sean, though for his part, Sean was doing his best to conceal the same emotion mirroring in his mind.

"Yep. I did. I suspect Werner didn't tell you boys about it because of the exact reaction you're giving me right now. I think he was afraid that people might discredit him for trying to find something a little off the historical radar."

"A little off?" Tommy asked with a huff. "I don't mean to beat you up about a project you sponsored, but there's no evidence that place ever existed, Malcolm. I mean, if it did, we'd have seen it with satellites or planes or—"

"A random farmer stumbling onto it, I know," Malcolm cut Tommy off before he could finish. "Believe me, I have all the same skepticism you do about this."

"But you funded it anyway," Sean said in a shrewd tone. "You must have seen something to convince you. You don't put your money into bad investments. Not usually."

"No, I don't," Malcolm agreed with a grin. "And I didn't on this one. I received information that changed both my mind, and Dr. Fischer's, about Shangri-La. Initially, when I approached him about being the lead on the project, he balked at the idea. Gave me the same reaction you two did, actually. He talked about how it was barely mentioned in some ancient texts, poems, things of that nature. I knew about all that, and the authors that talked about it in some of their fictional works."

"And yet you somehow managed to convince him."

"Which also means," Tommy added, "you must have found something, something tangible."

Malcolm nodded. "I wasn't sure if it had anything to do with Shangri-La or not, but I had to know more."

"Wait," Sean said, holding up a hand like a student in a classroom. "Let me guess this one. You didn't actually tell Werner he was looking for Shangri-La, did you?"

Their host's face reddened, and he lowered it in an admission of guilt. "I knew that once Werner got over there, he would find something. Whether it was Shangri-La or something else from another lost civilization, I knew he would succeed."

"Did he?" Tommy asked. Before Malcolm could answer, Tommy pressed on, his face red with anger. "Because he died, Malcolm. Searching for something that you sent him to find, except you didn't tell him what he was supposed to be looking for. Kind of important for us to know that sort of stuff."

"Yes. I know. You're right. But when you see what I have to show you, you'll understand why I was so insistent on this project. And while I have felt nothing but guilt since learning of Dr. Fischer's demise, accidents do happen, guys. It's unfortunate and tragic, but it could have happened to anyone, anywhere. I understand if you don't want to see what I have to show you, but I believe once you do, you'll understand why I was so interested in this. And why Werner was, too."

"Fine," Sean said, suspicion in his voice. "But why do you think Werner was killed? We haven't addressed that yet, or who you think did it."

Malcolm acknowledged the question with a nod. He'd been expecting that one and answered immediately. "I'm afraid Werner may have been killed by someone who was part of the expedition."

"The guide?" Tommy guessed.

"It would make sense. Of course, the Chinese government is always a suspect for these kinds of things. If they caught wind of what he was looking for—"

"You said Werner didn't know what he was looking for," Tommy corrected.

"True. But, it's possible someone learned of his expedition, followed them to the mountains, and then murdered him there."

Sean shook his head. "No. I don't think that's what happened. The Chinese aren't behind the killing, at least not if I'm betting on it."

"Why's that?" Malcolm wondered. He leaned forward and rested an elbow on the table, placing his chin in the palm of his hand with one finger reaching halfway up his left cheek.

"Because if they killed Werner, they would have also killed his guide and anyone else who might have been in the group. They only found one body, yes?"

"Correct."

"Then, there you have it," Sean said, holding out a hand as if he'd solved the case. "First people I would start looking into would be the guide he hired. Don't suppose you have a clue who that might be?"

"Unfortunately, no," Malcolm admitted. I tried not to be too hands-on with the project. Once I had Fischer on board, I felt it prudent to let him run the show as he saw fit. He knew better than I about the kinds of people to hire for something like that. I'm just the backer." He thumbed his chin for a second before speaking again. "Your theory makes sense, though, Sean. And I think I agree. If the Chinese had been behind the killing, then they would have executed everyone on the expedition."

"Unless they took prisoners," Tommy offered. His tone blended a splash of snark with a hint of concern.

"Yes, that is possible," Sean agreed. "Especially if Werner found something up in those mountains they thought was valuable."

"I certainly hope that isn't the case," Malcolm said with utmost sincerity.

Sean shook his head. "Probably not. Fischer was the one they needed. Not a sherpa or a local guide. Those would be low-value ransom targets—not to be too callous about it. But Werner was the one with the knowledge and resources. They would have kept him alive and eliminated anyone they deemed useless."

"Good point," Malcolm said with a nod. He ran a fingertip around the cold rim of his glass, his mind wandering in thought.

"Adriana and I talked about flying over there," Sean announced.

Tommy's head whipped around. He faced his friend with a bewildered scowl. "When did you talk about that?"

"This morning," Sean chuffed. "When I got your reply."

"Oh." Tommy almost sounded forlorn. "When were you going to tell me about this?"

Sean rolled his shoulders. "I don't know. I guess now? Adriana was going to look for flights."

"Why wouldn't you just take the plane?"

"Because I figured you were using it. And she and I were thinking about getting out of Dodge for a while."

"Oh, I see," Tommy said. "So, you thought you could just take off on a little adventure without me?" He pretended to sound hurt, but Sean knew better.

"Yeah, if you think you're going to get that old guilt trip routine to work on me, you're sadly mistaken."

Tommy chuckled at the comment. "It's almost as if you think I haven't known you for basically my entire life. I'm aware the guilt trip won't work."

"Then why are you trying it?"

"Habit."

Sean let out a "Ha." He shifted his eyes back to Malcolm. "So, I'm guessing you won't mind if we take a look around China to see what we can find, yeah?"

"And I'm coming with you," Tommy chimed.

All he received from Sean was a knowing smirk, as if that was the plan all along.

Malcolm looked pleased. He folded his hands over his knee and leaned back. "I thought you would never ask."

6

CHATTOGRAM, BANGLADESH

B enitzio sat in an uncomfortable red metal chair, waiting for the server to return with his beer, his second of the meal. He'd already scarfed down the fare the restaurant offered—in his case, he'd gone with a selection of staples featuring rice, fish curry, and lentils.

He watched the constant flow of cars driving by on the busy street. The vehicles stopped, moved a few feet or the length of the street if they were lucky enough to catch the light, and then returned to a stop to wait for what must have seemed like an eternity.

The pedestrians on the sidewalk mirrored the street, packing the narrow concrete walkways like tuna in a net. It looked as if the people didn't have a choice in which direction they moved, instead guided by the unified conscience of the masses.

Ju Chen returned and sat down across from him, her eyes steadily sweeping the scene behind her employer, as she always did when taking a seat. She always repeated the same habit no matter where she went, just in case.

"I saw that," Benitzio commented as he picked up the nearly empty beer bottle and drained the last few drops through his lips.

By the time he set the bottle down, the young waitress had

returned with a full one and placed it on the table before picking the empty one up and setting it on a tray.

"Thank you," he said, with a tip of the head. He reached out and wrapped his fingers around the cold bottle. The condensation tickled his skin. "That something you picked up in Chinese special forces?"

"I don't know what you're talking about," she said in a curt *I wish he would shut up* tone.

"Oh, come on," Benitzio urged, flashing his best begging smile. "You sat down and immediately looked around the area."

"So?" She stuck a fork into a dome of rice and shoveled a pile of the carbs into her mouth.

"You were checking for trouble," he continued, as if encouraged by her one-word answer. "Did you learn that in the military, or have you always been paranoid?"

She ignored him for a minute, stuffing two more spoonful's of rice and vegetables into her mouth before she moved on to the fish.

Without an answer, he decided to keep going. "I just assumed you picked up that little tick in the Chinese army."

She finished chewing a piece of fish before wiping the corner of her lips with a red napkin. Then she looked at him with a stern glare. "I check, yes. Did they teach us that? Probably. I already did that before I went into the CSF. I don't need someone to tell me to analyze my surroundings before I settle in. I've always been careful like that. Perhaps the military made me more prudent at that sort of prevention, but it's always been in my nature to take inventory of everything around me. When I walk into a room, I assess any threats that could be lurking in the shadows, or out in the open."

"Good," Benitzio approved. "And I agree, always better to be safe. You never know what kinds of enemies are out there and what they may be thinking."

She didn't say anything else, but he took her silence as a strange sort of agreement as she finished her meal in half the time it took him to stuff down a quarter of his.

"You never told me why you left," he said, adding to the list of things he didn't know about her. All Benitzio knew was that she was good and came with a dangerous reputation harnessed to her.

"No, I didn't," she said as she finished her plate of food in what was, to him, record time.

"Classified?"

"Something like that." Ju Chen picked up a bottle of water and drained half of it in a couple of gulps.

He laughed at the answer and turned his head to gaze out across the street, his thoughts meandering again.

"Did you get a response back yet?" She asked the question as though she already knew the answer.

"No," he said. "I didn't. And I don't think I will. I haven't spoken to anyone yet who understands the clue. The man meeting us here is might. After that, I'm not sure who to ask."

"And have you told everyone you asked what it is you're trying to find?" She peered at him through narrowed eyelids, dark slits that only allowed scrutiny through.

Benitzio sighed at the question, which gave her an inadvertent answer. "No. I didn't tell them what we were looking for. You heard Fischer's reaction when he realized we'd lied to him. No self-respecting historian or archaeologist in the world would go off on a hunt like this."

"You are."

He felt his face flush red with heat and blood, but he didn't take the bait. Benitzio calmed himself with a few short breaths and then counted to five before responding. "Not everyone has vision, my dear," he replied coolly.

"Or delusions of grandeur."

Benitzio forced himself to take a swig of beer before he responded. After he swallowed the lager, he wiped his lips and set the bottle down gently, though he really wanted to slam it against her face in a fit of defensive anger.

"Is it a delusion to desire wealth? What of prominence? The respect of your peers?"

"Somehow I don't think you care about the respect-of-peers part," she hedged. "Who are these mythical creatures you call peers? You haven't worked in the field in years from what I've heard."

She wasn't wrong, and that's what stung him the most. "It's true," he confessed. "I don't have any peers. The years I worked at the university were both a waste of my time and my talents. Not to mention the pay was abysmal."

His eyes grew vacant, and Ju Chen could sense a distant memory playing itself out in his mind.

"And this pays better?"

He cast a warning glance at her, but he found no malice on her face. "By miles," he said, disarming himself. "And you can always double dip. Find a buyer? Great. Or get money up front for an expedition. Just as good either way."

Ju Chen looked out across the sensory chaos of the city. She breathed in the smells of exhaust, curry, frying fish, and herbs. "If you can't figure out the meaning of that inscription, we have to find someone who can."

"Yes," he stumbled over the answer. "Of course." He did his best to sound convincing. "The sooner, the better."

"You promised an insane amount of money, Benitzio. The kind of money that allows a person to disappear forever. And then some." There was more to the statement, but she added nothing else.

"I assure you, the money we will receive for this discovery will be unimaginable." He clenched his jaw, fighting off the irritation simmering in his gut.

"I don't know," she countered. "I have a vivid imagination."

"Yes, well, that won't do us any good if we don't find the valley."

"Which brings me back to why we're here," she demurred. "Who is this person we're meeting? You've been coy about them."

"It's not my last option," he lied, and poorly at that. "But I do think he can help us. Just bear in mind, he's a little out there."

Ju Chen's right eyebrow climbed up her forehead. With her black hair pulled back in a tight ponytail, thin wrinkles stretched across the skin.

"What is that supposed to mean?"

A commotion behind her tore her attention away from Benitzio. She turned and looked in the direction of the noise and found an old man with a long gray beard. The wrinkles on his face looked like fault lines. His gray hair hung down to his shoulders, splashing over the auburn robes he wore.

Ju Chen scowled at the sight of the guy and turned around to face Benitzio once more. "Tell me he's not your source."

"Try not to read a book by its cover. Sometimes, when you're searching for the thing that can't be found, you must ask those no one else will ask."

"Waxing philosophical doesn't suit you."

She leaned forward, realizing she only had scant seconds before their contact arrived at the table. "He looks like some deranged shaman walking down the street in that outfit, and possibly like he hasn't showered in weeks."

"Hello, my friend," Benitzio said, standing as he ignored her to greet his guest. "It's been a long time."

"Yes, it has," the man said in a thick Bengali accent. He put his arms out wide as if to hug Benitzio, who begrudgingly returned the gesture. The two embraced for a few seconds before letting go.

Ju Chen wasn't about to stand up and repeat the greeting. And she was right about the man's bathing habits, or at least the body odor radiating from his flowing robes suggested it.

"Prabir," Benitzio said, pointing to his partner, "This is Ju Chen. She's working with me on this project."

Prabir beamed a broad smile at her. To Ju Chen's surprise, the man's teeth were remarkably clean, and fairly straight. It struck her that was probably the only feature of his appearance that she cared for.

He stuck his hands out wide again as if she could hug him as well, but she merely nodded her head in a sign of respect that couldn't have been further from what she actually felt. After a couple of awkward seconds just standing there with his arms extended wide, Prabir dropped them and looked back to Benitzio, who pulled a chair between himself and Ju Chen.

She fired him a scathing glare, thinking Benitzio had put the eccentric man between the two of them as a sort of punishment. If that was his plan, it worked. Prabir reeked of sweat and the grime of the city that seemed to permeate the air.

"My friend Prabir is a student of the strange and unusual," Benitzio began.

"Is that so?" Ju Chen groused. Sarcasm dripped from her lips like blood from a tiger's teeth.

"I suppose you could say that," Prabir agreed, noncommittally. "I am most interested in ancient religious and cultural studies."

Ju Chen gave Benitzio her best *are you serious* face.

He replied to her unspoken barb with a long, annoyed expression and then continued with the conversation. "He's been responsible for two of my greatest finds."

"And you didn't buy him a new outfit?"

Prabir's smile faded, and he puzzled over the Chinese woman for several seconds before speaking. "Ah, someone who only sees the beauty of the flower when the petals are in bloom."

The insult, if that was what it was, bounced right off her and sailed into the ether.

"Yes, I think you have that one pegged, my friend," Benitzio said quickly. "But we're not here to fix her issues." He warned her with a flash of the eyes.

He removed the rubbing from his satchel and spread it out on the table, holding down the top two corners so the erratic gusts of wind from passing cars didn't blow it away. Now that he considered it, Benitzio realized how important the copy in his bag really was.

"We found this the other day. It was engraved on a cliff in the Jiangxi Province of China, high up in the mountains."

Prabir's head snapped to the left. "What did you say?"

Benitzio leveled his gaze, peering into his guest's eyes with the intensity of a ravenous wolf. He tapped a finger on the rubbing. "I said we found this in China. Mount Sanqing to be specific."

Concern drained the life from Prabir's face. When he spoke, his voice carried a warning tone in it, like darkening clouds before a storm. "What do you think you are going to find, Benitzio?" He offered a mocking laugh before continuing. "Because if it's what I think you're looking for, surely you realize many have tried before. None have succeeded. What makes you think you're any different than them? It's a fairy tale. No? A fictional story by a poet."

Benitzio replied with a disarming grin, one that hinted at an ace up his sleeve. "None of them had you, my friend."

7

CHATTOGRAM

Prabir huffed derisively at Benitzio's pandering. "You think you can win me over with a little kissing up?"

"I was hoping the Spanish charm wouldn't hurt," Benitzio said with a shrug.

His comment elicited a laugh from the robed man. "You always did have a good sense of humor, Benitzio. And while I may be immune to your Iberian charms, I am not immune to curiosity."

He leaned over the rubbing and read the message. His face darkened again as he realized what he was reading struck a chord, something deep in his mind that perhaps he'd forgotten. He frowned, desperately trying to think of it. When his memory sparked, Prabir's eyes widened.

"Where did you say you got this?" He peered into Benitzio's eyes as if the stare alone could draw out the answer.

"China. Jiangxi Province."

"Yes, yes. The mountain?"

"Sanqing."

Prabir started nodding, and continued for several seconds to the point it was almost awkward, like Jack Nicolson's famous nod in *The Departed*.

"The sacred mountains," Prabir said, almost to himself but loud enough for the people at the closest table to hear if they'd been listening.

"What do you know of those mountains?" Ju Chen jumped in, finally finding a point of entry into the conversation.

Prabir looked at her mockingly. "What do I know of the sacred mountains and how they relate to the location of Shangri-La?"

Her eyes swallowed him from head to toe and back again. "Yes." She turned to Benitzio. "And who is this guy? This is your expert? The one we're hinging all our success or failure on?"

"Ouch," Prabir said, twisting his head to look at Benitzio. "Where did you find this one?"

"Former Chinese special forces," Benitzio answered. "Wasn't working for them anymore."

"Oh," Prabir said, as if that explained a great many things. He returned his gaze to her and bowed his head. "It's good to meet another warrior. You are wise to surround yourself this way."

She frowned, both irritated and confused. "What are you talking about?"

"He's former Bengali special forces," the Spaniard said, jerking a thumb at Prabir. He took another pull from his bottle and waited.

"I've never heard of Bengali special forces."

"Then it sounds like we're doing a better job of keeping things quiet than some of the others. Wouldn't you say?" He added a smug grin to the end of his comment, and there was nothing she could say against it.

For the first time since he'd met her, Benitzio saw Ju Chen lower her armor. Her shoulders visibly slumped, and while she didn't smile, she did look as though she approved of the new addition to their group.

"He's a well-trained killer," Benitzio went on. "More than that, however, is his knowledge of the ancient world, and the histories that books won't tell."

"He looks like a deranged monk."

"I get that a lot," Prabir said.

"If you're not a monk, what's with the outfit?" She asked the question with an accusing stare.

He looked down at the fabric and then back to her. "Call it a disguise. Seemed like a good idea at the time."

"Prabir isn't exactly free and clear of his—how should I say this—duties to king and country?"

"You deserted?" she asked, the same accusatory look filling her eyes.

"I didn't agree with the way my superiors wanted to do things. Or rather, they didn't agree with my tactics. A dead enemy is a good ally. They claimed I was too zealous." At the last part, he widened his eyes abruptly, and for the first time, Ju Chen saw the true crazy imprisoned behind them.

Prabir returned his focus to the rubbing on the table. "This mentions the Heart of Shambala." He cast a sidelong glance at Benitzio. "So, you believe you've located the key to gain entry to the forbidden valley, yeah? I have to say, man, that is the longest of shots. No one is even sure the heart exists, much less the valley."

"More than a thousand years span the tale of Shangri-La," Benitzio said. He stared at the beer bottle while he played with the corner of the label. "Maybe the later authors just thought it was a cool concept, something that would spark people's imaginations. Or maybe, just maybe, there is something to it." He pointed at the paper. "This came from the cliff in Jiangxi. Sorry if I miss my read on this, but it doesn't seem like a very practical joke to play on future generations to climb down ten feet on the side of a mountain cliff with a bunch of engraving tools just to place a clue there that no one would ever likely see."

"No," Prabir agreed. "I suppose you're right." He narrowed his eyelids for the next question. "Which brings me to my second point. How did you find this? You must have had some information. Something to cause you to believe you actually had a chance to locate the lost valley."

Benitzio nodded. "Yes, but not me. Our employer." Ju Chen flashed him a warning glance, but he disregarded it.

"Employer?" Prabir scoffed. "That doesn't seem like your style. Last I checked, you didn't work for other people. You prefer to be free."

"That's true," Benitzio confirmed. "Normally, I don't like to take orders from anyone. I've had enough of that to fill more than one lifetime."

"So," Prabir wondered after a few seconds of his acquaintance letting the answer linger, "why now?"

"A very good reason," the Spaniard said, only hinting. "Several million good reasons. And if you help us, we can share some of those reasons with you."

Prabir's head slowly rocked up and down. "I like good reasons. Especially millions of them. Who are you working for?"

"That's the tricky part. We don't know," Ju Chen answered for him.

The Bengali man whipped around so fast she was surprised it didn't crack his neck. "What do you mean, you don't know? How can you not know?"

"The benefactor has remained anonymous," Benitzio answered. As he did, he drew an envelope from the satchel at his feet and slid it across to Prabir, who stared at it blankly for a few seconds. "The money, however, spends just as well as anyone else's."

Prabir hesitated, then pulled the envelope closer, pried open the flap, and looked inside.

"That's a thick stack of money," he said, salivating.

"There's more where that came from. What's in there is only a taste. Our backer is loaded, and he desperately wants to locate Shangri-La."

"Why?" Prabir snapped. "Why does he want to find the lost valley? If he's so wealthy, why does he need it?"

"Maybe he just likes history," Ju Chen offered. "Or perhaps money isn't enough and he simply wants the fame that will go along with locating the fabled valley. We don't care what his reasons are. He led Werner Fischer to us. Now we have something we can work with."

She gave a nod to the rubbing. "Unless you aren't up to the challenge."

Prabir's eyelids narrowed at the goading, but he didn't push back. "So, someone paid this Fischer guy to look for Shangri-La?"

"That is correct," Benitzio answered.

"And someone else paid you to bump him off and steal whatever clue he helped you find?"

"Also correct."

Prabir nodded slowly, the pieces finally coming together in his head. "How devious," he said. "Count me in. But if you think about stabbing men in the back the way you did with Fischer, you may find yourself with the knife coming your way."

Benitzio's lips parted into a thin, devilish grin. "So, we have an accord?"

"Yes," Prabir said. "I think I have some time open on my schedule in the foreseeable future."

"So, do you know what this clue means?" Ju Chen asked. She didn't sound hopeful or despondent, merely curious.

"No," he said. "But I know someone who will."

"Good," Benitzio said with a nod.

Just then, the phone in his pocket buzzed once. He reached into his pocket and pulled the device out, looked at the screen, and blinked two times. "Please excuse me for a second," he said. "Important text message."

He stood and stepped away from the table. He mindlessly walked into the café, through the eating area, past the counter were two people stood in line ready to place their orders, and continued to the back of the rundown building until he reached the restrooms. The two dilapidated doors looked like an infant could break them down, but Benitzio wanted privacy, not security.

He pushed the men's door open and stepped into a bathroom from his worst nightmares. It would have made the vilest truck stop look pristine by comparison. The place reeked of detritus and urine. The toilet was missing a seat, and the stall's door looked like it had been ripped off long ago. The graffiti on the walls were as filthy as the bathroom itself, with lewd statements, threats, and more than a few phone numbers.

Benitzio distracted his mind from the filth with a quick thought about why someone would have taken the door away or put a stall in a bathroom with only one toilet, but he quickly lost that battle to his senses as the stench and visual assault continued.

He refocused his attention on his phone screen and unlocked it with Face ID. He tapped the message from his employer and read it.

In a matter of two seconds, what had been a hopeful sentiment in Benitzio's mind turned sour, and he felt a sinking feeling in his gut. His face drained, then flushed red as he rode the wave of emotions from discouragement to anger.

"That's impossible," he whispered to himself. "How?"

He shook his head as he read the message over and over, feeling a range of emotions battering him like sails in a storm.

He steadied his breathing, though the awful stench didn't make that task any easier. Benitzio had to collect himself before he responded to his employer. He didn't want to send anything that made him seem weak or incapable of completing the job he'd been given. But this message, this simple text, had thrown a monkey wrench into everything he'd been working on.

Finally, after a minute of contemplation, he tapped on the Reply bar on his screen and typed out his response. "Not a problem, sir. We'll get the job done. We're already on our way to the next clue." It was a half lie, but he figured, what could it hurt? The last thing he wanted was to come this far only to have the plug pulled. Benitzio had millions on the line with this deal. If he could find the fabled valley for his boss, money would never be a concern for the rest of his life.

Still, even after he hit the Send arrow, he didn't feel good about it.

He waited there in the john for the response from his boss. Someone tried to open the door but found it locked. Despite it being deliberately closed, the other patron knocked on the door and shouted something Benitzio didn't understand.

"I'll be done in a minute," he responded in English.

"Hurry up in there," a man said.

Benitzio looked down at his phone again. Still nothing from his employer. He hoped his message hadn't sparked doubt in the man's mind.

"I said I'll be done in a minute!" Benitzio shouted back. "Calm down!"

A string of profanity came through the door. Then more pounding from the man outside. The Spaniard felt his temper burning, both from the message he'd received from his boss and the idiot outside.

"If you don't hurry up, I'm going to break down the door."

Apparently, the man had eaten something that didn't agree with his digestive system. Benitzio's patience only lasted another five seconds. Then, he unlocked the door, twisted the knob, and pulled it open.

A short, dark-skinned Bengali man stood just beyond the threshold. He had a round face and dark hair cut close to his scalp. Anger brimmed in his eyes.

"About time," he barked, shoving the door open a little farther so he could hurry through.

"Yes, sorry about that," Benitzio said. Then he grabbed the man by the back of the neck, shoved him into the bathroom, and kicked the door closed with his heel as he spun around.

"What's wrong with you?" the man asked, whirling around with fire burning in his pupils.

"You needed the toilet," the Spaniard said. "Here you go." He stepped quickly to the man, grabbed him by the neck again, and yanked him into the stall.

"Hey!" The man protested and fought, but he was too small and too weak to keep the stronger Benitzio from taking his own brand of justice.

Benitzio kicked the man's left leg out from under him, dropping him to his knees. Then, with a strong grip on the man's skull, he bashed his face against the filthy toilet until he felt the victim's muscles go limp.

He let go of the man and let his head slump against the rim, blood mixing with the nastiness in the toilet before he slid off and onto the floor.

Benitzio stared down at the unconscious man for a few seconds, then straightened his shirt and walked out into the café once more.

He stopped at the table out by the street. The two people at his table looked up in curiosity.

"You okay?" Prabir asked. "You look flushed."

"Yes, I'm fine."

"Curry too much for you?"

"No," Benitzio said. "As a matter of fact, I enjoyed it. Just had a little trouble with another patron in the bathroom. They were being rude."

"Anything you need help with?" Ju Chen asked.

"Nothing I couldn't handle. He was full of *mierda* anyway."

The two at the table raised an eyebrow at the Spanish reference but said nothing.

"Well," Prabir segued, "I do think I know someone who might be able to help us. They're in China, so I hope you two haven't burned any bridges with their customs people."

"Not that we're aware," Benitzio said. "What do you have in mind?"

"An old friend of mine is a historian in Kunming. He knows all about this sort of stuff, especially ancient world history that most of the history books have forgotten. He's studied everything, including myths and legends like Shangri-La."

"You think he will help us?" Ju Chen asked.

"Probably," Prabir hedged. "He can be fickle. He's retired from a life of teaching this stuff, but I know he still keeps up with it. His library has some old stuff in it—scrolls, books, artifacts, you name it. If anyone knows what this seven stars thing is, it's him."

"Then I guess we're going back to China," Benitzio declared. "That works out since Shangri-La was supposed to be there."

"Indeed."

"But, we do have a problem."

"What's that?" Ju Chen wondered.

Benitzio held up his phone and looked at the screen. He'd received a message in the melee without realizing it. His employer had responded.

"Make sure you find it first," was all the man said.

"Our boss said," Benitzio began, shifting his eyes to the screen to read it word for word, "'It appears Sean Wyatt has entered the game. I hope you're making progress.'"

The two people at the table exchanged confused glances, then Ju Chen spoke first, "So? Who is Sean Wyatt?"

"He's a problem," Benitzio said. "A thorn. Nothing we can't handle. We proceed as planned, and visit Prabir's contact."

Deep down, he didn't believe his own words. Sean Wyatt was more than just a thorn. He was the whole thicket.

8

JINGDEZHEN, CHINA

The IAA jet touched down on the tarmac at Jingdezhen Luojia Airport at ten o'clock in the morning—local time.

The long flight from Atlanta passed without incident, and largely without much sleep as far as Sean was concerned. He typically found it easy to doze off while on a plane, but not as easy to stay asleep. Fortunately, he managed to scoop a few hours here and there and was awake enough when the wheels hit the ground that the sudden jarring didn't startle him. Not that he could have been asleep with the captain chattering every ten minutes on the descent.

Sean looked over at Tommy and shook his head. His friend was still out cold. Tommy, by the most severe contrast, could sleep in the middle of a heavy metal concert. Sean wasn't sure it hadn't happened at least once. The only way he figured Tommy couldn't sleep was standing up, but that had yet to be proved.

"Hey, Schultzie!" Sean barked in a tempered shout. "We're here!"

He sat on the opposite side of the private jet, lounging in the plush leather seat. Tommy's wife, June, had been unable to come along for the trip, as she had other pressing matters to deal with at Axis, Sean's former employer.

Longtime friend and Axis Director Emily Starks had June

Holiday working on a special assignment, and while she wasn't out in the field at the moment, that could change.

Sean turned his attention to his wife sitting by the window to his left. Adriana stared out the open window at the airport terminal as it passed by, along with neat rows of airplanes, all with the exact same markings on their exteriors.

"Weird not to see the different airline companies, isn't it?" he said, noting the oddity for himself. He'd been to China before, and he'd noted the same subtle difference between an airport here and an airport in most places around the world.

"Yes," Adriana agreed. "The state runs everything." She turned and leaned forward slightly so she could see Tommy. "Did you send your colleague a message to let her know we're here?"

Tommy was still trying to fully open his eyes. He looked like he could use a few gallons of coffee, and even that might not have been enough.

He blinked slowly as his first response, then nodded. His head looked like a cantaloupe on a toothpick the way it lolled around. "Yeah, I'll text her in a second. Just trying to wake up."

"What was her name again?" Adriana asked Sean.

"Daiyu," he said. "Daiyu Ling. She works for the National Administration of Cultural Heritage."

"That's a mouthful."

"I know," he laughed. "And I thought International Archaeological Agency was bad."

"It is."

"Hey," Tommy protested from across the aisle. "I heard that."

"That's why you put IAA on the plane, isn't it?" Sean asked. "Not enough space to spell it all out."

"Very funny, you two." He shook his head and finally seemed to be entering the realm of the living, or at least the semiconscious. "Sorry I couldn't come up with anything better while I was establishing an agency in honor of my recently deceased parents. If I'd known they were still alive, maybe my head would have been a little clearer."

"Yeah, but then you wouldn't have had the inheritance to get this whole thing going either, so..."

Tommy stared at Sean for five seconds. The blank look on his face made him look like he was sitting there while someone painted his portrait. "I think you just blew my mind."

"It ain't the first time. Doubt it will be the last." Sean passed him a wink.

"Probably not, buddy. Probably not."

Once the group disembarked the plane, they made their way across the tarmac to a black limousine waiting by a hangar.

A well-dressed woman in a red business dress stood next to the long car. The crimson skirt stopped just above the knees, and the fabric barely stretched over her shoulders in a cutoff style. The outfit was modest yet form-fitting, and she wore it to perfection.

Tommy waved to the woman as they approached the car, and she stepped away from the vehicle to meet the Americans halfway. Upon reaching them, she stopped and half bowed. Tommy set down his bag and did the same. Sean and Adriana copied him.

"Adriana, this is our colleague, the esteemed Daiyu Ling."

Daiyu smiled at his introduction and lowered her head humbly before stepping forward to shake Adriana's hand.

"A pleasure," Adriana said.

"The same," Daiyu replied in perfect English.

The liaison made her rounds of handshakes, exchanging a pleasant smile with each, and then stiffened her spine, standing erect and looking every bit the authority Tommy and Sean knew her to be, at least in the realm of Chinese history and culture.

"You've come during the best time of year to see the mountains," Daiyu said. "It can get colder in the higher altitudes during the winter months."

"I'm sure," Tommy agreed.

"My office was sad to hear about the incident with Dr. Fischer. He was a respected historian in many circles, especially here in China."

"Yes. It's a terrible loss. Not just for his family but for the entire history community."

Daiyu nodded. "He did so much to help restore our history here. The Chinese people owe him a tremendous debt of gratitude."

"Indeed," Tommy said, lowering his head as a silent tribute.

"Let's continue the conversation in the car," she suggested, motioning with an extended arm. "We can discuss things further while we're on the road."

"Sounds good," Sean said.

Within ten minutes, the limo pulled out onto the main road leaving the airport and headed into the city.

"So," Daiyu began, pulling a bottle of water from a cup holder. She sat with her back to the driver in black, plush leather seats. One leg crossed over the other as she twisted the bottle cap. "Who do you think murdered Werner Fischer?"

Tommy and Sean exchanged a confused glance, while Adriana merely grinned.

"What makes you think we think that?" Sean asked.

"Sean, I may not be a special agent or a government investigator, but I know foul play when I see it. This was murder. And I want to know just as much as you who did it." She raised the bottle to her lips and sucked down half of it in five seconds.

"We did think the circumstances surrounding Werner's death were suspicious," Tommy offered. He was always a careful sort. "The second I heard about it, I didn't buy the official narrative."

"Do you know anything about who he might have been working with?" Daiyu turned her head and looked out the window at the mountains outside the city, as if they might give up the answer.

"No," Tommy answered. "We haven't been able to dig up anything yet."

"I asked around," Sean added. "I have a pretty good network of contacts around the world. No one has heard anything."

Adriana had been listening quietly but decided to cut in. "I have also tried to find out all I could, but none of my contacts came up with anything. Then again, many of the people in my network lean toward the shady side of things."

The last comment seemed to spike Daiyu's curious side, but she decided not to jump into that rabbit hole.

"The only information I've been able to turn up regarding Werner's expedition," Daiyu said instead, "is the name of the company Werner hired to provide him with a mountain guide."

"You know the name of their outfitters?" Sean pressed. Hope cracked his voice.

"Yes. It's a small family business in the village of Wuyuan. They sell some outdoor and adventure equipment, camping stuff, that sort of thing. But they also provide guides for people interested in hiking through the mountains. That area is an ancient and sacred place. Many people, mostly pilgrims, go there every year."

Tommy took the information and ran with it. "So, if you know the outfitters, then we can possibly learn the name of the guide who was with Werner's expedition."

"Exactly."

"Well, that should help," Adriana said. "The guide can give us the description of anyone else on board."

"I should hope so," Daiyu continued.

"I'm not sure," Tommy admitted. "To be fair, he was a pretty close-to-the-vest kind of guy. He didn't share many details about anything, at least not until a project was done."

"Maybe he was being careful," Sean offered. "He may have been concerned someone was coming after him."

"Not concerned enough," Adriana muttered.

"So it would seem," Daiyu agreed. "Do you have any leads on who might have wanted him dead? Anyone in the archaeological or historical community that might have had a grudge against him?"

"No," Tommy said, forlorn. He searched the floor at his feet, as if it might produce an answer, but only more questions flooded his mind. "Werner was a good guy. Direct, sometimes abrasive if you didn't know how to take him, but I don't know of anyone who wanted him dead."

Sean took it from there. "The only thing we could figure was that maybe he found something he wasn't supposed to, or maybe something that one of the people with him wanted."

"That's the part that doesn't make sense to me," Adriana interrupted. "He had people with him, or at least one person. What happened to them? We were told that the guide was sent for help. Who sent him?"

"Yes," Daiyu said with a nod. "I have wondered the same thing. And I heard that story as well. If it really was an accident, why did the people working with him simply disappear?"

"Maybe they were afraid of the Chinese authorities. If it was Americans working with Werner, I could see how they might be afraid of the cops here based on rumors or simply propaganda from the media."

"True," she hedged. "But I think we can all agree that the most logical explanation is probably the correct one."

"Occam again," Sean mused.

From the blank look on her face, it was clear Daiyu didn't know what that meant.

"Simplest explanation is usually the right one," Adriana explained.

"Ah," was all she received for her efforts.

The sky overhead churned with thick charcoal clouds. A few raindrops streaked across the windows, signaling the coming storm.

The car slowed as it entered the city proper. Jingdezhen was a scattered place, so spread out that Sean wondered if the population number he'd seen online was correct. Supposedly, more than a million and a half people lived there, but it didn't look it. The city sprawled across the valley, surrounded and infiltrated by forests, with the hills and mountains bordering its limits. It was much larger than he'd initially believed, though most of what he'd read was about the sights around the area rather than the city itself.

The Sanbao International Porcelain Art Village was one place he'd considered visiting. From what he'd seen and heard about it, that spot was quieter and far less busy, with the exception of the tourists swarming over it, though that didn't seem to be a huge problem. Jingdezhen wasn't as popular as some of the other touristy spots in China, and it was, after all, a big country.

Daiyu took the silence as an opportunity to speak up again. "Did you want to eat breakfast here in the city, or would you prefer to get to the village outside the city limits where it's a little quieter and less busy?"

Sean and Tommy took the gentlemen's route and deferred to Adriana.

"Something authentic in the village would be good," Adriana said. "If we can get something quick for breakfast there."

"Excellent. I know a place in Wuyuan Village that has excellent food." Without segue, Daiyu shifted the conversation back to the reason for the Americans' visit. "Up until now, we've discussed what we think happened to Dr. Fischer." Her eyes panned the limousine's interior, meeting every other pair that stared back at her. She held the space just as a great orator would command an audience of thousands. Sean thought for a second that no one could keep the truth from the intense gaze of those walnut eyes. "We haven't, however," she went on, "discussed what he was searching for."

Tommy nodded, and Sean took the cue to let his friend speak. He was, after all, technically the boss.

After a deep breath, Tommy sighed, knowing how what he was about to say would sound to one of China's foremost historians. He pressed his lips together, pondering how to say it, then blurted, "We think he was searching for Shangri-La."

He grimaced, bracing himself for a laugh from the woman, or perhaps a passing insult. Neither came.

The expression on her face wasn't one of derision. Instead, Daiyu appeared concerned, almost frightened if Tommy didn't know any better.

Sean noticed it, too. An expert in reading body language, he knew that something was off. "Daiyu? Are you okay? You look like you just saw a ghost take your bourbon."

She maintained her statuesque appearance, probably a result of years of practice. Sean imagined she'd been trained not to show emotion, perhaps by parents or maybe in school.

Daiyu took a breath, then bowed her head once before she spoke. "Dr. Fischer wasn't the only one looking for the ancient lost valley."

Surprise filled the limousine's cabin. And every pair of eyes in the place stared back at her even more intensely than before.

"Who else is hunting for it, Daiyu?" Sean pressed. He noted the concern—no, fear—in her eyes. It wasn't something he'd seen before with her.

She looked out the window and over her shoulder as if not fully trusting the driver's ears. Then she pressed a button and lowered the divider between the front of the car and the seating area in the back. She gave the man directions for where to take them. He nodded curtly, and then she raised the divider again.

"He only goes by a single name," Daiyu began. "From what I understand, no one knows who he is."

The two men's faces twisted into scowls while Adriana remained stoic.

"How does no one know who he is?" Tommy wondered.

"I'm sure there are a few who do," Daiyu said. "But he keeps those people very close. Rumors are that he's made his money in the black market."

"Drugs?" Adriana guessed.

Daiyu's shoulders lifted and dropped. "Perhaps. Or it could be weapons. The name is all that anyone knows, and that those who serve him do so ruthlessly."

"Sounds like our kind of bad guy," Tommy joked but didn't laugh.

"This mystery man approached you?" Sean asked, trying to keep things on track.

"Yes," Daiyu answered with a nod. The answer seemed to bring back a bad memory, one that shook her to her core. "I was leaving my office one evening when a car pulled up. Two men in white shirts and black pants got out and forced me into the back. At first, I thought it was the government. I'd heard of that sort of thing happening before with the police, but I hadn't done anything wrong. Not that I knew of.

And sometimes here, innocence doesn't matter." She flicked her eyes toward Sean. "They didn't hurt me, but I never saw the man's face. They didn't even drive me anywhere. He simply told me who he was and that he had information regarding a clue he believed would lead to the lost valley."

"What did he want from you?" Tommy asked.

She uncrossed her legs and flattened her skirt, tilting her legs to the side. "He only wanted me to take a look at the clue."

"And did you?"

"Of course. I didn't have much choice." She could see the men brimming with impatience and knew their next question before they could ask it. "It was a drawing. He didn't tell me where he found it. I don't know who created it, and without tools from the lab, I couldn't verify its authenticity, but I can tell you this. I believe it was very old."

Silence filled the car for a few seconds before she continued.

"The drawing featured the landscape of eastern China, and it came with a riddle written on the bottom. To be honest, I'm surprised the ink hadn't faded more. Whoever possessed the map before him took excellent care of it. It was remarkably well preserved."

"And this map, and the riddle," Tommy said, "it showed the way to Shangri-La?"

"No," she said, shaking her head. "He believed the map was the beginning, the key that unlocked the door to the path leading to Shangri-La. The riddle alluded to the sacred mountains, the mountains where Dr. Fischer was..." She stopped herself. "Where he died. There was also a spot on the map that indicated where one might find a supposed mark of some kind that would show the way to the heart."

"The heart?" Adriana asked.

"Yes," Daiyu confirmed with a nod. "The Heart of Shambala. Another name for Shangri-La."

Something kept bugging Sean, and he had to steer things that direction. "I'm sorry. You said you were in the car with this guy, and you don't know who he was?"

"He wore a mask. It's common practice here in China. Many

people wear them, and since the pandemic, that has only increased. I could see his eyes, and his hair. He was Chinese; that much I know. He wore an expensive suit, too." She turned her focus back to Adriana. "The heart is purportedly the key to locating the lost valley of Shangri-La. An old legend suggests that when a person with the heart stands before the entrance to the sacred valley, the gates will be opened."

"What did you tell him?" Tommy had to know.

"I told him that he was chasing a fairy tale and that I wasn't able to help him. The only assistance I lent was telling them a general location of the area circled on the map, the place in the mountains near where Fischer went. Honestly, I just wanted to get out of that car. I felt at any second he was going to shoot me, or worse, have me driven out to the middle of nowhere and tortured to death. Fortunately, the conversation ended, and he let me go. I guess he believed that I didn't believe the legend, or maybe that the map wasn't authentic. I certainly played my part to that effect. Mostly because that's how I feel."

"You don't believe in the fairy tale?" Sean asked in a gruff tone.

"No. Many people throughout the history of our nation have searched for the supposed lost valley. None have succeeded. And now, nothing can go unseen by technology. If the place existed, it would have been found."

"Possibly," Tommy offered.

"What do you mean?"

He sucked in air through his nose. Turning his head to face the window, he stared out at the passing city. Rain continued to streak the windows in a sporadic rhythm. "We've seen things through the years that have caused us all to question the bounds of the science we understand, or think we understand. Things that don't make sense to the human mind, and yet we've seen these wonders. It's possible that Shangri-La is real and is being hidden by something, a powerful ancient technology, perhaps."

"Or simply the earth itself," Sean hedged. "You may recall the ancient temples discovered down in the jungles of Central America that no one could see, but that LIDAR was able to detect. Some things have been covered up over time."

"Yes," Daiyu said. "I remember hearing about your discovery of the ancient pyramid in the Sahara several years ago. I often wondered if there was anything to be found under the great deserts of the world. There is evidence out there that suggests many of those deserts were previously inhabited places with very different environments than their current ones."

"Shame you didn't get a good look at this guy," Sean said, tracking back to the earlier conversation. "Any chance you could pick him out of a lineup?"

"I doubt it," Daiyu said honestly. "He kept it dark in the car. And the mask made it impossible for me to get a positive ID on him. The only thing I have is his name, or at least the name he uses to intimidate people."

"Yeah?" Tommy chimed. "What's that?"

"He calls himself Lóng. It simply means the dragon."

9

WUYUAN, CHINA

The driver parked the limousine along the sidewalk in the little village. Nestled against the backdrop of the foothills and mountains, the place looked like the town time forgot. Many of the white-walled homes looked several hundred years old, with waterways and streams snaking their way between houses and shops.

Golden cole flowers sprayed shades of bright yellow across the emerald hillsides and the valley, wrapping the village in vibrant colors.

One of the things Sean noticed was the multiple clusters of buildings spread out throughout the area, making it look as though several smaller villages came together to form a single larger one.

As he stepped out of the limo, Sean felt immediately aware that he was getting out of a car that, by comparison, appeared garishly lavish when he noted the other vehicles parked along the street.

Noticing his apprehension, Daiyu said, "The driver will park somewhere else. He's just dropping us off here so we can get that bite to eat. The outfitters Fischer used aren't far from here. A five-minute walk at most."

"Thank you," Sean said, feeling better about the car. He noticed a few people already staring, and he preferred they look somewhere else. Getting attention wasn't his thing.

The rest of the group exited the car, and as predicted, the driver drove off and disappeared around the next corner.

The smell of pastries, onions, and noodles filled the air, mingling with the cool humidity of the late morning.

Sean took in a deep breath, inhaling the scents of the town that mixed with the nature around it.

"Up these steps here," Daiyu said, pointing to a white building with multiple cracks in the façade, "is the place I mentioned before. We can grab a quick bite to eat and then head over to the outfitters. They have excellent pancakes."

"You never said anything about pancakes," Tommy said with a gleam in his eyes. "I'm just curious. I've been to China several times, and I've never had pancakes."

"They aren't like the ones back in the United States," Daiyu cautioned. "There you put syrup and butter on them, sometimes fruit or powdered sugar. Yes?"

He nodded.

"These are more like what you would consider crepes. They're thin, savory pancakes, often with various herbs, spices, or vegetables mixed in."

"Sounds good," Adriana said. Her stomach grumbled from the all-out assault on her olfactory senses.

The visitors followed Daiyu up the old stone steps to the entrance. An overhang covered the front porch, and Sean stopped to look back out over the landscape. White and gray clouds hugged the mountaintops in the distance, presenting a constant threat of rain. He turned as Daiyu pulled open the heavy wooden door. The aromas smashed into him and the others simultaneously, driving them all into a ravenous frenzy. Sean felt himself salivating as he followed the others into the restaurant.

High ceilings supported by dark wooden beams and rafters featured red paper lanterns hanging throughout the room. A dozen wooden tables spread out in neat rows throughout the little restaurant. Only a handful of patrons hovered over their bowls of noodles or rice. Others ate thin pancakes, dipping them into various sweet or savory sauces.

"Have a seat at that table over there, and I will order us something." Daiyu issued the order and pointed to a table in the nearest corner to the door. It also happened to be the most isolated from the other customers.

"Thanks, D," Sean said, and led the way over to the corner.

As usual, he took a seat facing the doorway with Adriana sitting next to him. Tommy sat across from the two, but at an angle so he could keep an eye on everyone else in the room.

Daiyu walked over to the counter at the back of the restaurant where a squat man stood waiting for the next customer.

She looked at the offerings on a menu board over the kitchen area behind the man, and ordered several items. After she paid for the meal, Daiyu returned to the group and sat down next to Tommy.

"You still do that?" Daiyu asked Sean.

Sean allowed a smirk to cross his lips. "What's that?"

"Sitting so you face the door. I noticed you did that the last time we met."

"Yeah, he does that everywhere," Tommy answered.

"Look at you, Mr. Sitting Sideways," Sean retorted with a snort.

"I was just admiring the room."

"Uh-huh."

"Adriana," Daiyu said, turning the conversational attention to the Spaniard, "what do you do? And how did you get caught up with these two?"

Adriana took a playful look at Sean and then said, "I thought he was hot. So, I didn't kill him."

Daiyu burst out laughing. Then she nodded. "Yes, I suppose Sean is easy on the eyes."

"Hey, what about me?" Tommy asked, pretending to be offended. "What am I, chop suey?"

"Nice twist on the chopped liver thing, bud," Sean quipped.

"You liked that?"

Sean shrugged and held out his hand, flipping it back and forth. "It was okay."

"You are handsome, too," Daiyu said to Tommy, though it was in a voice she might have used with a sad puppy.

"Thanks for the pity. Can we just focus on Adriana and your question?"

"Right," Adriana said. "So, my jobs are a tad complicated. But the main thing I work on is recovering lost or stolen art from the World War Two period."

"Oh." Daiyu looked impressed. "Like the Monuments Men."

"Sort of like that, yes. Except we're decades removed, and things are much more difficult to track down now. I've spent years on a single project before locating an item. Sometimes I never find it. That's the nature of the game."

"What a difficult game that must be. I imagine it is fraught with its own perils, yes?"

"Sometimes." Adriana left it at that, unwilling to give up any more details about her unusual interests.

A young woman working behind the counter brought two trays of food over to the table and set them down. She asked if they needed anything else. Daiyu told her no, and the girl returned to her station.

The plates of pancakes, sauces, and rice steamed in the cool air.

"Go ahead," Daiyu said, pointing at the food with an open palm.

The group discarded the conversation for the moment and helped themselves to the feast.

Once everyone had something from the trays, Sean spoke up again. "Do you think the guides will talk to us? What if they're too afraid to tell us anything?"

"If they're still alive," Tommy added. "Could be whoever offed Fischer might not have wanted to leave any loose ends lying around."

"Good point," Adriana said.

"I have my moments."

Daiyu didn't dig into the food yet, instead watching the others eat as they spoke. "Up until now, I have not heard of any additional deaths surrounding Fischer's. That doesn't mean it hasn't happened. We'll know soon enough. The outfitters aren't far from here."

"You mentioned," Adriana began, "that someone came to you trying to find Shangri-La. Does that sort of thing happen often?"

"More often than you might think."

Adriana nodded understanding.

"There are the treasure-hunter types out there who think they've found the next clue to this or that. Shangri-La has always been a popular one. I get a fair amount of people asking me to look at things they believe will lead to the lost valley. Of course, the things they bring to me are usually fakes, or if authentic have nothing to do with Shangri-La. In all my years working in this career, I have only ever once met someone who had something credible to present regarding the disappearance of the sacred valley."

"What was that?" Tommy asked.

"About ten years ago, a man came to me with an idea. Many ancient cultures believed in a world beneath the world."

"Like a world of the dead?" Adriana asked.

"No, not in this case. The world beneath the world was another civilization, a place where ancient technology thrived, a sort of utopia. This man suggested that Shangri-La was such a place, that it was a world under the world."

"I've heard of this before," Sean said, flicking his eyes at Tommy, who agreed with a knowing nod. "The Cherokee believed in such a place, where an entire civilization dwelled inside the earth. To get there, you had to go in through waterways, such as a spring. The mouth of the spring was considered the gateway into the underworld. But you had to be taken in by a guide, one of the underground people. Only with one of them could you gain entry."

"And then there was the little matter of the guide stone," Tommy added. "You had to approach with a pure heart, and with a special stone of some kind. Although I've heard the history on that told without the stone, so it very well could be an added piece of romance to the legend."

Daiyu listened with intense interest. "This underworld of the Cherokee, you say people lived there in harmony?"

"Supposedly," Sean confirmed. "As I remember the story, the seasons are the opposite of here. The reason for that belief was that water in the winter coming from a spring is always warmer than the air and always cooler than the air in summer."

"What a fascinating bit of logic," Daiyu said dismissively. "It is interesting, though, that this sort of belief could spread across the ocean, all the way to the tribes of the Americas."

"It does make me wonder, though," Tommy said. "The piece of the legend suggesting the guide stone might apply to Fischer's quest. I wonder if the people who murdered him were after that stone, or whatever gets a person access to the gates of Shangri-La?"

"You're speaking as though this is a real place," Daiyu commented.

"It could be," Sean argued. "Even if it's a far stretch of the imagination. It's possible. Virtually anything is."

"True. And based on what I've seen you involved in before, I would say it's not only possible but likely."

They continued eating until the food was nothing but scraps and crumbs on top of parchment paper. When they were satisfied, and a little lazy from the meal, the group stood up and left the restaurant, heading back outside into the fresh mountain air.

"The outfitters is nearby, as I mentioned before," Daiyu said. "We go on foot from here. Hopefully, they can help us understand what really happened to Dr. Fischer."

"Lead the way," Sean said cheerfully. But his external demeanor hid the true fears in his mind. *I just hope the guide isn't at the bottom of a ravine, too.*

10

KUNMING, CHINA

Benitzio slammed his fist down on the table. The candle in the middle wobbled and nearly fell. Ju Chen managed to grab it before it tipped over and spilled wax everywhere. Some of the hot liquid splattered on her hand. She didn't even flinch. To her, it may as well have been a gnat landing on her skin.

The old man sitting with them didn't react so calmly. He stared at Benitzio with fear in his eyes, and surprise at the sudden outburst.

"I'm sorry," the man said. "I don't know where this place is. I already told you, I have never heard of it."

Benitzio tightened his jaw and took a long breath before he spoke again, collecting his words in the process. He took a breath of the musty air. It was laced with the smells of dust, leather, and paper, only slightly covered by the mild scent of vanilla produced by the candles.

"You are supposed to be an expert in ancient Chinese history. How is it that you don't know anything about this?"

"It's a long history," the man explained. "It's been around longer than most."

Prabir took his turn with the old historian, leaning forward and putting his elbows on the table.

"Please, excuse my friend here. He has a short temper." Prabir spoke in perfect Mandarin.

The old man across from him twisted his thin mustache thoughtfully between his finger and thumb, then leaned back in his seat.

Prabir had arranged the meeting with the historian in hopes that the man named Li Tah would be able to help them unravel the clue about the seven stars and where that might be. Prabir had known Li Tah for more than a decade, though their relationship wavered from hot to cold at the whims of the wind, or so it seemed.

Prabir knew that Li Tah looked at him as nothing more than a greedy treasure hunter—someone who didn't care about the history or the cultural implications of the past. He only cared about money, which was a fair assessment. Prabir made no illusions regarding his intentions. But he also knew that Li Tah couldn't help himself when it came to uncovering ancient mysteries. The man's curiosity always got the better of him, and Prabir used that prod.

"Li," Prabir said, "you have all these books in your study." He motioned around the dark library, lit only by candles, the windows closed to add effect.

When they'd first entered the old historian's inner sanctum, Benitzio made the comment about it being too dark to see anything, much less read. "I guess you never heard reading in the dark was bad for your eyes."

Li Tah had simply answered, "This is the way it was done before, and how it will be in the future."

Benitzio didn't fully understand the statement, though he couldn't ignore the dim, predictive overtone.

"Surely," Prabir went on, "you have something in your vast collection that could help us. It's of the utmost importance that we find this."

Li Tah sat with his arms crossed, unimpressed by the man's pleading. "For what? You seek the Heart of Shambala, Prabir. A fictional jewel that supposedly opens the gate to the lost valley of Shangri-La. Frankly, I'm surprised you're wasting your time with this. There is no hidden valley. There is no lost city. It's a fairy tale.

Even for someone as greedy and blinded by fame and fortune as you."

Prabir's head retreated a few inches, and he pouted his lips, pretending to be insulted. "Li, that's not a nice thing to say to your old friend."

"Is that what you are now?" The man snorted derisively. "The only time you ever come around is when you want something from me." The candle in the middle of the table played dancing tones of yellow and orange on his face. "You have never cared about history, only finding treasures that can fill your coffers until you've spent the money recklessly on temporary pleasures. And when it all runs out, you have to find something else. It might be easier for you to simply find a job. Have you ever considered that?"

Prabir bit his lower lip. "Yes. You are correct, Li. I have been foolish in the past. I've been like a drug addict looking for his next fix. But this time is different."

"How so?"

Ju Chen and Benitzio watched the exchange, concealing their concerns and their emotions as the duel continued. The Spaniard didn't like the way things were going, and if Prabir wasn't able to coerce the man to help, he would have to use Ju Chen's skills of persuasion, which were far less cordial.

Prabir considered his words but could come up with no good answer. Stumped for words, he stared down at the table for too long.

"It's not," Li Tah cut into his thoughts. "This is no different than any other time you've come to me for answers. You should, perhaps, invest in some books as I have. Spend more time in libraries and museums. Take some classes. Expand your knowledge. Then you will be able to find your own answers, and won't waste my time every instance you need help with something."

"Finding the heart will make the world a better place," Benitzio interrupted.

Li Tah turned his attention to the Spaniard. He stared at the guest, who stood off to the right of Prabir's shoulder. "And you are the one funding this little venture? I wonder what it is you hope to gain from finding this mythical relic."

"It's not mythical. It's real." Benitzio stood up a little straighter, doing his best to look as noble as possible. He sensed the curiosity from their host and continued before the man could shoot him down. "The ancients of this world had access to technologies and information that we can only imagine. We have no idea what they were capable of, what they did, and how they did it. Contemporary history tells us that the ancient peoples lived in caves and only built magnificent things with simple tools and brute force."

"And you do not believe this?" Li Tah asked.

Sensing the man's genuine curiosity, Benitzio went on. "I do not. I believe that the people from the ancient world, especially before the time of the Great Flood, were capable of things that we are just now beginning to understand, or trying to understand. I seek the heart so we may finally locate Shangri-La and uncover its mysteries, science and understanding that could change the world."

He was laying it on thick now. The only thing missing was a Sarah McLachlan song playing in the background.

"Go on," Li Tah said.

Sensing he finally had something, Benitzio continued while Prabir watched in awe at his associate's ability to schmooze.

"What if the lost valley contains cures for diseases that have ravaged our planet for centuries? Cancer, AIDS, the common cold. That virus that caused the pandemic all over the world. There could be a cure for any number of conditions in Shangri-La. And what about energy? What if they had a superior source of power back then that we have never even considered possible? Clean, renewable, free energy that could change the landscape of so many developed and undeveloped nations. What of their agricultural knowledge? What if they possessed the information that could double or triple our harvests? We could end world hunger within a single season. Does none of that sound noble or right? This is what we are looking for, Li. It is our duty as seekers of truth to continue to push forward, even against all odds. Is it likely that Shangri-La never existed? Certainly. But that doesn't mean we shouldn't try to find it. Especially if finding the lost valley could turn the world into a much better, more united place."

It was all Ju Chen could do to keep her jaw from hitting the floor and splashing into the load of BS he'd just spewed. Somehow, she managed to maintain her stoic expression, though perhaps allowing a single wrinkle to crease her forehead.

Li Tah stared at Benitzio for a long minute, assessing whether the man was telling the truth.

For what it was worth, Benitzio didn't believe for a second that the man bought any of it. He felt like the old historian could see right through his bleeding-heart speech. But the Spaniard didn't retreat. He didn't surrender. He stood there, resolute, with the conviction of a priest written on his face.

Then, Li Tah stood abruptly, pushing the chair back from the table. The sound of the legs scraping against the worn wooden floor reverberated around the room, accentuating the perfect acoustics of the walls and high ceilings.

The historian turned away from them and padded around his cluttered work desk festooned with books, papers, a magnifying glass, and even a few scrolls that appeared to be at least a few hundred years old—if not older.

With their host's back turned, Benitzio risked a look down at Prabir, who sat in the chair watching Li Tah with rapt attention. The Spaniard offered an unspoken question to his associate. Prabir looked up, knew what Benitzio was thinking, and merely shrugged, mouthing the words, "I don't know."

Li Tah ran his finger along several books on a shelf that was just above the top of his head and then stopped on one with a brown leather cover.

He pulled the tome from the shelf and returned to the table, holding the book with the same level of care and caution he might a newborn baby. He gently set the book down on the table so the two guests could see the cover.

No words adorned the cover, only a circular emblem. The

emblem was divided into four equal sections. One piece featured the image of a tree, another of a human hand, the third a bird, and the fourth the shape of a heart.

"What is that?" Prabir asked, staring at the aged book.

Li Tah ignored him, instead addressing Benitzio. "I discovered this in a monastery forty years ago, high up in the mountains of Tibet. I was there conducting research and I came across this volume. They had more scrolls than books in their collection, but this one stood out among all the others, as if calling to me."

Benitzio felt a wave of skepticism crash into him but pushed it aside, allowing the man to continue.

"Do you recognize this symbol?" Li Tah asked, his finger hovering over the emblem.

Benitzio knew there was only one answer that would fit, and if he got it wrong, their host might shut down and stop helping. He had to risk it. "The crest of Shangri-La," he wagered with a heavy dose of false confidence.

"Yes," Li confirmed. "This book contains the many legends of the lost paradise. It describes a place where humans and nature coexisted in harmony. There was no pollution, no fighting or wars. It was a utopia, according to this book." Then his face soured. "But such a place cannot exist. Human nature dictates that we feel fear, jealousy, hatred, all the things that lead us to painful experiences in this world. It is ingrained in us, and we cannot change that no matter how much we try."

"We've made progress, though, haven't we?" Benitzio said, venturing into a realm he felt unfamiliar with. Persuasion wasn't the best tool in his arsenal, but he had to try.

"Some might think so, yet how many more animals were added to the extinction list this year? How much fighting have we seen by armies, or even in individual countries? We have never been more divided, or so I keep hearing. People will always want more." He looked down at Prabir with a chastising splinter in his eye. "They will always covet that which they don't have. And they will continue to disregard the damage they do around them to get what it is they think they want or need."

"Finding Shangri-La could change all that," Benitzio doubled down. "We could finally change things for the better. Turn it all around. We simply need the tools, and the instructions. If we can show the world there is a way, maybe there is a better future for us all."

He could feel Ju Chen rolling her eyes in the shadows behind him, but he didn't turn to look.

"Hmm. Well said." Li Tah scathed Prabir with one more glare, then nodded. "You could learn from him. You know that?"

Prabir didn't make the same effort as Ju Chen to hide the eye roll.

The host leaned down and turned the cover, revealing the book's first page, all written in the artistic language of ancient China. He continued reverently turning the pages until he stopped somewhere in the first third of the book. Tracing the characters with his index finger, Li Tah read through the page until he found the line he sought.

"Here," he said.

"What does it say?" Benitzio asked.

"I have heard of this place," Li Tah answered. "The temple of the seven stars. You can find it to the west, on the other side of the country. The ruins of this temple are in Xinjiang, along the old trade route. It was once a thriving city. Now it is nothing but crumbling stones. If you believe that Shangri-La is real and that there really is a heart stone that will allow passage through the ancient gates, then this is the only place I know of—according to that clue you have—that could house the sacred gem."

Benitzio took a step closer and peered at the page. He couldn't read much of it, but he still looked at it as if he could extract some additional information from the faded ink.

"Xinjiang," Benitzio said. He turned to Ju Chen. "I wonder if the reference to the old trade route is meant to be the Silk Road. Do you know where Xinjiang is?"

She gave a single nod.

"Good. Then that sounds like where we're going next." He raised his eyes and met their host's gaze. "Thank you for your help, Li Tah." He said it with sincerity and bowed low to the man. "This has been very helpful."

"Just because this book says that is where you can find the heart doesn't mean it's true, or that the jewel even exists. But you do what you want. I have work to do, so, if you don't mind, I would like to get back to it."

"Of course," Benitzio said. "I wouldn't want to overstay our welcome." He turned and started for the door.

"Thanks again, old friend," Prabir said, standing to join his companions. "I look forward to seeing you again." He extended a hand, but the host didn't accept.

Li Tah merely stood there, leering at the man with an expression that could have unsettled a gargoyle.

Li Tah closed the book and walked back around his desk to return the volume to its resting place among all the others in his library. When he'd slid the book back into the vacant spot, he turned around and started to say one other thing to the group, but he found Ju Chen standing next to him. She held a silenced pistol in her right hand, with the muzzle of the suppressor an inch from his left temple.

Li Tah swallowed at the unexpected threat. His lips parted as if about to say something. Her finger twitched, and the gun clicked loudly. Blood sprayed onto the desk and the floor behind it an instant before Li Tah fell sideways onto his chair, then slumped down onto the hardwood.

Benitzio and Prabir were already at the door, about to exit, when they heard the sound. Benitzio spun around, concern smearing his eyes. "What did you do? I didn't tell you to kill him."

Ju Chen lowered the still-smoking gun and looked over at him as if she'd just squashed a bug. "No loose ends," she said. Then she walked to the door and out into the corridor, leaving the two men alone in the study.

They glanced at each other, suddenly aware they were standing in a crime scene, and hurried out the door behind her.

11

WUYUAN

A little bell tinkled over the door to alert the shop owner that customers had entered the building. Sean and the others followed Daiyu into the white building with a wooden sign hanging over the entrance. The shop stretched from left to right, filled with all manner of gear from tents and backpacks to sleeping bags, snowshoes, hiking poles, hats, gloves, and anything else an adventurer might need to explore rural China.

A squat man stood behind a register in the back while a woman of similar build to his right restocked a shelf with energy bars.

"I guess they must do pretty good business," Tommy commented.

"I guess so," Sean agreed.

"Yes," Daiyu confirmed. "The mountains here are a popular destination, both for outdoor enthusiasts and for religious pilgrims."

"Sounds like they're killing two birds with one stone," Tommy laughed. Daiyu's confused expression caused Tommy to rethink how he said it. "Sorry. That's a saying we have in the States." His explanation didn't seem to melt the ice in her eyes, so he stumbled forward with his words. "What I mean is they're serving two markets at the same time. It's good business. That's all."

"Why didn't you just say that?" Daiyu asked. Then she turned and led the way to the back where the couple now both stood facing the entrance as the new visitors approached.

"Hello," Daiyu greeted them in their native language. She introduced herself, including her position with the NACH. "We are here on government business, and I was wondering if you could answer a few questions."

Sean's Chinese wasn't what it used to be, though he'd never really been exceedingly proficient in it. Over the years, he'd learned many languages from modern ones to some of the ancient forms. Chinese, however, had eluded him for the most part. It had been required during his time with Axis, especially considering the difficult relations the United States had with China then. Still, he managed to pick up a few words and phrases in the conversation as Daiyu plied the shop owners for information.

The conversation quickly got out of hand, though, as the speech quickened. Sean couldn't pick out as many words and so gave up trying.

Daiyu continued talking with the couple until the man nodded and pointed toward an open door in the back-left corner of the shop. She thanked him, then the man walked to the door and disappeared.

Daiyu returned to Sean and the others.

"What did they say?" Tommy asked.

"He said two of his guides are out on tours, but there is still one here right now in the back, doing some maintenance on gear." Daiyu looked over her shoulder at the elderly woman behind the counter.

"Is it the same guy who went with Fischer?"

"I don't know, but we're about to find out. The man and woman who own the place believed he was the one who went out on that expedition, but they seem...a touch oblivious."

"Oblivious?" Adriana wondered.

"Yes, they hadn't heard about what happened. Or so they said."

"You believe them?" Tommy asked.

"I have no reason to believe otherwise until I do," Daiyu replied coolly.

Sean grinned at the comment.

Before Tommy could ask another question, the owner reappeared in the open doorway, and a slightly younger man appeared behind him. The owner pointed at the visitors, said a few words, and the guy from the back nodded.

He approached, walking around the maze of shelves and displays, stopping a yard away from Daiyu.

"I'm sorry to take you away from your work," Daiyu offered. "But I work with the National Administration of Cultural Heritage. Do you speak English?"

A worried look passed over the man's face. He nodded. "Have I done something wrong?" he asked so that the Americans could understand.

"No, no. Nothing like that. But we were wondering if you happened to know which guide was on the expedition with a Dr. Werner Fischer, the one who fell and died up in the mountains recently."

The man shifted uncomfortably. He was shorter than everyone standing there and had to look up to meet Daiyu's prying but easy gaze.

Sean knew she wasn't immune to using strong-arm tactics if needed, but Daiyu also knew how to relate to people in her own way. Her gaze disarmed the man and he visibly relaxed.

"I was the one on the expedition with Dr. Fischer."

Daiyu looked back at the others, trying to conceal her surprise. Collective relief settled over the group.

Though they said nothing, Sean, Tommy, and Adriana all believed that the guide might well have been murdered by whoever killed Fischer, if his death was indeed intentional.

"Can you tell us what happened?" Daiyu continued.

The man nodded. "Yes, certainly. I've told the police everything I know already." He looked at the Americans, befuddled as to why they were here with someone from the NACH, but continued talking. "Dr. Fischer booked the expedition a few weeks ago. I had never worked with him before. Honestly, I didn't know who he was until I did an internet search for him. When I found out he was a famous historian,

I signed up for the job. The owners"—he jerked a thumb over his left shoulder—"let us sometimes pick the jobs. Not all of the guides are the same. One of them is afraid of heights."

Tommy flung a sardonic look at Sean.

"Easy, big guy," Sean cautioned.

"Dr. Fischer's request was odd, but I knew where he wanted to go. Only me and one other guide knew of that exact location." He paused to think for a second and then said, "Usually, tourists or pilgrims want to see the religious sites, the famous spiritual places. Then there are the ones who are just here for adventure or sightseeing. They may be hikers or climbers, mountain bikers, kayakers. We get all kinds here. This is a unique area that offers many outdoor activities for visitors."

Daiyu lowered her head slightly to encourage him to get back to the point.

He took the hint and kept going. "When Dr. Fischer arrived, we did all the usual preparation, talked him through how things would go, how long it would take to reach the location he requested, that sort of thing. It wasn't bad. Just a two-day trip. And he offered good money, too. So I took him and his team up into the mountains."

"And then what happened?" Tommy pressed, unnecessarily.

He realized the man was just about to get to that before he could stop himself from speaking.

"We drove up to the trailhead and then hiked in. Took about an hour of walking with all the gear they brought. When we arrived at the cliffs, I set up camp and let them do whatever it is they were there to do. Dr. Fischer climbed down over the edge with a rope and was looking at something. I had no idea what they were doing. I listened to their conversations, but I didn't fully understand what they were saying. They were looking for something; that much I know."

"And did they find anything?" Daiyu asked.

"I guess," the man said with a shrug. "They got excited about something. All I saw was a piece of paper. It looked strange to me, though I didn't get a close enough look at it."

"Paper?" Adriana asked in Mandarin.

"Yes," the guide said, smiling bashfully. "He took it over the edge with him. It was a..." The man struggled for the word.

"A rubbing?" Tommy suggested.

"Yes," the guide said with bob of his head. "He used something to trace an engraving in the rock."

"And there was some kind of message on the paper after he did it?"

"Yes, but I did not get a good look at it."

Sean studied the man for a few breaths. "You speak exceptional English, especially for someone in a small town like this, away from most of the touristy areas."

"Thank you," the guide said with a sincere grin. "I learned because we have many English-speaking tourists who come to the mountains, and to the pottery village." His smile turned bashful, and he bowed his head slightly as if embarrassed. "I figured I would make more tips if I spoke better English."

Sean approved with a smirk and a nod. "Smart."

"Would you be available to take us up to the same place you took Dr. Fischer?" Daiyu ventured. "And of course, we'll pay."

"On such short notice," Tommy added, "I'll throw in fifty percent on top of your normal rate."

The guide looked at him, astonished. "I will have to check with the owners. They take a cut of my guide fees, but they had me doing some work in the back while the others are out on their tours."

"Great."

The man retreated to the back of the store and spoke with the owners. He pointed back toward the group, and Sean acknowledged them with a subtle wave.

The older man and his wife turned to each other, had a quick discussion, and then nodded to the guide.

He returned to the visitors with a pleased look on his face, bordering on eager.

"I can go," he said. "It will take a while to make preparations."

"That won't be necessary," Daiyu said. "This is a one-day trip. We just want to take a look at the site and come right back."

The guide bobbed his head. "Okay, whatever you want."

The man was about to turn around and return to the back, presumably to get a few things for the journey, when Sean spoke up.

"We do have another question," he said. "We were wondering if you could share the names of the people Fischer had on his team. He didn't come here alone."

"No, he didn't." Something about his answer stank of concern. "They weren't very friendly. And after Dr. Fischer...fell..." He stumbled over the words, and everyone could tell Fischer's death hung over the man. Sean wondered if anything had ever happened like that to him before, losing a tourist. "I called for help, at the request of the other two. The rescue teams arrived an hour later."

"What were their names?" Sean pressed. "The other two."

"Yes. I remember their names. I normally forget quickly, but because of the accident, I can't forget them. The woman's name was Ju Chen. She's Chinese." He flashed a look at Daiyu before finishing. "The man's name was strange. Benitzio. I can't recall the last name."

Sean's face drained, as did Tommy's a second later.

"Oh," Sean said. "Benny."

12

MOUNT SANQING

The cool mountain air wasn't the first thing that struck Sean as he stepped out of the guide's SUV. It was the sense of danger that he'd come to both appreciate and loathe—like a watchdog suddenly alerted by the faintest sound in the night.

He looked around as the cold mountain air settled across his skin. He listened but heard nothing but the others climbing out of the two vehicles.

Daiyu and Tommy rode up in Daiyu's car, thinking it best that they have more than one option for transportation—just in case. Sean agreed with the line of thought, so he and Adriana rode in the SUV with their guide, Bingwen.

Sean didn't see any trouble, but he knew that didn't mean it wasn't there. Out here in nature, there were a million places an enemy could hide. While Sean was always aware of his surroundings, he didn't live his life in a fight-or-flight mode. That usually switched on with a certain trigger. In this instance, it was hearing Benny's name back at the shop. The second Bingwen mentioned Benitzio, Sean knew at his core that Fischer's death was no accident.

On the drive up, he sent a quick text message back to the two lab rats in Atlanta. It was the middle of the night back in the eastern time zone, and Tara and Alex would be asleep. Even those two had to rest now and then, despite their seemingly constant availability.

Sean's message had been simple. "We may have a problem. Benny is involved. And someone named Ju Chen, a Chinese national. Can you find out more about her?"

Now, all he had to do was wait for them to do their thing. The two had a knack for finding the unfindable, especially in the digital realm. Sean knew that if there was anything out there on this mysterious Ju Chen, Tara and Alex would track it down.

Maybe there was nothing. It was likely the woman was simply another assistant, a researcher, or just a hired goon Benny picked up along the way. Whatever the answer, Sean was way more alert now than when they'd first touched down in China.

Bingwen got out of the SUV and walked around to the back. He plucked a gray day pack from the cargo area and handed some bottles of water to each person. "It's a decent hike up to the top," he said. "You'll need these." When he finished handing out the bottles, he continued. "It should take us about thirty minutes to get to the spot. There's a small clearing at the edge of the forest where we set up camp. Camping is frowned upon by many, but no one really enforces that rule. Not that it matters for us."

"Lead the way," Tommy said, cracking his neck to the right and left. "I could go for a good hike right now."

The guide closed the hatch on the SUV, locked it, and started up the hill, where a sign marked the beginning of the trail.

Sean stayed in the back with Adriana just in front of him, and before they joined the others, he grabbed her by the right arm and pulled her close.

She knew his touch intimately, and this wasn't a romantic gesture. Adriana sensed the danger before Sean said a word.

"Keep your eyes peeled," he whispered.

"I already am," she said.

"Oh?"

She looked at him as they slowly made their way up the trail, lingering behind the others a little more so they couldn't hear the conversation. Tommy was already intensely focused on the path ahead, as if it was a challenge he would conquer at all costs.

The look in her eyes showed surprise, and she almost cracked an amused smile.

"What?" he insisted.

"We're being followed."

Sean instantly snapped his head around and looked down the trail. All he saw was the gravel parking area and the two vehicles. He searched the forest on both sides but saw nothing.

"They aren't here yet," Adriana added. "They're hanging back. No need to follow us if they already knew where we were going."

She made a good point.

"I noticed them in the village, as we were coming out of the restaurant. They watched us all the way to the outfitters. They were still there when we came out."

"Did you get a good look at them?"

Adriana kept her eyes forward, apparently confident that they weren't going to be shot in the back. Yet. "One man. Chinese. About your height and build. Wore a black peacoat."

"Seems a bit too early in the season for that."

She rocked her head to the side with a shrug. "Not up here in the mountains." She pulled her charcoal-gray windbreaker tighter around her shoulders and zipped it all the way to her neckline.

"True," Sean said, zipping up his own jacket. "I guess it's one of Benny's thugs. Did he look like an observer or an assassin?"

She glanced over at him again, a confused question radiating in her eyes. "I've never known the two to be mutually exclusive."

"I suppose you're right." He looked over his shoulder again, quickening his pace a little so they didn't fall too far behind the others. Ahead, Daiyu easily followed the guide, her long stride engulfing the trail with ease. "But a tail means Benny knows we're here."

"It could be someone else. The dragon Daiyu was telling us about. He could have put someone on her before we were even in China."

"You're full of good points today, aren't you?" He passed her the cool grin she loved so much.

"Maybe it's the fresh mountain air."

Sean nodded. He did appreciate that. The area reminded him of some of the mountains back home in the States. The smell of conifers filled the air. "It does clear the mind. I can see why so many people consider this to be a highly spiritual place." His mind returned to the subject of their concern. "I think we can both agree that, if we're playing the numbers, Benny probably sent the tail."

"Agreed." Adriana stepped over a root jutting out of the ground. The tree's vein wrapped around an outcropping of rock and then dove back into the earth just beyond it. "I do believe Benny is behind that. Now I have to wonder where he is."

"No telling," Sean said. "But I do think it's odd that he knows about this and is on the same case at the exact same time."

"Yes. And this has happened twice in a year to you."

"Yeah," Sean huffed. His legs warmed with the climb and he felt his breath growing more labored, both from the exertion and from the higher elevation. "Odd coincidence."

Adriana hummed a short laugh. "I think we both know there are no such things."

"Indeed."

"Do you think Benny is working for Lóng?"

"The dragon guy?" Sean asked as he wrapped his fingers around a skinny tree to round a curve in the trail. "Anything's possible. Although Benny strikes me as the cowardly type. From what Daiyu told us about Lóng, I don't know if Benny has the fortitude to work for someone like that. Then again, he's a greedy cuss. That Spaniard —no offense."

"None taken."

"Thinks of only one thing. Money."

"What's his story?" Adriana asked, her breath shortening to quicker bursts. Up ahead, Bingwen and Daiyu continued to power forward, but Tommy started to lag back.

"Benny?" Sean clarified.

She nodded once.

"Yeah, I don't know. Used to be a professor. Pretty well respected, I think. At least early on in his career. Had a falling out with the university or something. I don't remember all the details. But he sold his soul, only cares about the money now. That run-in we had with him in Costa Rica was a prime example. If he'd gotten to that statue before me and Tommy, we would have never seen that thing again. He would have sold it to the highest bidder in the black market, and another piece of cultural antiquity would have been lost forever."

"Well, if he's so focused on that, perhaps he isn't as aware of the danger working for a man like Lóng. People are easily blinded by the glitter of gold."

Sean looked over at her with admiration. "You're so sexy when you talk like that."

She blushed and smiled back. "Philosophically?"

"Oh yeah."

"Hey, pick it up back there," Tommy half shouted. He stood at a turn in the trail, his chest swelling and releasing with labored breaths.

"Stop for a little breather, buddy?" Sean fired back.

"No," Tommy lied, blatantly.

"Yeah, okay, pal. Whatever you say."

Sean and Adriana caught up to him, and the three continued up the path.

"What were you two talking about back there, anyway?" Tommy wondered. "Discussing new window treatments, maybe adding some subway tile to the kitchen backsplash?"

"Why do you know what those things are?" Adriana asked.

Tommy's face reddened. "What? I don't. I just—"

"Sounds like June has you watching HGTV in your spare time."

Tommy pressed his lips together, unable to mount a response.

"You know better than to mess with her, Schultzie," Sean chastised.

All Tommy could do was hang his head. "Yeah, I know."

13

MOUNT SANQING

Daiyu and Bingwen reached the top of the mountain ahead of the other three, though only by half a minute.

Sean immediately felt overwhelmed by both the majesty and the terror of the view before him. The sweeping vista displayed the dramatic valleys and peaks in 180 degrees. It reminded him of a few of the national parks he'd visited in the States, as well as a harrowing journey to Bhutan many years before. He still recalled clinging to those high-up steps on the way to the Tiger Monastery, and a shiver trickled through him.

"This the spot?" Tommy asked, hands on his sides as he caught his breath.

"Yes," Bingwen confirmed. "We had a little camp set up back there," he pointed through the woods to a clearing no more than eighty feet in diameter. "Dr. Fischer fell over there." He changed to the other hand and aimed an index finger at the cliff where the rocks stuck out and then gave way to an empty drop.

Daiyu went first, walking over to the precipice without concern. Adriana followed, and then Tommy—after he calmed his breathing. Between him and Sean, Tommy was the more muscular, carrying an extra twenty pounds of weight, most of it sculpted into muscle. Sean had the more well-rounded athletic physique, lean and functionally strong. Both of them knew, though, that Adriana was in the best shape.

Sean lingered near the edge of the forest, only stepping a few yards away from it to keep a safe distance from the cliff. He felt a familiar tightness in his chest and a mild paralysis gripping his muscles, restricting his movement. And that was just from the other people being near the drop-off.

"Y'all be careful over there," Sean cautioned.

Tommy looked back at him and shook his head. "We'll be okay." He set down his rucksack and lay down on his belly, inching toward the cliff's edge. Daiyu, Bingwen, and Adriana watched from a few feet away as Tommy poked his head over the rocky lip and looked down at the ground far below.

He craned his neck to one side and shimmied a little farther, bracing himself with his palms on the ridge. "I think I see something on the rock," he announced.

The words carried on the breeze, and Sean felt his curiosity spike. He risked a step forward, unwilling to go farther.

"What is it?" Sean barked.

"Come over here and find out."

"You're hilarious."

"Come on. It's not that bad. Only a few hundred feet down."

Sean felt all his muscles tighten again.

Daiyu looked back at him. "Are you afraid of heights?" she asked.

"Oh yeah," Tommy answered for him. "He's been afraid of heights since we were kids. Not sure why."

"Because if you fall from a high place, the best-case scenario is as lot of pain," Sean said. "Worst case is death. Seems like enough reason to not push the envelope. Could you please get away from the edge?"

Tommy scooted backward a foot and then stood up. He dusted himself off and said, "Nope. I'm going to have to go over the edge to get a better look at it."

"Great," Sean said. "You do that. I'm going to look around."

Adriana faced him for a second and caught the look in his eye that told her his ulterior motive for leaving the cliffside. She gave a nod and returned her attention to Tommy as he dug out the rope he always seemed to bring along.

"I have a harness if you need one," Bingwen offered.

"Great," Tommy said. "That will make me feel a lot safer than the webbing I usually use to fashion one."

Sean rolled his eyes and disappeared behind a bushy tree. He returned to the trail and looked down the slope. No sign of trouble, but then again, he doubted a decent assassin would simply follow the beaten path. If it were him, he would go parallel to the trail to conceal his presence, using the many trees and shrubs for cover as he advanced uphill.

If Adriana was correct—and throughout the years, it was rare when she wasn't—the person tracking them would appear shortly.

Sean crept downhill, veering off away from the trail to his left. The optimal direction to flank the group at the cliff was to his right. The distance was shorter, more direct, and if Sean was in the follower's shoes, it would be the way he'd go.

He had a fifty-fifty chance of being right. But there were plenty of places to take cover in case he was wrong.

Watching his step, Sean picked his way down the slope, stopping every ten or fifteen yards to look around, hiding behind a wide tree trunk. His heart ticked at a steady rhythm. Sean had grown accustomed to battle energy long ago, working in the field for the ultra-covert Axis agency. His skills had only grown since his time with Axis, and like the proverbial fine wine, Sean felt like he was getting better with age.

He'd been on the move for ten minutes, surveying the forest in 360 degrees every time he stopped, always careful to check his six in case somehow their stalker had managed to sneak behind him.

Sean stopped again behind a particularly huge tree and looked back up the hill, then swept his gaze across the terrain, finally poking his head around the trunk to look toward the trail.

He froze for a second, then pulled his head back a few inches.

Beyond the trail, a man crept toward the top of the ridge. He moved quickly and silently, barely stirring anything around him. Sean spotted the gun in the man's hand, and the knife on his left hip when he stopped and looked around.

Sean slipped back behind his cover before the man could spot him. He inched his way around to the other side of the tree and watched the tail continue up the slope.

There wasn't much time. The guy already had a head start on him, and Sean doubted he could reach the gunman before the man made it to the top. No telling what the guy's plan was after that, but Sean had a bad feeling it wasn't to enjoy the view.

Pushing himself harder, Sean moved faster, bounding from cover to cover, making sure the man didn't see his movements. Fortunately, Sean typically wore drab colors in cooler weather, as was the case today with his olive-green jacket. The khakis would stand out a little, but with so many other browns in the backdrop, he hoped they were close enough.

Sean closed the gap, but with every step the gunman drew closer to his quarry, and the top of the mountain loomed just ahead.

Drawing his pistol, Sean lined up the sights, but he was out of range. As good as he was, there was only so much he could do from that far away with that particular firearm. He needed to get closer. And while he'd made long shots with a sidearm on plenty of occasions, none of them had been this far.

Sean moved ahead, stopping when it looked like the gunman was nearly to his next cover spot. He repeated the process over and over: advance, withdraw, wait. In the back of his mind, Sean hoped that Tommy and the others were done with whatever it was his friend had planned for the rope. He preferred not to think about it.

The game of cat and mouse intensified the closer Sean got to his target. The slope began to level out, and Sean knew he was short on time.

The gunman disappeared from view over the hillcrest. Sean abandoned a chunk of caution and hurried forward. He spotted the gunman, now holding the hunting knife in his right hand and the gun in his left. He lingered behind a tree, but Sean couldn't make out what he was doing until he angled up to his right. Then Sean realized the assassin's plans. Fear rippled through Sean's body.

No more hiding. This guy was about to cut a rope tied around the tree. Tommy's rope.

14

MOUNT SANQING

S ean didn't have a choice. He burst through the forest with his pistol raised, the sights bouncing with every step. The mad charge up the rest of the hill came with a battle cry loud enough to shake the mountains to their ancient foundations.

The assassin twisted his head around in time to see the berserk madman rushing at him with a pistol.

Sean's angle wasn't great. The target was between him and the others. A single errant bullet could hit someone he cared about, and on the run, his accuracy would be low, even for him.

The gunman raised his weapon, and Sean ducked to his right, changing the angle just enough that he felt safe enough to fire. He lined up the assassin's torso and squeezed the trigger. One. Two. Three. Four. Five.

The successive pops echoed through the forest.

Two of the rounds found their mark, one in the man's chest and the other in his left shoulder.

The impact drove him back against the tree where the rope was tied, and he struggled to raise his gun to return fire. Sean rushed forward, unleashing another three shots, one of which struck the man in the right side of his chest. He slumped against the tree, and the gun in his hand dropped to the ground. His drawn face showed the fight he waged against the pain and the coming darkness.

Sean knew that any second the gunman would be feeling a cold sensation sweeping over his body.

The man grimaced as he began to slide down to the ground, his eyes staring out at the approaching American who'd ended his life.

Daiyu, Adriana, and the guide all spun around at the sounds of gunfire.

Adriana at once drew her weapon and sidestepped, putting herself between the potential threat and Daiyu.

Bingwen merely ducked down, though he had nothing to hide behind.

Adriana saw Sean running toward a man sitting against the tree Tommy had used for his rope anchor. She moved forward, weapon extended and aimed at the side of the assassin's head, but she couldn't get a clean shot.

Sean and Adriana both saw the knife at the same time, as the wounded gunman raised the blade and in one last act of defiance, sliced the sharp edge across the rope.

"No!" Adriana yelled.

She launched forward, but Sean was closer. The now dead assassin hadn't cut all the way through the rope, but he'd frayed it significantly—to the point that the few remaining threads barely held on.

Sean took one last step and dove as the final thread popped. He grabbed the cord the second before it broke free. He squeezed it as tight as he could, then wrapped it around his forearm as gravity pulled Tommy's weight downward. Sean felt the jarring tug on the rope, and he abruptly jerked toward the cliff's edge.

He skidded on the hard rock surface until he managed to dig his heels into the edge of a rock in the dirt, then abruptly felt his upper body pulled upright and nearly over onto his face.

Adriana dropped her weapon and grabbed on to the rope just ahead of Sean. He felt the burden ease slightly, but they were still being pulled in the wrong direction.

"Would it kill you to maybe hold on to a ledge or something?" Sean shouted at his friend below.

"Hey!" Tommy yelled back. "What are y'all doing up there? Stop messing with the rope!"

"Are...you...just hanging from it?" Sean asked, straining against his friend's bulk.

Bingwen and Daiyu grabbed on to the rope ahead of Adriana, and both started pulling. With their help, Sean found himself gaining ground again, moving back from the ledge. Step by step, he continued moving backward until Tommy's head appeared over the rocky lip.

"What is going on?" Tommy shouted. Then he saw the rope in the hands of everyone he'd come with and realized it was no longer tied to the tree. "Sean? Is that the rope from the tree? Why are you holding the rope from the tree?" His panicked words came in a rapid staccato.

"Kind of...busy here, Schultzie. You could help by using your hands and finding a foothold."

Tommy didn't have to be told twice. He was already loosely gripping the edge, but now he clung for dear life while struggling to find the closest ledge for his feet.

Sean felt the weight ease again now that his friend was supporting at least some of it. "Almost there, guys," Sean said, encouraging the others.

Tommy reached one hand forward, now nearly over the edge and back to safety.

The air cracked near Sean's head. He knew what that sound was.

He turned his head and saw the gunman against the tree, somehow, miraculously, still alive. And he held his gun with an extended arm, aiming sloppily toward the group.

Tommy slipped and fell backward at the same moment Sean relaxed his grip on the rope.

The others tugged harder, but they were losing the battle for a couple of seconds. Sean tightened his grip and dug in his heels as the anchor. Tommy stopped dropping, but the gunman squeezed off another shot, this time sending the bullet ricocheting off the rock at Sean's feet.

"You got it?" Adriana asked, looking her husband in the eyes.

"Yeah. Go ahead."

"I'll handle it."

She dove toward the gunman, rolling on the hard, bumpy surface as she scooped up her pistol. Adriana bounced up to her feet and jumped to the left as the gunman fired again. The round missed badly and sailed off into the distant valley below. Adriana fired, once, twice, and a third time, but her shots went astray. Then she leaped off the rock and onto the dirt near the end of the trail. The assassin was only thirty feet away and raised his gun toward her.

On one knee, Adriana braced herself and steadied the weapon. She aimed at the man's head, right in front of the ear. Letting out a slight exhale, she squeezed her trigger finger.

The weapon popped, and the man's head snapped to the side, a new hole in the near side where the bullet plowed through flesh and bone just above his jaw. She didn't want to see what the other side looked like, but there was no time to think about it.

She scurried back to Sean and the others, latched on to the rope, and pulled.

Sean continued to back up, faster this time as Tommy appeared to be helping from down below, causing the rope to go slack several times until he appeared over the edge again, this time scrambling to pull himself to safety.

He swung his right leg over the edge first, but the look of sheer terror on Tommy's pale face showed that he still didn't feel safe. Not until he got his entire body back on stable ground did Tommy even look like he was breathing.

The rope went completely slack, and everyone let go. Every one of them breathed hard for air and flexed their fingers in and out to get the blood flow going again. Sean unwrapped the rope from his forearm and noted the red stripes it left on his skin.

He plopped down on the ground, exhausted from the climb and the subsequent salvation of his friend.

"You guys mind telling me what just happened?" Tommy blurted after he'd managed to catch his breath.

"Assassin," Sean said, jerking his thumb over his shoulder toward the dead man. "Tried to cut the rope."

"Why? Why would he do that? And who is he?"

Adriana remained standing while the other two in the group took a seat next to Sean to recover.

She walked over to the tree where the dead man sat while Sean gave an initial answer.

"Don't know," he said. "But Adriana spotted him back in the village. Said he was following us."

"Wait a second," Tommy protested, pushing himself up off his side and onto his rear. "What do you mean, she spotted him in the village?"

Behind Sean, Adriana kicked the gun away from the dead man's hand, just to be safe. Then she dug into his pockets. She found nothing there, then saw something on the man's wrist. She rolled over his hand and found a tattoo of a black dragon on his wrist. "That's interesting," she said to herself.

"That's what she told me," Sean confessed.

"So you're telling me that you two knew there was a guy following us, probably with bad intentions, and you never thought maybe the rest of us should know about it?"

Sean shrugged. "I just found out about it myself. That's what we were talking about on the trail before."

Flames erupted in Tommy's eyes. He surged toward Sean, grabbing at his chest. "I could have been killed."

Sean easily slipped his friend's grip and rolled over onto his feet, leaving Tommy grasping at air with his meaty fingers.

"Why do you think I went back down the trail earlier?" Sean said with a laugh. "I was doubling back to make sure no one was following us. And if they were, I could handle it."

"You could handle it?" Tommy spat, clumsily finding his balance as he stood. "I almost died, Sean!"

"Yeah, that's true. But you didn't." Sean slapped his friend on the shoulder and spun around. He walked over to where Adriana was investigating the dead man's pockets.

She stood as he approached.

"Find anything useful?" he asked.

"No," she said with a twist of the head. "Just a wad of cash. What I presume to be a fake passport. And a cell phone. Probably a burner. No way it's connected to a real identity."

Sean sighed. "Yeah, these guys never have anything as simple as a driver's license on them. Would make it so much easier."

"Excuse me," Tommy blurted, approaching from behind. "You two knew about this guy, and you didn't say anything to the rest of us?"

"We went over that, Schultzie. You're fine. Although I bet you can probably appreciate my fear of heights now, huh?"

Tommy fumed at the comment, but he couldn't stay mad at Sean for long. And his friend had a point. Tommy had never been afraid of heights in his entire life, and now he nearly died from a long fall.

"Anyway," Sean continued. "You're welcome."

"For what?" Tommy groused.

"Saving your life. Again. Also, you should thank Adriana and the other two. I couldn't have held you up by myself, big guy." He patted Tommy on the belly.

Tommy instinctively tightened his core, and his hard abs resisted the silly gesture from Sean.

"Fine," Tommy surrendered. "But you could have told me what was going on."

"Yeah, but then you wouldn't have gone over the ledge."

"Wait a second." Tommy thought hard for a second. "Were you using us as bait?"

"No," Sean said with a deliberately confusing bob of the head.

"I hate you."

"No you don't," Sean beamed. "So, what did you find down there?"

Tommy shook his head and held up his phone. "The engraving," he said. "It's real. It must be what Fischer was looking for. I took several pictures of it. We should be able to send those to the lab rats and find out what it means."

Sean stared at the pictures as Adriana and the other two huddled close.

"No ID on the body," Adriana announced. "But I did find a tattoo of a black dragon on his left wrist."

The others looked at Daiyu, who acknowledged with a nod. "Then he knows what we're doing. And where we were headed. I doubt he'll know where we're going next."

"We don't even know where we're going. Yet, anyway," Tommy chuffed.

"It's difficult to make out what the inscription says," Daiyu announced, indicating the picture of the tablet. "It looks very old."

"We'll run a depth-contrast analysis on it," Tommy explained. "The kids will be able to figure it out."

"Kids?"

"The IAA's crack research and analysis team," Sean bragged on his friend's behalf. "Couple of whiz kids."

"How old are these...kids?"

"Oh, they're adults. We just call them that because they're younger than the rest of us."

"Interesting."

"You'll find," Adriana offered, "there are more than a few enigmatic things these two do."

"I'm sure."

Bingwen hadn't said anything for minutes. While the others were talking, he continued to stare at the dead assassin by the tree.

"Is he..." The guide pointed at the gunman slumped on the ground.

"Dead?" Sean asked. "Yeah. I mean, I didn't take his pulse, but I doubt he survived the three rounds I plugged in him and the one my sweet wife added."

Bingwen stared at him in shock, and possibly a little horror. "Are you two secret agents or something?"

"No," Adriana said. "But if we were, we'd have to kill you. So..." She left it at that.

"She's kidding," Sean refuted. "We're definitely agents. Just not so secret."

Sean ignored the man's confusion and returned to the conversation. "I'm still waiting to see if they can find out anything about this Ju Chen character, too. We know enough about Benny, but I want to know who she is, and if she's going to cause trouble."

Tommy nodded, then returned his attention to the image on his phone's screen. The engraving was still surprisingly well preserved, and some of the details could be seen with the naked eye. Not enough, though, to get a full interpretation of whatever this was meant to be.

"Well, the good news is that we have whatever Benny has as far as leads."

"And the bad news?" Daiyu asked.

"He's got a big head start."

15

KARASAHR, CHINA

Benitzio slid a fat wad of cash across the counter to the man behind the register. "This should cover it."

The Chinese man frowned at the offering, but that quickly melted away as he realized the money was real.

"Yes," he said. "It should cover everything you need." His English was stunted and broken, but he spoke it well enough to get by.

Benitzio gave a curt nod of approval. "And you said you would provide us with an escort."

"Of course, my friend. Whatever you need."

The interior of the parlor stank of stale cigarettes and something Benitzio couldn't identify, though he believed it was probably hash or some other cannabis derivative. It had a pungent, skunk odor, with a chemical overtone.

"You want to keep this off the books, yes?" the rotund man asked with a crooked smile. One of his front teeth was missing, and his long black hair hanging in a rim around his bald head distracted only slightly from the dim shine from the light overhead.

This wasn't the usual rental place, but that's why Benitzio had chosen it. He couldn't be bothered with driver's licenses, passports, or any other hassles. Now that Sean Wyatt was on the trail, keeping his movements secret would be even more paramount.

Benitzio cursed himself for being sloppy before. He'd given his name and Ju Chen's to the outfitters in Wuyuan and now was rethinking the idea he'd had of eliminating all of those people, just as Ju Chen had killed their last contact.

"No loose ends," she'd said.

Benitzio knew she was right. He'd been sloppy. That wouldn't happen again.

The dimly lit room featured few pieces in the way of wall decorations. There were a few pictures of cars, some posters, but most of the walls remained barren. Benitzio had heard of this place through the mercenary he hired to take out Wyatt and the others in Wuyuan— come to think of it, he hadn't heard from the assassin all day and was starting to wonder why the man hadn't reported in.

"I'll send two of my best guides with you," the man behind the counter said. "They're both good with weapons in case you run into any trouble. And they know the terrain."

"Excellent," Ju Chen said in her native tongue. The man shifted his attention to her.

She could tell he was one of those types who preferred not to deal with women, and Ju Chen felt obliged to needle him.

"My men," the shop owner said, returning his focus to Benitzio, "will be ready and at your command within the hour. You can stay around here if you wish, or if you prefer to go get something to eat and return, that's fine, too."

Benitzio cast an unspoken question at Ju Chen. Her head barely moved a few millimeters from one side to the other, but he caught the subtle answer.

"We'll stay here," Benitzio said, realizing she must have had a good reason for not wanting to go and come back.

He figured hers was the same as his. This guy was so shady he made a shadow look bright. And Benitzio had just handed him a bunch of cash. It would be easy for them to leave and return and the man claim he'd never seen them before. While the money didn't belong to Benitzio, he had a feeling losing five grand in American currency wouldn't be good optics for his employer, the mysterious Mr. Lóng.

"Suit yourselves. There are some chairs and benches over there in the waiting area." He pointed toward the front of the rental place to three chairs and a wooden bench.

"Thank you," Benitzio said and meandered over to the corner, picking out a seat wedged against the wall. He sat down on the cheap, cracked vinyl cushion and sighed.

Ju Chen chose to stand, pacing back and forth, occasionally roaming to other parts of the shop, not that there was much to investigate. The simple room was a long rectangular shape, only twenty feet wide and sixty feet long.

Benitzio watched Ju Chen exploring the same path over and over again for ten minutes, until she finally stopped and decided to sit down, positioning herself across from Torres so the door was facing her.

"So, what do you think we're going to find?" she asked plainly.

Benitzio's eyes widened, and he looked over at the man running the rental shop for fear the guy might have heard the question.

"Shh," Benitzio warned. "There are too many eavesdropping ears around. Last thing we want is more people hunting for this."

Right on cue, the shop manager looked up from his laptop, suddenly interested in what the other two were talking about. He looked at them for a couple of seconds and then returned to his work, busily pecking away at the keyboard.

When Benitzio saw the manager focusing on his work, he continued. "Keep a sharp eye," he said. "I don't trust these guys as far as I could throw them."

"You would prefer to go to another place to get a vehicle?" Ju Chen asked.

"No. Anywhere else will require red tape. It would be unwise for us to leave a paper trail. Just be on your toes. Would hate to get Munsoned out in the middle of nowhere."

Her eyebrows lowered at the reference. "What did you say?"

"Nothing," he lied. "Don't worry about it."

Their guides arrived within fifteen minutes, which only made Benitzio question the shop owner's integrity even more.

Why had the man said it would take them longer to get here?

Maybe the owner thought the guys needed more time to prepare than a mere fifteen minutes, but Benitzio got the distinct impression that they were being played. He regretted their decision to come here, but there weren't any other options. Not in this two-star town.

"Where is the rest of your gear?" The first guide snarled the question, as though he'd been woken up and dragged out of bed to do this job.

"We travel light," Ju Chen replied in a serpentine voice. "We would prefer to not draw unwanted attention," she added.

The second guide looked at the first and simply grunted. He turned, motioning with a hand over his shoulder for the others to follow.

"I suppose if it's only one day, you shouldn't need much. A few supplies should be enough."

"Yes. Only one day." Ju Chen eyed the first guide with mistrust in her eyes. "We have water and food for the day. Just take us out to the ruins. We don't need anything else."

"Suit yourselves," the guide grumbled. He turned and followed his twin out the door, leaving the two visitors to decide if they should go along. "We leave at dawn."

"I don't like these two," Ju Chen said when the men were out of earshot. "Something about them. It's off."

"You think we should scrap the job? That's a lot of money to leave on the table." Benitzio acted like it was fine if she wanted to bail, but in his mind, he knew he needed her, and the two guides. He'd searched for someone else to do the job, but hiring someone else would draw that unwanted attention she'd referenced earlier.

"No," she said, reading his mind. "I'll keep a close eye on them. If they even think about doing something stupid, I'll take care of it."

Benitzio saw the killer in her eyes, the cold-blooded predator that had killed before, and had no problem doing it again.

"If you think you can handle it," he remarked coolly. He received daggers from her eyes, but lucky for him, those were the only kind.

"Just try not to get in my way," she cautioned.

"Hey, I don't want to get in your way. We're on the same team. I'm only giving you a hard time. Relax, Ju Chen. I know you'll take care of it. You're the best, or so they told me in the Mercenary Guild. I don't expect you'll have any issues with the likes of these two."

She measured the sincerity in his eyes, gave a curt nod, and spun around to head out the door.

As she walked down the steps and outside, Benitzio watched her as he would a lion that had come to him for a meal but left hungry. He had to be careful with that one. She could turn on him at any moment, and if he wasn't ready, she might devour him.

16

WUYUAN

Tommy's phone vibrated in his pocket as the group sat around a table in the corner of a darkened tea room.

They'd been waiting for several hours, making the best of their time by doing some online research into the mysterious engraving from the cliffs in the mountains. Tommy cursed himself for not bringing his rubbing kit along. He'd considered packing it but hadn't seen the necessity. That kit, though primitive compared to digital tools, would have come in handy.

Now that mistake was costing them valuable seconds, minutes, and maybe hours. He prayed it wasn't more than that.

Benny was out there somewhere. Tommy and Sean had both wondered out loud if Benitzio knew they were there in China. Both knew it was best to assume that to be the case.

Benny was a clumsy treasure hunter, despite the elegant Spanish exterior. He'd been sloppy in Costa Rica, and he'd lost as a result— luckily for the rest of the planet.

Still, he was more than capable of succeeding if enough of the odds were tilted in his favor, and at the moment they were.

"Hey?" Tommy said into his phone. "Thanks for getting back to us so fast." He pointed at the device and mouthed, "It's the kids" to Sean and the others.

"It's been hours, boss," Alex said from the other end of the line. "We just got to the lab a few minutes ago."

"You mean you two don't sleep there all the time?"

"Uh, no. That's really what you guys think, isn't it?"

Uncertain if he should confirm or deny, Tommy opted for silence.

"Your lack of an answer only reinforces that's what you think," Alex added after a few seconds.

"Well, you do stay there sometimes."

"True. In this instance, I wish we had."

"Hey, chief," Tara said into the phone. "How's China?"

"Good morning, Tara. It's not bad. Weather has been nice so far. Food is good. Only thing troubling me right now is the guilt your darling husband is shoveling my way."

Laughter erupted from the other end. Tommy glanced over at Sean, who listened in, along with everyone else at the table.

"You guys are on speaker with Sean, Adriana, and our friend Daiyu from the Chinese National Administration of Cultural Heritage."

"Hey, everyone," Tara said cheerfully.

"Hi, Tara," Sean and Adriana echoed.

Daiyu simply offered a quiet, "A pleasure."

"So, I guess y'all just got to the office. Probably don't have anything for us yet, so let me know when you—"

"Oh, we already have something," Alex cut him off. "You wanted to know about the engraving from the cliff. We started on it earlier this morning."

"Earlier?" Daiyu mouthed silently, looking at her watch. She did the math in her head, and the astonishment only increased. She knew it had to be before dawn back in the eastern time zone.

Tommy only shrugged in response.

"Yes. We've been working on a solution to the images you sent us. Thanks to the scans and analysis, we were able to determine the message in the inscription."

"Excellent," Tommy praised. "What are we dealing with here?"

"Well," Tara began, "it's a pretty cryptic message. It says, 'Seven stars cradle the Heart of Shambala, protecting the way for those who would seek the gates to the sacred valley.'"

"This is the first evidence I've ever heard of for the existence of a very real place like Shangri-La," Alex said. "Up until now, we've only had legends, stories passed down throughout history. You're certain what you sent us is authentic?"

"It's authentic, all right," Sean confirmed. "And the boss nearly took a spill over the cliff to get to it."

"Really?" Tara asked. "You okay, Tommy?"

"Yes, I'm fine," he answered with a scathing look across the table at Sean. "Close call, but I'm okay."

"We had a run-in with someone who didn't want us finding that little clue on the mountain," Sean said.

"Any idea who it was?"

"No, but we're pretty sure who hired them. And who was responsible for Dr. Fischer's death." He paused for a second before filling them in. "Benny Torres is searching for the same thing. And from the looks of it, he's ahead of us."

"Wow," Alex breathed. "What are the odds you run into him twice in such a short time frame?"

"Yes, it's all very strange. But can we please focus?" Tommy insisted. "The seven stars cradle the Heart of Shambala. That's one of the alternate names for Shangri-La."

"Correctomundo, chief. And based on the depth analysis, what we're looking at is something that was carved into that rock a long time ago."

"How long?"

"About twelve thousand years."

Silence surrounded the table like a fog. Tommy let out a low whistle. In the kitchen at the back of the tearoom, plates and saucers clanked as workers prepared drinks for customers or washed dishes from previous ones. The smell of mint, herbs, and various teas filled the dark room, mingling with the scented candles that spilled vanilla and lavender into the air.

"Twelve thousand years," Sean muttered. "That's a long time ago."

"Way before any of the earliest Chinese records," Alex included. "Then again, ever since we started working with you guys, we seem to encounter more and more stuff that contradicts the traditional historical timelines."

"Indeed."

"Hey, Alex and Tara. Adriana here. Were you able to decipher the meaning of the riddle in the inscription? I mean beyond the translation. What does it mean, seven stars?"

"Hey back, Addy," Tara said cheerfully. "Great question. And the answer is a little complex. We cross-referenced several potential results in the quantum computers and narrowed it down based on location. It took a little longer than expected, but I think we have the location this inscription is referring to. It's actually an interesting place. Used to be on the old Silk Road."

"What is it?" Daiyu asked, leaning forward to make sure Tara and Alex could hear her.

"The Shikshin Temple," Alex answered. "Or Shorchuk Temple as it was called by the first archaeologist to examine the site, Albert Grünwedel. He excavated the area during the third German Turfan expedition between 1905 and 1907. It's also called *Ming oi*, which translates to 'Thousand Dwellings' in the Uyghur language."

Daiyu raised both eyebrows, clearly impressed.

Tara continued where her husband left off. "It was a major religious center along the northern part of the Silk Road in the second half of the first century. But here's where things get really interesting. The origins of this place suggest it was a part of the city state of Arśi, now known as Karasahr. The temple ruins are about twenty-five kilometers from that town. It's believed that Arśi was the home of an extinct Indo-European language known as Tocharian A. Some know it as Agnean. It seems that this place was also extremely important in regard to the introduction of Buddhism to China."

Everyone at the table took a moment to process the information. Sean was the first to speak up.

"So, you guys think this is the place that inscription was talking about?" He looked over at Tommy, then Daiyu, and could see the curiosity in their eyes.

"It's the only one that makes sense," Alex said in a matter-of-fact tone. "Unless you believe it could be referring to something in another part of the world, however unlikely."

"If you think this Shikshin Temple is the place," Tommy said, "then that's good enough for me."

"It's actually in the dead center of China," Tara said. "The heart of the country. I'm not sure if that was by design, especially since borders and maps change throughout history. Still, pretty interesting that they put it there. I don't know if you'll find the Heart of Shambala there, but based on our research, it's probably your best bet."

"I can't believe I've never heard of this place." Tommy hung his head in disappointment.

Sean snorted a derisive laugh. "It's a big world, Schultzie. You can't know about *all* the history."

"True."

"Is there anything else we should know?" Adriana asked.

"That's it for now," Tara said. "If we get any more info, we'll let you know."

"Sounds good," Tommy concluded. "I appreciate you guys. You're the best."

"We know," Alex demurred.

Sean let out a laugh. "Don't get cocky, kid."

"I won't."

"Y'all take care. We'll be in touch."

"Same."

The call ended, and everyone at the table looked around at one another, as if waiting for someone to speak first.

Sean took the cue. "What is the best way to get to this place?" He searched his mind for a second, then found what he wanted. "Karasahr."

Daiyu took a long breath and looked down at the table for a second, a forlorn look in her eyes. "It's a long drive from here," she said. "By the time we get there, your old friend Torres could have already investigated the site and taken whatever he found."

"If there's anything left," Adriana offered. "Tomb robbers and temple thieves are rampant. Have been for thousands of years. If this place is as old as we've been told, it's unlikely anything of value is still there."

"Unless it's hidden," Sean said. "And it always is."

He looked over at her with a cryptic smile, then met the eyes of everyone else at the table before settling on Daiyu. "So, what have you got in terms of transportation that might be a little quicker?"

She flicked her eyes to the side, shrugged, and said, "Air travel might be tricky to that place. Not sure about the airport situation." Then an idea bloomed, and her face took on a mischievous expression. "You're afraid of heights, Sean. How do you feel about helicopters?"

17

KARASAHR

Benitzio slammed the door shut to the banged-up SUV and stared across the barren, landscape at the ruins of the Shik-shin Temple. He pressed the edge of his hand against his forehead, shielding his eyes from the bright morning sun. The air felt cold and dry against his skin. He raised a bottle of water to his cracked lips and took a drink. The cool liquid slithered down his throat like a chilly snake.

Ju Chen exited the SUV on the other side, keeping a watchful eye on the two guides.

The drive hadn't taken long from the town of Karasahr, but it felt like they were a million miles from any sign of civilization. She knew her cell phone was useless out here, but her sat phone would be fine. Benitzio also carried a satellite phone, in case of emergencies out in the middle of nowhere, though he doubted his employer, the infamous dragon, would send help if they were to find themselves in any sort of trouble.

Neither he nor Ju Chen had any misgivings about their roles in this drama. They were expendable, just like the guides leading the way toward the temple ruins. Benitzio watched the men closely as they opened the back of the vehicle and pulled out a couple of day packs. They didn't even bother handing Ju Chen or Benitzio their gear. The two men simply walked around to the front of the SUV and waited.

"So much for service," Benitzio complained under his breath.

He and Ju Chen removed their gear from the vehicle and slammed the door shut. Slinging their bags over their shoulders, they ambled to where the guides stood staring at the ruins.

The place looked as though it had been uninhabited for thousands of years. And from the looks of their surroundings, Benitzio had to wonder why anyone had ever established a city here to begin with. There were few natural resources within view, unless you counted dirt and rocks as resources.

"So, this is the place?" Benitzio asked.

The guide with a long Fu Manchu mustache and beard nodded with a grunt. "This is it," he said. "Not much here. As you can see."

"What is it you two are looking for?" The other guide asked the question, only barely turning his head an inch toward his two customers.

Benitzio shifted uneasily. "Information," he lied. "This is a historical expedition."

Guide Number Two huffed his derision. "And here I hoped you were looking for a buried treasure or maybe something valuable." He shook his head, and Benitzio knew the man was rolling his eyes as he turned away.

Ju Chen fired the Spaniard a cautionary glance and then nodded toward the ruins. "We should hurry. The day won't last long, and we don't want to get stuck out here in the night."

"Are you afraid, little girl?" Fu Manchu asked. "Do you worry about the spirits that haunt this place, the ghosts of the Silk Road?" He laughed, and his partner joined in the teasing with his own booming laughter.

Ju Chen knew better than to let these two idiots goad her into anything. She would bide her time. If they screwed up, she'd take care of it. One wrong move, and she could end both of them in less time than a lightning strike.

"The spirits that haunt this place are more threatening than the two of you," Ju Chen stabbed back. "See if you can keep up."

She took off at a brisk pace up the rise toward the ruins. Benitzio looked at the two men, surprised she'd said anything but happy to see the two guides put in their place.

He followed after her, catching up quickly. He looked back over his shoulder at the two men who continued to stare at them, now in disbelief.

"I think you pissed them off," he said with another over-the-shoulder glance. The men started marching begrudgingly toward them.

"They're going to try to steal it from us. You know that, right?"

Benitzio didn't look back this time. He merely nodded. "Yes, I was beginning to get the same impression. When they mentioned treasure, that was the last confirmation I needed."

"They're lowlifes. I wouldn't be surprised if they've done this sort of thing before. Taking a couple of tourists out to see the sights, then robbing them blind."

"Yes," he agreed. "It sounds like as long as we don't find anything valuable, we'll be okay."

"And when we do?" She looked over at him, wondering what his orders would be. Ju Chen already knew what she would do.

"They will try to take it from us. And then you kill them."

"Why not just let me kill them now?" She looked back toward the men, who were still out of earshot, lumbering forward.

Benitzio took in a long breath of the dry air. "Because we still may have use for them. What if there is something heavy that needs to be moved, and the two of us can't do it? Would be nice to have a little extra muscle around."

"Until that muscle turns on us."

"True. But I still say we wait. Just in case."

"Fine," Ju Chen relented. "But I'll be watching."

"I know."

The two continued ahead, passing between crumbling walls toward the first structure—a long dwelling that resembled a pueblo from the American Southwest. Hollow doors at either end and matching windows occupied the walls. The roof hadn't been around for centuries. More buildings like it dotted the Martian-like landscape. Craggy, dry mountains jutted up in the distance, stabbing the sky with jagged peaks. Domed rock outcroppings rose from the earth in random places around the abandoned dwellings.

In the center of the commune, the largest of the outcroppings towered over the rest of the structures.

"Where should we start?" Ju Chen asked. She stopped next to the first building and looked in through one of the windows, wary that there could be anything in there—a homeless nomad or a wild animal, though she hadn't seen much wildlife in this area since they arrived. Devoid of birds, insects, and anything else that moved, the landscape made Ju Chen wonder if any creatures inhabited this barren land.

Benitzio stopped and surveyed the landscape, thinking hard about the answer to her question. "Every archaeologist and metal-detecting hobbyist will have checked all these buildings. There's nothing in them. At least I'm fairly certain. This place has been here a long time. I highly doubt it hasn't been picked clean by thieves or historians."

"So, we need to figure out where they wouldn't have looked."

"Or..." Benitzio said, indicating the central structure. It looked as if a building had been carved out of the mountain's rock, shaped and cut into something more than just stone. "This building here," he motioned to the one she'd been looking inside, "looks like it was the main temple, maybe housing for the monks, too."

"Doesn't seem to be a very big place for a bunch of monks to live."

"There are other houses here." He pointed at some of the outlying buildings. They were smaller, but still large enough to house five or six people, albeit tightly. "But if I had to guess, I would say that over there is where we should look first." He pointed to the center of the commune.

An entrance appeared to be carved into the rock at ground level, and other cavities that looked more like windows dotted the surface in random places. Benitzio wasn't sure if the entrance was a natural cave structure or if it was man-made. What he did know, however, was that was where he would begin his search for the heart.

"Come on," he said, motioning to her and the guides as the two men caught up. "We'll explore that first, and if we don't find anything, we'll spread out and search the area."

He and Ju Chen trudged ahead, leaving the two guides to question each other with a glance before begrudgingly catching up.

The group arrived at the opening, and Benitzio stepped ahead of the others, peering into the darkened entrance. He swept over the exterior with a quick look.

"This must have looked very different a thousand years ago," he muttered. A sense of appreciation laced his voice. The historian in him couldn't hide forever. Benitzio, despite everything he'd done—the people he'd hurt along the way, his thirst for revenge or justice or whatever it was—couldn't hide his love for history forever. He'd always loved it, lived it, even dreamed about it when he was asleep. This place held stories, lives of those who had walked this earth centuries before. Maybe more.

Ju Chen's ears pricked up. Something was wrong. Not wrong. Different. A sound, distant and muted, caught her attention.

"Do you hear that?" she asked, interrupting Benitzio's thoughts.

"What?" Fu Manchu asked. "What is it?"

She held up a hand to quiet the man. "Shh." Looking down at the rocky ground, she listened more intently. Then her eyes widened, and she raised her head. "It's a helicopter."

"What?" Benitzio wondered, oblivious to the noise. He wrinkled his forehead and listened closer. Then he heard the thumping cadence and knew Ju Chen was right. "A helicopter? Who else knows we're here?"

Ju Chen turned on the two guides, scorching them with fire from her eyes. "What did you two do? Who did you tell?"

The men looked at each other, befuddled, and shrugged. The second guide shook his head. "The only ones who know we're here are us and our boss."

She inched closer to him and grabbed him by the tunic. "Who else did your boss tell? The Chinese government?"

"No." He spat and swiped at her hand. His fist hit her wrist and knocked it away. "We have nothing to do with the government out here."

"Then who is coming?" Ju Chen used the momentum of his blow to pick the gun from her holster, concealed in a black shawl that draped down over her right hip.

Before the guy could blink, the pistol was in his face, inches from his nose.

"Hey! What are you doing?"

Benitzio inclined his head, hearing the rotors' constant beating draw ever closer. "I believe, Ju Chen, that this is the appropriate time to get out of view and see what happens. Put the gun down, and let's see who else is planning a visit to the temple."

She held the pistol another few seconds, tempted to end the guide's life right then and there. Instead, she lowered it and holstered the weapon.

"Quickly," Benitzio urged. "Sounds like it's almost here."

He reached into his bag and took out a flashlight. Ju Chen hesitated, then did the same. The guides likewise found lights.

"Inside, now," Benitzio ordered. "We'll talk this out later."

The guides went in first, leading the way through the entrance into the tunnel.

Ju Chen started to go after them, but Benitzio held her back.

"Wait," he said. "For the opportune moment."

She nodded understanding.

"Stay behind me, though. In case anyone follows us in."

He turned and stalked into the passage, fully aware that the helicopter likely carried his greatest nemesis inside—Sean Wyatt.

18

KARASAHR

Sean looked out the helicopter window at the passing mountains and into the deep valleys surrounding the rise where they believed the Shikshin Temple ruins stood. He'd been staring at the landscape for most of the journey, mesmerized by the changes in terrain that central China offered.

Daiyu had been concerned about him flying in a helicopter due to his fear of heights, but Sean had been in a chopper before, even one with an open door next to a gunner operating a SAW machine gun. As long as he was clipped in, he felt safe flying. In this particular helicopter, no doors hung open, and so his fear of heights never crept in.

He recalled the first time he'd ever flown in one of these contraptions. The initial panic and wave of terror had melted within sixty seconds of liftoff, and he had felt like he was in an elevator in the sky, which sounded terrifying, but Sean didn't seem to be affected.

The chopper pilot guided the aircraft up the slight rise toward the temple site and then banked gently to the right, swooping around a hillside until the ruins came into view.

From above, it didn't look like much.

The Shikshin Temple ruins looked as though they'd been leveled by a nuclear bomb. There wasn't much left other than a collection of collapsing buildings and some rock formations that stuck out from the ground—the largest sitting in the center of the commune.

As the pilot swept the helicopter around the site, Sean noticed the light brown SUV parked a hundred feet from one of the buildings. He sighed silently.

"Looks like we have company," Tommy said, looking over from the opposite window at his friend.

Adriana and Daiyu sat across from the two men, and both looked out in the same direction to see the vehicle parked on the rocky hilltop.

Sean nodded. "Yeah," he said into the mic attached to his headset. "Only question is, how long have they been here?"

"Only one vehicle," Daiyu noted. "I would have expected more."

Sean shook his head, his eyes still fixed on the SUV as the chopper circled around it. "No, Benny likes to keep things close. No loose ends."

"Which explains Fischer's murder," Adriana added.

"Exactly. I'd be surprised if he has more than three or four people with him. He only had two in Costa Rica, and that was more than enough to cause problems."

Tommy faced his friend, beaming with a goofy smile. "Yeah, but nothing you couldn't handle. Right, buddy?"

Sean merely twitched his head to the side for a second, as if to say, "Maybe."

When the pilot picked his spot, he maneuvered around the site one more time and then dropped in on a flat piece of ground about fifty yards away from the SUV.

Once the aircraft touched down, the pilot went through the process of shutting things down and then gave the all-clear for the passengers to disembark.

Sean spied the SUV from a distance, watching it closely to make sure they weren't walking into an ambush. He couldn't detect anyone inside the vehicle through the tinted windows, but that didn't mean a trap wasn't waiting for them. Benny and his team could be hiding in one of the dilapidated ruins, or perhaps in one of the nearby caves Sean read about before they made the journey.

He removed the headset and opened the door on his side, then jumped down. He zipped up his jacket a little tighter against the chilly wind that blew over the hillside and combined with what the rotors overhead continued to produce even as they slowed.

Drawing his pistol, Sean stayed low and crept forward until he was out from under the spinning blades. Then he stood up straight, keeping his eyes on the SUV ahead. Adriana stayed close behind him, with Daiyu and Tommy bringing up the rear.

Twenty yards from the vehicle, Sean slowed his pace and checked the empty windows of the nearest building. If Benny had a sniper with him, he would have already been dead. That boded well, at least for now, but that didn't answer the question as to where Benny and his team were. *Had they already gone into the temple? And if so, was it possible they had already discovered the heart?*

On the one hand, that might not be a horrible thing. Sean and the others could wait outside, and *they* could be the ones to set up the ambush, then take the jewel from Benny when he came out unsuspecting.

Sean had no misgivings about that. He knew there was no way Benny hadn't heard the approaching helicopter, which could be easily detected from miles away. Unless he was deep underground, and even then, Sean knew how loud that kind of aircraft could be.

Adriana kept her eyes trained on the windows and doors of the nearby building, aware that a shooter could easily be hidden within.

"Doesn't look like anyone's in the truck," she said, holding her own pistol at arm's length, aiming it at the back window.

"No," Sean agreed.

He crossed the remaining twenty yards quickly, trotting over to the vehicle's rear before crouching down behind it. She ran after him, with Tommy and Daiyu in tow.

Sean turned his weapon on the building to cover the last two until they were safely behind the SUV.

Tommy breathed hard when he skidded to a stop. "So, no one's in the SUV? You think they went in?"

Sean gave his friend a sardonic look. "Figure that out all by yourself, Captain Obvious?"

Tommy shook his head and rolled his eyes. "What do you suggest we do? They could be anywhere. And we're sitting ducks out here in the open."

"We have no idea where Benny and his goons are. Our only option is to spread out and sweep the area. He can't have more than five people on his team. Unless he made a couple of guys ride in the back of this thing without seats."

Tommy looked in through the back window and smirked. "Yeah, he should have gone in for the third-row seating option." He frowned. "Then again, this truck is like twenty years old. Maybe they didn't include that in this version back then."

"Can we focus on the problem?" Daiyu interrupted.

Sean nodded. "Daiyu, you and Schultzie circle around that way," he pointed to the right of the building. "Adriana and I will go left. Sweep wide, checking every nook and cranny you can find around the perimeter. We'll meet you on the other side."

"Sounds good," Tommy said. "We gonna do like a go-team thing or something with hands in the middle?"

Sean simply shook his head and sighed. "You're an idiot."

Tommy smiled back. "And you're my best friend. What does that say about you?"

Adriana took the lead and sprinted out from behind the SUV, running hard to the left of the long building. Sean darted after her, keeping his pistol pointed in the general direction of the first door, then the first open window, then the next, and so on, ready to fire if necessary.

No gunshots rang out across the landscape, though, and within fifteen seconds, the two of them were on the other side of the building.

Sean poked his head around the corner and watched as Tommy

and Daiyu disappeared around the other side, running in a wide arc toward a smaller building to the east.

"Cover me," Sean said. "I'm going to check this building first."

She bobbed her head once, and he ducked into the open doorway. He turned on a flashlight attached to the bottom of his pistol and pointed the weapon around to every corner of the first room. Nothing but broken pottery and dirt occupied the floor space. He listened closely but heard no signs of life from any other part of the building.

Sean moved toward an archway separating the first room from the second and continued through the ruins until he'd gone all the way to the other side. He found nothing of interest—and no sign of Benny or his team.

He retreated to the doorway he'd come through and stepped back out into the bright light of day. Adriana still stood there waiting.

"Anything?" she asked, already knowing the answer.

"No. They must be somewhere else." He shuffled over to the back corner and looked out toward the middle of the compound. "If I had to guess, that's the main temple right there, carved out of rock. We'll check everything else, but that's gotta be where he went."

"Looks like a cave," Adriana commented.

"Yeah. It's always a cave," he complained. "Except this one looks man-made."

"Let's check the rest of the area. Just to be safe."

"Right. After you?"

She grinned. "I like it when you let me go first," she said and then took off at a sprint across the rocky ground, heading toward a rock formation jutting out on the hillside to the west.

He watched her for a few seconds. "She is so sexy," he muttered, then ran after her.

She slid to a stop behind the rock outcropping and pressed her shoulder against it, leveling the pistol in her hand in case a threat appeared in her field of vision. Sean hurried to her side, and then they repeated their maneuvers, working their way to the backside of the compound until they'd done a rough check of the perimeter.

Sean saw Tommy and Daiyu circling around on the other side and motioned for them to hurry up.

"See anything?" Sean asked once the group was reassembled behind cover.

"No. And that's what bothers me," Tommy said. "They're here. And if we didn't spot them, that ain't so good."

"Agreed. And way to use that accent to its fullest potential, Schultzie."

Tommy rolled his eyes.

"We'll have to check the central structure," Adriana steered. "Since they got in first, we'll have to be extra careful." She directed her comments at Daiyu, already trusting that Sean and Tommy appreciated the gravity and the danger of the situation.

"You won't have to worry about me," Daiyu reassured. She checked her pistol again and looked around the edge of the boulder. "I don't see any sign of them in the upper areas. That means they're hunkered down in the center, probably waiting for us to go in after them."

"Or they found a way out," Sean offered.

"What do you mean?"

He shrugged. "I doubt the Heart of Shambala is sitting on a table in the middle of that rock. If so, it would have been stolen a long time ago. That means it's hidden. More than likely, anyway. It's possible it really was on a table and someone stole it within days of its placement. My guess is something that powerful wouldn't have been left out in the open. There must be a secret entrance. Probably encoded or something."

"So, we should get in there before they find the door," Tommy said without a trace of confidence. It almost sounded like a question.

"Yep," Sean said. "Follow me."

19

KARASAHR

Benitzio stumbled over a section of the floor that jutted out of place. He cursed the craftsmanship of the long-dead builder and continued headlong into the darkness. Flashlight beams danced on the walls and floor ahead and all around him as he and his escort of three hurried deeper into the structure.

Their journey ended abruptly at a dead end.

In a near panic, Benitzio looked around, searching the room for a way out. He pointed his light into every corner of the space.

The tunnel itself had been cut from the native rock, the walls hewn smooth, though undulating across the majority of it. The ceiling had needed less work. Its jagged appearance appeared to be less of a concern to the ancient stonecutters.

Benitzio and his group had passed several doorways on their journey into this place, but he'd wanted to press on, certain they would find what they were searching for deep within the bowels of what he believed to be the actual Shikshin Temple.

He forced himself to breathe, and work on finding a solution. He recalled the clue from the cliff inscription. "Seven stars cradle the heart," he muttered out loud.

"What are you talking about?" Fu Manchu griped. "This is a dead end. We need to go back."

"We're not going anywhere," Benitzio said, mustering as much bravado as he could. "We're close. We just have to find it."

"We didn't sign up for this," the other guide said.

Benitzio searched Ju Chen for an answer to the problem. Her eyes narrowed for a second, and he immediately caught her meaning.

"Okay," Benitzio relented. "We go back out, but be careful." He fired a wicked look at Ju Chen, who gripped her pistol and slid it out of the holster. She stealthily snapped a box suppressor on the barrel and held the weapon at her side, ready for anything.

"You know what?" Fu Manchu asked. The guides stopped at the door. "We need to make sure we get paid." He and the other guard spun around with guns in their hands.

They never made the full turn.

Ju Chen unleashed the contents of her pistol's magazine into the two guides, cutting them down in seconds, before they could even manage a single shot. Her trigger finger twitched rapidly, filling the room with the deadly clicking sounds from the gun's barrel.

At such close range, the guides didn't miss a bullet, catching every one of them in their chests and abdomens.

The men shuddered as one, staggering backward against the wall, only separating as they slumped down on the hard floor.

Ju Chen stepped over to Fu Manchu and raised her weapon, lining up the sights with his forehead. Blood trickled from the corner of his lips as he looked up at her, his eyes full of pain and rage.

She sent a round through his forehead, then turned to the second guide. The man shook his head defiantly, but there was no mistaking the fear in his eyes. That fear evaporated with a click.

"You really are good," Benitzio said with only a hint of admiration.

"That's why you hired me," she replied coolly.

"We both had a bad feeling about those two. Now we need to find a way out of here."

He pointed the light around the room and happened to shine it up into the corners where the walls sloped upward in a dome shape. There, he spotted something unusual.

"Look," he said, excitement swelling in his throat.

She followed his gaze and spotted the shape of a star engraved into the stone. He turned, running the beam along the same line until he found another star.

"The seven stars," he said, continuing along the wall until he counted six. Back to the original one, he stopped.

"That's only six," Ju Chen informed. She kept her eyes on the doorway while Benitzio tried to figure out the problem. "We won't have much longer," she warned. "They'll be in here any minute. I'm surprised they aren't already."

She ejected the empty magazine from her pistol and slid a full one into the well.

Benitzio had to think fast. He knew they couldn't linger much longer, or it really would become a dead end. Sean Wyatt's reputation for violence was one that his friend Tommy Schultz had worked hard to cover up. None of the news articles about the IAA's work, how they operated, and how they were able to seemingly be given a free pass no matter what they did or where they did it, dumped a truckload of fuel on the anger burning in Benitzio's heart.

Some people called them heroes. Benitzio clenched his jaws at the thought. He knew what they really were. They were no different than him. They got paid for finding lost pieces of history. Did it make them better that they justified their payouts by bringing offerings of artifacts to the historical communities of the world?

Hardly.

"What do you propose we do?" Ju Chen said with urgency.

Benitzio wouldn't let himself panic. Not now. Not when they were so close. They were in the right place, but they were missing something.

His thoughts returned to Wyatt and Schultz. While those two had a penchant for aggression, they also had a knack for figuring out mysteries such as the one foiling him at this very moment.

The decision made, he simply said, "Follow me."

Benitzio hurried back through the passage, leaving the two dead men behind.

"Where are you going?" Ju Chen asked. The concern in her voice spoke directly to the threat looming outside the temple rock.

"Trust me. And stay quiet. They may already be inside."

He worked his way through the dark tunnel, navigating around the few turns until they reached one of the open doorways he'd seen before. Benitzio ducked inside and found a chamber that may have once been a cell for Buddhist monks centuries ago. Grooves were cut in the far wall, like a ladder carved into the rock. They led up to another level where Benitzio could see a dim gleam of sunlight radiating beyond.

"Up there," he said.

Benitzio climbed the ladder first and scrambled to his feet at the top to get out of Ju Chen's way as she followed close behind. He moved forward down the tight corridor, barely able to stand upright without scraping his head on the ceiling.

Up ahead, the passage curved to the left, and he found the source of light in a circular window along the wall.

He stopped when the doorway in the room below was out of sight. He held up a hand, motioning Ju Chen to stop, and nearly smacked her in the face with his palm.

"Sorry," he offered. "This should be far enough."

She scowled but realized his plan. "We'll let them go by," she whispered.

He nodded. "And then when they figure out the problem, we go in behind them and take the heart from them."

She nodded her approval. "Good idea," she admitted. "Risky, but better than trying to shoot our way out."

Killing his flashlight, Benitzio crouched down low and crept toward the edge of the second floor. He fixed his gaze on the doorway, watching and listening for Wyatt and his crew to go by.

"They'll be suspicious when they don't find us at the end of the passage," Ju Chen cautioned.

"Maybe. But they'll also wonder about the two dead guards. My guess is they'll watch their backs right up until they get out of this place. Then they'll focus their attention on the perimeter, wondering if we're setting an ambush outside."

"I didn't realize you were an expert on tactics now."

He shrugged. "I'm not. But I know how Wyatt operates."

A noise came from down below, and Benitzio held up a finger to silence the conversation.

He listened intently, focusing all his attention on the darkened passage beyond the door. At first, he didn't hear anything and momentarily thought he must have been hallucinating. Then a similar sound echoed through the corridor. It was movement, like the scuffing of a shoe on rock.

Then he saw the first traces of flashlight beams casting their radiant glow into the darkness. Benitzio retreated an inch, just in case one of the newcomers decided to thoroughly check the room.

The lights grew brighter.

Benitzio felt Ju Chen holding her breath as the wide circles of light darted and shifted around in the passage. She gripped her pistol, but Benitzio held out a hand to keep her from moving forward. His unspoken request was heeded, but not without reluctance.

Benitzio watched as someone stopped at the door and directed their light inside. He couldn't make out the face. Not that it mattered. There was no question in Benitzio's mind who was there.

He waited as the interloper scanned the room, flashing the light around until it stopped directly over Benitzio's head. It lingered there for several seconds, and he felt his gut tighten, hoping that whoever was down there hadn't spotted him.

Then the light swung around and disappeared into the passage, leaving Benitzio and Ju Chen in the dark.

The two remained in their hiding spot for another minute, until they were sure Wyatt and his crew weren't returning, before they dared to move.

"What do you propose we do now?" Ju Chen breathed.

"We're going to follow them. Those two know more about solving ancient riddles than anyone on the planet. As much as it pains me to say it, if there's a secret hidden in there, those two will find it."

"And then?"

"When they do, we kill them and take it."

20

KARASAHR

"Wait," Sean ordered, holding up his hand to stop the other three.

He saw the object protruding from the corner of the archway leading into another chamber and raised his pistol at it. Sean recognized the shape as a foot and leg, but who did it belong to? And why was it there?

Creeping to the left-hand side of the archway, he paused, shining the flashlight on his firearm down onto the face of a dead man with more bullet holes drilled through him than a firing range paper target. Sean raised the light and swept the room with it until he came to the second body to his left. That man had been similarly executed, with multiple gunshot wounds to the torso and a single shot to the forehead.

He cautiously stepped into the room and kicked away the weapon still held in death's grip by the guy with a Fu Manchu beard. Then he did the same with the second.

From just inside the archway, Tommy and the others stared in grim curiosity at the bodies.

"Who are they?" Daiyu asked.

"They look like hired guides," Sean guessed. "Not sure, though."

"Where's Benny?" Adriana asked. Her senses tingled, and she spun around, pointing her pistol and attached light back down the corridor.

"He's not in here," Tommy overstated the obvious. "That much is clear."

"Unless he found another way out," Sean chimed. "Addy, keep an eye on the tunnel, yeah?"

"Way ahead of you." She took a step away from the enclosed chamber, keeping her pistol raised and aimed down the corridor.

Sean and Tommy searched the room with their lights, scanning every nook and cranny in the place. It was Daiyu, however, who spotted the first anomaly.

"There," she said. "A star."

She kept her light fixed on the engraving. Adriana barely flinched, keeping her focus down the passageway.

Sean and Tommy both noted the object and continued their search.

"Got another one," Sean said.

"Same here," Tommy added.

They counted six stars encircling the room where the wall angled up into the domed ceiling.

"Where's the seventh one?" Sean wondered. "There has to be a seventh one, right?"

"I would think," Tommy answered.

Daiyu frowned and then slowly traced her light up the ceiling until she found something at the peak. "Look," she said, pointing upward with a lithe finger.

Sean and Tommy directed their beams onto the same focal point. There, hanging down from the ceiling like a man-made stalactite, was the shape of a star. It was held in place by a foot-long rod that appeared to be carved from the same stone.

"Okay," Tommy said. "Great. What does it mean?"

Sean knelt on the floor directly under the star and ran his finger over the thin layer of dust that covered it. Motes kicked up in the wake of his hand. He focused his light on the hard surface, searching for the thinnest seam.

"What are you doing?" Tommy asked.

"Looking for a trapdoor."

"You mean like something that leads to a secret passage?"

"Something like that."

"What makes you think there's another tunnel here?" Daiyu asked.

"I don't know. Gut instinct. The riddle says the seven stars cradle the heart. If it's not above, maybe it's below."

"Or maybe it's been gone for the last several hundred years because it was stolen," Tommy demurred.

"No," Sean said. "It's still here." He hadn't found anything unusual in the floor, but he knew it had to be there. "This spot," he pointed a finger downward, "is smoother than the rest of the floor. It must be held in place with something. Possibly underneath."

"Like a support?" Tommy asked.

"Yeah."

"Okay, but how exactly are we supposed to get it out of the way?"

Sean looked up. He traced along the upper edge of the wall with his light and then pointed it at the lone star hanging from the ceiling. "You got any of that rope left, Schultzie? Or did you not buy more after yours got cut up on that mountain?"

His friend frowned with a childlike suspicion. "What have you got in mind?" Tommy set his bag down and pulled out a long black rope coiled up in a figure eight.

"You really did buy a new one," Sean laughed.

"No," Tommy corrected. "I always keep a spare."

Sean fought off the urge to roll his eyes. "Seriously. You and the rope, man. I don't get it."

"You get it every time it bails us out of a tight spot, though, don't you?"

"Fair enough. But jeez. How many spares you got in your house?"

Tommy shrugged. "A few."

"Would you two mind hurrying up?" Adriana drawled from the corridor. "Getting tired of switching back and forth between gun hands."

"Sorry," Tommy offered and handed the rope over to Sean.

"Great," Sean accepted. He unwound the rope and then set about creating a loop. Once the lasso was complete, he started twirling it at his side, letting the slack go longer and longer until the loop nearly touched the ground.

"Twenty says you don't get it on the first three tries," Tommy quipped.

"What are you guys doing back there?" Adriana asked. She glanced back over her shoulder for a second.

"Nothing," Sean answered. "Just taking candy—" he released the slack and let the loop sail into the air. It wrapped around the star, and Sean pulled it tight. "From a baby."

All Tommy could do was stare at his friend's handiwork. "I can't believe how lucky you are."

"Luck is one of my superpowers," Sean said with a shrug.

"What exactly is your plan?" Daiyu asked, stepping close. "Are you going to try to climb up there?"

"No," Sean said. "But now that you mention it, I suppose that's another possibility."

"So, what then?"

Sean's response was a hard tug on the rope. He leaned back and used his weight to pull. It didn't take much.

The rod and star bent in Sean's direction, and the room filled with the loud thud of stone on stone. The floor at their feet abruptly gave way, and the three felt their stable footing disappear.

Tommy let out a yell. Sean reached out both arms to brace himself as they tumbled down the smooth slide.

Adriana whipped her head around and, for a second, lost her discipline. "Sean!" she shouted.

She retreated into the chamber, keeping her weapon extended with the light pointing into the passage. When she reached the new hole in the floor, Adriana looked down, shining her light into the opening.

"You okay down there?" she yelled.

She saw flashlights moving around but no sign of anyone. Then Sean appeared at the bottom of the eight-foot ramp. He dusted himself off and looked up at her. "We're all good. Found the secret passage. Come on down."

Adriana kept a watchful eye on the archway as she maneuvered around to the end of the ramp, then gracefully slid down on her feet like a pro snowboarder—without the board.

She hopped off at the end, landing upright. Tommy was smacking dust off his pants while Daiyu appeared to not care about getting dirty.

Sean waved his flashlight around in wide, slow arcs. He spotted a torch hanging from the wall to his right and walked over to it. He pulled a lighter out of his pocket and set the flame to the fuel.

"No way that's going to burn," Tommy warned. "Way too—"

The torch flickered and then roared to life. Sean looked back at his friend and merely shook his head. "Do you ever get tired of being wrong? Seriously. I'm asking for all of us."

Tommy lowered his head and pressed his lips together, withholding any response he knew would be destroyed by Sean's wit.

Adriana suppressed a giggle. "Come on, boys. You two can quibble later. Benny is still up there somewhere. Only a matter of time until he finds the trapdoor."

"Right," Sean agreed. "Seems like this is another passage."

This one, however, was taller and wider than the one above, easily wide enough to fit a compact car. The walls were smooth and featured intricately painted images of birds, camels, horses, and people.

Tommy and Daiyu closely analyzed the hieroglyphics as the group moved forward cautiously into the dark tunnel ahead. The blackness almost seemed to suck the beams from their flashlights, only allowing them to see things within a close perimeter around them.

"It looks like a history of this place," Tommy said. "The traders who used to come through here. Merchants."

"Yes," Daiyu agreed. She traced a finger across the wall's surface. "Spectacular," she breathed. "I had no idea anything like this existed, especially out here."

The group continued down the corridor. The drawings changed, and it appeared now as though the people and animals weren't going toward something, but rather away from something else.

Bizarre scripts dotted the walls between images.

"What is that language?" Tommy asked, directing his question at Daiyu.

Her head turned slowly from side to side. "I have no idea," she confessed. "It's not like any ancient Chinese language I've ever seen. And it's certainly not the supposed dead language we would expect to find here."

Sean's flashlight beam pierced through a domed archway into another chamber. He stopped at the threshold.

"Why are you stopping?" Daiyu asked, nearly bumping into him from behind. She'd been paying more attention to the glyphs on the wall than watching where she was going.

"Because there's more to this," Sean said, pointing at three lines of tiles below, each tile occupying about two square feet.

"What does it mean?"

"I don't know," Sean said, still staring at the images carved into the squares before his boots. The tiles covered the floor from the entrance of the chamber and stretched five meters into the next room.

"You thinking they're not just decorations?" Tommy asked.

"Maybe. Look at the designs. It looks like some kind of warning." Rudimentary images of the sun and moon, rivers, and mountains covered the stones. More than one featured a skull.

Sean checked the walls on both sides of the archway and then risked a step forward onto one of the tiles. He pressed down on it, half thinking it might fall away underneath him like in one of those movies he'd seen when he was younger.

Nothing happened.

He looked down at the floor and noted an image where it looked like a person was reaching out their arms for...a heart. The next relief displayed what Sean interpreted to be the same person, this time turning away from an altar. After that, the tile along that line showed a skull.

"They're timelines," Sean realized out loud.

"What?" Adriana asked.

"Each one of these is a series of options," Sean said. He pointed to the one on the far right. "That one shows a person turning away from this place and going back up to the surface. Sunshine and other symbols of a normal life follow. A river, the mountains, forest. The path in the center looks like, if you take the heart, you'll end up dead."

"And that one," Tommy took over, pointing to the path on the left, "is what exactly?"

Sean looked over the tiles, running his flashlight beam across the surface. "Looks like two options with that one. There's a figure taking the heart, but that one is in the middle. Retreating back this direction leads to a skull. Going the other way takes the person to a sunrise over a mountain, another day. If I had to guess."

"So, what are we supposed to do?" Daiyu asked.

Adriana stole a look back down the passage, fully aware that they could be ambushed at any second.

Sean answered by taking another step forward. He searched the archway for a sign of any kind of booby trap—poisoned arrows, spinning blades, a giant stone looming overhead that would drop and crush him in the blink of an eye. He knew most of that was ridiculous, but he'd seen stranger things in his time with the IAA. And from the looks of this temple, that wasn't going to change anytime soon.

He stepped again, and this time Sean felt the tile under his foot shift slightly. He stopped again and held up his hand for the others to do the same.

"What is it?" Tommy asked.

"This tile moved a little. Stay there for a second, and don't move. If there's some kind of trap, no reason for you three to get killed."

Worry streaked through Adriana's chest, and she started to warn him not to do anything, but it was too late.

Sean steeled his nerves, inhaled a deep breath, and raised his foot from the tile to take another step forward.

21

KARASAHR

Sean and the others sighed collectively in relief as he placed his foot back down on the next tile ahead.

"I guess it was nothing," he said. "False alarm."

Tommy had been holding his breath for several seconds when he exhaled. "Don't. Do. That. Okay?"

"Do what? Our jobs? We have to get in there."

"Just...be more careful. I don't want to set off some thousand-year-old booby trap."

Sean didn't say anything else as he continued through the archway and into a round, domed chamber. He checked to his right and left, wary that there could be something else waiting on either side to cut him down or smash him into the floor.

He started at the sight of two statues, one on either side of the entrance.

"What? What is it?" Adriana asked, stepping forward with her gun in hand, the attached light swinging the bright beam around to illuminate the statue on the left.

"Just a couple of statues," Sean said.

Tommy and Daiyu joined them and stared in wonder at the two figures. Facing the archway, a statue of a woman in unusual armor guarded the door. She held a short sword in one hand. The blade looked similar to a gladius. In the other hand, she held an astonishingly intricate rose.

To the right, a man stood guard in similar armor. The helmet was rounded, somewhat like those the Spartan soldiers wore thousands of years before, but without the plume on top.

It was unlike any armor the group had ever seen—sleek, curved, and smooth. And the figures wore boots instead of the sandals that so many other ancient warriors strapped to their feet.

"Who are they?" Adriana wondered.

"Guardians," Tommy guessed. "But what are they guarding?"

Sean had turned away from the statues, letting the flashlight play along the rounded wall. A story played out in front of his eyes in vivid colors. The walls and ceiling were covered in images of people wearing strange garments, clothing that may well have fit with some futuristic science fiction story. The tunics were long, with strips dangling from each side. They wore trousers that clung to their legs, and boots similar to the ones on the warriors guarding the room.

Images of grand cities and children playing in fields dotted the wallscape. The faces, foreign yet familiar, all wore a satisfied, almost grateful look. They were at peace with everything and everyone.

On the backside of the room, all the paintings merged to a single focal point where mountains stood on either side and sloped down into a valley where a grand palace sat in the basin. A gate stood between two pillars, blocking the way into the palace. The image of a red heart occupied the center of the gate.

"This is incredible," Tommy muttered. "I never get tired of finding this stuff."

"Me either," Sean admitted.

Daiyu's eyes wandered the wall until she found something dark in the middle of the room.

She pointed her flashlight at it and gasped.

A stone cube stood atop two steps that encircled it in the shape of a square. On top of the cube sat a metal ring, held in place by four prongs. The silvery metal gleamed in the flashlight beams,

Every pair of eyes fixed on the object for several seconds.

Sean tore away his gaze long enough to find a round basin made of stone just to the left of the entrance. A dark brown powder filled it halfway. He followed a trough away from the bowl and traced it around the entire chamber. He swallowed, uncertain if he should try it, then touched the torch in his left hand to the material.

The powder sparked, then roared to life. The flame spread through the trough until it encircled the room, bathing it in a fiery golden light.

"Whoa," Tommy exclaimed. "That's cool."

Sean flipped off his flashlight and set the torch in an empty holder behind the male statue.

The four explorers moved toward the altar.

Daiyu took in the images surrounding her as she approached the altar. In the firelight, the imagery seemed to come alive, and she couldn't be certain, but it felt like the figures and animals somehow moved as if animated by the flames.

"This is the story of Shangri-La," she blurted, as though unseen forces made her speak.

"What?" Tommy said. He tore his eyes away from the ring and looked around the room. "Is it me, or does it seem like the people in those paintings are watching us?"

"It's not you," Sean said. "The flames make it look like they're alive. And I'm not entirely sure there isn't something in the fumes from the fire that might help that hallucination."

"Hallucination?" Tommy sounded worried. "Did you just light some kind of psychedelic fire over there, Sean? Because I gotta be honest, I don't think this is the best time to take a bad trip."

"Or any trip," Adriana added.

When Sean ascended the first step, he peered at something he could only describe as magical hovering in the center of the metal loop. A metal cube shimmered like chrome in the dancing firelight, floating in midair. Defying gravity.

Sean took another step up to the top of the platform and stopped at the base of the altar. He craned his neck, poring over the object to make certain it was safe.

"I've never seen anything like it," Tommy observed.

"No," Sean agreed in a breath as he studied the object. Each side looked to be about six inches across. "How is it being held in place like that?"

"I don't know."

"With all the things we've seen in all our amazing adventures, I don't recall ever finding tech like this," Adriana confessed.

The four stood mesmerized by the gleaming cube as it hovered in the air, spinning slowly.

"It must be magnetic," Daiyu offered. "I've seen things like this people put on their desks."

"True," Sean agreed. "But not this old. And where is the power source?"

He searched the base of the altar but found nothing that answered his question.

Tommy leaned forward, getting a closer inspection of the cube. "Check out these markings," he said.

"They look like runes," Adriana added.

Each member of the group analyzed the mysterious spinning object, trying to figure out what the ancient dead language was trying to tell them.

"I'm going to touch it," Sean said.

"Maybe you should wait on that, buddy," Tommy cautioned. "We don't know if there's some kind of radiation with this thing. Or maybe it unleashes some terrible booby trap."

"Or maybe you shouldn't touch what doesn't belong to you, Sean," the familiar voice echoed in the chamber, and sent a sickening feeling through Sean's entire body.

He and Adriana reacted quickly, spinning around with guns in their hands in the fraction of a second. But it was too late.

"Don't," Benny warned from the doorway. The flaming basins on either side of him illuminated his face in haunting, flickering light. "And I wouldn't touch that cube if I were you."

To his right, a woman stood with two pistols extended. One aimed at Tommy, the other at Adriana.

"I always knew this day would come, Sean."

"Yeah?" Sean asked, his pistol aimed at Benny's chest. From this range, it was the logical target, but it was anything but a gimme. "What day is that?"

Benny took a step forward, unconcerned about the weapons aimed in his direction. "The day when I beat you."

"Beat me? You mean like with a stick, or maybe a bat? And if so, where is said stick or bat? I don't see any lying around."

Benitzio did his best to ignore the comment. "You were always one step ahead of me. Until today, Sean. Today, I will make my mark on the world."

"You mean stain," Tommy quipped.

"Nice one," Sean said, keeping his eyes locked on the interloper.

"Cute," Benny groused. "But your little jokes won't save you this time. I have more men waiting outside. There is no way out of here." He gestured to his associate. "My friend here is former Chinese special forces. She can cut you down before your trigger fingers can twitch once."

"And here I thought you knew us," Sean hedged.

Daiyu watched the scene playing out, listening to the interaction, but she didn't dare make a move for her own weapon. Neither did Tommy.

"If you wanted to kill us," Sean said, "you would have already done it."

"Oh, I know you believe that, Sean," Benny half agreed. "But the truth is I couldn't risk damaging the cube." He pointed a finger at the metal box spinning in the air over the altar. "And from the sounds of it, I don't think you four know what you're dealing with. Best to let me have that."

"I'm sure you'd love for us to," Tommy spat. "Not gonna happen, amigo."

"Ah, Tommy. How many years has it been since we last met? I

want to say five or six? Yes? Since you told me you weren't interested in taking on this project?"

Tommy drew in a deep breath. He remembered Benitzio's presentation, the offer of helping to find the lost valley of Shangri-La. It had been an easy offer to refuse, but he'd done it as professionally as he could. Benitzio, however, seemed to hold some resentment over the matter.

"Looks like you've found an investor, anyway," Tommy observed.

"Yes. I certainly have. He pays well. And he has vision."

"Lóng," Daiyu blurted. "You work for the dragon."

"I don't care what his name is. I'm well compensated. And I'm going to be the man who discovered the lost city, the ancient valley that no one in history has been able to find."

"You sound pretty sure of yourself," Sean said. "What do you think is going to happen here, Benny? Your girl there shoots. Then we shoot. Someone dies on both sides. One of them will be you. I can guarantee you that. So, how about you tell your lapdog to put her weapons down before someone gets hurt. And by someone, I mean you."

"I'm sure you would enjoy that, Sean. But I'm not stupid. Ju Chen won't be relinquishing her weapons anytime soon."

"So, what?" Tommy asked. "We stand here in a stalemate until Judgment Day?"

"You have no idea what you're looking at," Benny answered. "The cube holds the Heart of Shambala. And apparently, only I know how to interpret the ancient script engraved on it."

"How's that?" Sean risked. "We've never seen any language like this."

"No, I would assume you haven't." Benitzio reached into his back pocket and pulled out a folded piece of paper. He unwrapped it and held it aloft so the firelight surrounding them would illuminate the writing. "I found this years ago."

"It looks like printer paper," Tommy teased.

Benitzio ignored the barb despite the chuckle from Sean.

"It's a copy, idiot."

"And now he starts with the name calling," Sean added.

"Years ago, while on an expedition, I found what I believed to be the equivalent to the Rosetta Stone to a whole new ancient language, but I never knew what language. I'd never seen these markings anywhere before. Until I found this," he said, shaking the paper once.

Sean peered at the page and noted the faded ink in the lines. Even from a dozen yards away, he could make out the script. It was the same as the runes adorning the hovering cube.

"It belonged," Benitzio continued, "to an explorer named James Mattheson. Do you remember now, Tommy?" Tommy's eyelids narrowed as he recalled the name, and the presentation Benitzio had given about a supposed clue to the location of Shangri-La.

"I didn't see enough evidence," Tommy said. "I'm a historian. A scientist. I don't go after something unless I have a lot of cause. I had no way to authenticate that piece of paper in your hand. What you were asking was for me to invest in an expedition that had a low likelihood of success."

"And yet here we stand, on the threshold of the greatest archaeological find in history."

Sean bobbed his head. "Good point. Except that you're way over there, and I'm here. We both know a shootout will end up with a few of us dead. Like I said, one of them will be you, Benny."

"And one will be either your best friend or your wife."

"Yes. But you won't go there. You're afraid of dying. I can see it in your eyes and smell it on your skin."

"All true, Sean. Astute observations. I am afraid of dying. And I have no intention of dying here in this chamber. Which is why I'm telling you not to touch that cube."

Sean caught a hint of truth in the man's words, a warning that laced his voice like the scent of pine on a hot breeze.

"Please. Enlighten me."

Benny cocked his head to the side. "I have studied this note for years. Mattheson was close, but he never found what he was searching for. He laid the groundwork for this discovery. Not you. I put in the time, the learning, the energy. Not you."

"You going to get to the point sometime today, or can we just smile and nod and pretend to be listening?" Tommy asked.

Benny shut up for a second. His face grew long before he spoke again. "If you touch the cube incorrectly, it will destroy this entire place."

Tommy's head snapped to the right. He studied the floating box for a minute. Sean didn't dare take his eyes off the target. The second he did, the enemy gained the advantage. He was already miffed that he'd allowed Benny and his...whatever the woman was, to get the drop on him. He'd become distracted by the cube and cursed himself for it.

"Convenient for you," Sean said.

"What does that mean, exactly?" Daiyu asked, finally speaking up. "How will it destroy this temple?"

"There is more power here than you've ever imagined," Benny answered. "That cube holds the Heart of Shambala, the key to entry into the sacred valley. But the cube is rigged. Anyone who touches those symbols in the wrong order will trigger the trap."

"And I suppose you've figured out the correct sequence," Tommy jabbed.

"Yes."

Another convenience, Sean thought.

"What do you propose we do now?" Sean asked. "Let me guess. We put down our guns."

"That would be preferable, yes. But I know you won't do that for fear that my assistant here would shoot you where you stand."

"Correct."

"Unfortunately, there is no way out of here for you, Sean. I could have her shoot the cube, which would trigger the same trap. Standing here at the only exit, Ju Chen and I would be able to escape. But as the door closes behind us, you and your friends will be trapped."

Sean knew there was no way he and his crew could win. They were cornered, and without any leverage. Benny had position on them. And as any good poker player knows, position was everything.

"I'm willing to offer you a deal, Sean," Benny said. "Lay down your arms, retreat to the wall over there." He pointed to a spot farthest from the exit. "And I will allow you to watch as I open the cube. At least you'll get to see what's inside before you die."

"So, you'll kill us anyway?" Adriana mused in Spanish, the language she knew to be Benitzio's first.

"No," Benny denied. "I will extend to you the same courtesy you did me in Costa Rica, Sean. When you left me and my men there to die in that cave."

"I didn't leave you to die," Sean countered. "And you seemed to manage just fine."

"Only because of a little luck."

"What do you want with the jewel, Benny?" Tommy barked. "A few million? Then what? Off to the next one once you've blown all your money?"

"No, not quite. You see, the one who's responsible for putting me back in the game has big plans. The artifact is merely the key to a whole new world of possibilities."

Sean considered the words carefully. *What did he mean by that?*

"You can keep your guns," Benny offered. "But I want you to stand over there by the wall as I enter the passcode."

"Passcode?" Tommy asked.

"What do you think this is, Tommy? The ancient text on the cube must be entered just like a passcode on an entry pad. Look closer. Notice how each side is divided into four quadrants, each with their own symbol. Touch the wrong one in the sequence, and we all die. I alone hold the answer to that riddle."

Sean sighed. He knew his friend, Adriana, and even Daiyu would default to his decision on this subject. There was no way he would put his gun down. Both he and Benny knew that. This was an alternative, a way to get him far enough away from the altar so that Benny could do his thing, whatever that was, and still remain relatively safe. The problem was the only way in and out was blocked by a woman wielding two pistols. Without any way to know how effective she was as a shooter, Sean didn't feel willing to take the risk that she was just some random person Benny found on the street.

"And then what?" Sean asked. "After you enter the correct sequence, what happens next?"

Benitzio's face curled into a sickly grin. It was the single most untrustworthy expression Sean had ever seen in his life. He'd seen it before on other faces, all of them scoundrels, but on Benny, it took on a whole new sense of wickedness. "I guess you'll just have to find out."

22

KARASAHR

"I don't like it," Tommy whispered to his friend.

"I don't either, pal. But it's not like we have a bunch of options." He motioned toward the wall behind them. "Step back there. Like he said."

"Seriously? You're just going to let them have it?"

"We don't have a choice, Schultzie."

"I don't think that's a good idea," Adriana argued. "I'm happy to stand here until one of them dozes off. I can hold my own in that game." She focused her attention on the woman holding the two pistols. Adriana's sights lined up squarely on the center of the woman's torso.

"I agree," Sean said. "But we have no leverage. They're blocking the only way out." He needed more time, maybe a few seconds, possibly minutes, to find another option. Right now, he didn't see one. He wrinkled his forehead at a realization but didn't let anyone else notice, immediately returning his face to its usual, poker self.

"We're stepping away from the altar, Benny. Tell your bodyguard there not to shoot."

"She speaks English," Benitzio responded. "But she won't. Will you?"

Ju Chen turned her head one time to answer in silence.

"See? She won't fire."

Sean didn't trust the two, but he had no choice. He took the first cautious step backward, keeping his eyes and his weapon on the enemy. His friends hesitated, but when they saw Sean stepping away from the cube, they reluctantly followed.

"That's better," Benny taunted. "Keep going. All the way to the wall."

Sean stopped a foot away from the ring of fire that looped around the wall at a height of four feet. Adriana and the others did the same and watched as Benitzio approached the altar with his armed assistant.

Ju Chen kept her weapons trained on the group while Benny climbed the steps and stopped next to the metal ring and the anomalous cube hovering above it.

Sean and the others couldn't help but be enraptured as Benny reached out a hand and touched an edge of the slowly spinning metal box.

Immediately, a thump shot through the room. It felt like a bass subwoofer pounding out one beat, so deep it sank through every person's chest like a concussive blast.

The cube stopped spinning and floated perfectly still in midair.

"Don't screw it up, Benny," Sean heckled. "Would hate to have the roof collapse on all of us. Well, not you two, but everyone else."

"If you don't shut your mouth, that may happen." Benny offered the warning without so much as a glance in Sean's direction. His focus remained entirely on the cube hovering in front of him.

He tilted his head to the right and then reached out his index finger.

Sean wanted to ask if Benny needed to take another look at the page before touching the box, but he thought better of it. The slightest distraction could cause his nemesis to slip, and even though Sean didn't trust Benny as far as he could throw him—which he estimated to probably be around eight feet—he also didn't like to gamble when there was no way to know the odds.

Benny touched his finger to one of the squares on the cube, and the metal glowed with a radiant blue light. The object rotated, exposing another side to Benny, who analyzed the four symbols, then touched the one in the top-left corner.

The light pulsed. Sean couldn't decide if the light was coming from within the object or from somewhere around it. He searched for the source but only came up with more questions.

The cube spun again, presenting Benny with another set of options. He repeated the same process from before, and the cube responded the same, with a pulsing of light and then a rotation to present the next symbols.

While tempted to keep his focus on Benny, Sean knew his wife and the others were on that. So he took the opportunity to observe the room. The mural overhead danced in the firelight. Huge mountains, seven of them, loomed around the altar, surrounding it on all sides from above. Each of the mountains featured a body of water in front of it, which Sean assumed were lakes. Between the mountains and water, the stories of ancient people played out in vibrant colors.

Sean wasn't interested in any of that at the moment, no matter how much he wanted to be.

The fire continued to burn in the circle around the entire room, its fuel seemingly never-ending. But that's not what caught Sean's attention. There were no fumes other than a slight hint of something bitter in the air. The fuel burned clean, though he had no clue how. The ceiling overhead offered no ventilation for exhaust to escape, and by all rights they should have been blinded by a thick layer of smoke, or at least by the haze from burning some types of natural gas.

Yet the air above remained perfectly clear.

The cube continued to spin with every correct response Benny entered—until the final side twisted to face him.

Benny hadn't said a word since he began. Sean and the others, for all their resentment toward him, hadn't interrupted. Sean's companions watched intensely as Benny worked, each wondering how he knew what he was doing, and with such expertise.

After he touched the final symbol, Benny stepped back, and waited.

The entire room held its collective breath. The light brightened, glowing more radiant by the second until the chamber filled with a white hue that drowned out the previous blue color.

The cube began spinning again, this time on a vertical axis. Instead of the slow, methodical rotation it used before, it spun faster and faster. A loud whirring sound accompanied it, piercing the ears of everyone watching.

Ju Chen winced but didn't take her eyes off the enemy. Adriana and Sean also didn't surrender to the painful sound.

"Benny?" Sean shouted. "What did you do?"

Benitzio couldn't hear him over the noise. And he seemed unaffected by it. The Spaniard merely stood there, staring at the spinning cube as the shape blurred from the speed of its revolutions.

Sean directed his focus to the ceiling again. It seemed that as the spinning cube pulsed, it illuminated the lakes—one for every color of the rainbow. But one of the lakes flashed brighter than the others. Instead of yellow, it sparkled like gold.

A deep rumble pounded the room for only a second, much like the thump from before, only deeper, more powerful.

The bright white light that filled the chamber zapped away into darkness. Even the flames in the ring vanished. Only a dim blue light remained in the center of the room.

Upon looking closer, Sean couldn't believe his eyes as he watched the box unfold flat while still hovering in the air. Once it had completely dismantled, the color in the room changed as a bright red light turned ceiling and walls purple for a few seconds. In two breaths, the blue light was overtaken, and red bathed the chamber along with everyone in it.

Benitzio stared in awe for a dozen heartbeats before he snapped out of it. Reaching his fingers toward the spherical red jewel, he gazed at it as if it held the cure to his most terrible ailment.

When his fingers touched it, the gem began to pulse its radiant red light. The jewel's sides were cut flat, forming a sphere whose surface resembled the patchwork of a soccer ball.

Benitzio breathed heavily, fighting off the disbelief that must have surely coursed through his synapses.

With Benny distracted to the point of entranced, Sean broke free of the spell and reached out to Adriana. He motioned for her and the others to follow him, sidestepping carefully toward the exit.

If they could move subtly enough, they wouldn't be able to reach the door, but they could certainly cut off enough space to make it a fair race. Or fairer, anyway.

Unfortunately, Benny's lackey found the fortitude to resist the charm of the heart.

"Stop!" she shouted.

Benny's head snapped to the side, and he shook his head. "We could have been partners, Sean. If Tommy had only seen the possibilities. But he was too blind. Now you will all die here in this temple. And I will discover the legendary Shangri-La, along with all the riches and glory that come with it."

He lifted the gem from its metal cradle, and the entire chamber rumbled. Benny's eyes darted around, but he already knew what was going to happen next. He didn't know how he knew, but he spun and ran for the door.

Sean kept his pistol on the man, tempted to fire, but knew the consequences would be deadly for one of his own, maybe even him.

Adriana tracked him with her weapon, but the same restraint kept her from shooting.

"Shoot him!" Tommy barked. "What are you doing? He's getting away. Take him down!'

Ju Chen backed toward the door as the ceiling shook, raining dust and debris onto the floor below.

Sean and the others crouched in a huddle against the wall as pieces of the ceiling collapsed around them in huge chunks.

He looked toward the center where the blue light still lingered and realized the ceiling didn't seem to be crashing down onto the altar, or its immediate surroundings.

"Everybody!" he shouted over the raging destruction. "Into the middle of the room!" Sean pointed and the others reacted at once.

They rushed toward the altar, ducking and weaving their way across the floor. Tommy made it to the first step and hurried up. He turned to offer Daiyu a hand, but a piece of rock fell from the ceiling and struck her between the shoulder and neck. She let out an anguished yell and dropped to her knees, clutching at the wound.

"Daiyu!" Tommy shouted. He took a step down and grabbed her, looping his arm under her armpit and lifting with his bullish strength. She managed to muster enough power to use her own legs and climbed with him, using Tommy as a crutch.

Adriana reached the altar just before Sean, and the two jumped while covering their heads to make it onto the landing a mere second before a chunk of the roof collapsed right where they'd been.

Then, as quickly as it began, the chaos ended.

They pulled shirts up over their faces to filter the dust from the air as they breathed in deep gasps from the mad dash.

"Just try to calm down," Sean said. "Let the dust settle, then we'll find our way out of here."

He looked down at Daiyu, who sat with her back against the altar, her face pale, and it wasn't just from the blue light radiating from the flattened cube. Sean grabbed the phone out of his pocket and turned on the flashlight. He pointed it at Daiyu's shoulder and immediately saw the problem.

Her blood-soaked fingers clenched the area around her clavicle.

"Let me take a look," Sean said, lowering himself onto a bended knee.

She shook her head. "I'm fine, Sean. It's just a gash. Some stitches and I'll be fine."

"I know you're fine," he agreed in the way people do when there's a caveat. "I just want to take a look."

Daiyu hesitated, but surrendered after a few more seconds of contemplation. Her fingers pried themselves from the sticky wound. Sean assessed the gash in an instant. Under a tear in her shirt, a two-inch cut in her skin bled into the fabric, spreading farther down the garment by the second.

Sean's immediate concern of her bleeding out eased slightly. It didn't appear to be deep enough, or wide enough, to warrant that worry. Still, they needed to patch her up.

He sloughed off his rucksack and searched the main compartment.

"What are you looking for?" Tommy asked, copying his friend's activity with his own pack.

"I have a small med kit in here," Sean replied.

Adriana held Daiyu's clammy hand tightly to keep her from passing out. From the looks of it, that battle wasn't going Adriana's way.

"It's going to be all right," she said. "Just a cut. Nothing life-threatening." Adriana hadn't fully examined the wound, but she'd seen plenty in her life, and this one didn't scare her.

In under a minute, Sean found the medical kit, unzipped it, and removed a gauze pack.

Sean bit down on the packet, holding it with his teeth as he removed a small can of spray, popped the lid, and held it over the wound. "This is going to sting," he warned.

Daiyu nodded absently, then he depressed the button. The disinfecting mist coated the skin and the wound, sending a shock wave of pain through the woman's body. She squeezed Adriana's hand hard, clenching her jaw at the same time for several seconds until the stinging dissipated.

Sean ripped the pouch open, removed the fabric, then pinched the wound together before pressing the gauze down onto the bloody skin. He sealed the area by pushing down on the adhesive portion of the patch. Once the wound was covered, he grabbed an alcohol wipe from another pouch and began cleaning the skin around the gash.

Daiyu swallowed hard. Sean imagined the thirst parching her throat and remembered what it felt like to fight off shock from a bloody injury. He took out a water bottle from the side of his pack and held it to her lips.

"Here, drink," he said. "I'm sure you're thirsty."

He poured small amounts of water between her parted lips, allowing her to swallow slowly.

"We need to keep you hydrated while we try to find a way out of here."

He and the other two began scouring the room for an escape, an open doorway, a path, anything.

"Watch her," Sean said to Adriana, who replied with a single nod.

"Come on, Schultzie. Let's find a way out of this place."

The two stood, pointing their lights in separate directions, but before they even took a step, something overhead stopped them in their tracks.

The blue light emanating from the flattened cube and the ring below it cast its eerie glow onto the ceiling. Through the still-settling dust, Sean and Tommy could only stare at the confounding sight.

Rubble littered the floor all around them, fragments of the collapsed ceiling.. Yet, above, the murals appeared unaffected, as though nothing had happened.

Tommy and Sean couldn't pry their eyes from it as their minds struggled to find an explanation.

"What are you—" Adriana didn't finish her sentence as she gazed up with them at the perfectly intact artistry.

"Um, Sean?" Tommy muttered. "How is that possible? The roof was crashing down all around us."

"I know," Sean said. "I have no idea."

He lowered his eyes and rested them on the flattened cube. Sean cocked his head to the side and took a step closer to the object. The edges of the former box's sides were folded in on themselves in such a way that it now formed an arrow. *Or is that my imagination,* he wondered silently.

The chrome shimmered as if made of alien liquid, yet somehow still held its hardened surface.

"Look at the lakes," Tommy breathed in a near-reverent tone. He raised a finger, pointing upward.

Sean tore his eyes from the ring and the folded cube and gazed up at the ceiling again.

Adriana noticed it, too. Daiyu's breathing calmed, and she also tilted her head slightly against the altar's wall to look up at the ceiling.

Each of the seven lakes glowed as if spotlights shone onto them from below.

"What in the world does that mean?" Tommy whispered.

Sean shook his head. "I have no idea."

23

KARASAHR

"I don't understand," Tommy said, still looking up. He finally took his eyes from the mysterious mural and surveyed the room. "The ceiling fell down all around us. How is it still there?"

"It must be some kind of projection," Sean guessed. "But from where?" He waved his hand over the ring and the metal arrow, but that did nothing to interrupt the visual overhead.

"Those lakes were definitely not glowing like that before."

"No," Sean agreed. "They weren't."

"We need to get her out of here," Adriana said, gesturing with a nod toward Daiyu. "She's lost a lot of blood. I'd feel better about things if she had medical attention."

"Agreed," Sean said. "Tommy, start over there and search the wall for a way out."

"Roger that," Tommy chirped.

The two picked their way through the debris until they reached the wall in the direction of the doorway they'd used to enter. Any slim hopes they might have mustered shattered when the two found the archway and an impossibly large rock slab filling the cavity. This stone wasn't rubble.

"Whoever built this place designed this to keep intruders inside," Tommy noted.

Sean didn't let the somber realization drag him down just yet. "Split up. You go that way," he pointed to the right. "I'll go the other. Meet you on the other side. Look for anything. A vent hole. A drain. Any kind of opening that might lead back to the surface."

"Ten-four."

Sean turned his back to his friend and worked his way around the wall, carefully navigating the larger chunks of rocks and avoiding the smaller ones that could easily roll an ankle.

He switched back to his flashlight instead of the phone light and used the brighter beam to cast a wide light net onto the walls and floor around him, hoping to find any semblance of a way out. *Maybe a door opened in the floor. Or perhaps a piece of debris might have broken through to a secret passage.*

None of those thoughts proved fruitful or true, and by the time he met up with Tommy on the other side of the chamber, he didn't have to read the disappointment on his friend's face to realize the gravity of the situation. They were trapped.

A creeping feeling Sean learned to suppress long ago tried to crawl up his torso from his gut. Panic was something Axis training had burned out of him. More rigorous than anything he'd ever heard of outside of what the Navy SEALs went through, Sean's time with the agency forged steeled nerves and sharp wits that didn't allow for even the slightest moment of hysteria.

Tommy, on the other hand, hadn't gone through that crucible. Though, somehow, he managed to suppress his immediate and surely overwhelming concern.

"Well, this looks bleak," he grumbled.

Sean simply nodded.

"Any ideas?"

Sean didn't say anything right away. Instead, he turned his eyes upward, to the ceiling, where the strange projections still hung over them. *Was it some kind of hologram?* He didn't have the answer, and the fact they couldn't see beyond the projection caused him to wonder what was really above them.

Outside of a staircase leading to the surface, it didn't really matter.

"Come on. There's nothing along the wall." Sean managed his way back over to the altar with Tommy in tow and climbed the two steps back to the top where Adriana knelt by Daiyu.

The Chinese woman's eyes were closed, but her chest rose and fell in a steady rhythm. She had either passed out or was doing her best to relax. Either way, Sean had no intention of interrupting. The bleeding had slowed to the point where the bloodstain on her shirt no longer spread. He took that as a good sign.

He'd never been the best at field-dressing wounds, but he knew enough to keep someone alive for a while. In Daiyu's case, he doubted she would have died from the injury, but you could never be too careful.

Adriana stood up, lowering Daiyu's hand onto her lap. "She's resting for now. I think she'll be okay."

"You've been through worse," Sean said, his eyes drifting down to his wife's chest where a bullet had nearly taken her life several years before. That had been a hard day down under. He recalled the horror of seeing her shot, her body falling into the river, the desperate search to find her. He never wanted to go through that again. That fear made his acrophobia seem as silly as a child's fear of the boogeyman.

"I guess you didn't find a way out."

He shook his head dejectedly.

Tommy answered, too. "No. The exit is sealed. No chance we can move the slab that's blocking it. Whoever built this place didn't want anyone leaving."

"Or," Sean said, tilting his head back, "maybe they didn't want anyone leaving that way."

"What? We just looked around the entire perimeter. There's no other way out. And I checked the floor, too. Nothing opened underneath us."

"I know," Sean agreed. He studied the ceiling projection, shifting his focus from one glowing lake to another. "Did you notice how those lakes in the painting seem to be lit up now? They weren't when we first came in."

Tommy and Adriana followed his gaze.

"Strange," Adriana mused.

"Yeah. Strange," Sean echoed.

"I wonder why that is?"

Sean didn't answer right away. Instead, he returned his attention to the metal ring atop the smooth stone altar. "See these?" He pointed to a sequence of ancient rune-like characters carved into the ring, spaced out every few inches around to the other side.

He took his phone and began recording a video, moving slowly around the altar.

"What are you doing?" Tommy asked.

"When we get out of here, we'll need the lab rats to figure out exactly what this language is. Might come in handy later on."

"You mean *if* we get out of here."

"Have some faith, Schultzie. There's always another way."

"The eternal optimist, Sean Wyatt, ladies and gentlemen."

Sean finished his recording when he completed the loop, and he slid the phone back into his pocket. "So," he began, "what do you think this is about?" He pointed to the arrow formerly known as a cube.

"It's weird," Tommy answered. "I have no clue how it did that, the unfolding trick. And why is it an arrow now?"

He realized the question he'd asked the second after he asked it, and all three sets of eyes followed the arrow to a column along the wall.

"You think there might be something over there?" Adriana asked. "Perhaps a soft spot in the stonework?"

"I doubt it," Sean denied. "But during the whole light display thing that happened when Benny opened the cube, I noticed the lakes on the mural flashing in different colors."

"So?" Tommy debated. "There were lots of lights flashing during that display."

"Not like this. I wonder..." Sean cast his focus onto the metal ring and risked touching it with one finger. The metal felt warm, contrary to the temperature of the room. By all rights, it should have been chilly to the touch.

"Maybe you shouldn't touch that, buddy," Tommy offered. "No telling what might happen next. Although being crushed by a giant boulder is probably better than dying from dehydration, or starving to death."

Sean ignored his friend's pessimism and wrapped his fingers around the ring. He tugged to the left and marveled in surprise at how easily the thing moved. "This isn't just a ring," he said, leaning forward to inspect the four pillars that held the hoop in place. "It's a wheel."

"Okay..."

Sean twisted another few inches, and the three watched with wide eyes as the hovering metal arrow changed directions in synchronization with the wheel. When the arrow pointed in the direction of one of the lakes above, Sean and the others noticed it glow brighter.

He stopped the wheel, wondering what would happen next. The answer came abruptly and terribly.

Something that sounded like creaking metal echoed throughout the chamber just before a loud snap. Suddenly, a section of the floor beyond the arrow fell away, dropping into a black abyss.

"Whoa!" Tommy yelled in horror as he watched the stone slab disappear into the darkness. Ten full seconds passed before a thunderous crash rose from the pit.

Sean stared into the blackness, concerned but not as alarmed as his friend.

"Did you see that?" Tommy asked, clearly freaking out. He kept jabbing his finger toward what had been the floor. "It's just like in *Goonies*. Remember? With the bone organ and all that?"

"Except this isn't a musical instrument," Sean argued. "And we don't have the Fratellis after us."

"Is that supposed to be a joke?" Tommy jeered.

Sean rolled his shoulders. "Maybe. Look, we know how this works now. Sort of. You point the arrow at the wrong lake; floor drops away. Point it at the right lake, maybe a way out appears."

Tommy stared at his friend like his face was on fire. "Seriously? That's your plan? You're going to keep spinning this death wheel until the entire floor drops out from under us?"

"Ideally, no. I would prefer that not to happen."

"There are seven lakes, Sean. How do you know which one is the right one?"

"I don't," Sean admitted. "But I'm sure as heck not going to sit around here and die from dehydration."

Tommy considered his friend's words, fighting through the terror of feeling the floor drop out from under them. Eventually, he arrived at the same conclusion as Sean. "No, you're right. Better to die trying than doing nothing."

Sean knew he didn't have to check with Adriana, she would always back him up no matter what. Unless he was wrong. She had a knack for picking the right moments to correct him, usually gently but with a firm, unrelenting tone or expression.

She merely offered a nod of agreement. "Do it."

"Okay," Sean said. "One lake down. Six to go."

He gripped the wheel and turned it again, spinning it until the arrow pointed to the next of the remaining six lakes in the mirage above.

The same sickening sound clanked from below, followed by the deafening creaking. The next section of floor dropped from view, crashing into the darkness below.

After the shock of seeing yet another part of the floor disappear, Tommy turned to his friend with the most forced fake grin of all time splattered on his face. He chuckled uncomfortably. "Well, you're oh for two, buddy. Five lakes left and only two chances."

"Three if you count the altar where we're standing," Sean argued, briefly examining their footing, as if that would make certain they didn't fall.

He inched closer to the wheel, though, until his toes abutted the base of the altar. With the cavernous pits opening up around him, his fear of heights began to crawl up his spine like spiders.

Sean didn't wait for permission on the third try. He decided to try a different tactic, and instead of hitting the lakes in order, he spun the wheel around until the arrow pointed at one of the images on the opposite side of the ceiling.

He let it stop, waited, and cringed as the same sounds groaned throughout the chamber a moment before the floor collapsed from view.

Adriana reached down to brace Daiyu as the floor shook around them. Tommy pointed his flashlight into the chasm and then across it. "Just to be safe, buddy, maybe don't guess wrong again. I'm not sure what's supporting this thing now."

Sean sighed. He'd been incorrect three times straight, and now doubt crept into his mind like a thief, ready to steal all hope.

Seven lakes, he thought. *Those three were wrong. What is different about them?*

He returned to the moment Benny activated the cube, the lights, the sounds, and the imagery overhead. Sean recalled watching the lakes change colors, every color of the rainbow, except one. He turned his head toward the image in question and remembered seeing it turn a sparkling gold color, which was technically in the yellow family. Sean couldn't help but wonder why the others were different.

That had to be it. If he was wrong, they were going to die at the bottom of an ancient temple, probably never to be found. The movie played out in his mind in vivid, gruesome, horrifying detail as the telltale sounds boomed through the chamber and the floor gave way underfoot, casting them into the certain doom of the blackness below.

"Sean?" Adriana said softly.

He felt her fingers touch his shoulder and snapped back to the present. "Sorry. I think I know which lake it is."

"I certainly hope so," Tommy blathered. "You've struck out three times. And I don't want you hitting the golden sombrero."

Sean would have laughed at the baseball joke if circumstances hadn't been so serious. As it was, he knew there was likely only one shot left at this. Oddly, Tommy's use of the word *golden* felt like a sign to Sean, and he gripped the wheel one more time.

He turned it, steadily and constantly until the arrow flowing in the center lined up with the lake that had sparkled like gold.

Sean took a deep breath and removed his fingers from the metal.

A deep rumble roared through the room. The sound differed from the others, and for a couple of seconds, Sean wondered if he'd made a mistake.

Those doubts disappeared when the sound of stone grinding on stone filled the room. Tommy and Adriana whirled around and aimed their flashlights at the wall. Stone slabs pushed out from the wall until they jutted three feet out, and then stopped. More continued to spiral upward around the wall until they reached a spot where the domed ceiling took a sharper angle inward.

"It's a staircase," Sean said with an almost boyish wonder in his voice. He followed the slabs around as those near the top finished sliding into place. He couldn't believe he'd never noticed any seams, so perfectly fitted were the blocks. The last step stuck out just beneath a darkened opening.

"Look," Tommy said, pointing at the doorway. "It's a way out!"

He grabbed Sean and hugged him, squeezing tight with his big muscles.

"Okay there, big guy. Take it easy. We're not out of the woods yet."

He looked down at Daiyu. "It's going to be tough getting her out of here up that way."

"We'll just have to be really careful," Tommy countered.

Sean turned his head upward again and examined the new doorway. Something else struck him as he stared at it. The door appeared to be just below the lake. He couldn't be certain, but Sean wondered if that was another clue to the location of the entrance into Shangri-La. He noted the three mountains surrounding it, with one that appeared to be far off in the distance. The waters of the lake no longer shimmered like gold but instead displayed a crystalline hue like the lakes and rivers filled with glacier runoff in Alaska. Sean recalled looking into that kind of water from a drift boat while trout fishing on the Kenai River.

He doubted there would be any fly fishing going on in this particular lake.

Adriana bent down and spoke to Daiyu. "Wake up, Daiyu," she said gently. "We have to go."

Her eyes cracked but didn't fully open. She'd regained a fraction of color in her face, but she'd need medicine, some stitches or staples, and a lot of rest.

"That's it," Adriana encouraged. "Just need you to stand as much as you can. We're going to get you out of here."

"Adriana?" Daiyu mumbled.

"That's right. It's me. We're going to get you some help. Okay?"

Daiyu nodded but said nothing.

"Mind if I take the left?" Sean asked.

"Don't like that drop-off?" Tommy teased.

"You should be more careful. You're the one who nearly fell off a cliff this week. Not me."

"Maybe I should take the inside."

"Too late. Called it."

Tommy rolled his eyes. "It's not like calling shotgun in a car."

Sean and Tommy bent down and eased her up. She felt limp and heavy in their grasp, but their grip was strong.

The two stumbled through the rubble to the first step and together climbed up. Sean waited for a second to make sure the stone would hold all their weight, but the thing didn't even shudder in the slightest.

Adriana stood behind them, both hands up and ready to brace the others in case one tipped backward.

She followed them as they took the next step and the next, leaving behind the relative safety of what was left of the floor.

The gap between the steps remained consistent, but as the group ascended, the danger of the drop ballooned in their minds. Sean leaned toward the wall, using his weight to keep Tommy and Daiyu from sliding over the edge. Adriana also braced Tommy, keeping her hand on his hip from one step down as they continued to climb.

Two steps from the top, Sean finally started to feel hopeful. He didn't dare look down, or back over his shoulder. But he couldn't help noticing the abyss between the gaps in the steps. He swallowed back his fear, doing his best to focus on the block and not the air between and beneath the stone slabs.

Tommy twisted his neck slightly to get the circulation normalized. Carrying this much weight was difficult even for a muscular guy like him. Daiyu was barely conscious and only supported a small percentage of her mass, awake enough to put one foot in front of the other.

The slight shift caused Tommy to lose his balance, and he missed the next step by an inch, only catching it with the side of his right foot.

He yelped as he felt gravity pulling on him. Then, a strong hand pushed hard against his ribs while Sean latched on to his forearm and leaned hard into the wall.

Tommy found his footing again and exhaled the second-biggest sigh of relief he'd had this week.

"Easy there, big fella," Sean comforted. "Take it easy. You're good. One more to go, then we'll take a breath for a second once we're on the other side."

"Yeah," Tommy said, gasping for air. "A break would be good."

They managed to climb the final step without incident, arriving safely at the darkened doorway.

Sean risked venturing into the darkness first, pulling Daiyu and Tommy with him. Once inside and on solid ground, they lowered Daiyu to the floor and turned on their lights.

Adriana joined them a few seconds later, and after checking Daiyu's condition, looked into the passage ahead of the two men, who were stretching and catching their breath.

"Looks like we found our way out," she said.

"I sure hope so," Sean added. "Unfortunately, Benny has the heart. And we have no idea where he's going with it."

24

KARASAHR

"I have the heart," Benitzio said into the phone.

Ju Chen steered the vehicle into the town and toward the airport, where their aircraft awaited, a tool Lóng had bestowed to speed up the expedition.

"Really?"

Benitzio scowled at the question. "You hired me because you believed I could get the job done. The job is done."

"Well, not completely, not yet."

"How so?"

"Last I checked, you're not at the entrance to the valley. Yet."

Benitzio huffed, deliberately letting the man hear his derision. "That's a foregone conclusion, sir. We will be there before the end of the day tomorrow."

"You think so? It's two hundred miles from the nearest airport." Lóng's smooth, buttery voice did little to calm Benitzio's nerves. If anything, it set fire to the anxiety like a blowtorch to a fuel truck.

"When will you be there?" Benitzio asked. No one asked details like that of Lóng, at least as far as he knew. But in this instance, he felt no lines were being crossed.

A deep sigh came through the speaker. "I will be there on Friday. That is the soonest I can arrive."

"That's two days."

"I need two days."

The Spaniard knew he'd gone far enough with his insolence and dialed it back. "Very well, sir."

On the inside, he wondered why one of the most powerful men in China, and probably the world, needed so much time when he'd made quite clear that this expedition trumped everything else he had going on. If there were business dealings, Lóng could cancel. If he had family in town or a kid's recital to attend, they would forgive him. They were standing on the edge of the greatest discovery in all of history, and the man who'd dumped millions into the project said he needed two days?

"I must make arrangements," Lóng said. "Do you know where the gate is?"

The question caught Benitzio off guard. "What do you mean? I thought you knew where it was."

"I do." Lóng paused. "I'm surprised there weren't any more instructions where you found the heart."

"Instructions?" Benitzio grew tense at the thought. *Did I miss something in the chamber back in the temple?* He looked back over his shoulder through the rear window as if he could still see the place, but it was long gone, and they were nearly to the airport. "No, I didn't see anything there."

Another thoughtful pause filled the line with silence. "So, what was it like?"

"I'm sorry, sir?"

"The place where you found the Heart of Shambala, the keystone that grants entry into the sacred valley. What was this place like?"

Benitzio fumbled for words. "Well, sir. The temple was in ruins. The entire site, actually. It was all ruins."

"Yes, I know that part. What of the inside?"

"We arrived and began investigating the central rock formation at the site. Then we encountered trouble."

"Trouble?" Lóng didn't sound happy; the peaceful monotone he normally used elevated.

Not a good sign.

"Sean Wyatt arrived shortly after us. I don't know how he knew where to go."

"Wyatt?" The voice on the other end growled now, like a lion that hadn't eaten in a week and had just been challenged for control of the pride. "What was Wyatt doing there?"

"I wondered the same thing, sir. But you won't have to worry about Sean Wyatt anymore."

"Oh?"

Ju Chen flipped up the turn signal at an intersection where the quiet inlet into the town met a busier main thoroughfare.

She watched as dozens of cars rolled by, but stole a quick glance over at Benitzio when he mentioned Wyatt. Curiosity begged to know how her partner was going to handle this. She twitched at the thought of the word *partner*. She doubted he considered her that, but without her, none of this would be possible. She knew, too, that the wealth this venture would bring her would not be there if Benitzio hadn't brought something to the table.

Then again, she wasn't married to him. Who was to say she couldn't let him lead her to glory only to eliminate him at the finish line? Based on what she knew about Lóng, the man would probably appreciate a Romanesque move like that.

"We took care of it. Wyatt won't be a bother anymore."

"You killed him? You. Killed Sean Wyatt? Or was it your partner?"

Benitzio choked down the offense rising in his throat. "Is that so unbelievable? That I could take out Wyatt? He's not immortal, you know. He's a man. Flesh and blood."

"It would seem I have struck a nerve with you, Benitzio. I apologize. I didn't realize you had such a sordid past with Wyatt."

He knew. Benitzio didn't believe that lie for a second. The man knew everything, or at least that was the legacy he allowed to be passed through the ranks of the black markets and underworlds of the planet.

"Where is the body?" Lóng asked.

"What's left of it is in a secret chamber deep within the Shikshin Temple. We barely escaped with our own lives before the only way in and out was sealed by a stone I figure to be a couple of tons at minimum."

"So, you didn't see him die." It wasn't a question. And the line implied that Sean Wyatt was somehow still alive and roaming the earth.

Benitzio felt his voice catch. The light turned green, and Ju Chen steered their vehicle onto the main street.

"No. I didn't see him die. But I assure you: There is no way he escaped. The chamber was sealed. There were no doors, no windows, nothing."

"Describe the room."

Benitzio's frustration bubbled like water about to boil. He took a deep breath and exhaled slowly, audibly, so Lóng could hear the irritation. "It was a circular room. As I said, one door in and out. Inside, the ceiling was a dome. Probably thirty meters to the highest point."

"What else?"

This guy doesn't stop.

"Well, let me see. There was an altar made of stone in the center of the room. A ring of fire surrounded us in a trough along the wall. It wrapped all the way around."

"A ring of fire?"

"Yes. It wasn't like a fight-to-the-death ring of fire if that's what you're thinking." Benitzio waited only for a second before continuing. "Above the altar, a metal cube hovered over a ring that appeared to be made from the same material or element."

"A ring? A cube?" Lóng's voice sounded different. Instead of the probing, intense tone, he sounded...curious, with a hint of excitement.

"Yes." Benitzio changed gears to feed the monster on the other end. "It was spectacular. And the domed ceiling was covered in what looked like a living mural of Shangri-La's history, with mountains and lakes, people and animals, and cities that glistened in the sun."

Ju Chen kept her face forward but cast a sidelong *are you serious* glance at the Spaniard.

He didn't notice and continued laying it on thick. "Ju Chen and I got the drop on Wyatt and his friends. We allowed them to open the doorway into the secret passage. Then we hung back and waited, only following them when we deemed it prudent." He knew he'd shifted into more story than description of what his employer wanted, but he figured it might take the man's mind off his initial concern regarding Wyatt's demise.

"Once Wyatt and his friends were inside the chamber, we trapped them, forced them to stand back as I deactivated the cube."

"Ah," Lóng said. "So, Mattheson's code worked. Tell me. What was it like? The cube."

Benitzio twirled his finger at Ju Chen, urging her to hurry to the airport, as though that would save him from the onslaught of questions.

"Yes, the code worked. Did you have any doubts that it would?"

Hesitation. Then: "No. If I hadn't believed in it, then we wouldn't even be having this conversation."

"I suppose not."

"What happened next?"

"This floating cube defied gravity. It hovered in the air over the ring like those objects you see in novelty stores."

"Magnetic?" Lóng guessed.

"Possibly. I didn't exactly have time to stand around trying to figure out how the thing worked." He immediately regretted the comment, but it was too late to go back now. "The cube unfolded when I completed the correct sequence. The heart was within."

Lóng sounded like he was taking a drag of a cigarette. After he exhaled, he said, "You've done well, Benitzio. Very well, indeed. I look forward to seeing the heart. And rewarding your efforts."

Benitzio liked the sound of that last part. Had he detected a hint of malice in the man's voice? Or was it only his imagination?

Just when he thought the conversation was about to reach a merciful end, Lóng spoke up again.

"It sounds like an incredible experience. I must wonder, though, at what point you believe Sean Wyatt died."

Teeth ground inside Benitzio's mouth. His jaw tightened, flexing the muscles around his cheeks all the way up to his ears. "If Wyatt is alive, he won't be for long. I assure you. There is no way out of that death trap. The ancients who designed it made certain no one would get out of there alive with the heart."

"You did," Lóng countered.

"Only because we were fast enough. The doorway sealed seconds after we escaped."

Lóng made it plainly obvious that he didn't believe Wyatt was dead or that he couldn't have escaped the trap in the ancient temple. Benitzio didn't care at this point. The man could believe whatever he wanted, so long as he paid Benitzio what he was owed.

"I will see you at the gate. Coordinates will be sent immediately. I will arrive at noon on Friday. Do not be late."

"I—"

The call ended before Benitzio could finish his statement. "Won't," he said anyway. Looking down at his phone, he confirmed that the eccentric Lóng had indeed cut him off.

Benitzio stewed for the remaining ten-minute drive to the airport. When Ju Chen pulled up next to the hangar where a small crew prepped the private plane, she shifted the vehicle into park and then looked over at him.

"What is the problem?" she asked. Always direct, and never fluffy on the conversations, Ju Chen cut to the point. She knew something was going on, and from the abrupt way the talk with their employer ended, she had a bad feeling something wasn't right.

Benitzio remained silent for a few seconds before saying, "Nothing. Everything is going according to plan."

"Don't lie to me," she snapped. "What is going on?"

He tore his eyes away from the dashboard and looked over at her. A cold, distant stare filled his eyes. "We are to meet Lóng at the gateway to Shangri-La." His phone vibrated, and Benitzio checked it. The coordinates appeared on the screen.

"And?"

"And I don't like the way he sounded on the call." He measured her gaze. "I am of the opinion that our friend, Mr. Lóng, may try to kill us."

"Obviously," she agreed.

His eyebrows perked up in surprise. "You already think this?"

"Of course. Once he has what he wants, why would he need us around?"

"Was there any point in time when you were planning on telling me these thoughts?"

"You should not worry about Lóng," Ju Chen reassured. "That's why you have me."

His eyes narrowed for a fraction of a second, barely more than a twitch. "Yes," he said. "That is why I have you."

25

KARASAHR

Sean and the others had been walking through the tunnel for what felt like hours, despite his watch telling him only thirty minutes had elapsed.

The barren corridor walls offered no elaborate paintings, no ancient text. Only a path sheltered against the weather, but where it led, no one knew. Sean and Tommy required a break every four or five minutes to rest and stretch their muscles from bearing most of Daiyu's weight.

To her credit, Daiyu fought to stay semi alert and bear some of the burden, but it wasn't much. The weakening blood loss, and probably shock from the wound, still took a toll.

At the forefront of Sean's mind, the race against time charged forward, and he didn't allow their frequent breaks to last more than a minute before starting the journey again.

Just over thirty-five minutes into the passage, the group arrived at a barrier. Two stone slabs with a third serving as a header above them stood in the way of the tunnel.

"Looks like there's daylight just beyond," Tommy said, bending down to see through the two-foot gap between the columns. It was narrow, but they could fit through. Beyond, a pile of rocks blocked the exit.

Streams of light slipped through cracks between the stones like tiny beams of hope cutting through the darkness.

Sean stepped through the columns first and then turned his back to the pile of rubble to take Daiyu's right arm as Tommy turned her body sideways so she could get through.

"Easy now," Tommy said. "Sean's got you. Just a little farther."

"That's right," Sean urged. "I have you. Almost there."

He slid his arm under her armpit and looped it around the middle of her back, gripping her ribs tightly so she didn't slip. Then he pulled her through to the other side, adjusted his grip, and held her up with his right shoulder. Her head rolled to that side, hair brushing against his face.

"I'm...so sorry," she murmured.

"Don't worry about it, D. We got you. Almost there."

Tommy twisted his way through the narrow opening. Even with his bulky chest and shoulders, he made it through easily.

When Adriana joined them on the other side of the columns, Sean asked her to take the lead. "Take a look at that pile blocking the way, and make sure we don't risk a collapse if we remove them."

She nodded and slithered by him, making her way over to the debris twenty feet away. Adriana knelt down and examined the blockade, checking to make sure there were no tricks in play that would collapse the tunnel on them.

"Looks fine to me," she said over her shoulder as Sean and Tommy lumbered up next to her. "Honestly, I think whoever built this covered the exit this way to make it look unimportant. No one would think anything of a bunch of rocks heaped up in the desert."

"Always hide it in plain sight," Sean mulled, thinking—as he so often did—about the story of "The Purloined Letter" by Poe.

He looked at Daiyu. Her eyes blinked lazily, and not in perfect sequence. "We're going to set you down for a second," Sean said. "We have to move some rocks out of the way."

"I like rock," she drooled.

Tommy snorted slightly. Sean did, too. Even with the dire circumstances, they had to appreciate the humor of the moment.

Sean wasn't sure if Tommy realized it, but he felt like Daiyu was going to be okay. He'd seen dozens of wounds during his time in the agency—and since. One like this was almost never mortal, even without hours of real medical attention. So long as the bleeding had been stopped, she'd be fine. Eventually. That said, Sean's gratitude for the chopper filled his mind. They could get her to a hospital much faster than if they'd been in a car, and that time difference could be critical in terms of stopping infection.

They rested her head against the stone wall, and Sean turned to Tommy. "Keep her head upright. I'll help Adriana clear the blockage."

Tommy agreed with a nod and watched as his friends picked away the stones, some the size of footballs, others the size of baseballs. With every rock they pried from the pile, more and more streams of daylight sprayed through the cracks until huge rays shot through, illuminating the hard tunnel floor.

The work took a solid fifteen minutes to clear enough of the rubble away to allow passage. When they finished, the entire corridor filled with bright sunlight. Adriana and Sean stood in the opening for a minute, catching their breath and staring out into the light, allowing their eyes to adjust.

Sean winced hard. His eyes had always been sensitive to bright sunlight. He took in a deep breath of the dry, dust-blown air, and let the warmth of the sun wash over him. He only permitted twenty seconds of basking before he turned to the others.

"Stay here," Sean said to Tommy. "I'm going to have a look around." He looked to his wife. "Care to join me?"

"Sure."

The two stepped out of the tunnel entrance and found themselves at the base of a hill. They looked around, pistols raised as they traced over the area littered with the ruins of ancient homes, stalls, and shops. Out here, there weren't many places to hide. For them, or for an enemy.

He guessed Benny and his pet were already gone. They had at least a full hour's head start, and probably two when it was all said and done.

None of that mattered. Without knowing which way to go, Sean and his crew were down for the count. Again. It always happened like this. Just as it was with his favorite sports teams—even when they won, it seemed like they had to come from behind to do it. Just once, he wished he could play with a lead.

Then again, he'd always joked, you can't blow a lead if you don't have one. He must have heard that one a thousand times after the Falcons Super Bowl loss. His favorite American football team had made a habit of coming up small in big moments, perpetually disappointing the franchise for the better part of half a century.

At least I get the job done, Sean thought, pushing aside the trivial sports memories. *None of that really matters anyway.* Or so he told himself. Right now, it truly didn't matter, but it was funny the things a person thought about when under pressure.

"Clear," Adriana said. "I don't see any snipers."

"Same," Sean confirmed. "I'll get the other two, and we'll make a break for the chopper. It should be just over the hill directly behind us." Sean based his assumption on the topography around him. He'd seen the mountains in the distance directly ahead when they first arrived. The recon he and the others conducted gave him a broad view of the land. While they'd been walking through the passage for some time, several turns along the way caused the path to double back multiple times, gradually returning the group to the surface.

Sean returned to the tunnel and helped lift Daiyu off the ground.

"Sure is bright out there," Tommy said. "Always gets me when we come out of some cave or underground temple of certain doom like that."

"It's never certain, Schultzie," Sean laughed.

"I hope not," Tommy said with a chuckle that turned into a grunt as they helped Daiyu toward the opening.

Adriana took point as the two men continued assisting the injured woman up the hard dirt slope. At the top, they rested for half a minute while Adriana pushed on, her pistol at full extension sweeping dramatically from side to side as she checked the ruins of the ancient site.

No shots rang out, which Sean took as a good sign, within fifteen seconds of reaching the plateau. Exposed out in the open, a decent sniper would have taken the shot in less than ten. The fact none of them were dead meant they were alone. Still, something felt off, and Sean kept his pistol ready in his left hand just in case.

Right-handed, he preferred to keep his weapon in the other hand, but right now that one was occupied, and he'd practiced enough with both to be deadlier than most with both hands.

As he and Tommy continued their labor across the flat space toward the idle helicopter, Sean recalled his initial training when he joined Axis. The drills started off easy enough. Stationary targets, urban tactics, jungle tactics, gun ranges. He'd learned to hone his basic skills in those sessions. But it was the live fire training that made him one of the elite. High velocity paintballs were the initial tool of choice. *Man, did those suckers hurt,* he recalled. The memory caused him to feel a dull soreness from bruises that had long since healed. After the first day, he'd looked in the mirror at a black-and-blue torso, neck, and arms. While painful, those sessions taught Sean the finer points of using any cover he could find in order to survive.

After that, they'd gone through live fire drills with real bullets, much the same way the elite military forces used, except with one significant tweak.

"What are you thinking about?" Tommy asked when they were halfway to the chopper. They passed the rock formation in the middle of the compound, the place where their journey into the bizarre underground chamber began.

Sean snapped out of the past and returned to the present. "Sorry. I was just thinking about when I joined Axis. The training stuff. I think we're clear. If there'd been a shooter here, we would have already known it."

"That's good." Tommy vacillated for a few seconds. He stopped to rest again and adjust his arm. "You're not thinking about going back, are you? I mean, I know you told Emily you'd do whatever she needed if she was desperate."

Sean huffed. "So far, she's only done that one time. As much as she wants me back in, I think Emily knows how far she can push that offer. She'll respect my wishes as long as she can."

"Good." Tommy looked over at his friend, thoughtful perhaps about his own memories. "I don't want to lose you."

"I bet you don't, cowboy."

The two shared a laugh.

"Come on, Schultzie," Sean said. "Let's get this lady to a hospital."

They continued toward the helicopter sitting fifty yards away. Adriana arrived at the aircraft and stopped at the cockpit. She bent down, inspecting a heap near the skid. Her head snapped around and she raised her weapon again, checking every point surrounding her.

Sean felt a wave of concern rising and quickened his step. Tommy felt it, too, and kept up with him, scurrying across the plains like they were running a zombie three-legged race. For a second, Sean regretted not tying his right leg to Daiyu's. They might have been able to move faster that way.

He forgot all about that nonsense when they drew closer to the helicopter, and the mass on the ground Adriana hovered over came into view.

Sean and Tommy stopped twenty feet away from the aircraft, staring down at the dead pilot. The crater on the back of his skull told the tale of how he died—point-blank gunshot wound.

"Let's get her in the back," Sean urged.

"But Sean?" Tommy protested.

"Just do it, Schultzie." He fired a stern look at his friend, who understood immediately. Sean wasn't being callous. He was trying to make sure Daiyu didn't see the body and get hysterical. That was one of the last things she needed at that moment.

"Could you open the back?" Sean asked Adriana.

She nodded and pulled the latch, opening the rear compartment. The two men hefted Daiyu up and into the seat. Sean quickly climbed in after her and laid her out in such a way she'd be comfortable.

"You can fly this, yeah?" Tommy asked Adriana.

She nodded. "I haven't flown this particular model, but yes. I'm certified for rotors."

"Good thing your dad insisted on flight lessons."

"It's come in handy more than once."

Sean hopped back down out of the chopper. "Go ahead and get her started," Sean said. "We need to get moving."

"Where are we going?"

Sean bent down and rolled the body over. He checked the man's pockets but only found a wallet and a set of keys. He had no intention of robbing the dead, especially the innocent dead. Making sure the man's belongings were tucked away in his pockets, Sean left the pilot there on the dirt as Adriana fired up the chopper's engines.

For a few seconds, Sean stared at the dead man, hoping that he didn't have any family or small children that would grow up without a father or a husband. How many had suffered through that kind of loss in his time with Axis or with the IAA? There was no way to put a tally on that, and he knew it. Sean did what he believed necessary. But there were lines that got crossed. And there was the possibility of not knowing exactly when to stop before it was too late.

With a sigh, Sean turned away from the body and walked back to the helicopter's front passenger door. Tommy had already found a place to sit inside and was strapped in, prepped to fly.

He climbed inside, plucked a headset from the dashboard, and fit it over his ears.

"Where to?" Adriana asked.

"Nearest airport. Then a hospital."

"Got it," she said, checking gauges and controls.

The rotors overhead spun faster and faster, sending dust swirling out from the pressure. When everything checked out, Adriana lifted off the ground and steered the chopper toward the falling sun.

26

KARASAHR

Sean, Tommy, and Adriana sat in a hospital room under the pale light glowing in the bathroom. They'd kept it mostly dark since Daiyu came out of surgery. The doctors said her injuries weren't life-threatening, as Sean had suspected, but they still had to operate to align the bone fragments of what turned out to be a badly fractured clavicle.

The surgeons expected her to be fine but said she needed to rest. Sean didn't exactly have confidence in the small-town hospital in the Middle of Nowhere, China, but he also didn't have any other options. Flying to one of the larger metro areas would have taken too long. Not to mention all the other complications with going into a big city.

They'd made the right decision.

There'd been little conversation since Daiyu returned to the room after surgery. No one wanted to wake her up. She looked to be resting comfortably, though when the drugs wore off that might be a different story. And when the scalene block lost its effect, she'd probably be begging for the ibuprofen, or something stronger.

Sean didn't want to be insensitive, but after several glances with Adriana and Tommy, he knew they all felt the same pressing need.

Thankfully, the nurse appeared in the doorway with a cart of devices hooked to it. The woman said she was there to check on the patient, though her English wasn't stellar. Sean took that opportunity to pull the others out of the room and let the woman work, but the real reason was so they could talk.

He led the way down the hall to a small, empty waiting room surrounded with glass windows, opened the door, and held it for the others to enter before closing it behind him.

"Daiyu's going to be fine," Sean began. "But we're going to have to continue without her."

Adriana nodded her agreement.

"Yeah," Tommy said reluctantly. "I don't want to, but we can't let Benny find whatever it is that's out there. You guys saw what happened in that chamber. We're dealing with a power unlike anything we've seen before. And we've seen some weird stuff."

"Yes, we have," Sean said.

"Any ideas where Benny might be headed next?" Adriana asked. She looked to Sean then Tommy, but neither wore confidence on their faces.

"There weren't any clues in the chamber," Tommy said. "Usually, there is something that points where to go next. This place? Nothing."

"I wonder if Benny knows," she offered. "He mentioned something about—" She let the words hang in the room as a nurse walked by in scrubs and a face mask.

"Mattheson," Tommy finished. "He's a crackpot archaeologist. Years ago, he started publishing wild theories about the hollow earth, even hollow planets around us. Which I thought was interesting since he's not an astronomer, as far as I know."

Sean listened, but his mind ran wild with visions of what happened in the temple chamber earlier that day. The flashing lights, the sounds, the levitating cube, and finally, the glowing lakes all around.

His eyes widened, and he remembered he needed to send the video of the ring to the lab rats back in Atlanta.

"There might have been a clue after all," Sean said, trying not to interrupt his friend. The other two looked at him with muted expectations. "On the wheel, there were markings. Remember? Some kind of ancient language we've never seen before. I took a video of it and meant to send it to Tara and Alex, but I was so focused on Daiyu I forgot until now."

He tapped out a quick text to the artists formerly known as "the kids," then attached the video and sent it.

"Hopefully, they can make sense of it." He looked to Tommy. "You were saying something about Mattheson."

"Right. Anyway, he got way out of his lane when he started talking about space stuff, aliens, all that."

"Sounds like he wasn't ever really in a lane if you ask me."

"True enough," Tommy agreed. "The guy was out there on a lot of stuff. A real fringe character. To his credit, early on he published several papers on ancient civilizations from the antediluvian world. He posited that the civilizations that were destroyed in the Great Flood possessed technologies that far surpassed anything we have today. It was when he took a turn to the mythical side of things that his credibility began to slip away. His paper about his Shangri-La hypothesis got him laughed out of every reputable university and research facility around the world. No one booked him to speak anymore. He couldn't land a job, even at small community colleges.

"His reputation was destroyed." Tommy sounded almost sad about it. "Of course, the evolution of the internet and social media removed the gag from his mouth, and he started putting out videos on that and many other subjects. He published books with his own money, trying to create a new breed of followers who would subscribe to his theories. In the end, he found himself broke and alone. Last I heard, he was hiding out somewhere in Vietnam."

"What's he doing there?" Sean asked.

"Surviving is my best guess. If you saw your life's work laughed at, insane or not, you'd probably feel pretty broken. Not everyone has the fortitude to face that kind of failure, much less being laughed at by people you considered respected peers."

"I guess not."

Adriana listened closely while constantly checking the windows. She knew her husband had been doing the same, always on alert.

"Do you think it's possible Benny found this Mattheson?" she wondered.

"Sure," Tommy said. "Anything is possible. Especially now, with all the tech and tracking, can anyone really hide from the eyes that want to find you? I only saw a few of Mattheson's papers. The early ones were pretty good, actually. The man had some good ideas. But I'm one of the ones who stopped paying attention the second he started sounding cuckoo."

Sean's phone began buzzing in his pocket. He fished it out and checked the screen. "It's Malcolm. I better take this."

Tommy nodded, and Sean stepped out into the hallway.

"What's up, Malcolm?" He pressed the phone to his ear as he spoke.

"Hey, Sean. You guys doing okay?"

"We're good." Sean didn't think telling him about the injury to Daiyu would go over well, and it wasn't entirely relevant. Malcolm didn't know her anyway. "Still on the hunt."

"Any leads?"

Sean forced a quiet laugh. "I said it before, and I'll say it again: I like how you're always direct, Malcolm."

"Why beat around the bush?"

"Exactly. Yes, we're working on some leads right now, but nothing concrete. We had a good lead, but that's a dead end." Sean wasn't about to tell the man they found the heart only to lose it to Benny Torres. They might have been down to their last few chips at the poker table, but as the greats always say, you only need a chip and a chair to have a chance.

"I sent something to the lab back in Atlanta. I'm hopeful they'll be able to unravel what we found."

"Now I'm curious," Malcolm said, his voice rising slightly, quickening with each syllable. "What did you find?"

Sean explained the temple's inner sanctum, a chamber unlike any they'd seen before, with what could only be described as a living mural on the domed ceiling above. He left out the part about the narrow escape, Benny showing up, and the fact that they were in a hospital.

"But no sign of the jewel?" Malcolm pressed when Sean was done.

"We don't have it yet," he hedged, careful to mind his words. "But we will. I'm confident in that."

"Well, I trust you, Sean. You and Tommy are the best there is. Or is it the best there are?"

"I'm not the grammar police, Malcolm. You know that."

The man laughed. "All right. I won't bother you. Get back on the case. I'm sure you and Tommy will figure it out."

Sean checked his watch and roughly calculated what time it must have been back in Georgia. "Go get some lunch, brother. I'll catch up to you soon and get you a better update when I have something."

"I look forward to it. Later, Sean. And tell that pretty wife of yours I said hi."

"Will do."

Sean lowered the phone and ended the call. He stared at the screen for a few seconds, lost in thought, and then slid the device back into his pocket. Opening the door, he stepped back into the waiting room, where Tommy and Adriana looked at him with expectation in their eyes.

"What did he have to say?" Tommy asked.

"Nothing much," Sean confessed. "I told him we were working on a lead, but I left out all the stuff with Benny stealing the heart and all that."

"Probably for the best. He doesn't need those details. I know I prefer it when you don't tell me everything." Tommy's lips parted in a grin, and he chuckled in his chest.

"I assume you didn't mention Daiyu," Adriana ventured.

"No, I did not. No reason to cause concern. We can still finish this. Just have to be more careful." Sean felt silly even saying that. Being cautious guided his every move. Especially out in the field, he remained on alert every waking minute. People had gotten the drop on him before—almost always due to some extraneous circumstance.

This time, however, differed from the others. Getting distracted by the floating cube was one of the most unprofessional moments of his IAA career, or any other, in his opinion. Then again, Adriana also got switched off long enough for Benny to sneak up to the entire team.

"And get something back from the lab," Tommy said, peeling Sean back into the conversation and away from his thoughts.

"Right." Sean tried to recover from the internal analysis running through his head.

Tommy looked at the time on his watch and stretched his arms up high. "I'll stay here with Daiyu if you two want to get a room somewhere."

"I can't make you do that," Sean argued.

"We need sleep." Right on cue, Tommy yawned to hammer home the statement. He covered his mouth with a balled fist. "There's only one couch in the room. I'll sleep in there with her. You two find a hotel or something."

"You're sure?" Adriana asked. "I can stay."

Tommy shook his head dramatically. "Nope. It's all good. Besides, you may never get another chance to have a little private time in this part of the world."

Sean and Adriana rolled their eyes at him.

"I'm sure there's something close by. Call me when you wake up, or if her condition changes. It sounds like she's out of the woods, and I don't think there's any danger now that Benny is long gone."

"Yeah," Tommy agreed. "I'm sure he thinks we're still down there in the belly of the temple." He looked toward the door. "You two go get some rest. I'll be fine here. I can sleep pretty much anywhere."

Sean knew that to be true. He'd seen his friend pass out on the front row of a blues concert once at the famous Tivoli Theater in Chattanooga.

"We'll see you in the morning," Sean said as he opened the door and allowed Adriana to walk out into the hall.

Tommy returned to Daiyu's room and eased the door shut until there was only a crack left to allow light from the corridor to stream in. As the couple walked down the hall, Sean unconsciously reached out and took Adriana's hand. She squeezed it, looking down for a second with a smile as their fingers interlocked.

"I love you," she purred.

One of his favorite movie lines flashed in his mind. "I know."

She punched him softly in the arm and laughed. "Scoundrel."

He pulled her close. "That I might be, princess."

27

ATLANTA

"Kind of late for Sean to be sending us that video," Alex drawled. "That's all I'm saying. I mean, it's gotta be after midnight over there."

"Closer to two o'clock in the morning now," Tara corrected. Her eyes remained fixed on the computer screen. Data flowed by like a digital river of information.

They'd received the video from Sean more than an hour ago. The second the two saw the video, they wanted to know more. Burdened with an inflexible curiosity, Tara and Alex weren't the types to let a good mystery go unsolved. The second Sean's video ended, they set to work trying to figure out what the bizarre inscriptions meant.

The two replayed the video, pausing it every few seconds to create copies of the runes on paper. That painstaking effort took fifteen minutes, which didn't sound like much, but to a couple of people accustomed to getting things done quickly, it felt like a marathon.

Once the copies were complete, they fed the notes into the scanner, set the parameters, and let the computers do their thing.

Tommy allocated a significant portion of his budget to the lab in order to make certain his research team always had the best, fastest, and most up-to-date hardware and software available.

Surrounded by ancient artifacts set out on tables, and others enclosed in glass cases, the tech portion of the lab seemed like a contradiction—a crossroads where the very old met the most modern.

"Would be nice if it just spit out exact coordinates, wouldn't it?" Alex mused. He hovered over his workstation's keyboard, watching two screens flash though images of majestic mountains, lakes, and barren plains.

"Where's the fun in that?" Tara asked in a flirtatious tone. "You men always want things to be easy."

"And you don't?"

"I like a challenge. I married you, didn't I?"

He snorted and shook his head, keeping his eyes on the monitors for a few seconds before surrendering and passing her an admiring glance.

"I walked into that one," he said.

"Sprinted is more like it."

The computers made quick work of the runes, creating a key in under two minutes, then producing potential solutions for the inscription.

The message the machines deciphered turned out to be odd, as were nearly all of the codes Sean and Tommy discovered while in the field.

Upon the green waters the talon points to where horizons end. Pass through the eye to the sacred gate. As above. So below.

"Still nothing pinpointed," Alex said, shifting away from the conversation that seemed to only dig him deeper into a hole. He'd never been able to match wits with Tara. Part of him didn't want to. He loved how clever she was, how cute she could be when she teased him. Sometimes he had to pinch himself to remember he wasn't dreaming, that this woman had picked him, out of all the options in the world.

"This is harder than we thought it would be," Tara complained, shaking him from his admirations.

"Yeah. And what's the deal with that last part?"

"You mean the quote from the Bible? As above. So below?"

"Uh-huh," he confirmed. "The Shikshin Temple doesn't predate Biblical timelines, but it's possible the underground portion does, where the gang found that metal wheel."

"I considered that, too. We've seen several things through the years that cross over religious lines. Makes me think nobody has a monopoly on any of it."

Alex pondered the statement for a few breaths, then decided that was a conversation best saved for the firepit on the back porch with the stars twinkling overhead. He found the deepest and best discussions required a good venue.

"Maybe we're overthinking this," he offered.

"What do you mean?" Tara pulled away from the monitor, rubbed her eyes under black-rimmed glasses, and faced him.

The machines purred with their constant hum.

"Well, where are they right now?"

Tara shrugged. "Tommy and them?"

He nodded.

"China, last we heard. Although, you know those two. They could have been in China an hour ago and Russia right now."

He allowed the exaggeration and continued. "True, but let's figure they're still in China. If they're looking for Shangri-La, all the legends put the lost valley somewhere in China, or that vicinity."

"That's a big vicinity," she quipped.

"Indeed. But our computers are searching the entire world." He arched both eyebrows to urge her to the conclusion.

"I see what you're saying, but we might as well be thorough. No need to isolate down to the region when our computers can analyze every potential around the globe without adding so much as a minute to the workload."

He knew she was correct. "Yes. That's not what I'm saying."

"What then?" She cocked her head to the side, looking at him with a blank, genuinely curious stare.

"Let's work from the assumption that, if real, Shangri-La is somewhere within the Chinese border."

"Okay. That's reasonable."

"Now, look at the clue again."

She directed her attention to a printout on the desk. "Upon the green waters the talon points to where horizons end. Pass through the eye to the sacred gate. As above. So below."

Looking back to him, she rolled her shoulders. "What am I missing?"

"For the last hour or so, we've been trying to find a location based on that text, assuming the name of a place would pop up. Out of all the possible solutions our machines have offered, none of them are in China, and some of them don't make any sense at all."

He reached over to the desk and picked up a bottle of water, took a swig, and waited for her to speak.

"So," she tried to merge her thoughts with his. "What is it about Shangri-La? It's been called a sacred place, a holy place, paradise, utopia."

"All correct," Alex affirmed. "Exactly what I was thinking. And that led me to this thought—what if we should be looking for holy or sacred waters?"

"You mean like a river?"

"Or a lake. Think about it. Most rivers are pretty murky. Not clear. Same with oceans, except in places like the Caribbean or Fiji."

She smiled, remembering their short vacation to the Maldives. "Buddhist traditions honor several sacred lakes, in different countries."

"Exactly." He raised a finger, excitement building in his mind.

"So, let's search for sacred lakes in China."

She spun around in her chair and minimized the data rolling on the screen. Pulling up a search bar, she entered the keywords and waited for the results. The top link looked good enough, and she clicked it.

Alex shifted over to stand behind her as she worked.

The screen blinked and produced several images of nine lakes in Tibet that were considered the most sacred.

"Interesting they don't list any as Chinese," Tara noted.

"I would assume due to the government," Alex added.

"Probably. I still don't get why people think communism is the answer." She tossed her hair to one side and clicked on the first image.

The two read about the first lake, returned to the main results, and repeated the process with the second.

After reading the information about the first four locations, Tara hovered the arrow over the eighth.

"You going to skip those?" Alex asked.

"That one looks so pretty. The water, that little island, the green mountains in the background."

He bobbed his head. "You know, you're the kind of person who wins all the college football bowl pools. The ones who pick a winner because they like the mascot or the colors."

"Hey," she said, insulted. "I've only done that twice." Her hurt look turned cute, and she winked at him over her shoulder.

All he could do was shake his head as the screen flickered to a site with the description of Pagsum Lake. The images on the screen displayed spectacular, sweeping vistas of a clear lake surrounded by high mountains wrapped in green trees. Snow capped some of the higher peaks.

"That's...Tibet?" Alex muttered.

"Yeah. Tibet isn't just rocks and dirt and barren mountains, you know. Down in the southern parts, there are places that look like this."

"It's beautiful."

"Yep," she said with a nod, rocking slightly back and forth in her chair. She sensed a spark of excitement, too. "Basum, as it is also known, is a clear lake near Lhasa. The greenish color in the water is a result of the reflections of the trees surrounding the lake. The water is so clear and pure, it takes on the color of its surroundings."

"That's cool."

"The lake has also been called Draksum Tso, which means—" She stopped reading. Her mouth hung open, and Tara turned slowly to see her husband's similar response.

"Three rocks," he finished.

"Three talons," she managed.

Alex shook himself free of the cobwebs paralyzing his mind. "It can't be that simple."

"The best secrets usually are."

He looked down at the printout again, focusing on the section referring to the three talons. "Pull up more images. We need to see these three rocks."

She clicked, then scrolled, searching through the pictures until she found a satellite view of the lake. Her index finger clicked the mouse again, and she dragged it until the image covered the screen.

"There," Tara said, pointing to a short, thin peninsula jutting out toward the middle of the lake. "And there's another," she shifted her finger's angle to point out another.

"And there's the third," Alex said with a nod toward the screen.

Their eyes followed the tracks of the peninsulas toward a single focal point.

"That's it," Tara said. "That little island." She clicked on the image again and zoomed out. "Jeez. We didn't even have to dive that deep into it. The whole thing looks like one big eye. And that island—"

"That's where the gate must be."

She clicked on the information about the islet. A bridge allowed pilgrims to walk out onto the tiny island where an ancient monastery sits. Neither she nor Alex found anything about the current state of the monastery, whether it was still inhabited or active, or if it was nothing more than ruins. The images looked as though it could still be in operation.

"I wonder what it's like to live in isolation in a place like that," Alex breathed. "It's so beautiful there. No one to bother you."

"Yeah, but no internet." She paused and then started laughing.

While their lives were deeply embedded in the tech world, they both enjoyed their limited time away from all that and the big city. Getting out into the country was rare, but now that Tommy had them investigating the stranger mysteries in the world as part of their Paranormal Archaeology Division, those opportunities grew more frequent.

"You think this is it?" Tara asked.

Alex searched her eyes, but that quest didn't take long. He could tell she felt confident about their conclusion. "Yes," he said. "I think we found it. This meets all the criteria even without the three rocks thing. And what better place to hide the gateway to an ancient mystical city than inside a monastery."

Tara took several deliberate breaths as she considered the possibility. "Does that mean the lost city is underwater?"

"Probably. Like a freshwater Atlantis. In the mountains of Tibet."

Tara wore a look of uncertainty like dark curtains hanging over a window. "I don't know. That last part is weird."

"You mean in the clue?"

"Yes. As above. So below. That same text, or a variation of it, appears in several scriptures across multiple religions. I can't help but wonder..."

"If this was the source?" he guessed.

"Yeah." She turned to the computer and pressed one of her hot keys on the keyboard. "Analyze Lake Pagsum in Tibet. See if you can find any anomalies at the bottom of it."

"Of course," the computer said in its semi monotone British accent. "Running analysis now."

28

ATLANTA

D ave stood in the lobby of IAA headquarters, staring out through the tall windows that walled the front of the building. He stared out at the trees lining Centennial Olympic Park as they waved in the breeze from every car and truck that passed.

He'd been working for Tommy Schultz since nearly the beginning of the operation more than fifteen years ago. Every time he thought about that, it blew his mind.

Some people might have thought his job ordinary or boring, but not Dave. He was happy to have steady work, and even though all he did five days a week, seven hours a day was stand around and look through windows, he was just fine with that.

He took breaks now and then, always sure to let the receptionist, Sarah, know he'd be back in ten or fifteen minutes.

The two of them ate lunch together most days. Their backgrounds could not have been different. A sixty-four-year-old black man from South Carolina had seen a very different world than the thirty-two-year-old white woman from Nashville. Still, that didn't stop them from forming an immediate bond.

Sarah had never married, and Dave's wife had passed away when she was only forty-three. He'd never found the courage to remarry, but had found peace in his thoughts at this job.

"Dave?" Sarah said from behind the desk against the wall to his left.

He perked up, stiffening to push away from the column he'd been leaning against. "Yes, ma'am."

"You're never going to stop calling me that, are you?"

He smiled the childish way he always did when she said that. "It's how I was raised. Doesn't matter if I'm older than you. It's propriety."

She shook her head at him. "I'll be back in a minute."

She disappeared through a doorway to the left of her desk, leaving Dave alone with his thoughts.

He looked at her like the daughter he'd never had and hoped that —if he'd ever raised a girl—would she have turned out as kind-hearted as Sarah.

Dave held a locket in his right hand. The chain hooked around one of his doorman buttons so it wouldn't fall out of his pocket if he ever leaned over the wrong way. The picture of his wife within the heart-shaped necklace served as a bitter reminder of things past, and how life can be so unfair, but also of how love can endure anything.

He liked to think she would be proud of him, looking dapper in his security suit and captain's hat. Tommy was a great boss to work for and made Dave feel like every bit a part of the team as anyone else. That was something Dave admired about Tommy, how he treated everyone the same. Sarah was like that, too. Everyone, in fact, who worked for the IAA felt like they were part of a family, a group that took care of each other. Each member of the IAA payroll was an essential cog in the machine, and none of the cogs were more impor-tant than the others.

He appreciated the uniform, probably from his days in the mili-tary. That seemed like a lifetime ago. Fortunately, he'd been enlisted during a time between conflicts. The 1980s had been stressful with the Cold War and the looming threat of nuclear devastation always on the horizon, but he'd never seen a second of combat.

Through the years, he'd looked to training and exercise as an outlet for his emotions and continued maintaining optimal health even though he could have had every excuse in the world to let himself go and sink into the mire of depression.

A black SUV pulled up outside the building and parked along the circular drive where either deliveries were dropped off or the occasional high-profile visitor's driver parked to let their employer out at the front door.

He'd checked the schedule earlier in the morning, as he did every day first thing, and hadn't seen any appointments. With Tommy and Sean out of town and the other IAA agents fanned out across the globe, the only people in the building were Dave and Sarah, and the two researchers down in the lab.

A man with a buzz haircut climbed out of the passenger side. He wore a black blazer and matching tie, pants, and white shirt. Another guy walked around the back of the SUV and joined the first approaching the front door.

They arrived on the doorstep and the passenger reached out to pull on the handle.

Dave huffed a laugh, knowing the doors were always locked. When the boss was away, people could only get into the building with an ID card or a passcode. Ever since the attack several years before destroyed the original IAA building, Tommy and his team took security much more seriously.

Shaking his head, Dave wandered over to the door, his shiny shoes clicking on the hard floor. The sound echoed through the cavernous lobby, rising up to the second floor, where a loft overlooked the main entrance.

The SUV's driver checked the door as well, as if the other guy was somehow not strong enough to do it himself. The driver immediately realized muscle wasn't the problem.

He looked through the glass, frustration sagging the skin under his aviator sunglasses. His black, windswept hair made him look like he'd just jumped out of a cologne commercial—one of those obscure ones where a guy is standing in a full business suit by a swimming pool and then jumps in for no reason, all to the tune of some feminine whisper of a French name.

Dave shook his head again at the thought. "Who thinks guys watching football will buy that crap?" he muttered.

He stopped at the door and held up his hand in greeting, then pressed a button on a nearby panel to speak. "Afternoon, fellas. What can I do for you?"

"We're here to see a Tommy Schultz?" the passenger said, pressing on a button next to the door.

Dave nodded. "Well, you boys are out of luck. He's not here right now. Probably out conducting meetings or something." Dave knew Tommy wasn't in a meeting. Not in Atlanta, anyway. He was out of the country, but it was entirely in the realm of possibility that Tommy was sitting down with a few other people. Just because that happened to be Sean and Adriana didn't mean his statement was a lie. Or so he justified it.

"Is that so?" the driver said, unimpressed. "Well, can you please let us in so we can talk with one of the lab assistants? We represent the National Archives in Washington, DC. They have a piece they've been analyzing for us, and we're here to discuss their findings."

"Sarah and Alex?" Dave clarified.

"Yes," buzz-cut confirmed. "Sarah and Alex."

Dave nodded, splashing a wide smile across his face. "Well, now," he drawled in his deep, South Carolina accent. "Why didn't y'all say so? Come right on in."

He pressed the button to unlock the door and pushed it open to allow the men into the lobby.

They both nodded in curt, governmental appreciation as they passed.

"I'll show you right to them. They work down in the basement, you see. Always down there, those two. You'll have to have a card to get to that level. Tight security and all."

"Of course," the driver said, removing his sunglasses as he walked toward the back wall where the double doors protected the inner sanctum of the IAA and all its treasures.

"Head over to that door and I'll meet you there. Gotta pick up my card for that one. Don't always carry it on me."

The men said nothing and took the lead, walking side by side toward the doors.

Dave followed behind them, keeping one pace back as he removed the Taser from his belt, hidden just under one of his blazer's flaps.

"How long you been working here?" Buzz-cut asked, twisting his head to half glance back.

"Long enough to know BS when I hear it," Dave replied coolly.

Buzz-cut twitched his head at the odd comment, then started to turn around. It was too late.

Dave jammed the Taser into the man's side and pressed the button. The interloper shook violently as he fell to the floor, and the gyrating didn't stop once on the ground.

The driver whipped around, his reactions nearly instant to the attack. Dave shoved the Taser toward the attacker, but the man easily chopped his right hand across, knocking the electrical weapon from Dave's grasp and sending it skidding across the floor.

"That was stupid, old man."

Dave took exception to the barb, but he waited, measuring the enemy's stance. "You learn from stupid, son. Now, are you going to stand there and bark, little puppy? Or are you going to bite?"

The driver lunged forward with a fist aimed squarely at Dave's nose. The sixty-four-year-old twisted his shoulders, tilted his head back, and at the same time launched a jab straight into the attacker's throat.

The blow didn't have a thousand pounds of pressure behind it. And it didn't need to. Dave's knuckles smacked deep into the man's Adam's apple and cut off the airway enough for the driver to instinctively grab his throat.

Dave regained his stance, then drove his fists into the man's gut and ribs, over and over until the enemy doubled over, still desperate for air. Dave slipped behind the guy, wrapped his arm around the man's throat, and squeezed, using his left hand to brace the skull and keep the neck pressed into his forearm to cut off the air to lung passage.

Within thirty seconds, the man's body went limp. Dave knew enough to keep the hold for a few extra seconds before lowering the body to the floor. As the unconscious man slumped down, Dave found a gun inside the man's jacket. He drew it against the pull of the body and whirled around just as Buzz-cut propped himself up on all fours, attempting to get back into the fray.

"Don't. Move," Dave cautioned, brandishing the pistol. The long suppressor barrel wagged gently.

A door clicked open behind Buzz-cut, who remained on hands and knees. Sarah appeared in the doorway, turned toward her desk, and saw the spectacle halfway across the lobby floor.

"Sarah?"

She stared at him in shock, saying nothing.

"Would you mind calling the police?" He evened his breath, keeping his eyes on the would-be killer. "And let our lab rats know we have a problem."

29

KARASAHR

Two men with clean-shaven heads and wearing black blazers, matching pants, and white button-up shirts entered the little hospital through an unlocked maintenance door. Orderlies, custodians, and the occasional nurse used the side entrance to steal a quick smoke. Thanks to vaporizers, they could get their quick fix of nicotine and be back in the game without anyone noticing.

The assassins didn't know the full layout of the building, but it had taken little more than two passes around the regional hospital to find a discreet point of entry.

They'd received the call less than two hours ago. Apparently, this job was urgent. The payout on the contract was $50,000 American—nothing to sneeze at for a quick hit in a place where security would be almost zero.

These two mercenaries had worked together before, most of the time carrying out executions or other punishments for the Triads. Known only by the names Bolin and Donghai, these were the guys the gangs wanted whenever they needed two killers that worked with the same mind; as one.

The two entered through the side door and bumped into a man wearing a custodian outfit.

The janitor looked both men in the eyes, held up a cigarette toward them, and then died to the sound of a muted click. Donghai caught the body before it hit the ground. Bolin sheathed his silenced subcompact pistol and stuffed it back into the folds of his jacket, holstering it out of sight.

Donghai dragged the body over behind the staircase and stuffed it in the shadows where no one would see, at least for a while. By the time the dead man with a bullet hole in his chest was found, the assassins would already be gone, like ghosts among shadows.

The two men climbed the stairs to the second level. They continued up to the top floor and paused. Donghai touched the door latch while Bolin put his hand on the pistol grip, ready to draw at a moment's notice.

They communicated without speaking. Donghai opened the door, and Bolin stepped through, head twisting from one side to the other. Donghai followed, rechecking the empty corridor.

The nurses' station sat fifty feet away to the right. A quick look at the placard on the opposite wall told the two men that their target's room was to the left.

Bolin stalked in that direction, moving silently down the corridor. Donghai watched his back as he followed. If a nurse or doctor appeared, he would be polite and offer a subtle yet forgettable greeting.

The assassins preferred to have no witnesses, which was why the custodian on the first floor had to die. But killing a nurse or doctor on an open hospital floor would draw attention. While they didn't fear the local cops—especially in this small town—discretion remained the preferred means of operation.

Bolin noted the numbers by the doors he passed, counting down until he arrived at the mark's room.

Each man stole a quick glance down either end of the hall, then Bolin pulled the latch down and pushed the door open. They stepped inside quickly, evaporating into the darkness of the room.

Donghai drew his pistol and eased the bathroom door to the left wide open, checking the space with his weapon extended. Bolin surveyed the rest of the room with his weapon drawn, as well, and assessed no danger present.

A silhouetted form in the bed lay under sheets, shrouded in shadow from the moonlight glowing through a crack in the curtains.

The killers glided over to the bedside, Bolin taking the area closest to the window. He lowered his weapon down to where the victim's head should have been and waited as Donghai reached down and gripped the sheets.

In one swift and sudden move, he ripped the fabric away from the headboard to reveal...a body pillow.

The men's heads snapped up, eyes searching each other for answers to the same question. An epiphany struck them simultaneously. *They knew we were coming.*

The men spun around and looked to the door, expecting an ambush. But no threat lingered.

Donghai breathed hard, his brain working overtime to figure out what had happened. They couldn't go door to door searching every floor of the hospital just to find the mark. If she wasn't here, along with her American friends nearby, then the only option was to retreat and reassess. It was how they always handled situations such as this, though that almost never happened.

Since they'd been working together, the two killers had only been given bad intel one time. Now, it seemed, this was the second.

Without speaking, the two calmly returned to the door. Donghai opened it and checked down both ends of the corridor. *No sign of trouble.*

The killers hurried back down the hall without looking like they were in a hurry, then vanished back into the stairwell.

They would discuss a new plan when they were in the safety of their car, and perhaps after making a call to their employer. Getting paid was their only priority. No kill, no pay. They would get answers as soon as they were in the clear. Calling the employer on a contract only happened in this situation, when the intel was wrong.

The two flew down the stairs, around the landing on the second floor, and continued down to the ground level, where the body remained hidden under the steps.

Bolin pushed open the door and checked around the corner before continuing out into the cool, dark morning. The night sky above had yet to show the first signs of daylight, and wouldn't for another hour. The sleeping village surrounding the hospital remained quiet. No cars passed by on the street, and no pedestrians roamed the sidewalks.

Donghai passed through the door and quickly made his way across the lawn toward the parked sedan. He kept his weapon in its holster but his hand at his side, ready to spark the pistol to life if a threat appeared. Even in the stark hours, he and his partner stayed vigilant, ever on alert.

It was how they survived in this dangerous line of work.

They crossed the sixty-foot-wide lawn and climbed into the car, looking back toward the shrubs and trees, the hospital rooftop. Neither saw a sniper waiting in the shadows, and it didn't appear anyone had noticed their exit.

At least that part went according to plan.

There would be an investigation into the murder of the custodian when the body was discovered, but there were no cameras at the side entrance, and there had been no witnesses inside the building.

Donghai started the engine as Bolin took out his phone and called the number for their contact.

"Is it done?" the man's voice answered directly, without a hint of concern.

"We have a problem," Bolin said.

"Problem? What kind of problem?"

"The targets are gone."

"What do you mean?" the man asked, annoyed.

"We were given their exact location. The targets weren't there. We left. Please advise."

Silence spilled onto the line. Bolin couldn't even hear the man breathing over the steady hum of the sedan's engine.

"You're certain you didn't give away your arrival? They should have been in that room."

Bolin let the insult slide. But he wouldn't allow more than one. "You hired us because we know what we're doing. We're the best. No, they didn't know we were here. How could they have known?"

This time, Bolin allowed the man to consider his next words, and to ponder the situation. Moving a woman who'd just been in surgery would take time, and multiple people. And that was if the assassins had been spotted. The only other way the targets could have known was if someone had leaked the information about the attack.

"They couldn't. We are the only three who know about this little operation. They must have moved the woman to another room. I will have to figure out where."

"The sun comes up in an hour," Bolin said, offering the reminder. "If you want it done, you better act quickly."

He motioned for Donghai to drive.

With a nod, Donghai shifted the car into gear and accelerated away from the hospital. The driver stopped at an intersection flanked on both sides by empty lots where old buildings had been torn down and, as yet, hadn't been replaced.

"You have twenty minutes," Bolin remarked. "After that, the window will be—"

The car exploded in a flash of orange-white light, permanently cutting off the conversation.

SEAN WATCHED the burning car through binoculars from the playground across the street. Perched atop a slide, hidden from view by colorful plastic panels, he'd seen the assassins arrive and observed them as they entered the hospital through the side entrance.

He'd known they wouldn't dare go through the main doors, or through the emergency entryway. Too many witnesses lingered there. The side door was the best option.

While Sean had no way of knowing for sure if the killers would show up, it was the hunch he'd played, forsaking a good night of sleep to make certain his friends were safe.

Adriana crouched next to him, peering out through a hole in a yellow plastic panel at the inferno consuming the sedan.

"How did you know?" she asked.

Sean drew a breath and stuffed the detonator he held, along with his binoculars, into the black rucksack at his feet. "I didn't," he admitted. "But I had a feeling."

"You and those feelings," she commented.

"They've served me well in the past."

"Yes, they have." Adriana turned her gaze to the hospital and the room on the second floor, where they'd moved Daiyu thirty minutes before. She couldn't see Tommy in the darkened room, but she knew he was standing there, shrouded by the curtains—watching.

"So," she said, "Lóng is tracking our movements."

"It's more than that," Sean said, slinging the pack over his right shoulder. "He's ahead of our every move."

"Which means we're going to have to up our game."

"As always," he said with a grin.

He stuck his feet out through the opening where the slide descended to a rubbery mat below and then slid down.

Adriana followed and walked briskly with him back toward the front of the hospital and their rental car.

"What's our next move?" She glanced over at him, momentarily enjoying the way he walked. There was a kind of swagger to his step that she always found sexy, even if he thought he was just a goof.

His phone buzzed in his left-front pocket. "One second." He took out the device and checked the screen. "It's from the lab rats," he said.

"Do they have a location?"

The two continued walking to the corner, then veered left and crossed the street into a quiet, poorly lit block where they'd left their vehicle.

"Yes, they have the location of the gate. Well, they think they do."

The distant sound of sirens filled the air.

"I guess someone called the fire department."

"And the cops, I'm sure," she added.

"Mmm." He kept reading the text message. "Looks like we're going to Tibet." He frowned at the next part. "And it would seem someone tried to get into HQ."

"Someone?" She slowed her pace and looked at him more directly.

"Yeah." Sean matched her speed. "Alex said two guys tried to get into the lab, but Dave took them down."

"The doorman?"

"He's a security guard dressed as a doorman."

"Former Marine, right?"

Sean smirked. "No such thing as a former Marine, honey."

"So it would seem."

They arrived at the car, and he opened the door for her the way he always did. She appreciated that about him too, along with so many other things. But that Southern gentleman thing he had going on always sent butterflies through her gut, even minutes after they'd blown up a car with two Triad assassins inside.

She thanked him and climbed in, allowing him to close the door behind her. When he was behind the steering wheel, Sean started the engine and rubbed his hands together.

"So, where are we going next?"

"To the hotel for a nap," he said with a hint of cynicism. "Then it looks like we're headed back to Lhasa."

"Second time in a few years," she realized.

"Yeah. Something in the water there, I suppose."

Sean shifted the car into drive and steered it away from the hospital and the flashing lights that approached the burning wreckage.

30

TIBET, 40KM FROM LHASA

Benitzio peered through the windshield of the beat-up compact car. He surveyed the parking lot and the few dozen cars spread out in haphazard fashion. He'd wondered if there would be many pilgrims here, expecting a few hundred people or more. Instead, the sparse crowds seemed to be leaving after their morning visit to the holy site.

Believing in superstitions had never intrigued Benitzio. He only cared about what he could see, feel, touch, hear. Anything else was nothing but legend to him, fiction created to control the minds of the masses. Religion, he thought, was one of the original business models of humanity, and business had been good for thousands of years.

He'd never seen anything to make him think otherwise regarding the supernatural. His prayers were never answered when he was kid —not even when his mother was dying from a disease that started in her brain and gradually took away the movement of her legs and arms, and eventually her speech.

She'd looked at him from the hospital bed, the rare condition ravaging her body from the inside. "I wish God would just let me die," she'd said.

Those words still crushed him, and still drove him.

When his mother died three days later, after agonizing for more hours than he cared to count, Benitzio had vowed to never beg an invisible deity for favors. The thin spiritual ice he tread upon broke, and he fell through into the icy waters of unbelief and utter cynicism.

He felt free in that way. But an emptiness always haunted his soul. His ambitions and goals redirected to financial freedom, and perhaps a little fame that could open the right doors if he were so inclined.

A black SUV drove up and parked near the front of the lot closest to the path leading down to the water.

Ju Chen had taken her position more than an hour ago, just after arriving. She scoped out a location where she could hide out until Benitzio gave the all-clear.

She'd chosen a spot behind a building that contained bathrooms on either end, where they also sold religious trinkets in a stall at the front.

"That's them," Benitzio stated, watching the SUV from afar as it came to a stop. The red taillights stayed on until a flash of white from the driver shifting the vehicle into park.

Three men in long-sleeve black shirts and dark green cargo pants climbed out. The one on the passenger side opened the front door while the other two surveyed the immediate area.

With their matching sunglasses and pistols attached at the hips, they stood out among an otherwise peaceful collection of tourists. The men may as well have announced they were secret service for a high-ranking government official.

"Hardly subtle, I'll say that," Benitzio remarked. "Although I would have thought the man known as the Black Dragon would have more protection than three armed guards."

"He does," Ju Chen corrected.

"What?"

"White SUV ten cars to the left of the one that just pulled up. There's another one, seven cars to the right."

Benitzio looked first to the left. He immediately felt like a fool for not noticing the rest of Lóng's security forces.

Four armed men stepped out of each vehicle, sweeping around behind Lóng's ride before the man exited from the passenger side.

"Do you have eyes on Lóng?" Benitzio asked.

"Yes, but I don't have a clear shot. Eleven guards. All carrying sidearms. Inside a group that size, I might not be able to bail you out if things go sideways."

"Understood," Benitzio said. He didn't like the way she made things sound so dire, but this was the leap of faith he'd been preparing to take. "I'm going in."

He regretted saying it the second the words passed through his lips. *Stupid,* he thought.

Ju Chen offered no reprimand, probably because she was a professional, or possibly because the phrase got lost in translation.

Either way, Benitzio took a deep breath and opened the car door, a metal case in his right hand.

He closed the door and started walking toward the group encircling Lóng's vehicle. His phone buzzed in his pocket, startling Benitzio. He tripped over his toe, nearly losing his balance, but caught himself as he grappled with his pocket to remove the device.

In stride, he answered the call. "I see you brought a few friends," Benitzio said coolly.

"One can never be too careful," Lóng replied. "I just wanted to make sure you knew we saw you and my men wouldn't kill you as you approached."

"Thank you, sir. I appreciate that," Benitzio sniveled. *They don't look so tough to me.* He came nowhere close to believing that lie.

He peered through the huddle as he approached. His employer wore a black hood over his head. Under it, a matching baseball cap without a logo capped his skull. The hoodie was like nothing Benitzio had seen. The garment crossed over from shoulder to shoulder, the flaps flowing down to the man's knees on either side. They brushed against his loose gray trousers, though Benitzio thought the pants could be loose yoga pants.

With sunglasses covering his eyes, the man known as Lóng maintained an intriguing anonymity.

"I'll speak to you in a moment," Lóng said. "Oh, and tell your pet she should lower her weapon. I'd hate for anyone to get hurt."

"Yes, of course," Benitzio stammered. "Right away."

He tapped the screen to end the call, then spoke into the radio. "He knows you're here."

"Obviously. Lóng isn't stupid."

Benitzio cut the chatter as he neared the ring of bodyguards surrounding Lóng. Two of the men—hulking figures that looked like they could have played in the NFL—parted to allow Benitzio to pass through.

Lóng leaned up against the SUV with arms crossed over his chest, watching from behind black sunglasses with reflective lenses. The man had a thin black scarf, or gator mask, pulled up over his mouth and nose, though Benitzio couldn't figure why.

As Benitzio walked cautiously between the guards, Lóng stood up straight. It was the only fanfare the Spaniard received, which was fine by him. He didn't want to be showered with praise, and certainly not the other end of the spectrum—an abrupt execution. He knew men like Lóng played a cutthroat game. Benitzio's walk into the circle was more like a leap of faith. He had no choice but to trust Lóng wouldn't kill him right there.

Then again, Benitzio held one card up his sleeve.

"I'm glad you made it," Lóng said as the Spaniard approached.

"You didn't think I would?" Benitzio stopped eight feet away. The circle closed around him.

Lóng shrugged. The action caused the flaps dangling by his knees to rise and fall like twin capes. To Benitzio, he looked half-ninja, half-deranged poker player wearing a disguise to keep other players from getting a read on him.

"You could have kept the jewel," Lóng hypothesized. "It's priceless. Selling that would have made you richer than you've ever been in your life."

"Only a fool would try to stab you in the back," Benitzio replied. The groveling tone tasted like dirt in his mouth, but he knew it was the right thing to say.

"True," Lóng agreed.

"Besides, I'm playing a bigger game. I could make a few million off this." He raised the metal case. "Or I could make so much more from the treasures that await within the hidden city."

Lóng nodded dramatically. "Indeed."

Benitzio's face twisted slightly around his eyes, the wrinkles stretching toward his ears for a moment. His forehead matched the expression, cutting deep lines across his skin. Something was off about the man's accent. It didn't sound Chinese, or like any other Asian accent Benitzio had encountered.

"Is there a problem?" Lóng asked.

"No." Benitzio quickly shook his head. Probably too quickly. "I only wondered where you would like to see it. Perhaps out here in the open isn't the best place."

Lóng assessed the man, inclining his head.

The Spaniard felt fear slither through his body, raising the hairs on his neck. His employer saw through the lie. It was a minor one, a small infraction at best. Or so he hoped.

"We'll open it in the monastery." Lóng snapped a finger with his right hand, and two of the guards spun around and started toward the bridge leading to the island. "Most of the pilgrims will be gone for the day, but we'll need to clear out the rest. I prefer to have no distractions while we work."

Benitzio merely nodded.

"Also, enough of the cloak-and-dagger, Benitzio. Tell your shooter to join us."

So much for that plan, Benitzio thought. "You heard him," he said into the radio.

"Copy," she said. A minute later, she appeared carrying a long black case. It could have been for hauling around an electric guitar, but Benitzio knew what she kept inside. Her rifle would have drawn the worst kind of attention, from the wrong kind of people. Tourists would panic and call the police. From there, the future looked far more difficult.

Inconvenient as it was to carry a weapon that way, it was also the only viable option. She kept her sidearm concealed by a light gray jacket. That way, if Lóng or any of his men got the bright idea to screw her over, she'd at least be able to take a few of them with her.

The guards blocking her path parted as she approached, and she stepped into the ring to join the two men responsible for her being here.

"Ju Chen, I presume," Lóng said, greeting her with a respectful bow.

She didn't return the gesture. "You presume right," she offered, her tone and stance unyielding.

He grinned at the sassy reply.

"While I understand your desire," Lóng said to Benitzio, "to have your back watched in case I were to betray you, I hope you realize it isn't necessary. I have no desire to kill you or your partner. Besides," the man said, taking a step toward the Spaniard, "I still might need you once we get through the gate."

"If we get through," Benitzio said.

"*If* is why I need you here," Lóng remarked with a coy, devilish grin. "Without your skills, we may not be able to figure out the correct place to enter this cave."

Benitzio nodded, feeling empowered for the first time since meeting this man. "Yes, I figured that there are probably more clues within the monastery, wherever the gate is." He had no idea if that was true. It didn't matter. The more useful he could make himself to Lóng, or at least seem useful, the better Benitzio's chances of surviving. The crime boss struck him as the kind of guy who would happily eliminate the people he deemed unnecessary. All Benitzio could hope was that if he proved himself, the man might let him go once he had whatever it was he wanted.

"I've run an analysis on the monastery's structure," Lóng said. "There's a subterranean level I suspect may be a good starting point. Of course, my men will investigate the entire building first."

"Excellent. That should make our work quicker."

Benitzio turned to Ju Chen. "She's been invaluable on this project." He hoped the compliment would further entrench the assassin into Lóng's good graces. Benitzio knew she was just as capable of stabbing him in the back as Lóng.

She continued to eye Lóng suspiciously and cast a sideways glance at Benitzio. He caught the question in her eyes and wondered if she was thinking the same thing. Something about this man didn't make sense, but he couldn't put his finger on it.

Lóng ordered his men to move out. Then he turned to Benitzio. "Come. Let us see what this place holds in store."

The group moved toward the bridge, passing by the last few visitors as they exited the islet. Some of them wore unhappy expressions on their faces, and Benitzio wondered if it was because they'd been forced to leave before they were done with their tours or their religious rites.

Four of the guards took the lead, forging across the bridge in a protective wedge, with the other five remaining in the rear. With water on both sides, Lóng and his security forces had no concern about an attack from the flanks.

A breeze blew over the group, fluttering Lóng's hoodie. A chill rode the wind and sent a shiver through Benitzio's bones. He looked around, both out of concern and out of curiosity.

Green mountains towered into the sky, surrounding the pristine lake below. The clear water lapped against the bridge pilings in a steady rhythm. Trees reflected on the surface, showing off the green hue referred to in the ancient clue.

The bridge stretched fifty or more yards across the water before connecting to the rocky shore of the islet. A set of stone stairs led up to the top of the island, just behind an outcropping of evergreen trees. The roof of the monastery peeked out from the top of the islet just on the other side. Another set of stairs descended to the right of the ones attached to the bridge, but those steps dropped down into the water.

Benitzio had seen the pictures of this place before and wondered what those stairs were for, but assumed it had something to do with the religious visitors wanting to touch the holy water or something. And if that were the case, he figured they could have done that from the shore instead of walking all the way across.

All that simply added to the mystery of this place, and it peeled back the veil of cynicism from his mind, exposing it to a possibility that maybe, just maybe, the gate to Shangri-La really was here.

"Is the monastery still in operation?" Benitzio asked as they neared the islet's shore.

"Yes," Lóng answered with a sideways glance over his shoulder. "There are monks here all year. As you probably know, it was built in the fourteenth century, though we estimate that this location was used for other purposes much earlier."

Benitzio didn't have to ask how much longer. He knew if this island held the entrance to the lost city, it would have been here thousands of years ago.

"The monks won't be a problem," Lóng continued. "My men have taken care of it. We will be able to fully investigate the monastery without interruption."

Ju Chen and Benitzio shared a sidelong glance. Did their employer kill the monks? There was cruel, and then there was savage. The men who inhabited this place would be peaceful, gentle people —completely unable, and probably unwilling, to defend themselves. Unless they were some kind of secret order of Shaolin Monks, which Benitzio doubted.

More visitors streamed down the stairs as the guards in front led the way up. The people wore disgruntled faces, but they had no idea it could have been much worse. With the reputation Lóng carried everywhere, Benitzio was surprised the man hadn't simply killed everyone.

"If given the choice between rich or poor," Lóng said as they reached the top of the staircase, "I choose rich every time."

The comment struck Benitzio as strange until he looked down the hill and noticed the two guards who'd left earlier. They stood next to the entrance with four monks. The eldest monk accepted an envelope from one of the guards and bowed deeply in gratitude.

Benitzio's forehead crinkled. "Did you just—?"

"Bribe the abbot?" Lóng finished. "Yes. I did. I would prefer to be uninterrupted during our search. Fortunately, the monks of this monastery have needs. More offerings mean better food, and perhaps a few conveniences they're not always afforded."

Benitzio had figured the men living there had taken a vow of poverty, but if the money was going to the operation as a whole, maybe that didn't affect those vows. Or maybe they didn't take such vows. He suddenly realized how little he knew about this place, or of its religious dogmas. He'd have to be careful not to let that ignorance slip lest Lóng deem him expendable.

The group descended the hill via a collection of steps that wrapped around to the monastery's front entrance.

Benitzio studied the façade as they approached. Four red pillars held up the roof of the portico. Three windows with traditional Chinese frames divided into thirds looked out over the colonnade from within the white structure. Steep stone steps led up to the entrance. He also noticed a red trash bin to the left of the stairway.

"Nothing like a touch of the modern to ruin something otherwise ancient and pure," he murmured.

"What?" Ju Chen asked, her head snapping to the side.

"Nothing," he lied. "Just admiring the architecture and the surroundings. Whoever built this place sure could pick the spots."

Lóng bowed to the monks as he passed, following his guards to the base of the staircase, where he stopped and turned to Benitzio. "Are you ready?" he asked.

"Yes," the Spaniard answered without hesitation. In his twisting gut, all he could think of was what would happen to him if this was the wrong place.

31

TIBET

"Unreal," Tommy spat. He kept the binoculars against his eyes, the same as Sean and Adriana did from their positions on his left.

They watched Benitzio meet with the mysterious masked man but couldn't get a positive ID on him. Not that it mattered. They all knew it was the guy who'd funded Benitzio's expedition, including the one that killed Dr. Fischer.

"That Benny got here at all?" Sean joked.

"I mean, sure. Yeah. I'm surprised he could find his way out of a paper bag."

"He was right on our heels in Costa Rica, too, Schultzie. For all his downsides, Benny knows his history. And he can figure his way around the same stuff we do, just a little slower."

"Usually," Tommy corrected.

"Looks like eleven guards in total for the financier," Adriana said, diverting the boys back to their immediate concerns. "Plus the woman with Benny. He must have positioned her behind that building over there as some kind of backup plan."

Sean snorted. "Looks like that didn't work out so well for him."

"It didn't look like the man was angry about it."

"No," he agreed. "But it's hard to tell behind those sunglasses and mask. That guy really wants to maintain his anonymity."

"He should wear one of those Guy Fawkes masks then," Tommy huffed.

"Too gaudy," Adriana countered. "He's trying to lie low, not make a political statement."

"I was kidding."

She pried her eyes from the binoculars and turned her head slowly toward him. "I know," she cooed with a slight eye roll.

Tommy shook off the derision and returned to his view. He watched the group cross the bridge to the islet while other visitors left.

"Looks like Benny's finance guy bought themselves a private tour of the monastery," Sean noticed.

"Or they threatened the pilgrims."

"Nah. They look annoyed but not frightened. My guess is those first two guards that went over probably paid the monks for a few hours."

"It'll be tough for us to get in there unnoticed." Tommy took out a piece of gum from his pocket and popped it into his mouth. He chewed as he watched the group climb the stairs and disappear over the ridge to the other side of the island. White-capped mountains stabbed the gray sky above. Just beneath the snow line, dense forests of evergreens stretched down to the water's edge.

"Yeah," Sean remarked. "Most likely, he'll station some guards at the front of the building. They'll tell us we can't go in. If we're lucky, they won't be looking for us and we can work the tourist angle. We'll have to leave most of our gear in the car, though. Strolling up with a couple of tactical bags might give them the wrong impression."

"You think?"

"We split up," Adriana said. "You two take the main entrance on the other side. I'll go around back from the top of those stairs. Keep your earpieces hidden."

Their clear radio devices blended with their flesh tones, and were smaller than a typical earbud, but that didn't mean a careful eye wouldn't spot them.

"You sure?" Sean asked.

"I thought I was giving you two the harder job," she said with a wry grin. "But if you would prefer your wife to take the brute force angle, I can."

"No. It's not that. I just—" He stopped himself. "You're definitely the stealthiest of the three of us. That makes sense."

"Thank you."

"Well, their team is out of sight," Tommy interrupted. "We should probably move."

"Yes," Sean confirmed. "Move out. We drop off our gear at the car and get across the bridge. Hopefully, none of those bodyguards are under shoot-on-sight orders at the other side."

He stood up and grabbed his bag. They'd been hiding in a stand of trees for the last hour, surveying the area for trouble. It was dumb luck Benny showed up when he did.

Adriana collected her bag and joined him.

Tommy scrambled to get his stuff and hurried after them.

The three emerged from the woods just beneath the road that wound through the mountain pass and meandered alongside the lake.

After a quick stop at the SUV, each of them placed their gear bags in the back cargo area, only removing a few spare magazines and their primary firearms—.40-caliber pistols they concealed under windbreakers.

Sean watched the lot to make sure no one noticed what they were doing. None of the visitors leaving the parking area seemed to care. They looked more annoyed than anything, which only furthered Sean's assessment that the people had been told to leave.

Tommy pulled down an Atlanta Braves World Series cap over his head, then hung his jacket's hood over top of it. Sean and Adriana also wore baseball caps and donned sunglasses so they wouldn't be recognized. If Benny *did* spot them, the disguises would buy at least a few seconds. And depending on the circumstances, a few seconds could be a lifetime.

With their minimal camouflage on, the group left the SUV and made their way across the parking lot toward the bridge.

Most of the visitors were gone by the time they arrived at the water's edge. Sean scanned the area to his left and right, noting the bathroom close to the parking area, along with someone selling souvenirs in a stall.

The crew stepped out onto the bridge, gliding nonchalantly across the planks toward the islet shore.

Sean looked down into the crystal water. On the surface a short distance away, it displayed the most spectacular turquoise he'd seen in a lake. But directly under him, the water was without color or pollution. Nearly perfect in clarity, it allowed him to see all the way to the bottom some twenty feet or so below.

"This is clearer than some of those lakes in Montana we've seen," Tommy observed.

"Yeah," Sean said, refocusing his attention to the approaching shoreline. He couldn't allow himself to be distracted, not even by the pristine beauty all around him. He searched the trees, the rocks, and the shadows underneath the twin staircases leading up to the upper-middle section of the island.

If Benny or the mystery man he worked for had positioned a sniper anywhere in those spots, Sean could have easily missed them, and they would all three be dead by now. The fact they were still alive and getting closer to the islet boded well, at least for the time being.

When they reached the stone steps on the islet, Sean split off from the other two and double-checked the shadows underneath the landing at the top before casually, but quickly, rejoining his wife and Tommy.

"Clear under there," Sean whispered. "Just keep 'em peeled."

"Roger," Tommy uttered.

Up ahead, the path curled over the top of the ridge and then down the other side, curving around to the monastery entrance below.

Adriana stopped the two men, firing her arms out wide in a flash before pushing both of them down low.

"Four guards, front entryway," she said.

"Seriously?" Tommy asked.

Sean turned his head, showing Tommy the biggest *Did you really just ask that* face he could summon.

Adriana nodded, blinking slowly in irritation. "Yes. Two stationed on the near side of the portico. I saw the feet of the third on the other side."

"I thought you said four."

"Would you rather I say three and it turns out to be four? Or would you like to plan ahead with a slightly more difficult but less surprising outcome and be ready for it?"

Tommy pressed his lips together and nodded. "I see your point. And yes, four is good. Thank you."

"You're welcome." She nodded to the right. "I'll go that way. See you at the front."

Before they could muster so much as a "Wait," she scrambled away to the right, going slightly downhill before traversing along the hillside just below the ridge.

"You really need to know when to stop talking," Sean said with the all the mischief of a twelve-year-old kid.

He stood up and started down the hill, doing his best to look casual. Tommy caught up and stuffed his hands in his jacket pocket.

"Yeah, I guess you're right," Tommy said, figuring the guards would think two normal tourists would be talking as they approached. "I'm just trying to make—"

"Sure she knew what she was talking about?" Sean chuckled. "I imagine June has so much fun with you."

"What's that supposed to mean? June and I are great. I mean, sure, she's gone a lot."

"You're gone a lot."

"You know you're not making me feel any better, right?"

Sean laughed, careful to keep his voice low. They reached the bottom of the steps and continued toward the front of the monastery.

"Adriana loves you. June loves you. We all love you. So, pretty please, kick out the insecure guy in your head. You're a bad dude, Tommy. Look at you. You're way stronger than me. If I didn't know you, I would definitely steer clear of trouble in your direction."

The comment seemed to soothe Tommy's misplaced anxiety. "Really? That means a lot coming from you."

"Yeah, well, I do know you. So don't get cocky."

Tommy kept the smile to himself.

The two were like brothers, and they always would be. And as with brothers, their bond came with moments where one had to lift the other up, even if it was absurd to do so.

"Look at that," Sean whispered. "Four of them. I think you owe my wife an apology."

"I'll send her a box of chocolates."

"You'll be her best friend if you do."

They stopped at the bottom of the stairs and looked up at the four guards looming over them from the porch.

"The monastery is closed," the guard to the right of the steps said in mutilated English. He held out a stern palm.

The guy must have figured the two were either American or English, or from some country that spoke the language.

Sean looked at Tommy, then back up at the guard. "What do you mean? It's the middle of the day."

"The monastery is closed to visitors," the guard to the left said. The other two kept their arms crossed over their chests.

The way they stood made them look like judges, of what Sean had no idea. *Entry to the monastery for now.*

The one on the far left touched his right ear.

"Well, you know," Sean hurried to say, "if it's closed, it's closed. Nothing we can do about that. I do need to ask, however, if there is a restroom on the island we can use. I had way too much tea earlier, and I really need to use the facilities."

"Back on mainland," the guard on the right said.

The four men looked like they were cut from the same block of stone. Their broad shoulders stretched the fabric of their outfits to their limits. Though they all appeared to be less trim around the waist, the men would have been a force to reckon with in an American football game.

"Is one of you that guy that played football for the Las Vegas Raiders?" Tommy asked, trying to buy some time for Adriana to do her thing, whatever that happened to be.

The guards looked at each other, confused.

The one touching his earpiece said something into his mic. It was out of earshot, but Sean imagined he was getting the call from the boss to take out the two instigators.

He took a step over to the one on the right inner side of the steps —the guy Sean had already pinned as the leader. The man whispered something into the leader's ear, and the man nodded.

The man in charge started to reach inside his pocket, but his hand never made it. A click from behind opened a crater in his forehead. The guard who'd whispered to him received the next round, his through the front-left corner of his skull. By the time the other two responded, it was too late. They barely had a second to turn toward the threat before their lives ended to the suppressed click of a .40-caliber pistol.

Two victims tumbled over the porch and onto the ground behind an ornamental tree on one side and a large shrub on the other. The two men in the middle fell down the steps, their bodies flopping and rolling awkwardly until they reached the ground where Tommy and Sean stood.

Adriana emerged from the shadows, checked the entrance, and then gave an upward nod to the two men. "You two should move those guys out of the way. You know, in case some poor tourist doesn't know the place is closed for business."

Tommy and Sean shared a quick glance, then each grabbed a body by the ankles and dragged the heavy men around to the other side of the retaining wall in front of the building and left them out of plain sight, tucked under a dense bush.

Sean figured whoever was in charge of landscaping duty would have a macabre surprise when they showed up for work.

Adriana cleared the entrance to the monastery, checking the atrium just inside before popping her head back out as the two guys made their way up the steps, both a little out of breath from the effort required to move the heavy dead men.

"All clear just inside," she announced. "Not sure where the monks are."

"Hopefully praying," Tommy guessed.

"Would be nice if we could find one who could show us which way Benny and his group went."

"It's not a large facility," Adriana chimed. "Not a lot of places to hide. I'm guessing only a small contingent of monks stay here full time."

"That should make the chances of collateral damage lower."

She nodded. "There are three doors just inside the atrium. It would be best for us to get out of the open before the man in charge sends reinforcements."

"Good idea."

Sean held up a radio earpiece he'd stolen from one of the dead men. He'd been rubbing it on his shirt to get it clean, or *cleaner*. "I'll be able to hear what they're doing through this. Unless they switch channels."

"You got one of the radios?" Tommy looked at him as they climbed the steps.

"Yeah. Didn't you?"

"From a dead body? No. No, I did not. What is wrong with you?"

"What's wrong with you? He's not going to need it anymore."

"Can you two stop bickering and get inside?" Adriana said. She rolled her eyes and spun on her heels before stepping through the heavy wooden door into the building.

"We're not bickering," Tommy said, almost sounding hurt.

"Maybe we were a little," Sean joked as they followed her inside.

He took one last look out into the courtyard in front of the monastery before the door closed behind him and only the dim candlelight in the atrium shone inside.

32

TIBET

Candles burned all around—on shelves and tables, even on the floor next to one of the sacred statues in a corner. The flames didn't give off scent, except the bland odor of wax and string burning. The room felt warm and welcoming, almost cozy.

"Where are the monks?" Tommy whispered.

Sean held up a finger for silence and listened closely. He heard the sounds of chanting, muted by the door straight ahead. "Praying," he said, pointing at the door. "Not going that way."

This was the second time in two years Sean found himself in such a monastery, and he couldn't help but feel the similarities.

He stepped over to the door to the right and pulled it open. Inside, outer garments hung from a bar stretching across the tiny space. *Just a closet.*

The middle door abruptly opened, and a monk with a clean-shaven head walked through. He froze just as he passed over the threshold. His eyes fixed on the gun in Adriana's hand.

She held up her left palm as a show of peace, despite what the deadly weapon might have been saying.

He didn't look convinced, but after she locked eyes with him and nodded slowly, the man appeared to understand.

"Where did they go?" she breathed in as quiet a tone as she could summon.

The monk bowed his head and pointed toward the door to her left.

"There is a basement," the monk said in choppy English. He closed the door behind him, and the draft fluttered his orange robes around the ankles.

No one said anything, waiting for the monk to finish. They could tell the man had one more thing to add, and wondered what it might be.

"Below the basement is another level. You will find them there."

Adriana nodded. "Thank you."

"No," the monk said. "Thank you."

In his eyes they saw the fear Benny and his group had caused. They might have bribed the abbot to keep the monastery closed for a while, but this guy knew their intentions were less than pure.

"They are armed," the monk added as the three padded over to the door.

Sean nodded to the man and patted him on the shoulder. He nodded his appreciation to the monk and then opened the door, jamming his pistol through the opening. There was no way the monk believed they were with Chinese authorities. They were bluntly American in every way, except Adriana. There was no hiding her Spanish origins. Still, the monk didn't protest despite their absolute lack of official authority. The man must have been a good judge of character, or so Sean figured.

Adriana entered the stairwell through the open door. Tommy followed behind her, then Sean.

The steep stone steps led down into the monastery's underbelly. Candles lined the walls atop each step, and within shallow alcoves cut into the stonework every five feet. A musty, ancient scent filled the air and mixed with the faint odor wafting up from the burning wicks.

Adriana tiptoed down the steps with her pistol held at the ready, keeping her back toward the near wall. She moved with the stealth of a ninja—appropriate since her teacher was exactly that, one of the last remaining ninjas in the world.

She stopped at the corner where the stairwell turned to the right. Sean watched her from above and kept his head on a swivel, checking behind him every few seconds to make sure no one got the drop on them. Tommy stayed between them, his own weapon drawn and aimed down the stairs.

Adriana swept around the corner in a burst, gun barrel leading the way. Tommy and Sean moved as one, joining her on the landing with the same attack position across the floor.

The staircase turned and continued downward another floor to the basement. More candlelight flickered below, casting an eerie montage of dancing lights and ghostly shadows.

Adriana held up four fingers.

Sean nodded in agreement.

Four shadows wavering on the floor and wall near the base of the stairs. It was a dangerous thing to believe that the shadows belonged to more of the security team accompanying Benny and his boss. The last thing Sean wanted to do was accidentally shoot a monk.

He and the others would have to be careful. Collateral damage was unacceptable.

Adriana floated down the steps without so much as a squeak or scuff from her shoes. She stopped at another corner and waited, analyzing the shadows along the floor. The figures stretched across the floor and up the wall, which told her the men were close.

She waited for Sean and Tommy to join her on the next-to-last step.

Sean made eye contact with her and nodded, then bobbed his head to Tommy as well.

"Go," he ordered.

The three stepped down from the stairwell and into a rectangular room that spread out fifty feet in length and thirty feet across. Wooden tables and chairs occupied the center of the room near the stairs. Candles burned in alcoves along the wall and on the table.

Even in the gloom, Sean and his crew made out the guards in the shimmering glow of the candles.

One directly across from the stairwell in the corner caught his first bullet as Sean twitched his trigger finger and sent a round through the man's left shoulder. He turned, raising his weapon as he slumped against the wall. Sean fired again. A red stain splattered on the stone wall behind the man's head, and he fell to the floor.

Adriana rounded the corner and put another guard in her sights. She fired three quick shots into the man's chest, sending him staggering backward before he fell.

Tommy took the tougher of the first three targets, aiming for a guard a good thirty-five feet away along the far wall. He stalked forward, just as he'd done every time he trained with Sean at the urban warfare grounds at their favorite gun range. Keeping the weapon steady while moving at any speed was difficult, but he'd honed that particular skill to nearly the level of Sean's, and it was paying dividends. Although not for the guard who caught a round in the gut, one in the right side of his chest, and a third in the left shoulder.

The gunman stumbled back against the wall, desperate to raise his weapon and return fire.

Tommy strode forward, keeping on the offensive as he unleashed another two rounds.

Meanwhile, the fourth guard to his left lifted his pistol with both hands and took aim at the closest target—Tommy. With his focus on the farthest target, Tommy peppered the gunman with round after round. Two missed and ricocheted off the wall directly behind the guard.

He felt the threat to his left and started to turn his attack on the last gunman when Adriana and Sean both unleashed a blizzard of metal, ripping through the man's body with devastating accuracy.

The last round went through the man's cheek just below his right eye. He died before he hit the floor with a thump.

A sharp, bitter mist hung in the air, some still leaking from the silenced muzzles.

Tommy exhaled a lengthy breath. "Thanks," he said with a nod to his friends.

"No problem," Adriana answered.

The three kept their weapons free as they pushed forward.

Something wasn't right.

Sean's spider senses tingled. And not in a good way. This room was enclosed, with no windows and no other doors. He'd suspected there would be another stairway leading down to the level below the basement the monk had mentioned, but now Sean realized why the man said what he had.

The monk had been bought by Benny's benefactor. He told the Americans to come down here, to this room, where they would be trapped in what could only be described as the perfect kill box.

Sean started to spin around, but a familiar voice stopped him.

"That's far enough, Sean," the man said. "Drop your weapons. All of you."

Adriana and Tommy froze on either side of Sean, both realizing they'd fallen for the trap.

All three of them were so caught up in the idea of getting down to the lower level, they never considered it was a trick.

"I'm sorry," Benny said. "Perhaps you didn't understand me. I said drop your guns. Now."

Sean kept his head to the side, chin over his shoulder, with his old nemesis in the periphery of his right eye.

"Look at you, Benny," Sean groused. "You beat us to it."

"If you think you're going to get me monologizing long enough for you to figure a way out of this, you're mistaken. You're fast, Sean. A true American gunslinger if ever there was one. But each of you has a highly trained marksman already aiming his weapon at you. One wrong move and you all die."

"We both know that's going to happen anyway, Benny. Why make us wait?"

"Mmm. So true. Yes, your fate is sealed. It's the *when* that remains in question."

That told Sean everything he needed to know. He and Tommy,

Adriana too, had been down this path—following an ancient set of riddles and clues right up to the finish line, only to have some half-wit show up at the last second and try to steal the prize. In this case, Sean knew the prize for Benny was probably financial.

"Can't figure out the last part of the puzzle, huh, Benny?"

"Oh, it isn't that. My employer thinks that you and your little band might still be of some use to us once we're inside the lost city. I disagree with him, of course, but he's the boss, as you Americans like to say."

"You used to be a good historian, Benny," Tommy snapped. "You were a well-respected professor. What happened to you?"

"If I was so respected, why did you turn down my request, Tommy?" Benny fired back. "I came to you with this project. You said it was foolish, that it was a wild goose chase. And yet here you are, chasing the same geese. I can't help but appreciate the irony."

Adriana stood perfectly still with her back to the enemy. She kept her trigger finger ready, just in case.

"So, that's what all this is about? Revenge? You want to get back at me because I didn't fund your operation? I would have hoped you realized by now that the IAA doesn't do that sort of thing. We don't throw money at expeditions or research projects unless we take them on in house."

"You said Shangri-La doesn't exist," Benny barked.

"I know," Tommy admitted. "And until I see proof otherwise, I'm going to continue that skepticism."

"And yet here you are."

Tommy nodded absently. "Yes. Here I am."

"Boys," a new voice interrupted.

Something about the tone, the feel of the sound, caught Sean's attention.

"There is no reason why we can't all get along."

Sean felt compelled to twist his head sideways just a little more, but he resisted. Still, what was it about the new man's voice that sounded so familiar?

"Drop your guns," a woman to Benny's right ordered.

"You remember Ju Chen, right" Benny asked, the threat evident.

"Now, now, children," the new voice warned. "There's no reason we can't be civilized about this." He paused for a second. "Sean, there is no reason you have to die right now. I certainly don't want that, no matter how much your counterpart here might feel differently. I would prefer we work together."

A sickening realization crept into the back of Sean's mind. His breath quickened involuntarily. "No," he said. "That can't be."

Sean twisted his head a little farther, risking his life for a better look. Along the far wall near the staircase, three gunmen in outfits similar to the dead men on the floor stood with pistols aimed at him, Tommy, and Adriana. The woman called Ju Chen also held a pistol at full extension, her aim squarely on Sean.

Benny stood next to her with the smuggest grin Sean had ever seen sprayed on his face like grotesque graffiti under a forgotten overpass. None of them made an impression on Sean. He knew what he was facing in that regard.

It was Benny's employer that Sean needed to see, if he were to believe what his gut screamed.

The man in the flowing hoodie smiled back. It was the same easy grin Sean had seen before, and recently.

"That's not possible," Sean said, shaking his head.

"That I'm the mysterious Mr. Lóng? The feared Black Dragon of the Asian underworld?"

"No," Sean disagreed, forcing his wit against the rush of emotions crashing into his soul's shoreline. "I can't believe you wear your sunglasses indoors. Especially in a place as dark as this. It's lit by candles, for crying out loud."

Tommy spat laughter for a second, but it was timid and short-lived. Sean knew his friend also recognized the voice.

The man stepped from the faint shadows of the stairwell and removed his sunglasses, revealing the eyes Sean knew, or thought he knew.

"Hello, Sean."

Sean clenched his jaws while Tommy's mouth dropped wide open.

Adriana merely stood resolute.

After a short breath, Sean managed to answer. "Hello, Malcolm."

33

TIBET

"Malcolm?" Tommy breathed. "But—"

"Tommy, old pal. Don't go there." Malcolm took a step toward the long table and pulled out the chair at the head. He sat down and crossed his arms as he would have sitting down to dinner at a friend's house. "Don't be the guy who whines about 'How could you' or 'I thought we were friends' or 'But you hired us.'"

Tommy choked on the warning, but they were all thoughts he'd considered the second he realized the feared Lóng was actually their friend. Or had been their friend.

"I'll make this really simple for you guys. I like you. I really do." Malcolm opened his left palm to reemphasize the point, if there was a point to be had. "We go back a ways. And I appreciate all you guys have done and the effort you put in on this project. But in the end, I'm a money guy. I make weapons for a living, and until recently, I've done a good job of selling them."

"Until recently?" Sean asked.

"Yeah, before I answer, go ahead and put your guns down on the ground. Slowly, if possible. I really don't want to have my guys shoot you, Sean. Seriously. I would prefer to keep you alive—for now, anyway. We'll see how that sentiment holds for the foreseeable future."

Sean sighed, then bent down and lowered his weapon to the ground. Tommy and Adriana complied with reluctance.

"Now, that's better. Turn around. It's weird with you all standing sideways like that trying to have a conversation with me."

The three faced the man as requested.

"There we go. So, you three are wondering why I sent you out on this expedition. Truth is, I didn't think Benny could handle it."

Benny's head twisted to the side. His face drained of color. His expression turned from one of victory to ultimate betrayal.

"I mean, let's face it. You guys are the best there is. Right? That said, I had to hedge my bets and play both sides. Best way to make sure I get the outcome I want." He turned toward Benny, looking at the Spaniard over his shoulder. "Let's have a look inside the case."

Benny hesitated, like a child who'd been forgotten at Christmas. He set the metal case on the table and slid it in front of his employer without fanfare or grace.

"Thank you, Benny," Malcolm said with his Southern drawl.

Malcolm flipped up the clasps, then pried open the lid.

The dancing candlelight shimmered against the smooth red angles of the gem. The Heart of Shambala virtually glowed in the custom cushion within the case. Gently, he placed his hands on the gem and carefully lifted it out. He turned it 360 degrees, inspecting the perfectly symmetrical sides.

Inside the gem, a tiny light glowed. Benny hadn't noticed that before. He wondered how he'd missed it.

"Magnificent," Malcolm stated. "Absolutely magnificent."

"Shame you have no idea where the gate is," Sean chirped. "A key without a door is a useless key. Although I'm sure you could fetch a pretty penny on eBay for that thing. You'd have to get it authenticated."

"That's what I don't understand about any of this," Tommy cut in. "You're a billionaire, Malcolm. Why would you do this? You don't need the money!"

"Ah, Tommy," Malcolm said, raising a finger and holding the jewel with one hand. "That's where you're wrong. You see, governments make cuts sometimes. And occasionally, the military budget is one of the targets for those cuts. In the last year, I've lost twenty billion in contracts that our new Congress decided could be redlined. We were down thirty percent last year. Billions, Tommy. With a B."

"That's a lot of cornflakes," Sean interjected.

"Yes. It is."

"So, your plan was to locate the mythical lost valley where Shangri-La supposedly exists, and what, pillage it for its treasures? We don't even know if they had anything of value there, if the place was real."

"Oh, it's real, ye of little faith." He stood, cradling the jewel in his right palm. "And I'm not there for treasures of gold and silver, precious gems like this one. In fact, that's the genius of this key." Malcolm held the jewel aloft. "If anyone found this, it's highly unlikely they would look beyond the face value of it, what they could get at an auction house, or the marketplaces of antiquity. They would have never known what they sold. But I have my sights set on something far more powerful."

Adriana frowned a deep, dark look of disapproval and confusion. "If you're not doing this because of money, then why? What possible reason could you have for trying to locate the lost city?"

"Oh, don't get me wrong, my dear. In the end, it's definitely about money. Everything is about money."

"Not everything," Sean argued.

"Don't start with that noble nonsense of yours, Sean. In the end, you have to eat, just like everyone else. You have to have a car, a home, a bed, a retirement plan. Everyone does. So, in the end, everything is about money. You can spout off about true love or family or whatever all you want, but the truth is every single person on the planet is nine meals from doing something utterly desperate. Even criminal."

"So, you had Fischer killed." Tommy spewed the words through numb lips.

"Fischer didn't have to die," Malcolm countered. "But if Benny thought he was going to be a loose end, I gave him latitude to do what he thought necessary."

"We're all loose ends," Sean said, going to psychological warfare as best he knew how. He made sure Ju Chen and the three gunmen knew he was talking about them as well.

To her credit, she didn't even flinch. The three men didn't either, but they may not have understood what he said.

"So true," Malcolm agreed with a nod. "All of us are loose ends to someone. Expendable, every one of us. Which is why I am going to make myself indispensable, while at the same time making a ton of money."

"I suppose you're going to tell us all about it."

"Of course, my old friends. I wouldn't keep you in the dark." He carefully laid the jewel back in its case and reached into the folds of his robe-like hoodie, then produced a piece of paper.

He unfolded it and held it up for Sean and the others to see. The image featured an obelisk standing in the middle of a courtyard. A beam shot out of the obelisk's highest point, rising up to the top of the page in brilliant black-and-white detail. Strange buildings surrounded the courtyard, their architecture unlike anything Sean had ever seen.

"What is that?" Tommy asked, beating Sean to the punch.

"This is the Pillar of Light," Malcolm answered. "You've never heard of it?"

"No. Should I have?"

"Perhaps it hasn't entered the realm of the mainstream yet."

Sean chuffed. "Is that what you think we do? Mainstream? And here I thought you knew us."

"Who drew that?" Tommy wondered out loud. "It looks like the cover for a science fiction comic book."

"It certainly does, Tommy." Malcolm held it out and looked at it anew. "But that isn't where I got this. No, this drawing is much older, and comes from a time hundreds of years before comic books or science fiction."

"It's a copy. Right? Please tell me it's a copy."

Sean laughed at his friend.

"Of course it's a copy. And this pillar is the reason for this entire venture."

"Let me get this straight," Sean said. "You sent us all the way around the world to find an obelisk? Like the ones in Egypt or Rome or Paris or Washington?"

"Ah." Malcolm wagged a finger in the air. "Similar in appearance, yes. But they are not the same, I assure you. In fact, since my discovery of this artwork, I have come up with the theory that the obelisks you mentioned, all of them around the world, are replicas of this, the Pillar of Light."

Sean looked over at his wife and shrugged. "Honey, you ever heard of this thing?"

"No," she said, "not specifically."

He scrunched his eyebrows together. "Wait, you've heard of something like this?"

She tossed her head to the side with a shrug of her own. "Only legends about an ancient power source that could protect entire kingdoms from attacks. They were only stories, myths. I never found any concrete evidence about such a thing."

"That's because you didn't know where to look," Malcolm offered, stuffing the paper back in his hoodie-robe.

"And you do?" Sean asked.

"I do now. Thanks to Benny and Dr. Fischer. And you three, of course. You helped, I'm sure. And you may still have a way to contribute." His eyes wandered to the body on the floor nearest him. A pool of blood collected under the man's head. "Although you did kill eight of my men. I'm impressed, Sean. I really am. I always knew you were the best."

"I've never been the best at anything, Mal," Sean disputed.

"Ah. And always so humble. A real hero's hero." He picked up the red jewel again, and gestured with his head toward Sean and his companions. "Do me a favor, and move the table."

Sean and the others questioned each other with a shared glance.

"The table," Malcolm said in a harsher tone. "Please, move it. Do I have to explain everything to you? Just move it over there." He pointed at a random place off to the right.

The three did as told and pressed on the table's edge, sliding it across the stone surface to a loud scraping sound.

As they moved the table, a brown rug came into view beneath it. The table legs dragged the carpet from its position and exposed the edge of something in the floor.

"That's far enough," Malcolm said. "Thank you. Now, please, move over to the back wall."

Sean and the others retreated to the wall as prescribed and waited while Malcolm carried the jewel over to a spot in the floor where a curved gouge ran deep in the stone.

"Benny, would you mind doing the honors?"

Benny had remained quiet for several minutes, letting his rivals wallow in the realization that they'd been played all along. He snapped to attention at the sound of his name and walked over to where his employer stood holding the heart.

"Pull back the carpet, would you?" Malcolm requested.

Benny knelt down and jerked the rug away to reveal a circle of rings cut into the stone. The shape was three feet in diameter and featured five additional loops within, each containing shapes of the stars, the sun, the moon, mountains, forests, birds, and flowers. Each image portrayed a different time of day, season, or segment of a life cycle. Runes like the ones they'd seen before dotted the imagery as well. A divot the shape and size of the Heart of Shambala occupied the center of the relief.

"Spectacular," Malcolm exclaimed. "Absolutely spectacular."

Sean narrowed his eyelids. He studied the strange carving, noting the many details, including the arrow at the top of the inner circle where he assumed the jewel would be placed.

Benny hovered over the spot, examining it as well. "It looks like a wheel or a dial," he said.

"Yes," Malcolm agreed. "And note the three metal prongs sticking up at the bottom of the recess in the center."

He took the gem, carefully cradling it in his palm, then using both hands, lowered it into place within the wheel.

Malcolm stepped back and admired his handiwork, but the pleasure only lasted for ten seconds. When nothing happened, his pleased expression darkened. "What's going on?" He directed the question at Benny.

"What do you mean?" Benny replied.

"This is the gate," Malcolm insisted. "Did you bring the wrong jewel? Something is supposed to open."

Sean and Tommy snickered.

"You think this is funny?" Malcolm roared. He reached under his outer garment and drew a pistol, pointing it at Sean's face.

Sean reacted by arching his right eyebrow, as if the threat of death had no effect. He looked at the Walther with the little can on the end and nodded. "Nice pistol, Malcolm. Did you get that because it's the gun James Bond uses? As a guy who sells weapons for a living, you don't go with a bigger caliber?"

"This one is enough to kill you. Why isn't it working?"

"Beats me," Sean said. "Ask your lackey there." He indicated Benny with a nod.

"Good point," Malcolm said. He turned the weapon on Benny, who reacted much differently than Sean with a gun in his face.

He stumbled backward, instinctively putting up both hands in surrender. Like that was an option.

"Hey, what are you doing?" Benny complained.

"What is the problem?" Malcolm demanded. "Why isn't this working?"

Benny shook his head so fast the skin hanging from his bony cheeks jiggled. "I don't know. It should open the gate." The words couldn't spray out of his mouth fast enough.

"He doesn't know how to open it," Sean said, crossing his arms. "He's out of his element."

"Shut up!" Benny blurted. "You don't know me."

"I know you don't have a clue what you're supposed to do next."

Benny stewed, his face flushing with heat. "He's trying to turn you against me, Malcolm. You know that's true. Look at him. He's playing you against me."

"Oh, I know precisely what Sean is doing. I know how he works. And I also know he's probably correct. So, Benny, can you open the gate or not?"

Benny swallowed, choking down a gulp of fear and uncertainty. He didn't answer, instead shifting carefully over to the rings set in the floor. He breathed heavily, kneeling beside the strange wheel.

He inspected the runes, running a finger over the grooves and lines as if that would give him some hint as to what he needed to do next. His eyes darted back and forth as he tried to piece together the solution. Then, Benny pressed his fingers down onto the outer ring and pushed. To his surprise, the ring shifted, twisting slightly around the inner rings. The stone scraped against the surface of the floor around it moved relatively easily. He wondered if the thing had little wheels on the underside but kept that to himself.

Sean watched Benny as he lined up an image of the sun at the top of the circle so the arrow in the center pointed toward it. Feeling and hearing a click from within the floor, Benny stopped rotating the dial and lifted his hands away from it.

Everyone hovering around watched intently to see what would happen. Nothing.

Undaunted, Benny took the second dial from the outside and started turning it. He rotated the images of clouds, volcanoes, stormy seas, and majestic mountains until the latter's peaks stopped under the shining sun.

The floor clicked again.

In a groove now, Benny took the next loop and rotated the four scenes of a forest, one with trees full of leaves, one with skeletal branches, and two that looked the same but were on opposite sides of the wheel. He lined up the picture that appeared to be late spring or early summer and heard the click again.

The next images were the birds. One displayed birds flying with wings spread. Another depicted the creatures huddled in a nest, sleeping. One featured a mother bird with its eggs. And the last showed the little ones chirping with the mother hovering over them in the nest.

Benny lined up the soaring birds with the other images above the arrow and stopped when he heard the click a fourth time.

The last, the innermost ring, displayed four flowers in various stages of life and death. One bloomed, another looked dead, one looked like a sapling, and one's petals folded in on itself, as if waiting for the sun to rise before it opened.

Cautiously, Benny turned the last dial until the blooming flower aligned with the other images above. He stood up, waiting for the last click—what he thought certainly would open a secret passage or a trapdoor that would lead them to the lost city.

An acidic dread began filling his gut and rose in his throat. Then a loud thud shook the room, accompanied by a burst of air that blew out most of the candles along the wall.

Then, a loud scraping sound came from the base of the stairs. The guard nearest the stairwell looked to his left, finally torn from his targets by the sudden sound. A massive piece of the ceiling dropped to the floor, closing off the only exit from the room.

The gunman took a step back in surprise, but he didn't retreat far or fast enough. Another block fell from above, crushing him in a blink.

The remaining gunmen and Ju Chen rushed forward, away from the wall, as another row of blocks dropped to the floor, rocking the building to its foundations.

When the massive stones stopped falling, a thin mist of dust hung in the air, highlighted by the remaining candles that flickered hesitantly in the darkness.

Malcolm held his pistol tight, only cringing slightly when the blocks fell. He somehow managed to keep his composure while everyone else in the room seemed worried the next block would fall on them.

He drew a deep breath and shook his head.

"It would seem you've worn out your usefulness, Benny." Malcolm's index finger tightened against the trigger.

"No," Benny said, shaking his head vehemently. "Please. I brought you the jewel. Without me, you wouldn't even be here right now."

"And here, it would seem, is now trapped under an ancient monastery with no way out. I have you to thank for that, too."

"Malcolm. Please. Give me another chance. I'll get it right."

"No, I don't think so, Benny. And you don't get to call me Malcolm. After all, you're expendable."

Benny twisted and grimaced, retreating a step, then another. It wasn't far enough. Malcolm fired his pistol, dropping Benny to the ground in a heap against the wall.

He writhed in agony for half a minute before he stopped moving. Blood collected on the floor beneath him, staining the stone a dark crimson.

"Now," Malcolm said, turning away from the body. He pointed the gun at Sean. "Your turn, Sean."

34

TIBET

"What?" Sean asked bluntly.

"It's your turn," Malcolm repeated. "Get down there, and figure this thing out."

Sean shook his head in disbelief. "You're kidding, Mal."

"I'm not." He flexed his fingers on the pistol grip in a show of deadly intent.

"Mal," Tommy cut in, "you just saw what happened when Benny tried to make the thing work. We've never seen anything like this before. And there's no information about how to work it."

"That's what you boys do, isn't it?" Malcolm argued. "You figure out stuff like this. Well, now we're trapped. And the only way out is to decipher how it works. So, you can die now, or you can die getting crushed by a one-ton block."

"You think I'm scared of dying, Malcolm?" Sean demurred. "That gun doesn't scare me."

"No. I suppose it doesn't." Malcolm's eyes burned with a look Sean had seen before. It was a kind of insanity, a raging greed and lust unconstrained by any sense of human decency. "But I know what does scare you, Sean."

Malcolm turned to his remaining two guards and motioned

toward Adriana. "Take her over there. Stand her next to those blocks. If her dear husband screws this up, she'll be the next one crushed."

Rage pulsed from Sean's heart, racing through his body. If he had been a few inches closer, he'd have snapped the gun from Malcolm's hand, twisted it, and unloaded the entire magazine into his former friend.

But Malcolm wasn't stupid. He knew the venomous serpent standing across from him, and he was well aware of Sean's abilities. And his track record.

"No, Malcolm. Don't do that," Sean pleaded.

It was too late. The guards muscled Adriana over to the other side of the room next to the fallen stone slabs.

"Now, then. Make it work, Sean."

Tommy and Sean met each other's gaze, then Sean shifted his eyes to Adriana. The woman never showed an ounce of fear, even now. Only fire burned in her eyes—roaring flames that he'd seen in the past, just before she went berserk on an enemy. He was glad he'd never been on the receiving end of that fury.

"Malcolm, I don't know what this is," Sean protested. "We don't have a clue that tells us how this thing works."

"You have three minutes," Malcolm said in response. "Or I shoot her right here."

Sean searched Tommy's eyes for answers but found none.

"The clock is ticking."

"Okay. Okay. Take it easy."

Sean knelt down on the floor next to the dial and examined the images anew. He ran through the last riddle they'd received, the clue that brought them to this place. *Was there something about it he'd missed?*

The words didn't give him an answer right away. He stole a look over at Benny's still form only six feet away. He lay motionless on the floor, having received his reward.

Sean returned his focus to the dial, staring curiously at the images carved into stone. *It looks like Benny tried to line up all the best images, those that featured the best of times.* Sean bit his lower lip as he considered the information. *Does that mean I should do the opposite? Line up the stormy days and all that?*

He shook off the thought. *That's what they would want you to think. There has to be another way.*

"Two minutes," Malcolm said.

Sean sighed, rolling his eyes. "Not helping, Mal."

"Then work faster."

No, it isn't the opposite. What was it the last riddle said? It mentioned the eye, the gate, and...where horizons end.

Initially, Sean believed that the lake and the monastery were what the riddle referred to with that description. Surrounded by high mountain peaks on all sides, this lake valley truly was where horizons ended. The sun rose late and set early, but never truly on the horizon.

But is there another piece of that clue I could apply here?

"Ninety seconds."

Sean ignored Malcolm and reached out his hands to adjust the outer ring. He moved the sun to the right and kept moving beyond the image of the setting sun, past the engraving of the moon, until a blank slot aligned with the arrow.

He stopped and waited. Nothing happened. Then a loud click echoed through the chamber.

Sean felt his heart sink. *Strike one.*

He stretched out his fingers for the second ring. He started to turn it, then stopped. "This one stays," he whispered to himself.

"What?" Malcolm asked.

"Nothing. Just talking to myself. Would you mind keeping it down? I'm trying to not get my wife killed."

"One minute," was the only response Sean received.

The third dial confused Sean, with the two images that looked nearly identical then the others with trees in full bloom and after fall.

Sean turned the wheel until the two similar images were above and beneath the inner circle, then he stopped.

Another click.

"Tick tock," Malcolm warned. "Thirty seconds."

Sean sighed and began spinning the fourth ring.

"Where horizons end," Sean muttered, staring at the dial as he spun it. *How did this one apply? Was it possible Benny got this one right and not the others?* Sean realized with sudden fear that Benny's fate could have been sealed by only one mistake with this cryptic disc.

Horizon's end, he thought. Then he stopped the bird dial on the one where the birds appeared to be resting in the nest. "Dusk," he breathed. "The horizon disappears at dusk, when darkness falls. And just before sunrise."

He nodded at his work and spied the last wheel.

"Ten seconds, Sean," Malcolm said. He nodded to Ju Chen, who raised her pistol, pointing at Adriana's head.

"Hold on," Sean said. "You think I want to make a mistake?"

"Come on, Sean," Malcolm urged. "You're the best at this sort of thing. Well, you and Tommy."

Sean fought through the distraction. It was almost as if Malcolm wanted him to fail so he could watch Adriana die.

With only scant seconds to spare, Sean spun the last ring, stopping it when the flower with the folded petals aligned with the rest of the images above the arrow.

"And time," Malcolm said.

Sean stared at the wheel and waited. Another click.

He looked over at Adriana, meeting her brave gaze with his own terrified one. A sinking feeling in his gut told him it might be the last time he saw her alive. And if that were the case, he was ready to bumrush Malcolm against an onslaught of bullets. There weren't enough rounds in the billionaire's magazine to keep Sean from beating him to death if anything happened to Adriana. Maybe combined with Ju Chen's ammunition and that of the remaining two guards, but Sean would be on Malcolm before they could stop him. He'd get in at least one good punch. Or perhaps even wrench the gun from his hand and turn it on him.

After the loud click, nothing happened, leaving an odd pause hanging in the room. Then, as everyone waited for the first of a new set of stones to drop from the ceiling, a series of rapid clicks rattled from under the floor.

Sean looked down to the wheel again. Everyone else followed his gaze and watched as the rings started moving on their own. They spun, slowly at first, then faster. As the images circled the center, the gem radiated a dim red light. The light grew brighter with every second until it cast a scarlet hue throughout the room.

"What the—" Tommy mouthed.

Then the light disappeared, and the ring around it dropped out of sight. A blast of air shot through the room, extinguishing the remaining candles and casting the whole area into darkness.

The pitch black only lasted a second. As everyone's eyes adjusted, they looked toward the center of the room where the mysterious dial had been. Now, a faint beam of red light streamed up from a hole in the floor and painted a circle on the ceiling directly overhead.

Sean stared into the hole.

Malcolm did, too, unable to rip his eyes from the incredible sight. "Well done, Sean," he said, lowering his weapon. "I knew you were the best." He extended a hand toward Sean to help him up, then thought better of it when Sean hesitated.

Malcolm craned his neck to get a better overhead look of the shaft in the floor. A ladder with polished metal rungs led down a stone wall to the floor thirty feet below. At the bottom, the dial sat flush to the lower floor, the Heart of Shambala shining brightly.

"Seems like our only option is to go down that ladder," Malcolm theorized. "Unless you're too afraid of heights to try that."

Sean glanced over at Tommy, then Adriana. "I can handle it if you can, Mal," he said, redirecting his gaze to the billionaire.

"By all means, then." Malcolm waved his pistol toward the open shaft. "Lead the way, Sean."

Reluctantly, Sean shifted his feet toward the opening and dropped them through. He moved them forward until his toes touched the second rung on the ladder, then lowered himself down through the opening.

"You're next, Tommy," Malcolm stated, wagging the pistol toward the hole. "Ju Chen, take one of the guards down next. Then Adriana will go."

One by one, the group descended the ladder after Sean.

By the time Adriana climbed onto the rungs, Sean stood at the bottom in a wide, arced passage.

The sense of danger looming over him couldn't tear him away from what his eyes beheld.

Fifty feet away at the end of the passage, two stone statues clad in unusual armor stood on either side of a massive doorway. The door split in two, right down the middle. Runes adorned the surface, along with images of a spectacular, futuristic city with citizens in luxurious robes. The faces carved and painted in the relief looked as new as they would have thousands of years ago, the minute the artisans finished their work.

Sean and Tommy marveled at how well preserved the art was and struggled to understand how that was even possible.

In the center of the relief, an obelisk with a spark at its point and a beam of light streaming out from the spark stood at the center of the ancient city's focus.

"The guardians," Tommy drawled.

"Yep."

The two waited against the urge to go ahead of the group and investigate the gigantic door. The two pieces merged in the center. It formed a seam so tight it would have been difficult to slip a single sheet of paper through.

"Incredible," Malcolm said from behind them.

Adriana joined Sean and Tommy at the front of the group. Ju Chen shoved her forward to make sure she knew who was in charge.

Sean hoped the woman would come to regret that.

"Simply incredible," Malcolm continued. "I couldn't have imagined it in a hundred years."

"You should get out more," Sean quipped.

"Hmm. Perhaps. Well, go ahead. Don't just stand here. We need to figure out how to get through this gate."

"How about you figure it out and we watch you?" Tommy offered.

One of the guards slammed an elbow into Tommy's kidneys. He doubled over, coughing hard for nearly a minute.

"A simple no would have sufficed," he spat when he finally regained his breath. "I'm definitely going to piss some blood later with that one."

Malcolm walked ahead of the group, ambling over to the gate. He ran his fingers along the base of the pillar, tracing the engraved outline in the stone.

Sean and the others approached at the encouragement of the guards, and Ju Chen, who seemed unaffected by Benny's murder.

"That's far enough," Ju Chen said. She kept the group a couple of yards away, close enough to never miss with a bullet but far enough away that if all three decided to try something stupid, she would have time to mow them down.

"Amazing, isn't it?" Malcolm went on.

"Yeah," Sean agreed. And he meant it. If he wasn't being held at gunpoint, he would have marveled even more at the ancient wonder before him.

The guardians on either side of the doors each held long spears in one hand. The tips of the weapons were slightly curved, like miniature scimitars. Medium-length swords hung from their waists, also curved similarly to the spear points. The armor was unlike anything Sean or the others had ever seen. Their helmets were smooth and sloped back over the neck, stopping just above the shoulders. The guardians' faces remained concealed within masks. Within the helms, Sean felt as though the eyes hidden in the shadows watched the intruders' every move.

The armor worn by the statues displayed spectacular dragons with their mouths open wide as if screaming at an unseen enemy. The enormous guardians towered over the trespassers, as if warning them to leave before it was too late.

"This pillar," Malcolm said, pointing to the object portrayed in the stone relief, "is the entire reason we're here."

"You alluded to that earlier," Sean reminded him.

"Yes, but do you know what it's capable of?"

"Not really. I'm guessing you're about to tell us."

Malcolm's eyes widened with intense excitement. "The pillar is the reason no one has ever discovered Shangri-La, Sean. It's not only a powerful source of energy. It's a cloaking device. For thousands of years, the city and valley of Shangri-La has remained hidden from invaders. And not only that, but the pillar acts as a shield. Imagine if we had this technology in the United States. We could position pillars such as this one around the country. No enemy would ever be able to attack us again. No nuclear threat."

"And all for a price, I'm sure," Adriana added.

Malcolm snapped his head around. She expected a scathing glare, but instead, he merely rolled his shoulders. "Of course. Nothing in this world is free. The government has been milking the people of the United States for hundreds of years. I see no reason why I can't get a little piece of that. Do you have any idea what the American defense budget is?"

"Annually?" Sean asked.

Tommy burst out laughing, then quickly recovered his composure.

"Seven hundred and sixty-eight billion dollars," Malcolm clarified. "Plus or minus a few billion."

"That's a big plus or minus."

"Yes. Yes it is. And I see no reason why I can't scoop a little of that. What do you think Congress would be willing to pay to ensure that no enemy will ever be able to attack the United States again? What about the president? That would sure look good in a campaign speech, wouldn't it? They could cut five or ten billion off the top line and divert that money to, well, Barnwell. Ten billion a year seems like a small price to pay to make sure three hundred million-plus citizens are safe. Doesn't it?"

"Sure," Sean said. "It makes a ton of sense. And it doesn't matter how many people you killed or stepped on along the way to make it happen. People like Werner Fischer."

Malcolm's face darkened. He turned away from the guardians and shook his head as he looked down at the floor, as if trying to find a way to persuade Sean to see his side.

"In every war, Sean, there are victims. Winners and losers. Sometimes, casualties happen. You know that better than anyone. How many people have you killed to get the job done for Axis, or for the IAA?"

"I've never drawn innocent blood, Mal. That's the difference between us."

"I do what needs to be done, Sean. Don't stand there like you're so high and mighty, acting like you never sinned. I know you've sinned. You've done things! Horrible things!"

"You have no idea what I've done!" Sean barked.

Adriana and Tommy startled at the sudden volume in his voice, the darkness.

"You'll never know. Men like you believe you're killers, that you can do what guys like me have done. We take orders, and no one thinks we question them. But we do. No amount of training can ever take away the humanity of the person squeezing a trigger."

"How poetic." Malcolm raised his pistol, aiming it at Sean once more. "I appreciate the sentiment, but I'm afraid we're out of time. Open the gate."

"Open it yourself," Tommy replied in a sharp tone. "Or do you still need us to do everything for you?"

"Very well, Tommy," Malcolm said, turning the pistol toward him. "You open the gate."

"Point the gun at me, Mal," Sean ordered.

"You all have guns pointed at you. Doesn't matter which one. Open the gate, or I kill you now. Then Adriana. And last, Sean, I kill you."

"If you kill us, you won't get your precious pillar, or anything else beyond that doorway."

"Oh, I think it's cute you believe that. Now that we've discovered the gate, nothing will stop me from getting inside and claiming what's rightfully mine. Killing you three will only delay the inevitable. So, you can either open it for me and live a little longer, or you can die right here in this hole. The choice is yours."

Sean thought for a heartbeat, then ten more. If Malcolm was still dealing, that meant doubt lingered in the man's mind. He might still need their expertise once through the gate. On top of that, Sean's insatiable curiosity wouldn't let him not see the other side. Not after all they'd been through.

"Fine," Sean said. "I'll open the gate for you. Just don't shoot them."

"That's so much better, Sean." Malcolm waved the gun toward the giant door. "Now, how does it work?"

35

TIBET

Sean's two careers had depended on his ability to think on the fly, to come up with answers when there were no clear ones present. Some people might call that the ability to BS. Doctors called it fluid intelligence. He preferred to think of it as being able to innovate and adapt.

He stood there in the tunnel, studying the two statues—the guardians watching over the gateway into the lost city of Shangri-La. Distracting thoughts entered his mind, peppering him with curiosities. *What did it look like on the other side? Were there people still there, living underground in some ancient, high-tech society? Or were there only ruins of a lost civilization that had fallen by the wayside?*

None of those questions helped with the current situation. And reflecting on the clues they'd gathered along the way didn't seem to be of any assistance, either.

"The guardians," he mumbled. "What is it about these two?"

Sean meandered closer to the statue on the right. He inspected every inch of the impressive sculpture, from the toes all the way to the top of the helm. The male figure stood over him wearing a fierce scowl, from what he could see beneath the mask, even though only the mouth could be seen. Narrow, warning eyes stared out from underneath the mask.

Sean rounded on his heels and walked over to the other side as Malcolm and the others watched. The female guardian on the left wore matching armor and stood in the exact same pose. At his initial inspection, Sean didn't think there was any difference between the two, other than gender.

Returning his focus to the base, he noted the feet positioned on a round foundation. A circle looped around the feet. Sean cocked his head to the side and leaned down. Then he squatted like a baseball catcher, running an index finger along the seam.

He sensed Malcolm watching him from a distance, probably suspicious about what Sean would do next.

An idea emerged in Sean's head. He stopped running his finger along the base and stood up. "It's a turntable," he realized.

"What was that?" Malcolm pressed.

"Nothing. Just talking to myself."

"Well, hurry up. I don't want to stand here until Judgment Day."

Sean shook off his former friend's comment. The betrayal still roiled in his brain, burning his face with anger.

"If it's a turntable," Sean said in a quieter tone, "then which one do I turn?"

He strode back over to the male guardian and noted the same rim around the feet. "Tommy," Sean said, looking over his shoulder. "It looks like these are positioned on turntables. I guess we turn the statues to unlock the doors."

"Both of them?" Tommy asked.

Malcolm watched the conversation the same as he would have a tennis match, head turning back and forth.

"I hadn't considered that," Sean answered. "I was thinking only turn one of them."

"Oh yes." Tommy agreed. "That would make sense, too. Which means one could be wrong. And we saw how that worked out before."

"Right."

Tommy turned to Malcolm. "Let me have a look at the statues. I'm unarmed. What's the worst I could do?"

"You could sabotage everything and kill us all," Malcolm returned. "Especially if you believe there is no way you three will make it out of here alive."

"Will we?"

Malcolm's shoulders lifted and dropped. "That depends on you."

Tommy knew the statement was an offer of false hope. Malcolm wasn't going to let any of them live, maybe not even Ju Chen, though she remained a wild card in all this. Malcolm hadn't hesitated to kill Benny, but he'd allowed Benny's pet to live. Either Malcolm didn't believe the two were intertwined in their business relationship, or he had a plan for her.

"Sean can figure this one out on his own," Malcolm announced. "If he guesses wrong, well, then you'll get it right, Tommy."

Tommy felt like pouncing on the man and pounding him to a bloody pulp. "What happened to you, Mal?" Tommy asked instead. He kept his voice calm, patient, and sincere. "You were a good friend."

"Not as good as you might have thought, I suppose," Malcolm answered. "And we're running out of time, Sean. So, if you could go ahead and pick a statue, I would really appreciate it." He tightened his grip on the pistol to emphasize his point.

Sean said nothing. He simply turned and walked back across the face of the entrance and stopped at the female statue again. He pored over her figure, analyzing every inch of the stonecutter's work until he found something different. The eyes within the helm of this statue were softer, warmer. Welcoming? Sean craned his neck and looked under the mask at her lips. Instead of the angry scowl the male statue displayed, this female wore a smile—lips curled in a subtle expression similar to the *Mona Lisa*, as if keeping a great secret.

"It's the woman," Sean realized just above a whisper. "She's the guardian."

He searched the base for something to hold but found nothing. So, he grabbed on to the sculpture's arms with both hands and started twisting. He leaned back as he pulled, and found that the statue moved more easily than expected.

It swiveled as if on ball bearings and twisted inward toward the stone doors.

Click. Click. Click. Click.

The sounds came from under the guardian's foundation until the sculpture stopped. Whatever internal mechanism allowed it to turn reached a barrier that would allow it to go no farther.

A thunderous rumble echoed through the passage. Sean instinctively looked up, expecting a heavy stone slab to fall from the ceiling and crush him where he stood. None did. Then a grinding sound to his left shook the ground under his feet, nearly causing him to lose his balance and topple over. Everyone else put their hands out wide as it felt as if the entire place was going to collapse in on itself.

Sean wondered what the monks up above thought of all the noise —the stones falling, and now this. They must have believed they were either under attack or that an earthquake was going to sink their monastery to the bottom of the lake. *That would be ironic,* Sean thought.

Then, the doors parted, receding to their respective sides.

A bright light poured through the gap, nearly knocking out Sean's vision. He winced and held up his hand to shield his eyes for a second until they adjusted. Everyone behind him did the same.

Along with the light, a new scent burst into the room. It washed over Sean and filled his nostrils almost instantly. The sweet smell reminded him of walking in his grandmother's garden full of hydrangeas, azaleas, lavender, jasmine, and gardenias.

The doors continued to roll open until they stopped flush with the giant arcing frame.

Sean's vision cleared, and he found himself staring through the opening into a world unlike anything he'd ever seen before.

He shook his head as he peered at the spectacle, unable to form words that would express his wonder.

After a dozen heartbeats, Sean realized he hadn't taken a breath. He inhaled sharply and let it out with a long sigh.

"Very good, Sean," Malcolm said from much closer than Sean recalled. "Very good indeed."

For a second, Sean thought the man might pat him on the shoulder, but Malcolm wasn't stupid enough to get that close. The second he touched his finger to Sean's shoulder, Sean would take him down.

"It's incredible, isn't it?" Malcolm went on. It sounded as if he were about to cry. "Simply spectacular."

Sean ripped his gaze away from the opening and looked around. The guards had ushered everyone closer, corralling Tommy and Adriana within a few feet of where Sean stood on the threshold of a lost utopia.

Every eye stared blankly into the strange subterranean world. Green hills rolled toward a city in the distance, perhaps a half mile away and several hundred feet down. Unusual trees dotted the land, with thicker forests bordering the grassy knolls and ridges. Flowers of blue, red, yellow, and even green spread across more hills, and lined a pathway that led into the city.

"The city," Tommy breathed. "It's unlike anything I've ever seen before."

Sean snorted a laugh of agreement. "You can say that again, Schultzie."

The city looked as if it were made from stone. Three isosceles stones towered above all the others—rising from the city's heart to stretch two hundred feet up toward the sky.

The sky, Sean thought. *How is that possible?*

He found himself gazing up into the blue above, unable to reconcile how they were below ground yet somehow able to see the sky above.

A beam of light streamed between the three pillars. The light seemed to strike the sky and melt into the blue canopy.

The other buildings, while smaller in stature, were no less spectacular.

The structures featured round roofs and curved walls. Even from that distance, the detail stood out against the magnificent natural backdrop. A waterfall flowed from a cliff to the left, spilling down into a river that, like the path, flowed into the valley below and through the city.

Despite the epic beauty and magic staring Sean in the face, a different emotion tugged on him. It was the one that always warned him that something was wrong.

"Do you guys notice something weird about this place?"

"Other that it being awesome?" Malcolm asked. He laughed and took the lead, walking over the threshold and into the lost valley.

"No," Sean said.

"You mean weirder than what appears to be an ancient civilization with better tech than we have up above and that has somehow managed to allow sunlight to reach through the ground?" Tommy looked over at his friend just before one of the gunmen shoved him in the back, pushing him into the surreal underworld.

Sean stepped forward with Adriana, avoiding the nudge from the guards.

The warm air tickled their skin, and the scent of the otherworldly flowers tingled their senses.

Malcolm continued to walk ahead, his head turning from side to side as he took in the spectacle of it all.

"The sky almost looks like liquid," he said, marveling at the sight.

That's when Sean realized it—the first thing that bugged him. The sky looked like liquid, shimmering and alive. He let out a gasp, which drew the attention of Tommy and Adriana.

"What?" Adriana begged.

"The lake," Sean answered. "This entire place is under the sacred lake." He pointed up at the sky, and they followed his gaze above.

"That's impossible," Tommy said. "There's a lake bed under the water."

"Is there?"

Tommy scrunched his face into a thoughtful frown. "Yes. Of course there is. I read about the depths of it on the way here. It's been measured by scientists."

"And from looking at this, would you say our science has caught up with theirs?" Sean diverted his eyes from the sky to his friend, probing him with sincere questions.

"I...suppose not. But still, we've—"

"What if that pillar," Sean said, pointing at the center of the city, "is capable of producing an optical illusion that looks like the lake bed, is even semisolid like a real lake bed, and is also capable of allowing light through?"

"That makes no sense," Tommy argued. "On several levels."

"And yet here we are, looking up at the sky."

"Or," Adriana offered, "that isn't the real sky we're seeing. It could be that the pillar provides light the same as the sun, which allowed the plants to grow here. So, the lake bed is real, but the sunlight is not."

Sean bobbed his head. "That makes more sense, actually. Now I wish I'd thought of it." He passed her his trademark wink.

"So," Tommy reentered, "the lake is above us, and we're staring at a massive, millennia-old optical illusion?"

"It's not an illusion," Malcolm corrected, walking back toward the group and stopping a dozen feet away. "The pillar of light is the ultimate power on Earth."

36

TIBET

The group trekked down the winding path into the city, with Sean and his team in the lead, ushered at gunpoint by the remaining guards, Ju Chen, and Malcolm.

Despite the dire circumstances, Sean couldn't help looking around at this wondrous, alien place that somehow existed below the Earth's surface. He never imagined anything like it, except perhaps in his wildest dreams. That said, the same question continued needling his brain.

The path flattened as the group reached the bottom of the valley. Homes lined what passed for a street, each with several yards between the outside walls. No fences protected the patches of grass in front. As the group drew closer to the main gates of the city, the homes grew denser, taller, and larger.

It reminded Sean of the walk into the Emerald City that Dorothy took so many years before, except that had been fantasy—just a movie. This was real, and yet so surreal. Sean had difficulty wrapping his head around it.

But the question remained, and now that they were passing by dwellings and nearing the city's entrance, he had to bring it up.

"Where is everyone?" he asked, finally.

"I was wondering the same thing," Adriana admitted. "No people, no animals. Not even a bird."

"It's a ghost town," Tommy said, his words cryptic and harsh.

"Did you honestly think there would be people here?" Malcolm wondered. "This place has been forgotten for thousands of years."

"Still," Sean argued, "it seems like they would have had everything they needed to survive down here. The air is clean. They have light. Things clearly grow unimpeded." He noted the vines crawling up the city walls surrounding the inner parts of the town. More snaked their way up the walls of the homes the group passed. Grass had overgrown most of the fields and lawns long ago, though the path made of stone pavers at their feet seemed unaffected. By all rights, weeds should have been growing through the cracks to the point the stone should have disappeared.

"Is that really what's bothering you right now, Sean?" Malcolm asked. He continued walking behind Sean, a pistol in his hand aimed at Sean's spine. "I would be more concerned about the gun pointed at you, and not pissing off the guy holding it."

"What difference does it make? You're going to kill us anyway."

"Probably. But there's always a chance I don't. You never know, Sean."

Sean didn't believe that for a second. He knew Malcolm couldn't afford to risk letting Sean and the others out of this place. Especially him and Adriana. Either one of them would hunt him down, cut through whatever security forces he amassed, and eventually get their revenge. Malcolm knew that all too well. Which meant the only reason they were still alive at this moment, as Sean asserted before, was that Malcolm thought there might still be a use for their talents —perhaps with one last riddle before executing the three of them.

The group passed through the spectacular gate guarded on each side by enormous statues dressed exactly like the ones at the previous gate. These, however, stood facing away from the city, their weapons held upright. The figures stood at attention, their eyes staring out into the mystical landscape, waiting for enemies that would never come.

Or had they?

"It does make you wonder what happened to the people and animals, though," Sean continued. He looked into a window of a home to the left, just beyond the wall. A narrow path ran alongside the wall's interior, separating the home from the defensive fortification.

Sean imagined children running through the streets, playing whatever games this culture might have played. Now, however, only silence and a low-frequency hum occupied the air.

It struck Sean that he hadn't noticed the humming sound before, and he wondered where it might be coming from. His guess was the pillar in the center of the city. With every passing minute they drew closer to the towering beam, Sean realized the sound grew slightly louder, though nowhere near painful.

Tommy and Adriana noticed it, too, though Malcolm and his people either didn't, or they simply chose not to mention it.

With every passing step, Sean wondered more and more where the people had gone. How had they simply vanished without a trace? What could have caused them to leave this perfect place, this underground utopia where the outside world held no sway and posed no threat?

Sean craned his neck to see in through another open window, but the room beyond was empty. Only an empty sink, wooden table and chairs, and barren walls waited on the inside.

"It's like they all left at once," Sean commented to no one in particular.

"Left?" Malcolm laughed. "Why would they leave? It's perfect here."

"Perhaps they felt compelled to go to the world above and bring their knowledge to humanity in order to help it." Adriana offered the theory with a calm confidence that she perpetually radiated.

"That's your plan, isn't it, Mal?" Tommy jabbed. "To take the technology from here and use it up there?" He pointed to the rippling sky above. "Oh, that's right. You're going to use it for profit, extorting the taxpayers and the government for personal gain."

"This technology will make Americans safe," Malcolm retorted.

"We—and our allies, I might add—will never have to worry about an enemy warhead breaking through our defenses. Never have to fear any armed invasion. We'll be able to repel virtually any attack that comes our way. Will it make me rich?" He grinned. "Of course. But someone is always getting rich, Tommy. You're hardly a pauper out on a sidewalk with an eye patch and a tin cup. What's the IAA worth now? Hundred million? More? What are you worth?"

"I'm on a salary, Mal," Tommy spat back. "I don't live a lavish life."

"Says the guy who flew here in a private jet. Easy to be high and mighty when you're standing behind that nonprofit tax code, Schultzie. We private enterprise guys don't get that kind of benefit."

"So sorry for your struggles." Tommy laid the sarcasm on so thick it could have smothered a whale.

The street curved, slithering through the city. The humming sound swelled, but never to a painful level, as the group drew near the source. The noise felt almost welcoming, warm in strange way.

The street curved to the right, and for a few seconds the pillar of light disappeared behind an eight-story building with a mushroom cap-style roof atop it. Then, as Sean and the others continued around the bend, the three isosceles prongs came into full view.

Sean felt his mouth drop at the sight in front of him.

The city street straightened, leading directly into a massive garden that spanned at least five acres in either direction, left to right. Where the buildings ended, hedges protected the park and the finely manicured lawn that stretched from one end of the garden to the other. Beautiful flowers of every color in the rainbow lined the path and filled in huge square patches within the grass. Sean wondered what the designs looked like from above and figured there must have been some kind of animal woven into the planters' concept.

At the end of the flower-lined path, a gigantic temple rose from the ground. Its white stone façade glowed in the light from the pillar at its center. From right to left, the building's many spires towered high above the surrounding gardens. They reminded Sean of the stupas he'd seen in Asia, and of some of the architectural influences of Angkor Wat in Cambodia. These spires also featured several tiers rising to the conical tip of each one.

The center of the building stood three stories above the valley floor, standing above the rest of the temple to the left and right as the heart of the structure. A staircase made from the same white stone wrapped around the entire building, and Sean wondered if the designer had it in mind that this would be a place of welcome for all to come, no matter their origins.

He didn't even realize he was still walking until he was fifty yards into the gardens and surrounded by bright green grass, skinny palm trees, and acres of sweet-smelling flowers.

"We're all seeing this, right?" Tommy asked, cutting through the silence. "I mean, this isn't a dream. Is it?"

"No," Sean said. "And if it is, I would prefer you not be in my dreams."

Adriana snickered at the comment. Even in dire circumstances, Sean had a knack for making her laugh. He'd always said everyone has to go, that they can go with a laugh, or they can go with a frown. He knew which he preferred, though that kind of thing wasn't always optional in the end.

"That goes both ways, pal," Tommy quipped.

Sean forced a smile, but in his mind, he wondered what was going to become of all this.

The group kept moving along the path until they arrived at the base of the steps. Standing at the base, the building seemed even more enormous than first perceived. White columns supported a portico, all the way around to both ends. Many doors allowed entrance from multiple points along the exterior wall, but the main entrance into the heart of the temple featured the largest opening, and no doors blocked the way in.

A triangle-shaped portico jutted out to the top of the steps, beckoning visitors to enter through a twenty-foot-high opening in the wall beyond the stairs.

Everyone in the group stared into the temple's interior, where the beam of light originated and shot up into the sky.

"What are you waiting for?" Malcolm asked, his voice exploding the peace of the moment like one of his killer military drones over a Yemeni village. "An invitation?"

Sean turned around to face his old friend and noticed the guards were also enamored with the sight before them. These hardened men, probably mercenaries, stared in wonder at the temple.

"Sorry if I'm kind of taking it in, Mal. This is a pretty heavy moment."

"I'm sure it is. But if you don't mind, I would appreciate it if you would quit stalling." He brandished the pistol. "Keep moving. Pretty please."

Sean's eyes twitched at the derision, but he wasn't in a position to do anything about it. His fanciful mind, however, dreamed briefly of how many times he could punch Malcolm in the face before the man lost consciousness.

Instead, Sean took the first step, leading the group up to the landing where he could see clearly through the high archway into the temple.

He walked slowly, reverently, on white stone tiles that looked as though they were a hybrid of quartz and marble.

Once through the entryway, Sean found himself holding his breath for the umpteenth time, his eyes locked on the three isosceles prongs rising up from the open courtyard, as if they contained the white beam of light on three sides. In the center, an obelisk standing only four feet tall provided the source of the mysterious light. At the top of the obelisk, the pyramid glowed brightly, as if separate from the rest of the pillar.

A reflecting pool surrounded the beam and its source, reflecting the light in a circle that encompassed a hundred feet in diameter. A narrow stone walkway led out into the middle, perhaps for ancient ceremonies and rites held by high priests that were long since gone.

Sean muscled his gaze away from the light and turned his attention to the walls surrounding the temple's inner court.

Vibrant murals covered the surfaces, depicting people in strange clothing—robes, cloaks, tunics, trousers, jewelry, and armor that would have been right at home in some futuristic tale from another world.

"Look at those hieroglyphs," Tommy said, his voice full of wonder. "Spectacular imagery."

"Yes," Sean agreed.

The walls stretched two hundred yards lengthwise and about 150 feet across to the other side of the courtyard. Even at a distance, he could clearly see the images telling the story of this place—this lost, sacred city that once housed what many believed to be a perfect society.

Sean looked first at an image of a white-robed man with golden locks of hair down to his shoulders, surrounded by light and holding a pyramid exactly like the one at the top of the obelisk. A man in a green robe received the pyramid from the white-robed man.

On the next panel, the green man was seen showing the pyramid of light to other people who stood around him in awe at the spectacle. The story continued to show how the people built this place, and honored the pyramid in the center of this very temple, where its light was harnessed to create a bountiful city full of peace and joy.

Sean felt the happiness radiating from the faces, even if they were only paintings. The people loved their city and were grateful for the gift that had been given them.

Then, on the other side of the wall, the story changed. The people looked conflicted. Some turned their faces toward a picture of the mountains to the east and the gate leading out of the valley.

One of them, a woman in a lavender robe, took the light and journeyed out of the valley and into the realm above, where they tried to share the light with the world.

The imagery turned dark, pitting the woman against angry mobs. Some of the people were soldiers with ancient swords and spears that might have been the precursors to the original Sumerian weapons.

The woman fled the world, returning to the sacred valley to escape the darkness of mankind.

But when she arrived, Shangri-La was empty. The people were gone, and nothing remained except what they'd built.

The story of their departure from the city was displayed in vividly colored wall paintings, depicting people boarding bizarre silver ships. The boats looked like they were half yacht, half spaceship.

Then in the final panel, the woman with red hair and a lavender robe returned the pyramid to the obelisk. No further explanation told of what happened to her.

On the wall to the right of the northern row of murals, a different set of images took Sean's attention.

Five panels occupied the wall. In the center, an image of the obelisk mirrored the real one, complete with the three triangular prongs that stood around the light. The panels to the left of the center image showed a new being, a human in white robes with flowing locks of radiant hair. They approached the obelisk, and in the final scene, when they touched it, the light grew and seemed to surround them in radiant hope, peace, and love.

Sean stood dumbfounded at how the artwork could make him feel or perceive such things.

He turned his attention to the other two panels. These contrasted the other two, depicting a figure in flowing black robes and hair the color of the darkest night. They approached the obelisk, and when they grasped it, scenes of fire, destruction, and death surrounded them. People falling into an abyss, cities laid to waste, and mothers weeping for their children.

"What are you looking at?" Malcolm asked.

Sean didn't realize how much time had elapsed since he started reading through the imagery, the story of Shangri-La that no one outside these walls had ever heard before. He could have been standing there for hours and not realized it.

"The story," Sean said, pointing to the walls. "It's the history of this place."

"Great. Glad you got that out of the way. Now, if you don't mind, we should keep moving."

"To where?" Sean asked.

"Uh, out there?" Malcolm pointed his pistol's barrel at the center of the temple where the obelisk stood on a platform in the reflecting pool.

"What?" Tommy broke in. "You're not going to try to take that thing. Are you?"

Malcolm rolled his eyes. "Of course I am. That artifact is the source of the greatest power on the planet. I can't wait to get it into the lab and see what it can do."

Sean rounded on Malcolm with a scolding look in his eyes. "This isn't just about renting safety to the American people and its allies, Malcolm. Is it? You're going to weaponize this thing, aren't you?"

Malcolm rolled his shoulders, flicking his head to the side in a *you got me* gesture. "I'm sure going to try, Sean. Oh, don't give me that look. You know what I do. Did you really think I was just going to try to sell a shield? Why make money one way when you can make it two?"

Sean's eyes flamed and his nostrils flared. The visions of beating Malcolm into oblivion burned brighter in his mind to the point he could feel his knuckles crunching skin and bone.

"You should know," Adriana interrupted, "that this wall over here has nothing to do with the past of this place."

"What?" Malcolm turned to her. She stood with her back to him, facing the wall at the end of the temple, the one containing the images of both hell and paradise. "What are you talking about."

"It's a prophecy of sorts," she explained. "A promise and a warning."

"Are you going to start making sense, or do I need to just shut you up for good?"

He raised his weapon toward her. Sean instinctively took a step forward, but halted when one of the guards reminded him that another firearm was still aimed his way.

Adriana faced him, spinning around slowly on her heels. Her chocolate eyes remained calm, as if hiding a secret Malcolm would never understand or accept. "The one who is pure of heart may touch the light and be blessed. But the wicked will only bring about their own destruction."

37

TIBET

Malcolm peered at Adriana, suspicion darkening his eyes. "I think you're bluffing," he said after a minute of assessing her. "You're good. I'll give you that. But I think you're full of it."

He turned to the guard nearest him. "Retrieve the pyramid," Malcolm ordered.

The guard didn't hesitate. He walked across the floor to the stone pathway that seemed to float atop the reflecting pond.

He paused at the edge, then took a step out onto the walkway. Nothing happened. Filled with more confidence, the man continued across the bridge until he reached the obelisk. He turned back toward Malcolm, much like a child would have looked to a parent for approval before taking a cookie. Malcolm gave a single nod, and the gunman holstered his pistol.

The guard reached out both hands toward the light. He paused for a breath, then touched the surface of the obelisk's top with his fingertips.

Suddenly, the man shrieked the most haunting, terrible noise anyone had ever heard. The white beam pulsed, and the humming sound welled. The guard's body shook uncontrollably, twitching and convulsing faster and faster.

Sean shielded his eyes from the light as it seemed to grow, spreading out beyond the obelisk until the beam encompassed the entire platform atop the pool.

Then, abruptly, everything dimmed again. Sean kept his eyes protected for a few more seconds before he lowered his hand and twisted his head so he could see the pillar again.

Everything looked as it had before. Except for one staggering difference. The guard was gone.

"Where is he?" Ju Chen asked, speaking for the first time since anyone could remember.

"He was standing right there," Malcolm breathed.

"The light consumed him," Adriana explained. She left it at that, allowing Malcolm and his remaining team members to reach their own conclusions.

It didn't take him long.

A twisted grin of pleasure crossed his face, curling his lips. "I was right. This is the greatest power on the planet. Incredible. Imagine if we can harness this energy, the weapons we'll be able to build. I will have every government in the world eating out of my hands."

"You just saw what happened to that guy, right?" Sean asked, pointing at the pillar. The hum had returned to its calm, constant background noise. "You can't seriously be still thinking about stealing it. It's not worth it, Mal?"

The obsessed look on Malcolm's face never changed. If anything, it intensified. He turned the pistol on Sean and kept it there. "Well, let's see if you are pure of heart, Sean. Or if your sins will find you out."

Sean remembered the quote from the Bible. Despite all he'd done in his life, he always believed he was serving the side of justice and good. Now, that belief would be put to the ultimate test.

"You want me to retrieve it for you, like it's a toy you left in the attic?"

"Yes," Malcolm said, his voice even and cold. "Be a lamb, and fetch it for me." He twisted around and pointed the gun at Adriana. "Or she dies."

"You're going to regret pointing that at her," Sean cautioned.

"I doubt it, old friend. Hurry up. Or I kill her and then Tommy next."

"Don't trust your own self-righteous ideas, Malcolm?" Tommy spat. "Or do you know you'll face the same fate as your goon?"

"Let's just say, I want to play things safe. Now, Sean. Bring me the artifact."

Sean saw Malcolm's finger tighten on the trigger. He wasn't playing games.

Sean weighed the consequences. If he grabbed the artifact from the top of the obelisk, it could kill him, but if he didn't, Malcolm would kill Adriana. Then again, if he killed her, and Tommy, he'd be left with only himself to retrieve the thing. And Sean knew Malcolm wasn't brave enough to take on that challenge.

That would mean he'd never have what he wanted, the ultimate power as he'd called it. Without Sean, Adriana, and Tommy, Malcolm had no chance. He wouldn't be able to use the artifact to create anything destructive, and there was no telling how many lives might be spared.

All those thoughts raced through Sean's head as he stood there, staring at the pistol in Malcolm's hand.

"Well, Sean? What are you waiting for?"

Sean wanted to take a stand. He wanted to protect the rest of humanity from this monster he'd once called friend. In the end, though, his love for Adriana and Tommy overcame all. And even with the artifact in Malcolm's hands, there was still a chance, however slim, that they could put an end to his sinister scheme.

"I'm going," Sean said. "Sorry if I'm a little hesitant to go pick up the magical artifact that just incinerated one of your men."

"You done worrying about it?"

Sean answered by turning away and walking toward the narrow stone bridge. He didn't pause like the guard before. There was no need to hesitate now. He accepted his fate. He would either be disintegrated, or...He didn't know what the other possibility was.

He strode across the walkway and didn't stop until he reached the obelisk. The humming seemed to wrap around him like tentacles. Sean stared down at the artifact. The bright light didn't seem as blinding as before. He stared into the beam as if in a trance.

Sean didn't feel afraid, despite thinking maybe he should. Instead, he felt strangely...welcome?

"What are you waiting for, Sean? Pick it up!" Malcolm yelled across the reflecting pond, goading Sean.

Sean drew a breath and exhaled, then reached out his hands and touched the artifact.

He closed his eyes as his fingertips made contact with the sides of the pyramid, uncertain what would happen next.

He waited, but all he felt was a warmth radiating through his fingers, hands, and arms. He inhaled, held his breath, and then let it out. Opening his eyes, Sean realized he was okay, at least for now. The same reaction the artifact gave to the touch of Malcolm's mercenary hadn't consumed Sean. Not yet.

He blinked rapidly, trying to muster the courage to lift the artifact off its stand. He wavered between thinking he shouldn't and knowing the consequences if he refused Malcolm's order.

Sean slid his fingers down the sides of the pyramidal artifact—and found a seam at the bottom. Working his fingers under the object, he pried it off the plinth. He'd expected it to be heavy, but instead it seemed to only weigh a pound.

He lifted the artifact with ease and stared into it. The light swirled and pulsed, but he felt no pain, sensed no trouble. His heart filled with warmth unlike anything he'd felt before. Then the light swirled and changed colors, melting and churning through thousands of hues like a liquid kaleidoscope.

Sean's breathing calmed into a steady rhythm, and he turned away from the pillar and faced his former friend.

Malcolm wore a gloating, smug expression like a tacky Christmas sweater—without the humor.

Holding the artifact in gentle hands, Sean trod carefully across the bridge and back to where Malcolm stood.

"Attaboy, Sean," Malcolm spat. "I knew you could do it."

Sean stopped a few feet short of the billionaire.

Malcolm holstered his weapon and nodded to Ju Chen. "Keep an eye on him, will ya?"

She nodded and trained her weapon on Sean's head.

He knew she wouldn't miss from that range. And even though that only left one gunman to watch Adriana and Tommy, they wouldn't be able to take him down before one or both caught a round, likely a kill shot.

Malcolm held out his hands, waiting for Sean to hand him the object. Sean hesitated, knowing that the second he placed the artifact in Malcolm's hands, the man would no longer need him, Tommy, or Adriana.

"Well?" Malcolm insisted. "What are you waiting for? Give me the artifact."

Sean glanced over at Adriana, then Tommy. With regret dripping from his eyes, he extended the object to Malcolm, placing it in his palms.

For a few seconds, Sean hoped the artifact might consume Malcolm the way it had the guard he'd sent to his death a few minutes before. Apparently, Sean surmised, that trick only worked within the confines of the three triangles and the platform on the water. Once removed, he guessed, that little trap no longer applied.

Malcolm's eyes lit up as he stared into the artifact. The light no longer swirled with all the colors Sean had seen, but burned a pure white as it had before.

Sean still had his fingers connected to the object, unwilling to let it go just yet. "You know, Malcolm," Sean said, "if I let this go, it could kill you the same way it did your hired gun."

"Thanks for the warning, Sean. I'm willing to take that chance."

Malcolm started to pull the artifact away, but Sean didn't relent.

"Let go, Sean. Or I will kill your wife."

"No, you won't!" a familiar voice shouted from behind Malcolm and the others.

Malcolm turned his head around, keeping his fingers still on the pyramid, and saw a ghost standing under the archway, leaning against the wall.

Benny held a pistol in each hand, both pointed directly at Malcolm. Blood trickled from the corner of his lips, and crimson stained his jacket on the left side.

"Benny?" Malcolm and Sean said at the same time.

"Let it go, Lóng," Benny ordered, using Malcolm's alias.

"Benny. Let's talk about—"

The pistols in Benny's hands popped, cutting off whatever Malcolm was going to say.

38

TIBET

S ean sensed what was about to happen before Benny squeezed the triggers. He dove to the right, yanking the artifact from Malcolm's hands. Sean hit the ground and rolled backward until he dropped off the stone tiles and into the reflecting pool.

He let the artifact fall to the bottom of the pool as chaos reigned amid the hail of gunfire.

The lone remaining guard turned to open fire and peppered the wall and floor around Benny as he dove for cover that wasn't there.

Ju Chen found herself split between masters—and chose simply to run toward the far wall.

Malcolm avoided most of the initial onslaught, but one round gazed his leg, and another clipped his left shoulder. The two wounds stung. The one in the shoulder carried a sharper pain with it. Still, Malcolm managed to squeeze off five shots, pinning Benny back into the entryway around the corner where he took cover.

Sean pulled himself out of the water and rushed Malcolm, charging the five yards in under a second. Malcolm, on the floor, sensed the threat, turned his body, and tried to aim, but it was too late. Sean swung his right foot with all the power of an international soccer star and kicked the pistol out of Malcolm's hands.

The gun clattered on the tiles twenty feet away and skidded to a stop close to the water's edge.

Meanwhile, Ju Chen tried to escape around the pool, hoping to reach the backside of the temple. She didn't anticipate Adriana chasing after her. Just before Ju Chen rounded the pool's corner, Adriana lunged, plowing her shoulder into Ju Chen's midsection.

The two women crashed to the ground hard, jarring the pistol out of Ju Chen's hand. She twisted and kicked, extending her leg to drive Adriana off her, but the Spaniard writhed out of the way and dropped her elbow into Ju Chen's abdomen, crushing the air from the enemy's lungs.

Behind them, Tommy scrambled for the pistol Sean had kicked from Malcolm's hand. He sprinted for the weapon, but just before reaching it was slowed by several clicks to his right. Rounds ricocheted off the ground around him, spraying stone chips across his arms and face. Some of the minuscule chunks stung his cheeks. With a last effort, Tommy dove toward the pistol, scooped it into his hand, and rolled on the ground, extending it out to fire three wild shots at the gunman.

The guard retreated, trying to get back to the entrance, but that put him into Benny's line of sight.

The sound of thunder roared through the temple. The ground shook, and the blue swirling sky overhead blinked and then vanished, replaced by a brown, cavern-like ceiling one might have found in an enormous cave.

"What was that?" Tommy shouted.

Sean raised his fist and drove it into Malcolm's face.

Malcolm raised one arm to deflect a blow but couldn't stop the third. Before Sean realized his opponent was only using one arm to defend, Malcolm had pulled a knife from his pocket and slashed Sean across the chest.

Falling back with his skin screaming, Sean grimaced and rolled to his feet. He checked his shirt, sticking fingers inside to see how bad the cut was. Fortunately, the knife tip hadn't gone very deep. The wound wasn't mortal, but he'd definitely need stitches.

Malcolm crawled to his feet as the temple shook all around him. He held the knife out threateningly toward Sean, begging him to come get another taste of steel.

Off to their right, Adriana brought her fists down together into Ju Chen's face, crushing her nose in a single, devastating blow.

Ju Chen struggled and wormed, trying to get out from under the Spaniard's straddling grip. But Adriana's legs were stronger. She raised her fists again, brought them down, but Ju Chen managed to twist to the side just enough to throw Adriana off her and into the water.

Adriana emerged and took a breath, but had only time for one. Ju Chen lunged into the water feet first, striking Adriana in the jaw with her heel.

The blow dazed her and sent the temple spinning around her in a dizzying vortex. Ju Chen grabbed Adriana by the back of the head, wading through the shallow water, and shoved her facedown into the liquid.

Adriana struggled, unable to free her head from the woman's death grip. With only seconds of air left in her lungs, Adriana reached down to her side where she kept a small blade tucked away for emergencies. She ripped the knife from its sheath and with a powerful backhand, swiped the blade through Ju Chen's right forearm.

The Chinese woman screamed in pain. Her fingers loosened at the severing of the tendons. She grabbed her forearm with the left hand for a heartbeat, just long enough for Adriana to regain her bearings.

Adriana spun around, and in a single deadly movement, drove the knife into Ju Chen's chest. The woman grunted. Her knees buckled.

But Adriana didn't stop there. She waded around behind Ju Chen, grabbed her by the back of the head, and shoved her face into the water.

The Chinese woman resisted, trying to muster the strength to stand and take a breath, but Adriana was stronger. Using all her weight and muscle, she fought through Ju Chen's struggle until she felt the muscles begin to give way. The woman's body started trembling, and then after two big twitches, went limp.

Adriana kept her enemy's face under the water another ten seconds just to make certain, and then let go. She stepped back, watching the body float to the surface, facedown, before finding the edge of the pool and climbing out.

She looked over at Sean, who was in the middle of a knife fight with no knife, and then to Tommy.

Tommy took aim with the pistol and fired at the last gunman as the guy retreated toward the entrance. In the shadows of the archway, Benny also aimed his weapons. Realizing that if Benny missed, he would be in the line of fire, Tommy darted to the left and out of the way as the guard opened fire again to give himself some cover for the retreat.

He backed his way right into a bullet from one of Benny's pistols, spun around, and fired toward the second threat. Tommy slid to a stop, took a position on one knee, and shot the guard three times in the back.

The hulking man shuddered from the rounds, tried to whirl around in one last effort to defend himself, and caught three more rounds from Benny and Tommy, dropping him to the ground like a bleeding bull in an arena.

The trembling continued. One of the giant triangular pillars cracked, and then fell with a magnificent splash into the reflecting pool.

"This place is gonna collapse!" Tommy shouted at Sean.

Sean stood between the exit and Malcolm; their eyes locked in mortal struggle.

"It's over, Mal," Sean said. "Put down the knife. You can still get out of here."

"So sentimental, Sean," Malcolm sneered. "Always trying to be the good guy. Don't you know good guys finish second?"

A powerful crack broke the air. Behind Malcolm, the temple wall rent in two, revealing the source of the sound.

"This place is done for," Sean cautioned. "You still have time to get out."

The look on Malcolm's face showed a man Sean had never known. He was foreign, a stranger wearing the expression of a man obsessed with power and money.

Sean shook his head.

"Sean!" Tommy shouted as Adriana ran to him. "We have to go!"

Sean nodded. "Leave it, Malcolm. This is where it belongs."

"It belongs to me, Sean!"

With a step backward, Sean retreated from his old friend. "You don't have to do this, Malcolm. People can change."

"Why would I change? No one changed for me!" Malcolm turned and dove into the pool.

Sean shook his head one last time, turned, and ran to join Tommy and Adriana at the exit.

Benny stood there, leaning against the corner just inside the archway. Blood ran down into his pants now, and only a faint trace of color remained in his face.

He held the pistols at his waist, generally aimed at Sean and others, but in a nonthreatening way.

"Benny," Sean said. "Let's get out of here. We don't have much time."

The temple shook all around them. Beyond the exit, Sean saw parts of the ancient city were crumbling, too.

Benny shook his head. "No, Sean. It's too late for me. You were always the better man. I wanted to be number one for a change."

"It's not too late. You can make it. Come with us."

"No. This is what I deserve. I'm sorry." Benny's voice was distant, sincere. "I'm sorry I killed Fischer. He didn't deserve that. I was jealous. Of you. Of him. Of everyone who'd ever had anything I never got."

"Benny."

"Go, Sean. I'll take care of Malcolm. You and the others get out of here." He waited for a second, and when the second isosceles pillar crashed into the end wall, he mustered his last scraps of strength. "Go!"

Sean nodded and motioned for the others to leave.

They took off toward the stairs but were stopped when Benny shouted, "Sean?"

He slowed down and looked back.

"I did beat you here," Benny said with a feeble grin.

Sean nodded. "Yes. Yes you did."

Adriana tugged on his hand, and Tommy on hers, as the three fled the crumbling temple.

A HUGE CHUNK of rock crashed into the ground a few feet from where Benny stood. He winced, but nothing frightened him now. He was dying, and he knew nothing would change that. Every breath hurt, and his side burned where the bullet had entered his body.

He knew he had minutes, if that.

Malcolm emerged from the pool, raising the artifact high over his head. He placed it on the edge of the pool and climbed out, then picked it up and started for the door. He tucked the object under his armpit like an American football, rushing between falling debris all around him.

He reached the exit and stopped just inside the shadows.

"Hello, Lóng," Benny said, raising the pistols with the last remnants of strength he could find. He found great satisfaction in using the man's fake name.

"Benny? Listen. About before—"

One of the pistols clicked, and spit a cloud of smoke out the muzzle. The bullet burrowed into Malcolm's abdomen. He grimaced in agony, still clutching the artifact under his armpit.

"You betrayed me, Lóng, or should I say, Malcolm." He fired again, this time blasting a hole in Malcolm's knee.

That one dropped the billionaire to the ground. He braced himself on an elbow, shrieking in horrific pain.

"This is what you get for stabbing me in the back," Benny said. He raised the pistol, aiming it at Malcolm's head. And squeezed the trigger.

Red mist erupted from the back of Malcolm's skull, and the man slumped to the ground. The artifact slipped from his grasp, settling a few inches away from the body.

Benny dropped the pistols and slid down to the floor against the wall, watching as the temple collapsed around him.

He crawled over to the artifact, still glowing a bright white, and reached out to touch it. In his mind, he saw his mother as he felt the warmth of the little pyramid against his finger. He knew he wasn't going to make it out of here alive, but he just wanted to feel the thing he'd searched the world to find. The light swirled in myriad colors, and Benny felt a strange peace as the view of everything around him faded.

SEAN and the others ran as hard as they could up the path. They didn't dare look back into the city, no matter how much they might have wanted.

On his best days, Sean could run a nine-minute mile. But that was on a flat surface. The sprint back to the tunnel exit was uphill.

Tommy huffed for air next to him. Adriana took the lead, easily chewing up the path with her long strides.

"Almost there, Schultzie," Sean encouraged.

They saw the tunnel up ahead, only another minute or two away.

Huge rocks fell from the ceiling all around them. One boulder smashed into a palm tree fifty feet away, crushing it to splinters in an instant.

"Keep going!" Sean urged.

Tommy dragged his feet, but forced himself forward.

"The doors are closing!" Adriana yelled, pointing toward the tunnel.

"Great," Sean muttered between breaths. "Gotta pick it up, Schultzie. Leave it all on the field, brother!"

Tommy mustered the last scraps of endurance in his gut, and pushed his legs harder.

Fifty yards to go, and the doors were halfway closed. If they didn't make it through, they would be trapped in the valley that was hell-bent on self-destruction.

The ground shook under their feet, nearly throwing them off balance. Tommy stumbled, but Sean reached out and steadied his friend, helping him maintain stride.

Twenty-five yards from the tunnel exit, the gates only had an opening about ten feet wide.

"Come on!" Adriana pushed. "Nearly there!"

Ten yards and closing.

The gap between the doors only offered five feet of space.

Adriana reached the exit first and dove through to the other side.

She looked back at the two men as they lumbered forward. Sean put his hand on his friends back and shoved Tommy through the opening, his shoulders grazing both doors as he stumped between.

Sean twisted his body to the side and leaped. His legs were on fire, and he didn't have as much strength as he hoped. He landed on the other side of the doors, but his feet were still between the gates as they closed in.

He felt a strong hand grab his right wrist, and a familiar, more feminine hand latch on to the other.

Tommy and Adriana pulled Sean the rest of the way through the gates, just as the massive stone slabs slammed shut.

Tommy fell back onto his tailbone, gasping for air.

Adriana also took a seat, looking to her husband to make sure he was okay.

"You're bleeding," she said.

Sean shook it off, catching his own breath. "I'll be okay. Just a scratch."

With his shirt soaked red, she didn't believe him at first, but seeing that he didn't seem concerned helped alleviate her fear.

"Well," Tommy huffed as the ground continued to rumble. "I hope those monks can find a way to get us out of here."

"Yeah," Sean agreed. He looked back at the closed gates to the lost city of Shangri-La, and his head drooped. "I guess now it really is lost for good."

"And maybe that's for the best," Adriana offered. "Evil hands would always want to hold that artifact. It would cause more death and destruction than it's worth."

Sean recalled the murals surrounding them in the temple, along with the warnings that came with them. "Yeah," he said with a sigh. "I think you're right."

39

HONG KONG

Sean and his team sat at a table in a quiet teahouse near the waterfront. They watched the boats bob by in the early evening moonlight, sipping cups of tea from ornately decorated porcelain cups.

Tommy shook his head after a sip. "Nope. I still don't understand the whole tea thing."

Sean and Adriana laughed.

Daiyu offered a mocking scowl. "Unrefined American," she muttered before raising her own cup to her lips.

"I'm glad you're doing better," Tommy said with more than a hint of ire.

"Well, I have you three to thank for that." Daiyu bowed her head gracefully.

"You also have us to thank for the injuries, so, maybe it's a wash?" Sean offered.

"I suppose you're right."

She set her cup down on a saucer and leaned back. Her injured arm hung in a sling.

The three adventurers had waited for hours in the basement of the monastery until, finally, one of the monks found someone in the local village who could move the stone slab away from the stairs.

While the possibility that they could have been permanently stuck down there was very real, Sean never really figured they would have to wait more than a day before someone went down there and saw what happened.

It had been an endeavor in patience, and in medical toughness for Sean. He ended up using his shirt to seal the wound across his chest and prevent further bleeding, though he never believed it was life threatening.

"I wish I could have seen it," Daiyu mused, staring at her teacup. "I imagine it was incredible."

"It was," Tommy agreed. "And it's a shame there isn't anything left now."

"You said there was an artifact, some kind of pyramid. I'm unclear how this object brought about the destruction of the ancient city."

"You and us both, sister," Sean quipped, raising his cup in a toast.

While he took a sip, Adriana spoke. "The obelisk was a sacred gift to the people of Shangri-La. But in the hands of the wicked, it only brought death and chaos."

"As if the artifact could detect the intentions of the person holding it?"

"Something like that. It's possible that Malcolm could have escaped with it and brought it to the surface. There's no telling what end of trouble he could have caused if that happened."

"But it didn't," Tommy inserted.

"No," Adriana affirmed. "It didn't."

Daiyu shook her head, thoughts swirling a million miles an hour behind her dark eyes.

"Well, I'm glad. I have to say, it's hard to believe your friend Malcolm was the much-feared Lóng."

"I know," Sean said. "I guess it goes to show, sometimes you don't really know someone as well as you might think. We probably won't find out all the cookie jars he had his fingers in for quite some time."

"His underworld operations will fall to the next in line," Daiyu explained. "That is the way it always goes. There is always someone waiting with just as much, if not more, ambition."

Sean knew she was right. He'd seen it happen with cartels, gangs, Mafia, all of them. Heavy lies the crown, and yet someone was always waiting on the sidelines, ready to put it on.

"So, you're going back to America tonight," Daiyu said. "Is there anything else I can do for you before you leave?"

"No, I don't think so," Tommy declined. "You've been such a big help. Anytime you want to come visit us, you always have a free place to stay, and any resources I can provide." He raised his shoulders. "And if you, you know, need a job if the whole thing here in China doesn't work out—"

"I appreciate that, Tommy," she smiled, cutting him off. "Thank you. But my home is here."

"A boy's gotta try," he said in an aww shucks tone. "We could use someone like you at IAA, but I understand."

The group finished their tea in silence, only occasionally making mention of the lights on some of the boats, or of the sky overhead as a random cloud passed by, momentarily blotting out the moon.

When they were done, Sean and the others stood. Daiyu escorted them, broken collarbone and all, out to the street, where a car awaited them.

"I guess this is goodbye," she said. Regret brimmed in her eyes. "It's a shame our countries are so mistrustful of each other. There is so much we could learn and share with one another."

"I know," Tommy agreed.

"Perhaps someday that will change," Sean hoped. "The future always has room for people who are willing to let go of fear and greed in order to achieve great things."

"What a beautiful thing to say, Sean Wyatt. I shall miss you. And your lovely wife." She turned to Adriana. "Thank you for your help. I look forward to seeing you again."

Adriana nodded. "And I as well, my friend."

The driver opened the car door. Tommy climbed into the front seat and Adriana into the rear.

Sean lingered on the curb for six heartbeats, then turned back to Daiyu. "I would hug you, but the broken clavicle and all."

"It's okay, Sean. I know."

Sean nodded. "I'll see you again." He started to get into the car, stopped, turned to her, and said, "Oh, by the way, We left you a gift at the hostess stand."

"A gift?"

He winked at her, climbed into the backseat, and closed the door.

She watched as the car drove down the street and disappeared at the next intersection. Then Daiyu walked back into the café and stopped at the hostess stand. "I'm sorry to bother you, but I was told you have something for me? My name is D—"

"Yes. It's right here. Your American friends said to hold on to it until they were gone." The young hostess in a white shirt and black pants smiled up at her, then ducked down behind the pedestal. She popped back up a few seconds later holding a black metal case.

"What in the world?" Daiyu wondered.

"I didn't open it. They told me only you can do that."

Daiyu accepted the case, thanked the girl, and made her way back to the table by the water, where they'd been drinking. She set the case down on the table and flipped up the clasps with her good hand, then raised the lid.

Her eyes widened at the sight. She snapped her head left and right, hoping no one else had seen. Alone on the back deck, she returned her gaze to the beautiful jewel resting in a foam cushion.

The red gem glimmered in the city lights, almost winking back at her the same way Sean did.

She closed the case and locked it, shaking her head.

"Thank you," she whispered. "I wish there were more people out there like you three."

THANK YOU

I just wanted to say thank you for reading this story. You chose to spend your time and money on something I created, and that means more to me than you may know. But I appreciate it, and am truly honored.

Be sure to swing by ernestdempsey.net to grab four free stories, and dive deeper into the universe I've created for you.

I hope you enjoyed the story, and will stick with this series as it continues through the years. Know that I'll be working hard to keep bringing you exciting new stories to help you escape from the real world.

Your friendly neighborhood author,

Ernest

AUTHOR'S NOTES

Hello there again, reader friend.

It's that time where we separate the magic from reality, and discuss the elements of the story that are true, and those that I made up from the swirling maelstrom of ideas in my head.

Locations

Every general location such as a city, village, province, or region in the book is real. I tried to include true details as well, such as local festivals or customs. Topography descriptions such as mountains, rivers, trees, and even the weather should be relatively accurate based on the season this story took place.

There are some locations that aren't real, or at least I don't know of them. Usually, when it comes to eateries, bars, coffee shops, cafés, and things of that nature, I create my own in a place I've seen—whether during online research or in person. As an example, someone might put a bookstore on a corner along the Stroget in Copenhagen, but if you visit that spot you'll find something else. I like to employ these kinds of ideas with real places, as I've done with the location of the IAA headquarters in Atlanta. (It's where I tailgate for football and soccer games).

The Shikshin temple is a real complex along the old trade routes of antiquity. Sanqing Mountain, and the monastery at the end of the story are also real. As to the secret passages, tunnels, and the gateway to Shangri-La—I'll leave that up to you to decide.

History

For every thousand words I write, there is typically an hour of research that goes along with it. Just seems to be how the math works out. That means this story features around 93 hours of research, give or take.

I do this to make sure I get geographical and historical references correct, or as accurate as I can make them.

In the prologue, I took real characters from history, and very real circumstances to apply them as the catalyst for this adventure. An example of this, I was using the infamous general, Qin Zongquan and his quest for power. He was so desperate, he would have tried anything—even searching for something that may have only been legend.

I always try to make sure I get dates and timeframes correct, but there are occasions where historians disagree on specific years.

The Story

What a fascinating tale, the legend of Shangri-La. I have always wanted to write this story. In truth, it probably would have been the first I wrote had I not discovered the idea revolving around the ancient wall on Fort Mountain in North Georgia so many years ago.

Shangri-La has always intrigued me, as all the lost city legends do.

I'm of the mind that where there is smoke, there's usually fire. Not always, but usually. When so many different sources agree, however, it's at least worth investigating.

As with Atlantis, Cibola, and others, these places were likely real at one point—perhaps embellished or exaggerated—but real none-theless, and lost to our limited sight through cataclysm, time, or both.

What truly lies beneath the Earth's vast surface? What other incredible legends could be waiting for us to discover.

There are places like these out there, treasures that are beyond the understanding of our feeble minds. Does spectacular technology of the ancients exist, kept from us under the sands of time?

I like to think so.

And if it does, how could we use it to make our planet better, and perhaps expand to new ones?

That's for brighter minds than mine to figure out, but I hope we get to see it.

Thanks for taking the time to read this story. I appreciate it, and hope you'll join me in the next adventure.

OTHER BOOKS BY ERNEST DEMPSEY

ACKNOWLEDGMENTS

As always, I would like to thank my terrific editors, Anne and Jason, for their hard work. What they do makes my stories so much better for readers all over the world. Anne Storer and Jason Whited are the best editorial team a writer could hope for and I appreciate everything they do.

I also want to thank Elena at Li Graphics for her tremendous work on my book covers and for always overdelivering. Elena definitely rocks.

Last but not least, I need to thank all my wonderful fans and especially the advance reader team. Their feedback and reviews are always so helpful and I can't say enough good things about all of them.

Made in the USA
Coppell, TX
04 February 2022

72902707R00194